Laurent and the Beast

Kings of Hell MC #1

K.A. Merikan

Acerbi & Villani Ltd

This is a work of fiction. Any resemblance of characters to actual persons, living, dead, or undead, events, places or names is purely coincidental.

http://kamerikan.com

Cover design by
Natasha Snow
http://natashasnow.com/

Table of contents

Chapter 1 - Beast

Brecon, Maine, April 2017

From the corner of his eye, Beast watched his father share biting kisses with his girlfriend, Martina, and then lean forward to kiss the man who was taking her from behind. The beer had a bitter aftertaste, but Beast had more nevertheless, tapping his teeth against the glass bottle so hard he feared it would break from the force of his jaw clenching.

Heavy beats exploded within the old walls of the former asylum, drumming under the high ceiling. The splash of violet and green illumination licked the shapes hidden beyond its reach, making even the most mundane of things appear phantastical. In the corner of the large room, hiding in the violet glow, the three lovers moved as one, transformed by shadow and smoke into one monstrous body that pulsed at break-neck speed, twisting and shuddering, as if it were about to leave the shadows and attack Beast with all its ferociousness.

It was moving quicker now, caught up in a rhythm that would have to end soon. Two pairs of thick limbs wrapped around the quivering flesh of the woman in the middle, furiously thrusting to completion before disintegrating into separate bodies.

Beast stayed on the sidelines with his arms crossed on his chest, quietly watching over the buffet of flesh that he could sample if only he wished to. And the truth was that he'd love to join the shameless club party the way he used to. He'd go for Spike first. The handsome hangaround had a thing for bikers and never missed an opportunity for the dick of a patch, always there to open his legs at parties, the elegant suit he wore to work forgotten in his Portland home.

If Beast could have his way, he'd stuff his cock into that wide-open mouth and watch a dark flush spread down Spike's face and spill over his chest. And the worst thing was that were he to say this out loud, Spike would already be kneeling in front of him, ready for the taking. Beast was positive the guy had already crossed all the other members of Kings of Hell MC off his bucket list, and there was no end to the suggestive glances thrown Beast's way. But Beast would not be a freakshow, or a pity fuck, or yet another patch in Spike's collection of sexual partners.

He would not be someone's shortcut into prospecting either.

Beast doubted any of the hangarounds would ever want him anywhere near them unless out of morbid curiosity or to gain favors. And Beast was not about to be someone's sugar daddy, all the while wondering if they were even attracted to him. No. This was better. Watching would do.

While he was looking away, King, Beast's father, Martina, and the male hangaround all finished. She slid off the third wheel's lap and stumbled into King's arms, sharing yet another kiss with him. She pulled down her skirt and walked back into the light with her hand resting against the wall for support, looking dizzy, though whether it was from the double-teaming or having too much liquor—Beast didn't know. She waved at him and stumbled right after, thankfully grabbing the nearest chair for support instead of rolling onto the collection of bottles and glasses on the dirty coffee table.

A heavy hand landed on Beast's skin so abruptly he barely kept himself from wincing as the mangled nerves of his scarred shoulder cried out in alarm. He knew who it was before his father even spoke.

King's fly was still open, which made Beast immediately look up into the handsome face that always reminded him of his own long-lost good looks. He used to be a mirror image of his father. Too bad good genes stood no chance against fire. Looking into King's masculine, ageless features was a daily reminder of what could have been if Beast hadn't been disfigured in an accident twelve years ago.

His old man on the other hand could easily be one of those hot fifty-somethings Hollywood seemed so fond of. His hair and beard still a golden shade of blond, lips pink and plump as a young man's, and his body buzzed with vitality despite all the violence, alcohol, and sleepless nights it'd been subjected to all of King's life.

"Got laid yet?" King asked, presenting Beast with two rows of perfectly white teeth. "I am gonna ask you every day until it happens," he said, digging his fingers into Beast's aching flesh until he struggled not to flinch from the warning sensations his damaged nerves were sending his brain.

But Beast couldn't show weakness, not this long after the accident that left his body a minefield of pain—yet another reason why casually fucking someone during a party seemed more alarming than exciting. What if they touched Beast too firmly and made him cry out? What if they started talking about the president's son being a weakling who squeals in pain when he's being touched? The club was the only family Beast had. His only reason to be. And he could not put his position here in danger, because King would not hold him up, were he to fall.

"Just relaxing," Beast said in the end, cooling his neck with the empty bottle.

King's mouth stretched into a wider smile, and he slapped Beast's back. "Only your dick's relaxed, am I right?"

Beast forced himself to smile, and his gaze trailed over the cluster of sofas and chairs the party spun around. At the beginning of this evening, Beast's closest friend, Knight, and his girlfriend Jordan had seemed back to normal, but the mood must have deteriorated throughout the last few minutes, because they now sat turning away from one another and alternated hissing over their shoulders.

Sometimes, Beast considered dipping his toe into finding a regular partner—if there was a man interested in him enough—because then he could actually teach a guy how to touch him and not have to do it over and over again every time, like he would have to with every new casual lover. People didn't want to put effort into a heavily tattooed man with burns and a shady life when there were so many easy lays to be had at the click of a button. And then Beast thought of Knight and Jordan's relationship and shuddered, immediately losing interest in any kind of romance. Being with someone would only bring him more trouble and annoyance than remaining celibate ever could.

King groaned. "Are you in one of your *moods* again?"

"My moods?" Beast asked, as if he didn't know what his father meant. King was the kind of guy who believed not smiling all the time made you sulky. And Beast was just fine. He felt completely normal. Watching couples who actually had a romantic and sexual connection had only hurt him in the first few months after he realized he wasn't ever going to have that again. He was thick-skinned now, and he had the scars to prove it.

King raised his hands in mock-defeat and laughed. "Okay, okay. At least get yourself another beer."

Beast squeezed his hand around the bottle, stopping only when he realized that cuts were the last thing he needed in his collection of imperfections.

With the music so loud they all needed to shout in order to hear each other, Beast hadn't noticed a fight starting on the other side of the vast room, but two men shoving each other eventually caught his attention and pulled him away from King. One was their VP, Davy, the other—Gyro, a newcomer who got invited by one of the girls. Barely anyone noticed what was going on yet, with the band playing almost too loudly, but Beast was on it, rushing through the middle of the crowd of people engaged in a mating dance that would soon move to the sofas or to the bedrooms nearby.

"The fuck is this, anyway?" Gyro yelled and pushed at Davy so hard, Davy's favorite racoon hat fell off. Things were about to get ugly.

Davy's eyes opened wide in fury. "You don't come to an orgy and expect to only be covered in pussy. A guy stroked your shoulder! Get over yourself, motherfucker!"

Not this again. Beast wasn't in charge of vetting new people, but at times like these, he wished he were. That he could handle it all himself if some of his brothers lacked the sense of responsibility required for the job and allowed some homophobic trash in the clubhouse. At least this fight would give him something to do instead of sulking that he hadn't gotten any action for so long.

The music stopped. First the guitar and base, with the drums going strong in the silence for another two seconds before the guy realized things were heating up beyond the stage. Gyro's voice was loud and clear in the void left behind by the lack of heavy metal.

"You call yourself a biker club? You're all a bunch of dick-loving pussies," he growled and tossed a bottle at the wall, his intoxicated body swaying to regain balance following the rapid movement. The bottle broke into a million pieces, but the sound of shattered glass drowned in the onslaught of shouting and noise as the bikers turned their attention to the insults thrown at them.

Joker pushed a girl off his lap and stood up, jumping over the backseat of the leather sofa, nimble like an acrobat in his bright green shirt that surely hid a collection of weapons that could be used on the offender who'd come here to break club rules.

"We're outlaws. We do what the fuck we want! You have a problem with me fucking a guy when I feel like it? Maybe my dick should go into your ass then and show you what it's like, huh? Wanna be converted?" Joker hissed, pushing back his bright, spiky hair that had gotten slightly tousled throughout the party.

Gyro's eyes went wide, and before Beast could get to him, the fucker pulled out a gun. A small thing, one of those women were encouraged to carry in their handbags, but no matter how small the firearm, it could do a lot of damage. "You better stay the fuck away!"

The atmosphere got dense as cooling tar. Hangarounds scattered, shrieking in fear as they hid behind furniture or fled the room, some without their clothes on. The sheer sense of panic was sour in the air, and Beast's gums itched for violence.

He ducked and moved behind the sofas, intent on approaching the fucker from the back. The cigarette butts and dirt littering the floor were disgusting against his fingertips, but he progressed toward the enemy as quickly and silently as possible, his head pulsing harder. The longer he took to disarm the fucker, the more dangerous the situation would get. Beast couldn't have that. Not in his home.

"Come on now, don't be an idiot," said Rev, their sergeant-at-arms in a calm, steady voice. His reliable personality was one of the reasons why he played the club lawman, and maybe he would provide enough distraction for Beast to attack the piece of trash from the back.

"Me? You guys are fucking laughable. You don't even carry your firearms on you?" Gyro hissed with a slur to his voice, and Beast clenched his teeth. At this point during a party, all the club members were too drunk to take out an armed enemy without it being a risk to everyone else, but if Rev kept up the negotiations, the situation could still be diffused. No one needed a dead civilian buried on club grounds, just because he'd had too much speed and considered himself untouchable.

Knight must have noticed what Beast was doing, because after their eyes met for a split second, Knight casually pushed back his long hair and stepped closer to Gyro. Inevitably, Gyro turned the gun at him, but at least it drew attention away from Beast.

"How many bullets do you have in that tiny gun of yours, asshole? How many people can you shoot before someone bashes your brains in?" Knight asked in a low voice.

Not exactly the approach Beast would take when talking to an armed man who was either drunk or on drugs, but it would do as distraction. The moment the fucker opened his mouth, all his attention on Knight, Beast leapt at his legs and cut him down like a tree.

Gyro let out a high-pitched yelp, but as soon as he hit the floor, the gun went off, followed by a rumble.

Beast twisted Gyro's hand to make him let go of the firearm, then delivered a powerful punch by slamming his elbow into the twisted face. Plaster-smelling dust unexpectedly blew into his face, and the room exploded with loud cries. Beast's head shot up, and in the pale, powdery cloud he saw a man struggling against a large block lying among scattered pieces of rubble. The subdued light was barely enough to illuminate the ceiling, but with his heart beating furiously Beast noticed a large dent in the sculpted decoration above—the source of the debris that rained to the floor in chunks rather than tiny pieces.

Lizzy, the band's frontman, jumped off the stage, screaming for someone to call an ambulance for his father, but barely anyone listened in the commotion. More people were fleeing the room now that they weren't at risk of taking a bullet, and Beast was left calculating if they should all evacuate.

Gyro squirmed under him, trying to free himself out of Beast's grip. "I'm sorry!" he screamed, now sounding not only regretful but frightened for his life. Too late for that.

Rev, was by Davy's side, lifting the pieces of wood and brick off alongside Lizzy, Knight, and Joker. "I told you this place isn't safe! We either actually invest and renovate, or we have to move!" he growled, tossing a large chunk of debris so hard it hit the nearest wall and fell with a dull thud.

Only seconds later Beast realized it was King Rev was arguing with. "It's only stops being safe when someone shoots at the ceiling, for fuck's sake!"

"And what, a chunk of the ceiling would fall off in a normal building? Get a cold shower," hissed Rev, straining his muscles as he and Knight lifted the large piece off Davy, who screamed out as if someone was pulling his nails one by one. Lizzy, who tried to help his father get out from under the heavy slab of brick, was so pale Beast feared he'd faint at any moment.

Pushing Gyro firmer against the ground to keep him still, Beast looked at them, still confused by the choking dust and chaos around him. "What happened?"

King looked to him with a scowl. "The bullet dislodged something in the ceiling—"

Rev butted in with a snarl, spreading his thick arms away from the naked, tattooed chest. "The ceiling is falling apart. Look at this, Davy's leg is fucked!"

And to make matters worse, only now Beast realized a loud, ferocious barking was resonating from the corridor where Hound, his dog, had been locked away for the night.

"I'll just be on my way! I didn't mean to shoot! I forgot I even had it on me," Gyro kept squealing like a piglet that knew its time for slaughter had come.

Martina was already speaking to the emergency services on the phone, but due to the drunken slur in her voice she had to repeat herself and got more frustrated by the second. Davy's face, twisted in pain, and red behind the white beard, dominated Beast's thoughts. Davy was like an uncle to him. It was him who'd taught Beast survival skills and the enjoyment of camping out in nature. And now he was down because of an idiot who did not respect the rules of his hosts.

Beast grabbed the fallen gun and pulled up Gyro with a single upward tug. The fucker's confidence melted away, replaced by a fear so intense he was shuddering and barely able to stand upright. To think that someone this pathetic was the source of Davy's pain was an insult on its own. Beast's eyes met King's. Wordless understanding passed between them, and King nodded, giving Beast permission to deal with Gyro as he saw fit.

"Prospect," yelled Beast, already forcing Gyro away from the circle of people formed around the wounded club member. "Who's the pussy now?" Beast hissed into the man's ear when he noticed tears streaming down the guy's face.

Jake, their prospect, was already on Beast's toes, following him just like Hound did on their walks.

"What do you need me to do?" Jake asked, his blue eyes wide, the young, still boyish face flushed. He used to play football in high school, and he now looked as excited as if he scored a touchdown.

"Come with me," Beast said and pulled back Gyro's arms, forcing the bastard to walk in a bent-over position. His heart was breaking for Davy. Beast of all people knew the value of good health, and he hated thinking of all the things their VP would have to go through when he was so close to retiring.

Jake ran ahead and opened the double doors leading to private quarters where only club members were allowed. The light went on, blinking in yet another testament to the building's deteriorating state. It was likely the dampness that caused constant problems with electricity, but the falling ceiling was the last straw. Gyro was guilty of pulling out a gun in their clubhouse, on a senior club member at that, but consequences wouldn't have been so dire if this building wasn't slowly turning into a death trap. Beast had been suggesting a change for a while now, but after tonight, everyone would finally see how urgently they needed to either renovate the old building or move.

As they approached the room where Hound had been locked for the time of the party, the barking grew louder, drilling into the anxiety centers in Beast's brain. It was likely Hound sensed the chaos and was frightened of all the noise, but he still needed to check up on his dog.

"Prospect, the cellar," he said, easily subduing their prisoner, who didn't even attempt to twist away, shuddering like a frightened rabbit. It was too late for apologies or mercy.

Jake gave the man a long look full of pity. He needed to get over that if he wanted to become a patched member one day. The way to the cellar was a maze through disused rooms where rubble and old furniture lay covered in dust. Jake had to pull away a medical cabinet on wheels to access the hidden door.

"Please, I don't swing that way. I mean— no offense! I was too drunk!"

Looked like he was sober now. *Good.*

Beast pushed the fucker forward, sending him into a tumble down the old stairs. The sound of the body hitting steps and finally the floor farther down did nothing to relieve Beast's anger. Nothing could make this better. "You were a guest here. We can't tolerate this. You don't get to hurt our VP and just walk away," he said, switching on the single light bulb, which illuminated the small empty space that smelled of mold and rat droppings. He was down in the cellar within three long steps.

Gyro gave Beast a nervous smile as he tried to pick himself up from the floor, only for Beast's boot to help him down. "I— I *could* swing that way if it... helps," he finished in a trembly whisper.

Beast sneered, mildly disgusted. "No," he said and grabbed Gyro's collar, pulling him all the way up. A quick punch sent Gyro stumbling to the floor with a shocked yelp, but Beast was not done. Over and over, he made the fucker stand, and no matter how Gyro crawled away or flinched, Beast's fists did their duty, slowly turning Gyro's face into bloodied tenderized meat. Jake watched on, completely silent as Beast kneeled next to Gyro, who stayed down after the last punch, seemingly unable to pick himself up anymore.

Blood ran fast through Beast's veins, and even looking straight into the eyes visible through swollen slits he felt no remorse. Gyro should be happy he would be leaving the clubhouse alive. But that did not mean he could leave Davy a cripple and walk out of this with just flesh wounds. Before Gyro could react, Beast pulled on his right hand, the same that sent the bullet into the ceiling, and rested his forearm against the edge of a cement block that had been here since forever. Beast pushed down using the block as leverage, and the bone broke with a sickening creak. Gyro gave a frantic scream, only to still, passed out on the bare floor.

The moment silence enveloped the room, Hound's barking seemed to reach even here. Beast took a deep breath and finally looked back at Jake who stood straight, like a soldier awaiting orders.

"Take care of this. Drive him to town and leave him close to the hospital. Make sure you're not on camera. And then find out for me who vetted this fuck."

There was some kind of 'yes, sir' from the prospect, but Beast didn't wait to acknowledge it and climbed the stairs.

Hound's alarmed growling was coming his way, along with whines, when he reached the right door and opened it, only to have the massive Rottweiler's body rush past him and into the corridor. Beast expected his pet to rush toward the room where the accident happened just minutes ago but Hound looked back at Beast, as if signalling he wanted to be followed, and rushed the other way, stirring the worst of feelings in Beast.

Was there an intruder somewhere in the house? With the sheer size of the former asylum that has served as the Kings of Hell Clubhouse for the last fifteen years, it was easy to overlook things happening in the disused parts of the property. They once had a bunch of teenagers who came over wanting to spy on the orgy. That thankfully didn't end in blood, and out of the whole mess they got Jake to join their ranks.

Beast wondered whether he shouldn't go back to the armory and get himself a gun but ultimately decided against it. There would be police and emergency services coming for Davy, and he didn't want to run around with a firearm, no matter how good their relationship with the local police was.

Hound moved as if he were following a clear trail, but Beast couldn't smell anything apart from dust and dampness. They were leaving behind the shouting and even the sound of the ambulance approaching, and eventually entered a corridor so disused it had a thick layer of dust on the floor. Now even Beast could see faint footprints in the dust, and next to them, dark droplets that could be blood.

Hound smelled the traces, looked back and broke into a run, which had Beast following him with the worst of expectations as to what he would eventually find. His heart beat faster as they ran down the dark hallway.

The building was a labyrinth, and this far away from where they all lived and worked, it wasn't even wired anymore, so he breathed in the smell of mildew and followed Hound through the darkness in hope he would not stumble.

Windows in the doorless rooms on both sides of the corridor were the only source of light, now delivering a faint red and blue glow of the approaching ambulance. For all Beast knew, this could have been a gothic castle, something out of Bram Stoker's *Dracula*, with bloodthirsty monsters waiting for their next victim in one of the endless hallways, and yet he only ran faster, listening to the steady tap of Hound's paws.

Without any hesitation whatsoever, Hound rushed inside one of the rooms and gave a growl so vicious something inside Beast mourned his decision not to take a gun with him. But no one shot at him when Hound let out a single bark. Beast pushed past the empty doorway, jumping over a fallen chair, only to see someone hiding in the shadows.

Judging by the long, wavy hair and small stature, Beast at first thought it was a woman, but then the person spoke with a distinctly male voice.

"I… I'm not certain where I am." The stranger took half a step out of the shadow, and into the flashing light coming from outside. His accent was distinctly foreign. French maybe?

Beast took him in with a scowl. Blood covered the stranger's face, hair, dripped from his chin, from the tips of his trembling fingers, and stained the outfit that looked as if he'd stolen it from the set of a costume drama. Knee-high boots, fitted pants, a vest worn under a tailcoat.

"What the fuck are you doing on our property, boy?" hissed Beast, watching the soft features of a very young man. "Whose blood is this?" he asked, still cautious. In his experience, a non-threatening presence could hide an adept fighter, so he was not taking any chances as he joined Hound in front of the stranger, who was so short in comparison to Beast's own six foot five form that his red-stained head only reached Beast's pecs.

The stranger backed away into the corner, whimpering in fear the moment Hound growled at him again and lowered his head, but Beast wasn't having any of it and grabbed the boy's arm. "Is the blood yours then? Someone attacked you? Where?" he asked, not hesitating to pat the intruder down, to make sure there were no weapons hiding under the fancy coat.

The boy tried to weasel out of his grip, but he didn't seem adept at using force. "N-no. I don't think it's mine. I don't know. Is this hell?"

Beast groaned, staring at the silly-looking young man, whose white shirt was completely drenched in red. Someone must have died to produce this much blood.

"You will explain yourself to King."

Chapter 2 - Laurent

Brecon, Massachusetts, April 1805

With a tin lantern in hand, Laurent was braving the April chill with his heart in his throat. Tonight would be the first time he'd be alone with Mr. Fane, without the danger of someone intruding on their private conversation. So far, they've only ever met at Mr. Barnave's bookshop, but Laurent was sure they shared a special connection. So many times had Mr. Fane spent hours choosing books that it felt as if what he'd been really after was conversation.

Or, if Laurent was a capable judge of those things, possibly something much more than conversation. The way their eyes would meet sometimes and linger without a word, or the way Mr. Fane stood closer than it was strictly necessary or proper made Laurent recall the book Mr. Barnave had explicitly forbidden Laurent from touching. Which of course made Laurent even more interested in its contents. Always too curious for his own good, he'd read the book from start to finish, earning himself a caning when Mr. Barnave noticed the volume has been misplaced.

Still, Laurent took the strokes with a sense of contentment, because days later the book ended up sold and taken from the store under some gentleman's coat. The prints included inside the story still lingered in the corners of Laurent's mind, and that, Mr. Barnave could not take away from him.

It had been an illicit publication made up of prints depicting the life of a man who engaged with lovers from all walks of life, sometimes even men. And the illustrations did not hesitate in showing those unions either. Naked men, entangled like husband and wife, touching each other in forbidden ways, kissing and mating like beasts, without a care about morality or the laws of God.

Laurent wasn't sure if he was destined for a life of sin or if the book irreversibly colored him thus, but never in his later years did he look at a lady and wonder what it would be like to share her bed. Instead, he would sometimes marvel at the strength of the men working in the harbor, secretly admire the thick forearms revealed by rolled-up sleeves, and wonder what it would be like to lay in bed naked with one of them. How it would feel to have male hands touch him in intimate ways, for a man to lay on top of him, and press his—

In all fairness, Laurent wasn't entirely certain how two men were to connect this way, as the book wasn't about detailed explanations, and it hardly provided much reading material, but nothing had been the same since he'd held it in his hands for the first time. He was aware of the social consequences of his cravings, of course, but fear of discovery had never been enough of a deterrent, and as Laurent grew older, he became convinced he would sacrifice a lot to lie with a man. Possibly. Maybe. Most likely.

How was he to know if no man ever approached him this way, and he never approached another man, unsure how to go about it? He was a grown man of almost twenty years, and yet his life has been spent on assisting Mr. Barnave at the bookshop from early morning until nightfall. At least making deliveries all around Brecon kept him from developing a hunched back or ending up thin as a reed.

So if only the sparks of interest that he was sure he felt from Mr. Fane were real, Laurent was about to take matters into his own hands and experience them against his skin.

He tried not to harbor too much hope, but the delivery of books to Mr. Fane was yet another opportunity for developing a more intimate, personal connection. He was certain Mr. Fane liked him. Not only did he visit the bookstore frequently to share his thoughts with Laurent, but he also once bought Laurent a whole basket of the sweetest apples upon a chance meeting at the market. To remind Mr. Fane of that time, Laurent brought two apples to share with him. He hoped he was not overstepping by offering such meager food to someone who likely enjoyed sugar and marzipan everyday, but deep down Laurent knew Mr. Fane would appreciate and understand the gesture. Eating them together would feel like sharing a secret.

With the walk from Brecon to Mr. Fane's property taking such a long time, Mr. Barnave agreed for Laurent to stay the night and return to town in the morning. Of course, Laurent's employer assumed he would sleep with the horses or house servants, but if anything were to happen between him and Mr. Fane, it would happen tonight.

Laurent spared no effort in dressing and grooming himself, and despite the long trip through the woods, he chose his best clothes. A pair of light brown breeches, knee-high leather boots, the slightly old fashioned waistcoat with yellow stripes, and Laurent's pride and joy—a stunning, brilliantly blue tailcoat that widened his shoulders and nipped in at the waist. He'd purchased it from a used clothing seller with money he'd collected in tips and then drained his pockets to have it fitted to his size.

It was worth every dime.

A double set of porcelain buttons ran along the front of the coat, and the wide lapels left enough room to fit Laurent's most prized possession—a brooch his mother had given him upon their parting seven years ago. It was a composition of a Cupid's bow with arrows, two hearts with two doves, and a burning torch depicted in silver and colored with red enamel to symbolize both romantic love and blood spilled during the revolution in France, which had been still causing chaos and sudden arrests when Laurent left for the Americas.

He'd considered pinning it into the knot of his neckcloth, but he worried the muslin would flop over the pin, making it go unnoticed. And it mattered, because if it became a talking point, he could tell Mr. Fane the whole story of the family feud between his mother who favored the revolution, and his grandmother who believed the King was appointed by God and should not be judged like ordinary men. That in turn could lead to a conversation about what they both valued most in life, and Laurent could say he considered freedom a cause worth dying for.

Laurent's great grandfather used to work in the gardens of Versailles and passed many stories of Louis XIV to his daughter and Laurent's grandmother. In his words, the king had been godlike himself, and Grandmother even owned a small print that depicted the king, which he kept in a frame above her bed. In honor of a man so breathtaking and so beloved by his grandmother, despite the fashions of the day, Laurent wore his dark brown hair in long waves that reached all the way down to his shoulder blades. It was his one eccentricity.

He didn't own much, but he was lucky to be graced with a handsome face and lustrous, healthy hair. Secretly he wondered if the long locks communicated that in the arms of the right man he would be as pliant as a woman, but that hope was only based on his own interpretation of things he barely understood.

The shadows cast by the trees in the weak illumination of the lantern, transformed the forest into a place where werewolves lurked in the gloom and ancient spirits waited for a lone traveler to make a false move. He knew such things were only fairytales, of course, but a handful of men have perished in the woods around Brecon in the past few years, and whatever had taken them might as well come for Laurent himself.

He almost wished he wouldn't have to use the lantern, because the contrast of light and dark made everything beyond the trunks closest to the road sink into the shadows, making everything even more ominous.

But he couldn't risk falling down and ruining not only his Sunday clothes but also the items Mr. Fane asked him to deliver. So he persevered, telling himself there was nothing to fear. Wolves were rare in the area, and the light in Laurent's hand would surely scare off any predators. The lost men had surely owned no such commodity.

No matter how carefully he worked on distracting his mind, after an hour of marching along the hardened road between Brecon and Mr. Fane's residence, he still sensed an itch of fear whenever shadows shifted, and some small animal made a sound in the darkness where the lantern's light couldn't reach.

Everything was blurrier in the dark, and for some time now Laurent's eyes had been becoming terrifyingly fallible in the best of conditions. He felt secure enough in the shop and around Mr. Barnave's house, which he knew by heart, but stepping his foot outside, even to do deliveries, was becoming more difficult every day.

He didn't dare tell anyone that with each passing week, letters turned blurrier, and objects in his close proximity seemed so unclear that sometimes he had a hard time recognizing people he did not know very well. With the seven years of his indenture about to come to an end, his whole family left behind in France and barely ever writing him letters, his situation was beyond dire. Having worked as a clerk for most of his life, he had no other skill. And what good was a clerk who could neither write, nor read, or worse yet—one that would ultimately lose his eyesight entirely?

He knew there were methods to help with ailments of the eye, but spectacles were expensive, and he couldn't expect Mr. Barnave, as good a master as he was, to buy a pair for Laurent, especially not so close to the end of their contract. Mentioning it could deny Laurent even the smallest chance of finding employment in Brecon once he was free of the obligations of indenture. It didn't help that Laurent's feelings on the matter were getting graver by the day.

With the rapid progression the illness had made in the recent two years, reducing Laurent to having to remember all the titles in the shop to the letter and using a magnifying lens when there was no one to witness it, he became certain his eyesight was on an unstoppable path to complete darkness. There was no hope left, and once the term ended and he became a free man again, he would be left with only the clothes on his back and with a condition deeming him unable to find work.

At least things located farther away were still within the grasp of Laurent's eyes, and he was glad to see the woods clear ahead of him. He sped up, eager to reach a place with more illumination. The moon was exceptionally large tonight, although curiously tinged, as if rusty water had stained its pristine surface.

When he reached the last of the trees, Mr. Fane's house came into view with its white facade grand enough to be a town hall, two sets of steps at the front, a colonnade framing the porch, and a large balcony in the second floor. It was magnificent, so beautiful in its symmetry enclosed with an elegant fence of stone and metal.

Laurent licked his lips, trying to calm his furiously beating heart. Not a single candle was lit in the mansion, which struck him as somewhat odd, but then again, maybe life looked different beyond the borders of his town? He's never been in the countryside in his life, briefly passing it by on the way to La Rochelle where Father signed Laurent off to the captain of a ship heading to the Americas just weeks after he and Mother had another child.

A light breeze carried the scent of flowers, and he took a deep breath, closing his eyes and simply enjoying the way his long hair slid against his cheeks. Like he hoped Mr. Fane's fingers might tonight. It was so peaceful. Maybe he'd be allowed to spend more time out here, if he managed to forge a close friendship with Mr. Fane?

"Laurent, you're early."

Laurent swallowed a yelp that almost escaped his lips, but he recognized Mr. Fane's voice in time. He pulled up the lantern and looked around, frustrated just how poor his vision of things nearby was. If Mr. Fane knew of this, would he still have invited him?

"Good evening, Mr. Fane." Laurent took a few steps in the direction of the voice.

The light touched a huge rock that laid on its side by the tree line and was tall enough to be the size of the head of the legendary cyclops. Mr Fane's graceful body stretched on a dainty bench, which has been positioned in such a way that the sitter could watch this marvellous proof of geological development of the region.

"Good evening to you as well. I hope you are not overly exhausted after the march, but I could not spare my chaise tonight," Mr Fane said, slowly getting up and supporting his long body with a gracefully-looking cane that he likely didn't need at all. It was merely a sign of his status, just like the expensive, perfectly tailored clothes he always wore.

Laurent hugged the bag with books to his chest. "Not a problem at all, I've enjoyed the walk. Sitting at the desk from dusk till dawn is not ideal for a man of my age. And you, Mr. Fane?" He squinted to work out the pile of overturned dirt and grass by the rock. Laurent held his lantern higher to see better, but it was futile. "Surely, you haven't been gardening, have you?" He laughed out loud at the absurdity of that concept.

Now that Mr. Fane approached, the face that seemed so symmetrical from afar was starting to blur, but Laurent was determined not to show any worry or hesitation.

Mr. Fane looked back at the stirred ground. "Ah, this. It's nothing worth watering," he said with a wide smile. "Have you told anyone other than Mr. Barnave where you were heading tonight?"

"No, I— pardon me if it seems too sad, but I don't have many friends. I have books instead." Laurent looked up at the darker spots on Mr. Fane's face—his eyes. Laurent was a man of reasonable height, but Mr. Fane was more impressive in that quality. "I am not a loner though! I just… rarely meet a man who knows enough about books to keep me entertained in conversation." He dared a smile but stopped both breathing and talking when Mr. Fane's warm fingers skirted over his jaw and pushed some of the long hair behind Laurent's ear.

It felt as if time stood still, and when Laurent finally managed to inhale, he sensed the full power of expensive perfume barely anyone around Brecon could afford.

"I understand perfectly, dear Laurent. I consider you a fine young man. Well-read, polite, with an intelligence far surpassing his station. Your progress is quite remarkable."

Even Laurent's ears were beginning to heat up, and he was glad that it was so late in the evening, because the red blush surely staining his pale face would make him look like a farm worker after a day's work in the sun.

"That is beyond kind, Mr. Fane. I'm not sure if I deserve such praise." But he did. He knew he did. There were things one should say for the sake of modesty, but Laurent would not deny himself the pride he had in how far he'd gotten from his humble beginnings at Mr. Barnave's bookshop. He absorbed knowledge like a sponge did water, and he was bold enough to take action where others backed away.

If only Laurent could make Mr. Fane see that he was worth the attention, there might still be a good future in store for him. Employment within Mr. Fane's residence, perhaps? Laurent wouldn't dare wish for unconditional patronage, but if a man of wealth as vast as Mr. Fane's took a liking to him, he'd surely help a friend in times of need? Laurent knew how to make himself useful, and he could weave himself into the cloth of Mr. Fane's home if given the chance.

Mr. Fane crooked his head, standing so close Laurent could smell the sweetness of his breath, and it sent his heart galloping like a frantic stallion. "Please, do call me William when we are alone," Mr. Fane said eventually and started walking toward the gate.

Laurent followed, drunk on this new privilege, and when he tripped, too eager to keep up with Mr. Fane, the man was there to hold him up. The fabric of Mr. Fane's coat was so fine where it brushed against Laurent's hand. "Are you sure, sir?" he asked out of politeness, already eager to whisper the name into... William's ear. Because William suggested they would be alone. And more than once at that!

"Absolutely. I do believe we have a lot in common, my friend," William said, gracefully moving toward the nearby gate that led into the vast courtyard. Seeing its expanse made Laurent wish he'd arrived in a carriage after all, even if only to experience such a grand entrance.

"I've read each of the books you have ordered... William." Saying the name out loud had Laurent so exhilarated he could hardly breathe. "I can't wait to discuss them with you in the future. I hope that's not too forward. I know you must be such a busy man."

William nodded as they passed the gate, making their way toward the front steps. A shudder went through Laurent when he realized William intended to let him through the main door, not the one meant for servants. Almost as if they were social equals.

"Oh, we definitely shall, although I believe there are other things we could talk of if you fancy," William said, touching his fingers against the back of Laurent's coat in the briefest caress. It might not have been much, but the contact left Laurent's skin burning and yearning for more.

For a moment, Laurent feared he wouldn't know how to act around servants, unsure of his position as neither guest nor employee, but when they stepped into the house, there was not a single soul to greet them. No matter how strange it was, Laurent found it a relief, because he wanted William all to himself, without the need to impress anyone but his host.

"Anything you wish," slipped out of Laurent's mouth before he realized it sounded all too eager. He shouldn't sound like a pup just because he found William's presence so desirable.

He barely even registered the fine hall that was now gently illuminated by his humble lantern. Its high ceilings and sculptures of gods frozen in sensual poses in small alcoves along the walls made the house only seem quieter. They were Greek deities, with attributes, and when Laurent faced the handsome yet mature face of Dionysus looking at him from a fresco, it distracted him so much Laurent forgot to study any of the other figures. When Laurent looked up into the light and shadow that was William's face, he was completely mesmerized.

Something cold and rounded touched the underside of his chin, and it took him seconds to realize it was the smooth grip of the cane. A shudder trailed down his body when William leaned down to him.

"Anything?"

Laurent struggled to catch his breath, so he laughed nervously instead. "I would not damage books."

"Nonsense, Laurent. Why would you even say such a thing, you sweet boy?" William whispered, and even this tiniest, softest of sounds carried up the tall walls of the hall.

Laurent couldn't take his eyes off William even though he couldn't truly see him from such close proximity. "You need to know, William, that I do have boundaries." Ones that didn't include being touched all over. In that matter, his heart was open. And did William just call him 'sweet'?

William hummed and leaned back, trailing the handle of his walking stick down Laurent's neck before directing him into one of the three doors leading from the hall. "What other boundaries do you have?"

Laurent swallowed, navigating the corridor based on what he could see far away and remembering any potential obstacles. "I believe a man should have an open mind to live his life to the fullest."

"A man of my own persuasion, I see. No man should deny himself what he thinks rightfully his," William said, leading Laurent down a walkway where their combined footsteps resonated in the silence.

"I do not mean to be rude, but where are the servants? I believe a house this gloriously clean must be taken care of by many."

William pulled on Laurent's shoulder and directed him to a staircase that had been beautifully crafted in stone and dark wood. The balustrade was of an intricate design that cast long shadows in the faint lamplight. Columns topped with sharp arches stretched tall toward the sky, making the stairs reminiscent of a gothic tower without keeping the space truly enclosed. It spiraled upwards in a gentle curve that left space in the middle, which was now occupied by the statue of a gargoyle perched on the postument with its bat-like wings spread wide.

Laurent felt a sense of unease when the sculpture's ghastly features sharpened in the light, but he didn't dare question Mr. Fane's choices in art. Perhaps the sculpture had been transported all the way from the Old World, and asking about it would have made Laurent seem uncultured.

Fane ignored the statue and dove straight into its shadow, touching the wooden panels. Something clicked, and a section of the wall moved, revealing itself as a hidden doorway. Cool air swiped Laurent's face, and when the glow cast by the lamp snuck into the space behind the secret entrance, a hidden flight of stairs leading to the cellar was revealed. The walls beyond it were curiously naked, too mundane for a man as fine as the wealthy William Fane. William closed two locks on the door as soon as they stepped inside.

"Ah, they are not allowed to come here."

Laurent got a queasy feeling in his stomach when he looked down the stairs, where light died in the pitch-black gloom. But then again, if they were to do something illicit, wouldn't it be better to make sure no servant heard or saw them? He held the books closer to his chest. "Oh." His mind began to wander and draw on the only experience of the forbidden that he had. "Do you own… books that should not necessarily be seen?"

William was silent for a few moments as he took the lantern out of Laurent's hand and led him down the stairs. Just as they neared the floor, an intense, fruity smell started dominating the air, as if the walls had been impregnated with perfume. "Those things are not spoken of. We need to be cautious about what we do in these rooms."

Laurent smiled as his heart fluttered erratically in his chest. Never in his wildest dreams had he imagined he'd be taken to William's secret rooms, nor call Mr. Fane by his Christian name for that matter. "Do we? What are they for?" He looked down the corridor with a low ceiling and several doors on each side. All the walls were covered with beautifully carved wood, but there were no other decorations, which made the place look unfinished. Were those William's private chambers?

"Speak your mind," William said, opening the last door and leading Laurent inside. Fire buzzed in the fireplace, but the room itself, with a low ceiling and wood-covered walls, was curiously empty. A large bed made of solid wood stood in the corner, a chest of drawers, some trunks, a piece of furniture covered with fabric, and not much else, leaving the bare wooden floor empty. The scent of perfume and incense was particularly strong here, so strong in fact it was choking Laurent a bit, but he did not want to displease his host by saying he disliked it.

From his throat, all the way down below his navel, shivers crawled up and down Laurent's body. He pulled an apple out of the bag with books and presented it to William with a hand that was pathetically trembling.

He was a man who would reach out for what he wished for so dearly. He would show William his intentions and deem himself worthy of the man's attention. "I brought this one just for you."

William made a small sound and gestured as if he intended to take the apple, but instead took hold of Laurent's wrist and pulled on it. Laurent couldn't even think anymore, but he wished so dearly that his eyesight were still good enough for him to watch William's handsome face from up close. To be able to see the secret message undoubtedly hidden in his eyes. William's healthy teeth crunched through the fruit's skin, and he took a bite of the apple.

Laurent gasped, too stunned to do anything else. William Fane eating out of his hand? He wasn't wrong about where this evening was leading to, was he? William took him to a secret room, one that contained only a bed and some storage. There was no other explanation for this turn of events. First, William would bite into the apple, then he would bite into Laurent's lips.

"I like you so very much, William," Laurent choked out, weak in the knees already.

William hummed and continued eating as his fingers moved lower—there was no other way to describe it—*caressing* Laurent's arm. "I am loved by many."

"But do those people have lips like mine?" Laurent whispered, with his heart in his throat, so terrified of rejection he could faint any moment.

William pressed his mouth to the side of Laurent's hand, making him drop the core to the floor. "Certainly not, but I have not tasted yours yet," he whispered, pulling Laurent closer as the incense, and the perfume, and the warmth of the fire made his head spin faster.

There was no need to ask William about his intentions. The cards were on the table, and while the game of seduction was still being played, the stakes were becoming at once both impossibly high and irrelevant.

Laurent gave half a second to throwing the bag with books to the bed and took the tiny step needed to have his lips connect to William's. His indenture might not be over yet, but he had never felt as free in his life as he did in that moment.

William's hands were surprisingly strong when they grasped Laurent's shoulders, keeping him in place for William to ravage. His touch spoke of an unsatisfied hunger, and as his fingers wove themselves into Laurent's hair, the moment felt almost *too* perfect. Laurent pushed closer to William, giving a sound he never heard himself utter before, broken yet lusty, and so sinful anyone who heard it would know he was engaged in illicit acts.

William's warm tongue licked its way deep into his mouth, teasing him with a ferociousness he could hardly keep up with. His heart pounded with the ruthless desire of a beast, and he put his hands on William's chest while trying to reciprocate the kiss with the same skill William was offering, but it was a losing battle. William's tongue had ways of caressing Laurent's cheeks from the inside that made Laurent's toes curl in his boots and shivers go all the way down to his rapidly stiffening prick.

William pushed him away so suddenly Laurent lost his footing and sat on the bed, watching the magnificent lines of his host's body move in the warm light of the fire. He pulled off his ivory and golden coat, placing it on top of the chest of drawers.

"I… I've never met a man who… you see, this is very new to me," Laurent babbled, running hot and cold all over. Everything was happening so fast, and his mouth still tasted of the apple he'd given to William. Laurent would forever think of that kiss whenever he ate apple pie or even smelled it.

William's mouth stretched into a smile, and he unbuttoned his waistcoat as well. "Would you take off my shoes, Laurent?" he asked, leaning against the wall.

Laurent swallowed, unsure what to make of the request. Was that something lovers did for each other? Would they be *lovers*?

"Y-yes. If that's your wish." Laurent got down to his knees, not in the least worried about staining his breeches when he was so excited about the glorious man towering over him.

He grabbed the bottom of the shoe and tugged, just firmly enough to take it off without causing discomfort. The stocking-clad foot trailed down his chest and almost touched him between his legs, as if this was yet another way to seduce him.

"I have wanted you in this room for quite some time now," William whispered.

"You have?" Laurent asked, overwhelmed with feelings he couldn't name when he pulled the other shoe off. "I have to confess to thinking about you many times as well. No one has ever talked to me the way you do. And when you were at the store as a customer, Mr. Barnave wouldn't dare shoo me away to other tasks."

William gave a short laugh. "Do you reckon he knows why I wanted you to spend the night?"

"No! Never. I've never done anything to suggest such things." The thought hit Laurent with the heat of an iron poker, and he stilled, kneeling on the floor and unsure what to do. No matter how much he craved to know carnal delights with another man, he was beyond overwhelmed.

"Ah, that is very well indeed. A flower for me to pluck," William said, urging Laurent to get up by holding his jaw gently.

The words sent a shiver down Laurent's spine, but he let William guide him up. "Do you have… much experience in these matters?" When this had been still merely a fantasy in Laurent's mind, no worry reached his starved body, but now that William called him a 'flower to pluck', he wasn't all that sure how he felt about it. A plucked flower was only good for so long before being thrown away.

"Quite enough," William said, pulling on the cravat Laurent had so meticulously fastened earlier. The knot came undone, and William's warm hand trailed down his chest. "I will teach you things you've never even imagined."

Laurent took a step back, but William didn't let go of the neckcloth, holding Laurent with it as if the dainty fabric were a collar. "That is… what I want. Very much so. But I'm afraid nerves are getting the best of me, and I would much rather if we had a chance to get better acquainted first, William."

"Nonsense. We are quite well acquainted already. Are you forgetting all of our conversations?" William asked, pulling on the neckcloth, as if to tug it off.

"I know, but this type of connection is new to me. I'm not even sure how to go about these things." Laurent grabbed William's wrist. The sweet scent in the room was beginning to make him sick. "Could we please kiss again?"

William went silent in a way that had worry choking Laurent. When he spoke, his voice was no less pleasing than before, but there was a hint of impatience in it, and with his face a blur right in front of Laurent, it was impossible to know what the fine lines on William's face were telling him. "You agreed to visit me here, in my private chambers where I don't invite many guests. Does that not prove my interest in a sufficient manner?"

"It does!" Laurent was quick to answer. "But I didn't know what coming here meant, and I do, I do still want to… learn. It's just that we have all night, so maybe let's not rush so much?" He leaned in for a kiss, in an attempt to appease William.

William exhaled against his lips but didn't move to touch him. "Why would you be wooing me if you didn't intend to follow through? I will not be manipulated like this.'

Laurent slid his arms to William's sturdy shoulders. Why was he so confused? He did want to be touched by William. Hadn't he dreamed of a night spent in William's arms, their limbs entangled, their mouths dancing together as if no air was needed?

He took a deep breath and leaned into William's chest. "I'm sorry. Please forgive me if I'm being rude."

William exhaled, as if he was still angry yet tried to rein in his emotions. "Thank you. Your apology is accepted," he said, pushing Laurent back on the bed and immediately following him to the fresh blankets.

Laurent dared a trembling smile, hoping to make up for the earlier fiasco. His hands drifted back to William's chest on their own accord, and just touching the man, even if through a layer of silk, was calming Laurent down in the most pleasant of ways.

He was being silly. Hadn't that first kiss turned his world upside down? Didn't he want so much more of that? Didn't he want to touch William's naked skin? He couldn't wait forever, if he were to reach out for this forbidden fruit. And how long would his eyesight still last him? There were no guarantees that he could still attract a man once his eyes gave up and drowned him in lifelong darkness. This could be his one chance to find happiness, and he wouldn't let insecurity take it away from him.

William shifted on top of him and pushed up one of Laurent's hands, entwining their fingers as they kissed. William's lips, while sweet and still tasting of apples, felt more aggressive than before, almost as if he was about to take a chunk of Laurent's meat and chew on it.

Laurent did his best to answer in the same fervent manner, even though his fingers were beginning to hurt from the strong grip. William's weight on top was surprisingly pleasant, robbing him of breath, and making him imagine all the ways in which they could connect tonight. His grip on

William's shoulder strengthened when he started worrying over the pain the lovemaking could bring. But if William was experienced, wouldn't he know how to go about those things?

William groaned, pulling apart Laurent's legs and rocking his hips against him. There was no denying that he was aroused by what they were doing, and it both frightened and excited Laurent in turn. His head spun, and he wasn't sure what to think, lying flat on the bed still in his Sunday best. But it was William Fane, so who was he to ask him to get off for just enough time that would allow Laurent to take off his coat and waistcoat?

Laurent's heart rattled when he thought of the stiff cock in William's breeches stabbing into him later. It was all happening too fast, but he still went with it, knowing that there was no running away now. That he was almost twenty years of age and he would finally fulfil his potential, Goddammit!

A metal cuff closed around his wrist, and he whimpered when William bit on his tongue, drawing blood.

Chapter 3 - Laurent

Something in Laurent withered.

And when he looked up to see an iron shackle around his wrist, for a few moments he was too stunned to realize that the other end of the short chain was attached to the thick bed frame.

"There. I thought you'd never stop your theatrics," William said, holding Laurent's other hand down.

"My-my theatrics?" Laurent whimpered, struggling against the grip, still unable to comprehend what was happening. "What are you doing?" All excitement drained out of his body, and he thought back to the two locks holding the cellar shut.

The lack of servants.

The questions about whether anyone knew Laurent was coming here.

William laughed and patted his palm against Laurent's cheek, as if he were a little boy. "*Oh, I'm so scared, Mr. Fane. Can we just talk over dinner*?" William mumbled in a high-pitched, sugary tone before suddenly leaning down over Laurent and all but barking his next words. "No. We cannot."

The mockery cut right through Laurent's heart. He couldn't believe what was happening. "How can a man be so cruel?" Laurent choked out, forcing himself not to cry, sure it would be the source of yet more humiliation. "My employer knows I was coming to your house! Get off me, and I will forget this ever happened!" He shoved at William's shoulder with his shackled hand. William held his other hand so hard Laurent worried his wrist would snap. And of what value would he be if he wasn't able to write anymore?

William just held him down, crooking his head in an expression of curiosity, but the handsome lines of his face transformed into a grotesque mask beyond the veil of blur. "No, you were eaten by wolves. My servant will make sure someone finds the books in the woods. And your bloodstained coat. No one will know you were here."

Blood drained from Laurent's face when he realized the meaning behind those words. William wanted to *keep* him here? For what? He knew the answer, since it surely wasn't for conversation. He'd planned this. It was why he had Laurent walk through the forest at night. So that he could later claim that Laurent simply never arrived at his property and possibly even join the search party in a perverted mockery to the justice system. The betrayal of a man Laurent thought of as a potential friend and lover cut deep, but the fear for his life was much more visceral.

Someone so twisted could not possibly be human.

"You're a monster!" Laurent yelled, breathless with panic. What had been the struggle of a moth in a puddle of tar before, became a ferocious battle for freedom. The iron shackles rattled with each move he made, digging into his flesh, but it was no use, and the rough metal sawed at his skin. "What inhuman beast does such a thing? I've done nothing to deserve this!"

"Didn't we just agree that a man has the right to take from life what he wants? I happen to want pretty young men." William moved one hand down Laurent's thigh. It made Laurent thrash harder, knocking his knee into the sensitive place under William's arm over and over.

Laurent's eyes went wide, and realization trickled down his back like water from a melting icicle. This wasn't the first time William had done this.

"The right to take from life? Not at the cost of another!" He would not be enslaved by this man! Hadn't seven years of indenture been enough? All he wanted was to be his own man, on his own terms. He would rather die than be a shackled whore waiting for his master!

His hand got so sweaty he managed to slide it out of William's grip, and he smacked William in the face, putting all his strength into that single desperate hit. He wasn't even thinking of ways to escape or fight William further. His mind was a blur of fear as if the sickness of the eyes had taken over his thoughts as well.

William spat a curse and hammered his fist into the side of Laurent's head. It was as if the whole world trembled, but Laurent managed to get one of his legs free and kicked the heavier body back. His first instinct was to roll off the bed. With his whole being burning like a furnace, he tried to rush for the cane resting on the chest of drawers, but iron dug into his wrist with such force he feared it broke his wrist.

The impact of the pull sent him staggering back toward the bed, and one of the chests piled by the bed fell over when Laurent landed on the floor.

Its contents spilled out along with even more of the sickeningly sweet smell of incense and perfume. But there was something else hidden in those smells, revolting like a decaying rat hidden in a bed of roses. No matter how much Laurent squinted, he couldn't see the elongated shape well enough. A doll covered in fabric? There had also been a dull thud and a clang. The metal object fallen next to the other one was a large hoop with a chain attached, like a shackle or… a collar?

William roared with laughter, leaning against one of the bedposts, like a ghoul about to tear into the flesh of its victim. The imminent danger prompted Laurent to take the risk. In the warped, blurry reality of Laurent's failing eyesight, he reached out to the bundle of red fabric and sweet-smelling particles that turned out to be dried flowers. Laurent touched something soft and cold as a raw chicken leg. He stalled, because his mind could not comprehend why there was hair on meat, or why was meat being kept in a place so warm, so far away from the kitchens.

William laughed. "Say hello. Did you know Marcel Knowles?"

Laurent screamed out when he moved his palm farther up the object and touched stiff, lifeless fingers.

It was an arm. A severed human arm.

Laurent couldn't stop screaming, which then turned into sobbing as he backed away, too petrified to stand up. This was a nightmare from which he couldn't wake up, and he could still taste blood where William had bitten his tongue, which meant it was real, and he never *would* wake up.

Marcel Knowles had disappeared in the area during a hunting trip three months ago, and Laurent remembered him well, because he was a handsome man, the son of a local baker, who always had a good word for anyone.

"Oh, God! You killed him! You sick, sick bastard!"

"I didn't kill him," William said dismissively. "I was out of town for three days. He was dead when I came back, but still warm. I buried him under the rock. With the others. That is where you will also go once your body breaks," William said, opening his breeches. He stood far enough for Laurent to see him quite clearly, and the serenity of his expression, marred only by the odd tinge of cruelty playing around his eyes, was so neutral. As if they were discussing Plato, not talking over a severed limb.

"No! Please! I've been nothing but kind to you!" Laurent cried, unable to comprehend that such a vile creature walked the earth, that he were an admired member of society. And still, in his desperate state, Laurent wondered whether there was anything that could save him, if there was a weapon hidden somewhere for him to pierce the demon's heart.

"I was wondering if I shouldn't preserve the hand in salt, but then again, I do have a ready supply of the likes of you," William said, opening a drawer and producing large scissors with blades so sharp their very sight made Laurent cower by the bed. Cold and hot worms were drilling holes in his skull until he could barely think anymore.

Between the stench, the severed arm, and the blades on show, Lauren's mind was twisting and turning like a cluster of eels, and each time he tried to grab at a thought, it slipped through his grasp.

The initial chapters of his life barely contained anything, and yet the rest of them, all the pages he'd been so long waiting to fill with something meaningful, something other than servitude, were about to be torn apart.

He did not deserve this.

He did everything right. Worked hard and tried not to feel sorry for himself despite the curse of his failing eyesight. He would not allow William to do this. He would not be enslaved by this disgusting monster!

"What are you going to do with the scissors?" Laurent asked in a voice so calm he surprised himself.

William approached and picked up the metal collar off the floor, making the chain jangle menacingly. The closer he was, the more his face resembled a warped reflection seen in moving water. "I heard nails grow even after death. What do you think? Does Marcel need his cut already?"

William was mad. Never in his life had Laurent encountered such pure, remorseless evil. Would Laurent's own sanity be his key to safety, or was he about to spiral into madness as well? His insides were already twisting painfully.

He assessed how far the shackle would allow him to move, and it wasn't much.

William sighed and approached him with the open scissors in hand. "Do not worry. I will let you experience a man's touch before you die. Unless you make me really angry, but I can't quite have a new boy down here every week. Not for the things I want. People would start talking."

The thought of the vile creature on top of him now made Laurent want to retch. How was it possible that he hadn't seen the evil hiding in William's eyes? Not only was his eyesight failing, his thoughts had been clouded by Laurent's own illicit lust, and now he would pay the highest price for that blindness.

In his other hand, William waved the collar, as if offering it to Laurent. "When I put this on you, you will forever do as I please, but I like a bit of a struggle that first time."

Did the collar have spikes to torture a man until he obeyed? What was William on about? Laurent needed to do something and quickly, before the rush of fire in his veins ran out. He frantically searched his mind for any clues, any ideas from books he'd read, but when William approached again, Laurent bolted at him on his knees and bit into his arm like a rabid dog, all finesse forgotten.

A loud shriek resonated through the room, and both the scissors and the collar fell to the floor with a dull clang. William's face twisted into a nightmarish shape and he descended on Laurent like a harpy, both hands squeezing around Laurent's unprotected neck. They pressed down hard, thumbs digging into Laurent's Adam's apple, nails tearing at skin as William's mouth stretched into a devilish grin full of pale fangs.

"Me? You're trying to hurt *me*? You little boy cunt! You will regret having teeth! I will pull them all out one by one so you feel better on my prick!" William yelled.

The scissors glinted nearby, and Laurent reached for them, stretching his arm despite it being his one free hand. All instincts cried out for him to use it to stop William's hands from pressing down, from cutting his air supply, but Laurent looked into the grotesque mask of a face above him and did as his survival instinct bid him.

His fingertips brushed against the open blade that turned out to be as sharp as Laurent had imagined, but the shallow cuts were nothing in comparison to the pain caused by lack of air or the earlier punch to the head. His lungs ached as if a thousand needles pricked them all at once, and his blurry, distorted vision darkened at the edges.

William yelled more threats and profanities, which couldn't penetrate Laurent's mind anymore when William pulled him up by the neck and bashed his head against the floor. But even as it resonated with pain and rattled him to his core, the brutal shaking moved Laurent those few inches farther away from the bed.

Laurent grabbed the steel scissors and swung the blade across William's throat.

Warmth splashed across his face, and the hands around his throat first tightened, then let go when William pulled his limbs in, hands frantically pressing under his jaw to suppress the flow of bright red. His mouth opened wide, like a dog's about to howl, but all that came out was a gurgle accompanied by yet another splash of blood.

The whole house shook, and a bone-searing screech tore through the air. The door rattled, as if someone were attempting to open it by force, but all of Laurent's attention was on the distorted monster above him.

He could not risk that the wound he inflicted was one William could recover from, and when his tormentor frantically rose to his knees, Laurent stabbed the open scissors into the vulnerable stomach that was now only hidden by a linen shirt. The screech that reminded Laurent of the sounds made by birds of prey drilled into his ears as he stabbed the two blades into flesh over and over, even after William toppled over Laurent and then dropped like a log over him. His mangled flesh squelched loudly, replacing William's shrieks, but Laurent continued even when the torn innards began to stink.

"I hate you so much!" Laurent sobbed, disgusted by the coppery scent penetrating his nostrils and the hot dampness soaking through his clothes.

Blood was warm on his skin, soaking into him like a balm that would never wash off, leaving a distinct scent of murder on his flesh. He must have lost it for a few moments, because one moment William was still thrashing over him, and the other—still as death.

The house was no longer shaking, and the intruder that had tried to invade the room only moments ago was making no more attempts. Surely, some of the servants would have felt the ground shaking, but would they even search for their master all the way down here? Could it have been Laurent's frantic imagination?

Everything was deathly still.

At first, Laurent was too stunned to move, but then the need to have William off him became so visceral he screamed out in panic, as if he were still being attacked, and he pushed the lifeless body to the side. Blood from William's stomach covered Laurent's chest, the precious tailcoat, his hands, and his hair hung in sticky streaks, as if dripping with raw egg.

What was he to do now? His knees were soft, his fingers trembled, and he stared at the carnage he'd caused in disbelief. He gagged the moment he swallowed some blood-infused saliva.

Only when he tried to crawl away from the body was he brutally reminded of the shackle digging into his wrist. Laurent whimpered like a kicked dog, and looked at the metal cuff in panic. William had put the key to it on the chest of drawers, along with his other things, and it was far beyond reach.

What would happen if Laurent was forced to stay here with the body, and the severed arm too long? He was sure he would go mad. A terrible vision in which he feasted on William's corpse to survive longer made him spring into action and get up.

He started pulling on the chain frantically, hoping the iron ring attached to the bed could be somehow pulled out of the wood, but Marcel had been bigger than him, so if he hadn't managed to free himself, Laurent surely wouldn't either.

He twisted away from the dead body, angry that his eyes were welling up, because it made his vision even less clear, but he leaned in to have a better look at the shackle. He couldn't discern much detail by watching it, so he employed his fingers instead, probing the iron cuff around his wrist.

It wasn't too tight, so there was some hope left for him, and despite the sense that William had somehow cheated Laurent into believing he'd died and was about to attack from behind, Laurent persisted. Moment by moment, he twisted his hand in the cuff, adding some spittle as lubrication.

His progress was slow, but the more he focused on the task at hand, the more subdued his anxiety became. When he reached the point where his hand was at its thickest, the pain on his joints intensified, but he trudged on, knowing that survival was within reach if he only freed himself. At worst, he'd dislocate his thumb.

But then even that wasn't necessary. He ended up rubbing some skin off the side of his hand, but that was a small price to pay.

He took a deep breath.

He'd killed a man. A man no other than Mr. William Fane. Would anyone believe Laurent that he was only defending himself? They surely would if they saw this room? They would also find Marcel's arm, and they couldn't possibly assume that Laurent brought it with him, could they?

His throat was becoming too tight to breathe. It would only take hours, maybe days until someone discovered what happened here, and Laurent would be found guilty somehow. He would end up dead for killing a man in selfdefense, just because no one would ever suspect the good-hearted Mr. Fane of being the ugly monster that he was on the inside.

Laurent covered his mouth and slid down the wall with a sob. His whole life was melting away because of the one thing he'd tried to reach for, and he hadn't even tasted freedom out of his indenture at the bookshop. Fane had never cared for him and was a cruel madman, attracted only by Laurent's looks. Surely, none of their conversations had mattered to the murderous villain.

There was a tap, loud and clear, as if someone rapped their fingernails against glass.

Laurent looked up in panic, getting back to his feet. "Is anyone here?" he asked, stumbling forward to grab the bloodied scissors. Was there someone still held captive here, or was this a threat he needed to deal with?

He froze when his gaze fell at the tall object—like a door, or a wardrobe—covered in thick black fabric. He'd noticed something of the shape and color when he came in, but now he saw it with perfect clarity, even though the walls next to it were blurry.

He approached with caution yet stepped back when the knock came again, repeated three times in even intervals. Laurent swallowed hard, watching the curtain in silence.

"Who's there?" he asked, grabbing the scissors in a way that would allow him to use them as a weapon once more. His skin covered in itching goose bumps as he waited for an answer.

And then it came. The curtains parted with a whiff of air so hot and dry it could have come from an open fire, forcing Laurent to close his eyes and lean his head down as the scorch wove its way into his nose. His skin stung from the heat, but when he looked back, the fireplace was completely extinguished, as if the single blow of air made the buzzing flames die.

Where did it come from then if not from the fireplace?

Laurent looked up and stepped back with a yelp, holding out his weapon, but the figure opposite him did the same. Only then he realized he was staring into a mirror. His reflection was covered in blood beyond recognition, but even with the fear twisting up Laurent's insides, he was shocked by the clarity of the image. He hadn't seen this well since he was a child.

He stared into his own brown eyes that so often lately were only a blur. Tears left streaks on his blood-streaked face, and he wasn't sure why he was crying, too overwhelmed to assess it.

Was the mirror dark magic, or a brilliant new invention that could be used instead of spectacles? Or was the clarity simply his mind playing tricks on him? Because right before his eyes, the mirror image began to darken, as if the surface had soot covering it from the inside.

Laurent couldn't move, frozen in place as the mirror became black as tar, only to spill over like molasses from a pot. The thick goo drizzled down the wooden wall and into a puddle that started suddenly boiling. Laurent stepped back, still too shocked to do much but squeeze his hand on the scissors as the substance rose tall, taller than him and formed a distinctly human-like shape.

Was his mind already playing tricks on him? Was he descending into madness? Or was this Fane's evil soul coming back from beyond the grave to finish what the body couldn't?

"Please leave me be," Laurent whimpered, taking a few more steps back when the tar on the figure seemed to stiffen, rapidly drying. He cried out again when small cracks began to appear on the monstrous figure, and whatever was under the black 'skin' glowed red like molten iron.

Laurent dashed for the door, but when he grabbed the handle, it burned him, as if the flames of hell burned right behind the door.

This was it. He'd be suffering eternal damnation for his crime.

When the figure spoke behind his back, its voice shook him to the core. Raw and oddly sexless, like the screech of iron against rough wood. "Face me, Laurent."

Laurent was afraid to look back, afraid to face the unknown creature whose sheer presence caused his skin to burn, but there was no other way out, and he slowly turned around.

It had a towering presence, a giant among men and yet oddly slender, with legs that were more like the paws of a dog than human feet and a pair of long spiraled horns growing from the sides of its head. With burning white eyes, it watched Laurent.

Laurent leaned his back against the door that offered no escape, and tears once again spilled down his face. "He was going to force himself on me, and then kill me. I had the right to fight back!" Every time he breathed in, the scent of burning wood and sulphur overpowered the smell of rot and flowers.

"I know," the creature said in the same monotone voice. It stepped forward, and Laurent winced, watching the thick claws on the three large toes drag over the floor, leaving behind smoke originating where its paws had stood. "He was a greedy man. But now he's dead, and you are in need of my intervention."

Laurent swallowed, looking up into the eyes of a creature he could see with perfect clarity. "I am? Can you make all of this go away?" He pointed around the room.

The creature smiled, or at least its charred mouth curved into a grimace resembling a smile. "I can take this responsibility off your shoulders. I can take you to a place where you will be able to live the way you wish, and where this man's death will not send hounds after you."

Laurent's mind worked with the same ease with which his eyes did when looking into at the creature. "Somewhere else altogether? Somewhere where I can be free? Be the master of my own destiny?" He knew now what this creature was. "Are you the devil?"

The being shook its head, as if amused, and some of the char fell off its face in thin pieces, revealing the scorching insides. "Am I the lord of the Underworld in the way you Christians see it? No. Am I a devil? Perhaps I am. And I have the power to give you a new life. A life where you can have all you've ever dreamed of."

Laurent swallowed. Would a creature like this possibly judge or criticize him for making a request that his contemporaries would consider immoral? "A life in which I can freely satisfy my desire for men without repercussions?" He stood taller, squeezing his fingers on the scissors so hard it hurt. He was so, so sick of always being the servant, bound to someone, and now almost a slave or captive.

The creature watched him without blinking. "Yes."

"A world in which I would not go blind?"

"Yes."

Now came the hard part. "You would not give this freely. What do you want from me?"

"I do not demand your soul, mortal, if that's what you're asking," said the creature, revealing its burning hot throat when it laughed. "I need a human to do my bidding for a short time. If you don't fail, you will be free when accomplish your task. You will go to the Kings of Hell. You will find Beast and make sure he is in King's house on the day he reaches the age of thirty and three. Make sure the King himself lives until then. Keep the details of your task secret from Beast."

Laurent dropped the scissors in resignation. "I… I am a bookseller's assistant. How can I have any power over a beast, or a king?"

The creature watched him in silence, as if weighing his words, but in the end, it extended its large hand, unfolding all five fingers that ended in sharp obsidian-like claws. "You have that power, Laurent. That is why I choose you."

Laurent held out his hand despite the fear of being burned, despite the fear of even more indenture. Tonight he'd killed a vile man while attempting to ensure a better future for himself. Maybe this had been his destiny from the start? "I will find Beast, make sure he is where you want him on the day of his thirty third birthday, and I will not let King die. I will keep the details of my task secret from Beast."

The creature crooked its head and leaned its massive body toward Laurent. Its heat was prominent, yet this time Laurent was not afraid to burn. When the large hand closed around his, it felt strangely similar to something hot wrapped in thin slices of bark. "And in exchange, I will make you free in a world where you can fulfil your desires for men without fearing the law. You will gain your sight back. You will be able to forge your own destiny. But if you fail, you will come back to this very room and suffer the consequences of what you've done. Kneel, Laurent."

Laurent swallowed, but went to his knees without protest. With his head bowed, he watched the smoke slowly swirling from the floor beneath the creature's paws. That was the last thing he noticed before a burning heat descended on the back of his neck, filling his head and his whole body.

He was in hell.

Chapter 4 - Laurent

Laurent's whole body went from burning to cool in a split second. As if he had been dropped into a lake, but he didn't choke on water when he opened his mouth in a desperate gasp for air.

He was on stable ground.

On a thick carpet.

He looked back, only to face his own blurry reflection in what was the tall mirror the devil used to enter the human world.

He was no longer in the cellar. The ceiling was taller, and a grand window to Laurent's side let in enough light for him to survey the room, which was as huge as the Brecon market hall or a whole floor of a building, with no walls to divide the space. It could have been a chamber used for storage, but he spotted no dust, and the furnishings were organized in an orderly fashion.

A set of beds... or perhaps heavyset sofas was right in front of Laurent, covered in black leather and gathered around a table made of glass. Its sharp edges glinted in the faint light coming through the window, and Laurent stared at it, struck by the nonsense of using such an easily breakable material for the tabletop. Surely, it would crumble the moment one put a heavy cup on top.

He got up on shaky legs, taking in the room filled with furniture that had sharp edges poking at him from each side. This couldn't possibly be hell though, could it? It felt far too tangible.

He turned around to face a painting of a naked dark-skinned woman who lay with her backside turned to the viewer with no allegorical explanation for the flesh on show. Just a beautiful woman in the sheets.

Laurent stumbled back, struck by the audacity of such a shameless piece of art. Maybe this *was* hell after all.

He looked to the side when he noticed something stirring in the corner of his eye, only to spot another stark naked woman. This one was most definitely real, unless hell had moving sculptures. She groaned and rolled over to the side on a bed that could fit at least five people sleeping comfortably.

Laurent took a few steps her way, shocked by how… large the woman seemed. She was likely taller than him once she stood straight.

Her hair was a wild color that in the faint light seemed almost as blue as his jacket. Could this be? Was she a succubus awaiting a man to lure into her arms and drain him of energy?

He would not be that man.

The buzzing that had been present in his ears since the creature touched him finally stopped, and he heard distant sounds, a low, rhythmical rumble trailing from the floor into his legs in a primitive, ritualistic song with no melody.

On the door behind the sofa, was another painting, this one with a crude image of a skull in a crown and crossbones underneath it. The picture was framed by words from top and bottom, and the writing—large enough for Laurent to discern— read 'Kings of Hell Motorcycle Club'.

That did make sense. After all, if the creature had sent him to the Kings of Hell, should he not have expected debauched women and dark spaces filled with deathly paraphernalia? From one of the shelves on the wall, a green crystal skull grinned at him, a golden crown firmly placed on the side of its head.

Laurent approached the door with a deep breath. It was time to find the king.

The prospect of making noise in the presence of a woman who could be a demoness out for his flesh made his heart thump, but he managed to open the door without waking her.

The moment he slipped outside, the distant buzz he'd heard earlier became much more pronounced, drilling into his ears with a metallic sound that fluctuated continuously, and it struck Laurent that it might be the devil playing fiddle.

He stood in the vast corridor of a grand mansion, faced with a row of large drawings hung in between doors, each depicting a scene grizzlier than the one before. Skeletons forced themselves on barely-clad women, men ripped apart their own flesh, played instruments and did ungodly things Laurent did not want to witness despite having just made a pact with the devil. And instead of aiding him, his eyes picked up bits of the paintings farther away from him, only to let the detail creep into blur as soon as Laurent stepped closer.

Happy to hear the odd music die, he was quick to run down the corridor, as if the monsters left the frames and chased him. He hesitated when he reached spiral stairs made of metal, but then took a careful step onto the skeletal structure. If the king of hell himself could walk down those stairs, it would surely hold Laurent's weight as well.

The stairs squeaked unpleasantly when he descended, but they didn't seem wobbly, so Laurent just focused on getting to the landing quickly. He was about to rush all the way down when a loud bang tore through the air like a legion of soldiers shooting all at once, and he half-expected the whiff of gunpowder to reach him as he stumbled, falling to the smooth, gray floor. It felt like no stone he'd ever touched, but his mind wouldn't stay occupied with such trifles for long.

Loud cries erupted from the walkway ahead of him, and he fought off the pain in his knees, getting up, ready to find a way out. He could surely come back once the soldiers were gone, once the danger was not as pronounced as it seemed now. Whatever this world was—whether one of the circles of hell or another realm entirely, Laurent was determined to survive and do the devil's bidding.

He scrambled against the wall in panic when two naked people, a man and a woman, ran down the corridor, screaming as if their limbs were being torn off. Maybe they were being tortured? Laurent curled up with his hands over his ears, ready for another shot to go off, but instead there was only more shouting and commotion.

He couldn't simply wait until danger caught up with him, he forced his legs to move. As he passed yet another door, a vicious barking erupted behind him, making him yelp and fall against the opposite wall. He swallowed a sob and turned around, terrified of the beast hidden in the locked room. The dark house was full of hidden horrors and Laurent's mind wasn't clear anymore, swallowed up by the fear blooming inside of him.

The lights blinked above, and only then did he notice how odd the lamps were - not chandeliers with candles but long glass sticks that must have been filled by liquefied sun to emit an illumination so powerful. The walls around him and the floor seemed to perpetually pulse with the echo of sounds that were utterly foreign to Laurent's ears. There were voices, but also an ever-present buzz in the background that Laurent could not name. He wasn't ready to face the king of hell. He needed more time.

Laurent spun around when the door rattled under the weight of the beast on the other side, but it didn't break, still keeping the hellhound at bay. Could this possibly be the monster Laurent was to keep in the house until the day of its thirty third birthday? How would he even know how old the creature was?

Unwilling to face it just yet, he ran down the corridor when voices came closer, chasing him farther into the tangled innards of the mansion, with no way to leave in sight.

The barking became louder, more vicious, now accompanied by a tubal roar that sent shivers deep into Laurent's flesh, pushing him down the corridor, away from sources of light and into the dark corners where he could perhaps find shelter from the evils of this realm.

The scent of dust reminded him of Mr. Barnave's attic, where he'd slept just last night, but this provided little comfort when the beast and its companion closed in on him in their chase. The stomping of their feet was getting louder with each moment that Laurent spent desperately trying to discern shapes in the dim hallway where furniture and rubble had been left to rot.

When he got to a choice of two ways through this graveyard of forlorn items that poked and prodded at him with their blurry limbs, he turned into the dustier one in hope that something within it had so far prevented the monsters from entry. He sped up, ignoring all the aches in his body left behind by work and the struggle against Fane's superior strength. The growl of the beast made him open the nearest door in hope of hiding inside, but all of a sudden he was faced with a flash of red and blue light changing as if he were in the devil's kaleidoscope.

He wanted to get away from the blinding colors, to rush back into the corridor and find a different hiding place, but the loud barking had him first freezing, then stumbling back, all the way to the window. He swiped the chamber with his gaze, but it was painfully empty. Not a single piece of wood that he could use to protect himself if the beast threw itself at him. Nowhere left to run.

He took a step toward the window in hope that it could serve him as an escape route, but the ground was too far away to jump, and he didn't know how to open the strange lock either.

The beast didn't give him enough time to solve the puzzle. It leaped inside, barking as if it wanted to eat Laurent alive, and all he could do was back away into the corner and pray for a miracle.

It was a dog of magnificent proportions, tall and muscular like a mule, covered by a shiny black coat with brighter markings around the huge teeth and on its paws. It could tear Laurent to shreds if it fancied, and Laurent pushed his body against the wall, stiff with the fear of a lamb about to be snatched by a wolf. But beyond the growling, he heard footsteps very clearly. They were heavy and firm, like those of a heavyset man rather than the clomping of devil's hooves.

Laurent stopped breathing and shrank, pulling on the lapels of the damp coat in an attempt to protect himself with the only armor he had.

And then a true beast entered. No, a giant.

At first glance, he seemed like a void of black. All his clothes, the trousers and the shirt were that color, but so were his hands, and his face—the color of tar with pale spots for lips, eyes, and just the tip of his nose. He was a giant of a man, even taller than the creature who'd transported Laurent into this realm, with fists like loafs of bread and shoulders strong like those of an ox.

There was no point to hiding anymore. He needed to act first and show that he wasn't afraid, even if he was in fact utterly terrified. "I… I'm not sure where I am." He took half a step out of the shadow and into the faint light coming from outside.

The monster snarled even more ferociously than its hound in a voice so hoarse as if his throat was spiked with needles. "What the fuck are you doing on our property, boy? Whose blood is this?"

The humongous dog was quick to threaten Laurent as well, and as soon as it growled, Laurent returned into his corner with a whimper. His head was spinning, and every time he looked up at the human-like creature who could be over six feet tall, he felt so utterly defenseless. He didn't understand anymore why the demon had chosen him of all men to send into this realm.

The giant reached him in long strides, grabbing Laurent's arm and leaning over him as if he intended to suck out Laurent's soul through his lips. The moment he came into the light, his dark face blurred, features further distorted by Laurent's defective eyes. Not wanting to offend the hunter who chased him down, he looked into the broad face, and there were indeed eyes in the oval-shaped hollows, although Laurent could not discern their color. Regardless of his poor eyesight, he now realized the giant's skin was not completely blackened but rather painted all over with some kind of hellish alphabet.

"Is the blood yours then? Someone attacked you? Where?" the giant barked, sliding one of his oversized hands over Laurent's hips, only to slip it under the tails of his coat.

Laurent pushed at the giant's arms, intent to at least signal that the indignity of being patted down like a cow was something he would not stand for, but it was like shoving a massive boulder.

Should he admit to his crime? Would he be rewarded for it in a place where skulls were decoration? He couldn't confess until he was sure.

"N-no. I don't think it's mine. I don't know. Is this hell?" he asked in exasperation when the huge hands of the giant were finally off him.

The man released a deep groan and stretched to his full height. He was so tall the tip of Laurent's head barely reached his collarbones, and now that Laurent was close, he realized how odd the giant smelled, too. Without even a hint of sweat or sulphur, the man's odor was one of ale, musk, and lemon peel. No man smelled this clean unless straight out of a bath.

"You will explain yourself to King," the giant said sternly.

Laurent swallowed, suddenly self-conscious about his own state. Just hours ago, his biggest worry was if Mr. William Fane noticed his enameled pin, and now he was about to meet the king of hell, covered in blood. Maybe the king would like him that way.

"You will take me to your king?" Laurent tried to speak in a more confident manner, but it was hopeless next to the frightening dog and a man taller than any other Laurent's ever met.

The giant stared at him in silence. "You know King?" he asked in the end.

Laurent swallowed. It seemed that the rules of language were different here. "I know *of* him."

The giant sighed and pulled something out of a pocket in his trousers. The item, which looked very much like a small black notebook, was then pressed against his ear, and moments later, he spoke.

"King, we have an intruder in the clubhouse. Come to mine immediately. I'll get him there," the man said, already pulling Laurent back to the door.

Laurent took a deep breath, but it didn't help at all when the giant dragged him along the corridor with the strength of a bull. "Please, don't manhandle me. I was intending to meet King before you apprehended me."

"You should have requested an audience then," hissed the giant, walking back through the same corridor Laurent had run through earlier. "He doesn't like to be surprised."

Laurent wanted to speak but pushed his body against the giant when the humongous dog rushed past him, brushing its muscular body against Laurent's legs.

"I didn't mean any disrespect," he tried, feeling so weak against the body that seemed to be made of pure muscle. All the creature needed was horns.

"I don't care what you meant. You are on our property. You've come here covered in so much blood you might as well have skinned someone! You should be glad I didn't blow your brains out. You're not even local, are you?"

"I did not skin anyone!" Laurent raised his voice as panic seeped under his skin. Would he be tortured? Should he just admit to his crime and spare himself the pain? "I could say if I was local if I knew where I was," he said, throwing the giant a bone that could either be his salvation or source of yet more antagonism, depending on how proficient the man was at detecting attempts at manipulation.

The giant stopped in the dusty corridor and looked at him. The dog barked from the end of the hallway, as if calling them over, but it went quiet when the giant shushed it with a gesture. "What do you mean? Did someone bring you here?"

Laurent swallowed, sizzling in the fire of the giant's scrutiny. "I was sent here voluntarily." Was that an agreeable answer though? Maybe he should pretend he was dumb and knew nothing? It could be easier to navigate that position until he understood this new realm better.

"By who?" asked the giant, walking Laurent down the hallway with less aggression to his movements.

"I don't know. Please, I'm confused," Laurent said, keeping the submissive posture and voice. The new tactic seemed to work much better than confrontation.

"What's the last thing you remember? Do you know whose blood this is? Do you work at a living history museum?" the giant asked, taking Laurent into corridors he hadn't seen yet. It was much darker here, and he struggled with the worry that he'd end up stumbling again. But the giant's grip on Laurent's arm was secure enough that he would keep Laurent upright if that happened.

"A museum… where you keep the living?" He didn't like the sound of that at all. Damned souls locked behind glass for an eternity while demons came to gawp at their naked bodies. His mind was getting fuzzier by the moment.

"Okay, okay. You are fucking confused. Did you hit yourself on the head? Does it hurt?" the giant asked, following his dog down a flight of stairs and into a corridor similar to the first one Laurent saw, less messy and lit by the same strange lamps. Then again, they were all melting into an enormous labyrinth, and he wouldn't be surprised if it truly was the rooms that were moving while they were only trying to catch up with them.

"I… it does hurt," Laurent whispered when he thought of the place on his head where Fane had punched him. It still throbbed with pain.

The giant exhaled and finally stopped at one of the entrances. There was a curious plaque by the handle and he tapped it a few times. The lock clicked, stunning Laurent into backing away slightly when he realized the item must have worked as a key would.

"Maybe we can have a doctor look at you later, or something," the giant said.

It was a curiously kind thought to come from a man who spewed such rotten words just minutes before. "You have doctors here?" Maybe just to patch up those who were tortured, only so that they could be tormented again.

But the giant didn't get to answer, because another huge man was already approaching. "Who the fuck is that?" the newcomer bellowed in a voice so pleasant it was unbecoming in relation to such vile language.

The giant faced the other stranger. "He says he is looking for you."

Laurent straightened up to take in the man before he could come so close that his features became distorted. "Are you King?"

Chapter 5 - Laurent

Laurent would have suspected the man's identity even without being told, because King had the kind of presence that made people want to stand and listen. His facial features were symmetrical, handsome the way only a mature man could be, and short golden hair adorned his head like a laurel. He was wearing black though, just like his… soldier?

When King came closer, the features worthy of a medieval monarch turned into a flesh-colored fleck in front of Laurent. "This is the first time I see him in my life. And what is he wearing?"

"Says he hurt his head. We need to see if he's not injured," the giant said, finally pulling Laurent into the chamber. It too was rather large and sparsely decorated, with burgundy walls and gray sofas of a similar type as the one Laurent's seen in the mirror room.

The massive dog cut across the room, all the way to a large pillow where he rested after making several circles around it. But it was what stood next to his fabric nest that had Laurent's mouth go dry. A bookcase so full some of the volumes were stacked on top of others. His enthusiasm dimmed somewhat when he realized that if Hell had books, they might be filled with empty pages, to mock anyone who reached for a novel to soothe their mind.

King let out a barking laugh. "He must have. Only someone not right in the head would be walking around dressed like that." He pushed something on the wall, and a light as bright as a dozen candles illuminated the room all at once. "Jesus, fuck! He's covered in it! It's like he's been on a zombie killing spree or something!"

"I did not kill anyone!" Laurent was quick to say, once he decided that was the best course of action.

"Then what happened?" asked the giant, pulling him into a short hallway with three more doors. He headed for the open one and once again switched on a bright lantern above with a tap on the wall. It was a chamber completely covered by ceramic tiles—black on the floor and a grainy sort of gray on the walls. Under a large mosaic of colorful glass was a bathing tub, also covered by gray tiles from the outside but white and smooth on the inside. Behind it stood a translucent screen that revealed a collection of colorful items and metal piping, then there was a chair made out of white porcelain, and a cupboard housing an empty washbasin on top. Above it hung a small, flat cabinet.

The space overwhelmed Laurent with its oddity, the smoothness of the surfaces and complete spotlessness. Was this where he would have his audience with King? He only claimed to need one so that he could find the man and start organizing his plan, but he was smart enough to improvise.

Laurent looked up at the two men. "I don't remember. I'm not sure." Showing confusion has been the best strategy so far, so he would stick with it for now. Not that he wasn't actually confused—because he was, and it was giving him a headache already.

King stepped closer and Laurent tried not to scowl. He hated that moment when people's facial expressions became unfocused, particularly so in moments of vulnerability, when being able to read facial cues could be a matter of life and death. "We just need to know what happened. We can't have you running around covered in blood."

"Just tell us, and I promise you'll be fine," the giant said, leaning against the wall. When Laurent took a few steps back, in the bright light he could see his face much more clearly. There were indeed rows and rows of writing obscuring his features everywhere but around the pale eyes, lips, and nostrils. But there was something else under the ink as well, as if the skin had been somehow twisted, chewed through by a vicious dog, particularly on the left side, where—Laurent only now noticed—one ear was missing. The man's left arm was also completely black, as if covered in the tar that had poured out of the devil's mirror.

"I'm afraid I don't have any recollection," Laurent said quietly, all too aware of the danger he was in. Fane had been tall but nothing like these men. If they were even men, because Laurent wasn't entirely certain.

King took a deep breath and stepped even closer. "You think you can lie to the Kings of Hell, boy? I will ask you one more time. Is there a dead body somewhere on the premises that you want to tell us about?"

"I asked him, and he won't tell. Hound only led me to him," the giant said from his place by the door.

"Why the fuck does it have to happen tonight, when we have cops and medics on the premises? Fuck," hissed King and kicked over an empty bucket.

"Let's just be calm about this. You know they're all paid off and won't investigate beyond the public rooms. If those teenagers could have sneaked into the disused rooms, why couldn't he? Maybe someone left him here to cover their tracks? It's obvious he must have had some kind of head trauma. Can't you hear how weird he talks?" the giant asked.

King sighed deeply and grabbed the front of Laurent's coat with no regard for getting blood on his hand. "Maybe it's 'cause he's foreign. Are you some kind of exchange student? Ah, fuck this. Get me the cuffs. He's not going anywhere until I find what this fucking DNA all over him is."

At first Laurent was not certain what King meant, but then the giant reached to the back of his trousers and retrieved a pair of shackles connected by a short chain, and his curiosity turned into terror.

He backed out so rapidly he stumbled into the bathtub and hit his head against the wall so hard his teeth creaked. "No! Please! No shackles! There is no need for that!" As he struggled to get out of the slippery tub, the fear of that moment when Fane changed from man to monster in front of his eyes came back with a vengeance. He needed a weapon.

A metal pipe ending with a tear-shaped weight seemed like the ideal choice, even if it was connected to the wall, but when Laurent picked it up, it felt disappointingly light in his hand.

King raised his arm. "Shut the fuck up. You're on my property, and I can do what the fuck I want with you. Don't even try to hit me with the showerhead, or I'll have Hound bite off your hand!"

"I will not be a prisoner! I came here—" Laurent wanted to say that he came with good intentions, but if his story was that he didn't remember, then he couldn't let the two men know he'd been lying all along. He let go of the showerhead, and grabbed one of the items by the bathtub instead. This one turned out to be a glass bottle of solid weight. He threw it at King and jumped out of the tub, attempting a dash for the door.

The bottle burst into pieces and covered King in a green slime. With the distraction, Laurent felt a ray of hope, but the moment the dark-stained arms of the giant closed around him and forced him face-first into the wall, he knew there was no way out. He screamed in fear when his left hand was pulled back. Cold metal touched his skin, already burning and reminding him of the touch of William's hands.

And then the shackles dropped with a loud clang.

"King, take a look at this," the giant said, painfully twisting back Laurent's left arm.

Laurent let out a helpless sob.

"Christ… His hand's fucked up. Like he's pulled out of someone else's cuff already," King said, looking over Laurent's wrist. Fresh blood started dripping down Laurent's fingers where the barely-formed scab got ripped off in the struggle. "This is some fucked-up shit." King circled Laurent and leaned down to look into his face. "Listen, kid—"

"I am not a child!" Laurent swallowed another sob. "It's you who's unnaturally large!"

King chuckled and put his hands on Laurent's shoulders. "Until we work out what's happened to you, you can't leave, but we won't cuff you, okay? Calm down, and we won't harm you."

Laurent took a deep breath and nodded slowly, forcing himself to ignore the pain in his arm.

The giant groaned, looking at the messy floor. "But you will clean this up, because I'm not gonna. Now strip. We need to see if you're hurt anywhere else."

"E-excuse me?" Laurent choked up, twisting his body to look up at the man behind him.

The giant showed him the glass screen in the corner. "Go on. Take off your clothes, you can take a shower, and we will see if you need a doctor."

King nodded and even smiled. "Get all that blood off you. If nothing else, then it will at least help with your smell."

Laurent looked down at the dark burgundy stains covering the whole front of his body. He'd known they were there, yet somehow it only hit him now that it was the dark blood that had oozed out of Fane's stomach, and the bright one that spurted at Laurent from his throat. He was feeling sick again, and he rushed to undo the buttons of his beloved tailcoat.

"He's in shock. He's trembling like an engine in winter," King whispered to the giant, but Laurent was more than aware of the words. He was going blind, not deaf. But it was true, he could barely handle unbuttoning his coat.

"Yeah. We should have Jake call any museums and theatres in the area. He might be their employee."

"If he is, he's had some kind of meltdown. We can't be pulled into his shit. We've got enough on our plate as is."

Laurent carefully put the ruined coat over the edge of the tub, and continued disrobing, disgusted by the blood that soaked all the way to his skin. He was sure there were clots of it in his hair, and he needed to wash them out so badly he itched all over.

"You remember your name?" the giant asked.

Laurent pulled his boots off, already worried how he would save all of his clothes from such terrible damage. "My name is Laurent Mercier."

The silence that followed made him look up from the buttons of his breeches that always gave him a bit of trouble.

King sighed, but he didn't seem to be speaking to Laurent. "Give me a break."

"You think Knight would know him?" the giant asked, and despite his earlier anger, he started gathering the green slime and pieces of glass with a small shovel.

"I don't even know anymore. This is some first-class bullshit."

Since he wasn't being spoken to anymore, Laurent took off all his clothes and put them in a neat pile on the edge of the tub. At least a layer of bodily fluids was off him, but he was all too aware of his own nakedness, the red stains on his body, and the blood still dripping from his hand.

"Will… someone draw a bath? Or… do I… I mean, I could do it myself. Please, instruct me."

"Just get into the shower," the giant said, but seeing Laurent's confusion, he gestured at the screen in the corner.

Laurent approached it, only now noticing the screen was a door with small handles molded out of the glass. He expected the slabs of glass to be heavier and colder, but it must have been some kind of infernal invention that did not exist in the human world yet. As instructed, he entered the large space inside. He could easily stretch out his hands to the sides if he wanted to, but how would that help him clean his body—he had no idea.

"Just lift the big lever. The temperature's set."

"This one?" Laurent pulled on a strangely light lever that looked like made of silver but was definitely not. Cold water assaulted him in a flash, and it wouldn't stop hitting his flesh. He squealed and cowered in the corner, but it was no use. The water reached him there as well.

With the two men watching him like hawks, he curled into a ball, forced to endure the shock and get used to the cold temperature. Or perhaps it was the temperature that adjusted for him, because gradually it reached a pleasant heat, as if some good soul added freshly boiled water to the cold in perfect proportion.

"Just use any gel you want," the giant said from beyond the screen, and it turned Laurent's attention to a metal shelf containing a whole array of bottles. They all looked like made of glass, but upon touch they turned out to be something else altogether, a type of resin perhaps?

He grabbed one of them, and worked out that he could unscrew the top, releasing an intense scent of pine. This had to be the first thing to bring him any happiness since his doomed arrival at Fane's. He poured some 'gel' straight onto his head and began working it in as the water kept lavishing his body with pleasant warmth. The liquid created a foam, much like soap, but was endlessly more pleasant to use and smelled nicer too!

"How much water do I have?" he asked as he pulled his hair away to one side over his shoulder, not even caring that his bleeding hand stung.

But something changed in the atmosphere behind him, and before he knew it, King was opening the door, and he grabbed Laurent's neck with one massive palm.

"What are you really doing here?" he yelled, slamming Laurent against the wall.

The ruined sense of safety paralyzed Laurent as the big, masculine body forced him out of the water. The giant joined in, but instead of putting his huge hands on Laurent too, he grabbed King's wrist.

"What do you want from this kid now?"

King was panting, and he wouldn't loosen his hold on Laurent's neck, as if frozen in his vicious rage. He furrowed his eyebrows, but Laurent couldn't work out much more with King's face having morphed into a tangle of colors from up close. "I…"

"Can't you see someone's hurt him? Stop scaring him!" The giant stood in a way that would allow him to block any punch coming Laurent's way.

King let go of Laurent and laughed all of a sudden. "I just thought he might snap out of his amnesia. You know, like when you scare someone who has hiccups." He backed off, and as soon as his hand was gone, Laurent stumbled back into the warm shower, too stunned to think. Something was terribly wrong, and that sense twisted up all his insides. He couldn't *see* well, but he could sense the lie.

The giant closed the translucent doors, locking Laurent in and just staring at King for several moments. "Maybe you should check how it's going downstairs," he said in the end.

King's nostrils flared, and his gaze darted to Laurent in a way so intrusive it felt like a stroke with a cane. "Just don't let him go anywhere."

Laurent looked down at the pink water circling the drain.

"I'm on it," said the giant, following King with his gaze until he left the bathing room. They were both silent until the door into the corridor opened and closed, but even then the water remained the only sound in the room.

Finally, Laurent dared to glance through the glass, but his throat was tight, as if he could feel Fane's hands around it. The giant was still there. Leaning against the sink and watching. Even the warm water and pine-scented foam in Laurent's hair couldn't help Laurent calm down.

"I'm sorry about this," the giant said in the end, crossing his arms on his chest. "Were you held somewhere against your will? There's cuff marks on your hand."

"No, I scratched myself. In the woods." Laurent looked down to his bruised wrist and bleeding hand with a sense of righteous anger suddenly rising within his chest. That monster William Fane had intended to keep him in his basement and rape him over and over again. He deserved the end Laurent had given him.

The giant remained silent, but he approached in slow, steady steps until only the shower doors kept him from Laurent.

Laurent swallowed and rubbed his face with the soap and water. "Is it still on me?" he whispered.

"What?"

"The blood." Laurent stepped closer to the glass so that the giant could see him better.

An odd silence followed, but in the end, the giant asked, "who gave you that brand?"

Laurent stilled, and so did his heart. "What brand?"

The giant's voice was lower when he answered. "The brand on your nape. Who marked you?"

Laurent stepped back from the glass that was steaming up so much he could barely see the giant anymore. He reached back to his nape and ran his fingers over ridges in his skin that haven't been there the last time he touched. They felt hot and yet didn't burn him. His breath sped up, and he remembered how the devil touched him.

Of course the devil would mark him as his.

"Laurent? Don't faint," the giant said. "Just tell me who did this. As long as we don't know who you are, you will need to stay here, so it's in your best interest to tell me."

"I'm not going to faint! I'm fine!" He started rubbing his face in hope he'd gotten all the blood out. "Why is my hair still sticky?" he whispered, imagining Fane's blood thickening in his long mane, forming ugly, tangled knots that could never be washed clean. It was getting difficult to breathe, and the steam wasn't helping. His wounded hand stung when he touched his hair. Everything hurt. Everything was against him.

"Because you put half a bottle of shampoo into it. What the hell's wrong with you? You either tell me what I need to know, or we both wait until you do. Stop pretending like you don't know how to wash your head, because I'm not doing it for you!"

Laurent sucked in his lips, set on remembering all details that were being mentioned. The goo was 'shampoo', and he'd used too much. He decided waiting was the answer then, because he would not be disclosing details of his mission to King's soldier-monster-man. At least the running hot water was helping wash out the goo, and with it, all traces of pink in the water eventually disappeared.

As he was finishing up, the giant briefly disappeared out of the room, only to return with a bundle of fabric. "I'm still waiting. We have all fucking eternity, if you want to stay with us."

Laurent was torn between talking back to the rude creature and being polite to appease him. At least he finally felt clean. "I don't know about the brand. I'm still… confused as to where I am." He gently pushed on the door, but only then remembered to pull down the lever that stopped the water from falling. Without the remains of Fane on him, he felt more like himself again.

The giant passed him the bundle of black fabric. It felt off to the touch, soft, with tiny strings sewn onto the surface of it, as if it was to imitate animal fur. "You are in the clubhouse of the Kings of Hell motorcycle club, just twenty miles away from Portland."

Laurent covered himself in the fluffy blanket that soaked up water off his body. It was so nice to the touch he even patted his face with it before looking up into the giant's face, now wondering if he wasn't just a large human after all. He would still not reveal his poor eyesight to the man, just in case he used it against Laurent.

"That is… in the District of Maine?"

The giant slumped against the wall. "We're in the state of Maine."

Laurent hugged the blanket tighter around himself. "I'm sorry, I'm very confused. Would you possibly have a piece of cloth to wrap my hand in? I would hate to stain your blanket."

"What blanket?" the giant asked, sounding confused. "You're not wrapping yourself naked in any of my blankets. I don't know you."

Laurent cocked his head and held up the edges of the fluffy black cloth he'd wrapped himself in. "This one. It's surely not a sheet, is it?"

The giant exhaled. "Oh, so now you don't know what a towel is? Very funny. I'm having such a great time dealing with your shit. Come here," he added gruffly and opened a drawer in the cupboard.

Laurent sighed. He tried, he really did, but it seemed like nothing he knew was valid in this… place. That wasn't even hell? He didn't understand anything. He was wary, but the giant hadn't hurt him so far, so he did step closer.

The monstrously large paw pulled on his forearm and made him rest the hand on the edge of the washbasin. Only then Laurent noticed there was a hole in it. Before he could think, the giant splashed a cool, stinging liquid on his injured hand and wrist, causing it to ache as if the substance contained spirit.

He yelped and tried to pull away, but the giant held him in place as if Laurent's strength was comparable to the wings of a butterfly. "It hurts!"

"Someone branded you and you didn't even notice. This should be a piece of cake for someone as thick-skinned as you," the giant said, but started quickly wrapping Laurent's hand with an unusually papery-feeling cloth.

Laurent bit his lips to keep from whimpering. He had to stop thinking about the man as an inhuman being, even if he was monstrous. He hugged the towel with one hand. This was no normal place, whatever this club was.

"So rude," he mumbled in the end when the pain subsided.

"*I* am rude?" asked the giant, adding yet another layer of cloth and tying the ends to secure the wound dressing. "You're the one who came here uninvited and won't even admit what he's doing here. And you keep lying to me even as you're using my bathroom."

"I would have found my own way," Laurent said, but it didn't sound as convincing as he'd have wished. He despised being a prisoner, but on the other hand, he only had the bloodied clothes, the pretty pin, and nothing more. Not a coin to his soul.

The giant let out a growl and shoved more cloth at Laurent. "Put this on. If you won't talk, then dress like a prisoner. Just imagine those are orange."

"No! Am I not a guest?" Laurent squinted at the man, trying to see his facial expressions better, but only got confused by all the blurry writing on his face. He did grab the clothes though, which ended up with his towel falling to the floor.

"Not until you talk. We can't have a stranger spying on us. It's all your choice."

The clothes were of a baggy fit, too large for Laurent, particularly the trousers, which felt oddly soft to the touch. With a fastening at the ankles and a string to tighten them on the hips, he managed to put them in place, although with so much loose material around his legs, Laurent likely looked like a beggar straight out of the *One Thousand and One Nights*. The shirt, shapeless and with sleeves so short they only reached his elbows, didn't flatter him either, but at least he would be covered.

He let out a deep breath and squeezed some more water out of his hair, happy to see no pink residue. "I'm not a spy." Laurent shoved at the man's chest. It wasn't his intention to hurt him but to see what reaction it would provoke. Granted, it was a risky way to conduct himself, but he desperately needed to establish on whom he could count in this godforsaken place.

The man didn't even budge, and worse yet, Laurent's aching, abused wrist hurt from the impact.

"Are you trying to provoke me? It's not gonna happen. I've dealt with men much worse than you, kid," the giant said, pushing Laurent back into the corridor and toward the door across the small hallway.

The light came on, revealing a new chamber. It was of a good size, with a bed and pillows lining a space by the window, but what struck Laurent the most was the sheer number of books on shelves, and even in piles on the floor.

He couldn't help himself and walked forward, only to stumble over one of the heaps. The giant was there to save him from the fall though, and having his massive arm around the midsection was both unnerving and comforting.

"I'm sorry, I'm still a bit overwhelmed."

"Then go to sleep. Maybe once you wake up, you'll finally talk," the giant said grumpily.

Laurent pulled away from the touch, but the bars in the window filled his heart with dread. What if there were men like Fane in this 'club', and what if they fancied to hurt him after all? How could he agree to stay here as a pliant prisoner when he was still to find the 'Beast' he was sent for?

He turned around and smiled. "Thank you for your kindness," he said, set on taking the first opportunity to make a run for it.

The giant whistled, and the sudden tap of paws against the floor had Laurent's heart sink. The huge dog appeared in the doorway and sat down as soon as his master gestured for it to.

The giant leaned down and placed his hand on the dog's nape before glancing Laurent's way. "See him, Hound? Keep him here. If he leaves this corridor, rip his throat out," he said firmly and Hound tapped its huge paws against the floor.

Laurent hugged himself and couldn't help wincing as if he'd bitten into a lemon. He backed up until his knees hit the bed. "There is no need for this."

The man stretched. "I think there is. I don't trust you, and he will be my eyes. I will know if you try as much as step foot out of here."

Laurent thought back to the dog's vicious barking and swallowed nervously. He would find a way out. After all, he was much smarter than that dog.

"Don't make faces at me," hissed his captor, and Hound gave a loud, terrifying bark. "Don't you think we're soft just because we took pity on you, you little shit. If I discover something incriminating, there will be no tears shed for you!"

Laurent didn't have an answer to that either, because what could he say to contradict the truth? He was now in a place where he knew no one, but even back in Brecon he had no family, no close friends, and only an employer who had already expressed the wish to pay for yet another indentured youth to replace Laurent at his bookstore. He would fend for himself in this new world and find a way to fulfil the demon's wishes.

"Yo, Beast!" someone yelled outside, startling Laurent with a rapping coming from the main entrance to this set of rooms. "Beast, open up! King said there's a Mercier in there?"

Laurent's eyes went wide, and he stared at the man who was in fact *the* Beast Laurent has been sent here for. He sat down on the bed, too overwhelmed for words, and already hating the baggy clothes.

Beast grumbled and stepped out of the room, followed by his dog. "Remember, he will be watching you. Better be good, boy," he said before shutting the door behind him.

"I'm a grown man!" Laurent raised his voice in frustration, but all he got in return was silence.

He curled his shoulders, trying to not think of the monstrous animal that was to guard him. There was bound to be a way to go past it. As he weighed his options, Laurent swiped his gaze over the empty walls, stopping on the only decorative element he could spot. It was a picture. Incredibly lifelike, it showed a piece of woodlands, with bright rays of sun coming through the treetops. Below was a sort of table, and under it in large, thick letters, it read April. A calendar then.

But when Laurent stood up to look at it, now frustrated he left his magnifying glass in the pocket of his tailcoat, something was odd about it. The paper was silky smooth like of the paintings of the skeletons he'd seen upstairs, and as he predicted, the rows of numbers blurred in front of his eyes.

He stepped back in frustration and got all the way on the bed for the right distance. He squinted once more, and he could finally work out the biggest numbers.

2017.

April, 2017.

At first his mind went blank, but then it finally dawned on him with all its terrifying implications. This wasn't Hell. This was the future.

Chapter 6 - Beast

The sound of the ambulance rattled in Beast's head long after the vehicle left. With the party disbanded, the club members gathered for an emergency meeting in the small circular studio with no windows where they had their round table, and under it—hidden compartments for the cargo of jewelry and other valuables they transported for their business associate from New York City, known as Mr. Magpie. The studio was located in the oldest part of the building, which had originally been a wealthy man's countryside villa, and so he imagined the room used to have some kind of elaborate decoration until the hospital staff stripped it of all finery, replacing gold paint and ornaments with bare white walls.

Beast wasn't able to focus much on the proceedings. His mind kept drifting off, replaying the image of pink-tinged foam and water trailing down Laurent's pristine back. The boy's chocolate brown eyes kept glancing back at him over the graceful curve of his shoulder, from behind the curtain of thick, long hair, his cheeks rosy from the flush of heat.

It'd been a while since anyone this attractive visited Beast's apartment.

To be honest, it'd been a while since there had been a man staying overnight in Beast's apartment, period. A very long while. So long in fact that Laurent's presence was interfering with Beast's thoughts and making his mind descend into the gutter more than usual. In situations when he should focus on the problem at hand, not on a boy who likely acted strangely due to an injury and shouldn't demand so much of Beast's brainpower.

Maybe Beast shouldn't have left him alone after all? What if Laurent suffered some kind of brain hemorrhage while he was away, and he'd find the pale body cooling on the floor once he got back?

He dismissed those thoughts, trying to listen to King's tirade about their clubhouse being in excellent shape and in need of just little tweaks, but even as he repeated his father's words in his head for better comprehension, his mind offered him the round buttocks glistening with running water, and lips so kissable it was making Beast uncomfortable. Laurent had two small beauty spots on one side of his lips and their only purpose seemed to be drawing more attention to the mouth that was already occupying too much of Beast's thoughts. He really shouldn't think this way about someone who was effectively their prisoner.

He was around attractive men all the time, so why couldn't he focus? At thirty two... well, almost thirty three he shouldn't be ruled by his cock like this. Then again, he didn't think he'd ever met anyone remotely as attractive as Laurent in real life. There were plenty of good-looking people, but Laurent had the kind of face you'd expect to look at you from a billboard. With a slightly rounded nose, big, striking eyes framed by long eyelashes and cheeks like juicy apples Beast could bite into expecting nothing but sweetness. He seemed like a surreal presence that didn't belong in their crumbling clubhouse, and even less so in Beast's apartment.

He snorted when he thought that Laurent was a runaway from a high fashion mogul's dungeon.

King went silent and zeroed in on Beast. "You got something to add?" The deep frown suggested King wasn't talking about anything that deserved Beast's smiles.

Beast stalled, glancing at his brothers, who seemed to have focused all their attention on him.

"I'm sure he's damn sorry Davy's stepping down as VP," Knight said and patted Beast's back. Heat flushed Beast's face when he realized that he'd missed this part, but then again, it was no wonder. With Davy's legs crushed by the fallen ceiling, rehabilitation would take long, even in the most positive of scenarios where he wouldn't have to actually lose the limbs. Davy had been a part of the club from the beginning. He'd started it with King and their sergeant-at-arms, Rev. He was also the oldest of them all, and the years of indulgence and fighting had been catching up with the poor guy. Maybe they should have seen his retirement coming, even if no one wished for it to happen this way. He was now at the hands of doctors, with his family, and all that was left to the rest of them was waiting for news.

"It's a damn shame. Davy was a fine VP," Beast said in the end.

Knight nodded at Beast, his thick eyebrows gathered into a frown. He wasn't happy that he hadn't gotten to meet Laurent in the end, but he still had Beast's back at the meeting. It was ridiculous, but there was something about Laurent that made Beast want to keep to himself, even if that desire made him into a dragon guarding his pile of gold. He had no intention of pursuing the guy, but he didn't want to be reminded of the reasons why any advances on his part would be rejected.

At least unlike King, Knight never made Beast feel any less just because Beast's skin was all fucked-up. No one would dare say it to Beast's face, but between him and Knight—roguishly handsome and with long flawlessly-messy hair—he was definitely the ugly friend.

King gave a deep sigh. "We will have to make nominations and vote. I need a VP who can take the weight of responsibility the way Davy always did."

The men around the table murmured their agreement. Joker even raised a glass of beer, though it was unsure whether he was toasting his approval of the vote or to Davy's health.

Rev had a few sips of beer and tapped his thick, cigarette-yellowed fingers against the tabletop. "I think we need some young blood to assist you. Beast would make a fine second in command."

Beast's heart thumped, and he looked up, surprised that Rev would not want to step up himself. Then again, he'd always been the kind of man who preferred to be out of the spotlight. The sergeant-at-arms function was likely the height of his ambitions when it came to club hierarchy.

King went silent for once, and it gave enough time for Knight to but in. "Oh, man! So right." He clinked his glass with Rev's. "He always deals with shit when it hits the fan. He's an obvious choice for VP. And he's got no other position, so it's not like we'd have to then fill another one." The eagerness in his voice made Beast's heart soar, but he kept his face straight, listening on. He didn't want to get his hopes up like last time when he volunteered to become their road captain, only for King to push for Knight instead.

For as long as Beast could remember, his father never ever tried to elevate him or reward his sacrifices for the club. And the club was Beast's entire life, even more so since the accident, and to see others climb the ranks while he remained unrecognized was like a slap to the face. Slowly, he raised his gaze to meet King's blue eyes.

Joker shrugged. "Yeah, I vote for Beast too. Even tonight he went in and dealt with whatever stuff had to be done. And then he found the intruder as well. He's the prime choice."

King raised his hands. "We're not voting yet. And Gray's still on the run in New York, so how can we?"

Rev groaned and rolled his eyes. "He's my son. I can text him. It's not like it's confidential information."

Their latest member, Fox, gave a sharp nod. "That's a good idea. I know Beast hasn't officially occupied any of the other ranks—"

"But that's long overdue anyway. He's done all the things he could have, and he's always done them excellently, even if he had no rank to his name," Rev said, causing the room to go quiet as he pressed the buttons of his indestructible old Nokia.

Jake stepped out of his spot by the wall where he'd been standing straight as an arrow. "If I could just say, Beast dealt *so* efficiently with Gyro today."

If glances could kill, Jake would be a pile of dust left behind by the scorching heat of King's gaze. "Anyone asked you, Prospect?"

"I just thought it was worth mentioni—"

King slammed his fist against the table. "And I think you should shut the fuck up and go help with the rubble if you don't know your place in a meeting. What part of 'only a patch gets a voice' don't you understand? Dismissed."

Prospect nodded, and his shoulders slumped. He muttered a 'yes, sir', and left the room quickly.

Beast licked his lips, feeling a flush crawl up his neck. "I would be honored to take Davy's place," he said in the end, knowing a declaration was expected of him. With King's eyes drilling into him, he could not stop thinking of the intricate brand on the back of Laurent's neck that caused an outburst of anger in King earlier. What was the significance of that symbol?

And why did King have the same one on his nape?

Rev's phone buzzed, and he opened the message with a nod. "Gray says aye," he said, showing the screen to everyone. The message contained only those three letters.

Beast swallowed, catching Knight's gaze. His best friend grinned in encouragement, and Beast spoke. "I think that considering what happened to Davy, we should rethink the matter of the clubhouse. Some of you guys have kids, and they sometimes play in that room. What if a piece of the ceiling fell on Fox's daughter?"

Fox frowned, leaning back in the chair, his face serious as if he were attending a funeral. That was exactly the reaction Beast wanted.

King's face was stern. "Have we actually voted?"

Rev shook his head at King. "Who's backing Beast becoming our VP?" He raised his hand, and all others around the table followed, filling Beast with such exhilaration he had to work hard on keeping it in.

All eyes turned to King, and in the end, even Beast's father raised his hand for half a second. "It's done then." He threw Beast the 'Vice President' patch across the table and smiled in a way that seemed almost sincere. "Let's go celebrate our new VP and drink to Davy's health. We can talk about the clubhouse another time."

Beast grinned, although he didn't want to admit just how happy the appreciation had made him. He would raise the topic of the clubhouse again soon, but this wasn't the time to spoil anyone's mood with serious talk any further. "Let's."

Chapter 7 - Laurent

Laurent all at once loved and hated the clothes Beast had given him. He hated their shape, their size, and the way they made him feel small in comparison, but then again, the fabric of both the trousers and shirt felt so soft to the touch he couldn't help but enjoy the way the clothes enfolded him.

Hours must have passed since Beast left, and Laurent couldn't sleep, sweating into the sheets and constantly worried someone would approach him while he dreamed and snap his neck. He couldn't hear any sounds but the odd buzz that just hung in the air and was starting to sink into the background. But Beast likely hadn't yet returned to his rooms, and despite the furry monster guarding Laurent, he would need to relieve himself, and soon. There was no chamberpot in the bedroom, and with no other perspective in sight, he decided to take a leap of faith.

With his heart in his throat, he peeked out into the dark corridor, but the dog was nowhere to be seen, and the door to the large main room remained closed, so he was safe to pass to the bathroom. He would have appreciated if Beast told him that, not left Laurent to suffer with a full bladder.

On the wall of his room, he found the switch that illuminated the space and couldn't help but play around with it for a while to work out how it sparked fire so quickly and efficiently, but it was no use. His physical needs were more pressing than his curiosity of this new world and its inventions.

The future was an amazingly advanced place. He thought back to the shower-bath that seemed to hold an unlimited amount of water, as if the tank above were the size of a granary.

His clothes were still on the edge of the bathtub, blood drying into the expensive fabric and making his heart ache at the possibly permanent damage to his best outfit. He pushed them all into the tub and looked at the levers above it, which looked very similar to those in the shower. If he could at least soak the clothes in cold water overnight, maybe they could still be salvaged. After a moment's thought, he poured some of the pine 'shampoo' over them as well.

He looked around for a chamberpot, thinking that if it wasn't there, he could always relieve himself into the shower, since it had some sort of draining system. But as he took his time examining the room on his own and wondering what new devices people could have come up with, it hit him that the 'porcelain chair' was strikingly similar to the drawings of self-cleaning lavatories he'd seen in books about newest technological advances. Granted, no one had one in Brecon, but maybe in 2017 the convenience such devices offered was no longer a luxury affordable only to the richest of men. He approached the lavatory and wondered at the lid that wasn't even made of porcelain but the same light, resin-like material as many other items in the room, like the shampoo bottle.

He was relieved to finally urinate into the little pool of water, but with Beast not present, he took his time to take in the unfamiliar surroundings full of things he had no names for. As he turned to look at the stained clothes in the empty tub, he leaned against a metal piece on the side of the lavatory. It unexpectedly dipped under the weight of his hand. Surprised by the sound of gurgling water, he stepped back, only to watch more clear liquid flood the basin and wash away his urine.

Laurent laughed out loud when he thought of how this room was filled with freely available water in any amount one wished for. Maybe there was even no limit to it? Maybe people had worked out a way to perpetually pump water with no effort on their part? His excitement grew by the second, but there was no time to waste when it came to his clothes. Using the knowledge acquired during his earlier bath, he plugged the drain with a rubbery item laid out seemingly for that purpose, and then filled the tub with a bit of water. It was incredible how easy drawing a full bath was in the future!

The water that came out of the pipe was lukewarm, but as Laurent moved around the lever, he worked out that moving it to one side made the liquid colder while turning it the other way, caused hot water to pour out of the pipes. He chose the lowest possible temperature, to not have blood stain his garments permanently, and watched the pine-smelling gel create a thick, white foam over his jacket. He didn't know much about those matters, but he had watched the woman who did his and Mr. Barnave's laundry at work several times, and he knew the garments should soak first.

Proud of his work and discoveries, he inhaled the intense scent of pine. Since Beast wasn't anywhere to be seen, maybe he'd even taken the dog with him, and had only left Laurent with empty threats? That would be typical of a man as rude as the gruff, swearing giant.

Laurent peeked out into the narrow corridor and approached the closed door that would lead him into the main chamber. He put his ear against it, but no sound of dog paws tapping against the floor could be heard. In fact, he could hear no signs of Hound's presence at all.

Laurent went back into the bedroom to don his boots, just in case he managed leave Beast's rooms and explore the area. Perhaps he would then meet some friendlier souls, but with the hideous, oversized trousers pooling at his knees, he surely looked ridiculous. For once he was happy there wasn't a mirror in sight.

The boots moved the offendingly excessive fabric higher up his leg, making him look like he was wearing some type of trousers from the Orient. All he needed to complete the look was golden jewelry and a saber. Sadly, he had nothing that could be considered a weapon, and a long brush he found in the bathing chamber was made of the same resin as many other items and was not hard enough to be used for that purpose.

Not yet willing to go back to the main room, Laurent chose to explore the last door in the corridor, but it turned out to be locked, which only spiked his curiosity, but left him with no choice but to go out the same way Beast had used to lead him in.

Through a room that was possibly guarded by the vicious dog.

Only now did Laurent realize that all the things he'd done since leaving the bed—putting on boots, looking for a weapon—had been meant to put off the decision that could cost him his throat. It still ached from Fane's attempt at suffocating him, but remaining Beast's prisoner was not an option. He needed to continue his mission from a more dignified position.

He took a deep breath and opened the door to the main room oh-so-slightly, just to see whether the dog was waiting for him, quiet and ready to attack. But no salivating muzzle tried to push at the slit between the door and its frame. Was liberty really at arm's length?

He stepped outside, into the large room bathed in the first morning light. The weak illumination made everything even more gray, but the early hours would be Laurent's advantage. The heels of his boots tapped against the floor as he made his way ahead, for the door that would offer him salvation, but he was only halfway through when a low growl tore through the air and trailed down Laurent's spine, turning his legs into lead. Focused on his goal, Laurent had forgotten the nest of pillows and blankets hidden behind the bookcase, but the dog was there, already raising its black body off the bed.

If Laurent were quick enough, if he could run up to the door before Hound could, he'd be free in seconds. He'd also need to close the door behind him so that the monster didn't follow, but the decision had to be made. Now.

Laurent ran. With a yelp escaping his lips, he dashed to the door with the dog's growl on his heels. He leaped over the sofa and slammed into the door from the impact. With a sense of victory, he pressed on the mechanism that should open the door, but instead of a green flicker that appeared when Beast had done so, a red one flashed along with an unpleasant buzz, and nothing happened. The door was locked, and the dog so close he could sense it behind him.

The bark had Laurent staggering back, but Hound wouldn't let him regain his composure. He got to his hind legs and pushed the front ones against Laurent's stomach with all the power behind his combined muscle and weight.

Laurent tipped over, stiffening his neck in just the right moment to avoid hitting the back of his head as he suffered a hard landing on the floor. Hound's reddish muzzle was just inches from Laurent's face, long teeth on show, strong paws pushing down on Laurent's chest. When the dog barked, the sound drilled painfully into Laurent's ears.

Tears filled Laurent's eyes, and he wasn't even ashamed of them. Who wouldn't fear those jaws so close to their face? He would die eaten by a dog after escaping a long and painful death at the hands of William Fane. How pathetic was that?

He whimpered, stiff as a piece of wood and curling his hands into fists.

Hound leaned in, causing Laurent to close his eyes as the huge teeth came closer, and the animal's putrid breath teased his nose. The dog sniffed him, rubbing its hairy muzzle against Laurent's cheek, as if probing which piece of flesh it wanted to bite off first.

But then it laid its full body weight on top of Laurent and placed its head on his chest, watching him with large brown eyes.

Laurent didn't dare look back, but he exhaled deeply. At least his throat was still intact. But then minutes passed, and nothing changed. The moment he tried to move even an inch, the heavy lump of dog let out a growl of warning, which was convincing enough to make Laurent lie still.

All that was left for him was to try and bear the weight and watch the sun come up outside the window with steel bars in it. By the time he heard steps and voices behind the door leading out of the apartment, he was dying to get out from under the dog that would have surely suffocated him at some point with its weight alone.

The footsteps ceased somewhere by the door, and Laurent's heart fluttered with gratefulness when he heard the lock budge. He glanced to the door just in time to see Beast enter in the company of a slightly shorter man with handsome features and wavy black hair.

The newcomer's eyes glinted, and he laughed out loud. "Oh, no. Did you leave him like this?"

Beast's lips thinned as he walked farther into the room, letting through a young woman with distinctly foreign features and full cheeks. She reminded Laurent of the Chinese he'd seen sometimes in the harbor, only unlike theirs—her hair was pale as beach sand. She wore a blue garment so tight and short her body looked like wrapped with bandages, and her entire legs were on show, so perhaps she was a woman of ill repute. That was the only explanation for wearing undergarments when men were present.

"This was an accident, and won't happen again. I'm sorry. Please, he's so heavy."

"Oh, wow! Is he French?" The woman said in the same accent that Beast and the other man had. She did not sound Chinese at all. It was all becoming too confusing, and he was out of breath because of the dog.

The handsome man grinned widely and scooted by Laurent. "Are you actually from France? What's your lineage?"

"Knight, you're scaring him," the woman said, putting a stack of cloth on one of the chairs. When she bent over to do so, the bandage-like garment trailed up her thigh, revealing the bottom part of her buttocks along with—Laurent looked away, flushing furiously—a piece of pink cloth between her legs.

"I'm pretty sure he's scared of the big bad dog," the handsome man, Knight, said. Had people in the future adopted common words as names? Laurent would just assume nothing and follow the lead of his hosts.

Beast loomed over Laurent, glaring at him with his pale eyes, yet not asking Hound to set Laurent free. "Good. Maybe he's ready to talk now."

Now that Beast was here, Laurent was more confident about actually trying to push at the dog's paw, but he quickly abandoned that idea when Hound frowned at him and made an unpleasant grunt. "Please, Mr. Beast, I've done nothing wrong. This is a misunderstanding."

The woman laughed out loud and looked at Beast. "*Mr. Beast*! Oh, my God! Did you make him call you that?"

Beast put his thick arms across his chest and leaned down his head, making some of the dark blond hair that grew only on top of his skull slide over his forehead. He combed it back with an annoyed sigh. "Don't be silly, Nao. I just want to know where he's come from. It's not my fault he refuses to answer."

Knight pushed at Hounds body, but the dog growled at him too. "Oh, come on, Hound. I've known you since you were a puppy!"

Laurent sniffed and looked up at Beast. "Because I don't have the answers to those questions."

"How can you not know?"

Nao approached, and as she kneeled on yet another side of Laurent's body, her face morphed into a blur of color. She was even wearing face paint, it seemed. No one's lips could be that particular shade. "Maybe he has amnesia, or something?"

"Thank you for the understanding," Laurent said, eager to please her. If he couldn't have Beast like him, he needed to endear other people to himself. "All I wanted was to go to the bathroom, Mr. Knight, and I misjudged the doors when this monster attacked me."

"He's talking weird," Knight said, even though it was *his* language that contained strange and unnatural words.

Beast's mouth opened into a grin that had Laurent's skin breaking out in goose bumps. "If he hit himself on the head so hard then there's surely bruises on his head. Maybe we should shave his hair and look for them."

Laurent went silent as the words sank in. His hair was still damp from the wash, and felt strange to the touch, but he would still not want to lose it. The long strands were one of the few things that he got to have a choice on, and having this freedom threatened had him wishing he could sink into the floor.

"No, please. You can just touch it, and you will sense the lump."

Knight watched him in a strange silence, and Laurent's stomach was twisting into intricate knots.

Beast scooted down and roughly dove his fingers into Laurent's mane, making him stiffen when the digits pressed on the aching spot. Beast gave a low grunt.

"Do you even know where your parents live? Anyone we could contact?"

"It's all a blur."

"How old are you?" Knight asked.

"Nineteen," Laurent said, but quickly looked up at Beast, hoping this would be his chance to find out how much time it would take him to complete his assignment here. "What about you, Mr. Beast?"

Nao laughed and got back up again. "Oh, he's just precious."

"Christ, drop the mister," hissed Beast and whistled, which prompted Hound to finally get off Laurent and let him breathe again. "Makes me feel old."

"But how old exactly? You can't be forty, surely?" Laurent asked, knowing that when one suggested an age too advanced, the other person would most likely reveal their true years.

Nao shook her head. "God, you make him sound like a grandpa!"

"Beast will be thirty three by the end of August," Knight said, finally providing some useful information. It was April now, according to the calendar, which meant that this torment would take about four more months.

Laurent swallowed, slowly sitting up. "I'm sorry… Beast. I'm sure there are still many happy years before you."

Nao put a hand over her lips, stifling a laugh. "Okay, I'll be going. I brought you some clothes, Laurent, and by the looks of it, you need them badly."

She grinned and waved at them all before exiting the room and leaving Laurent with the two monstrously big men and an equally oversized dog. Once she was gone, Beast stepped back and gestured for Laurent to get to his feet. "Take off your shirt."

Laurent stood up, but stepped back, looking between Beast and Knight. "I… I don't need another bath."

Knight cocked his head to the side. "Why do you want him to undress? I mean, I know *why*, but—"

Beast's large body went rigid, and his face snapped in Knight's direction. "There's something I need you to see. Nothing more to it."

Laurent sighed deeply, knowing there was no way out of this humiliating process. He pulled the oversized shirt from under the waistband and then over his head.

Knight snorted. "Oh, yeah. I see what you mean."

Laurent pouted in frustration. Why didn't *he* understand then if it was so obvious to his hosts?

The shirt barely came off when Beast caught him by the shoulders and twisted him around, lifting the damp hair off Laurent's nape. A sudden realization came over him, and he stiffened, feeling the two pairs of eyes prod at the mark left behind by the devil. A deep shudder went through his body as fear took over. What if the presence of the brand made him a witch in their eyes?

"You see this?" Beast asked calmly, answered by a hum coming from Knight.

"It's like your dad's!"

Beast's hands tightened over Laurent, and he exhaled heavily before letting him go. "But what can I do if he doesn't remember, or at least says he doesn't? I can't exactly draw information out of him?"

Knight cleared his throat. "I bet Joker can."

Laurent looked over his shoulder in panic, only to see Beast shake his head and Knight reach for Laurent's nape.

"Whoa! Touch it! It's like… hot." Knight pulled on Beast's hand and placed it on Laurent's nape, as if Laurent were some freak of nature to be poked and prodded at. He hid his face in his hands and curled his shoulders.

He had no idea how his skin could be unnaturally warm if Beast's fingers touching it seemed to leave scorching hot traces. His palm was huge, and it not only covered Laurent's nape with ease but also spread to his shoulders. It was also rough, with an uneven surface and tiny bumps that rubbed against Laurent with the gentlest touch.

It was gone before he could get used to its presence.

Beast huffed loudly. "Look, there's this, and he's been kept somewhere by force. Someone hit him on the head and tried to choke him. It must be some kind of..." His voice trailed off into a whisper, and Laurent couldn't catch the last words.

He looked over his shoulder again. "May I dress?"

Knight was watching him, and despite his face seeming quite fuzzy, Laurent could discern when the dark eyebrows furrowed at whatever he'd heard. He held out his hand in a gesture Laurent understood, so he turned around and squeezed it in greeting. "I'm Travis Mercier, but my friends call me Knight."

Laurent dared to smile at the man, overwhelmed that they in fact shared their last name. "Laurent. Laurent Mercier," he was eager to say.

Knight grinned so widely Laurent could recognize it from up close. "Where is your family from?"

"I…" He wasn't sure if he should mention it, but it was too exciting a connection to pass on. "A small town east of La Rochelle."

Knight gave a yelp and slapped his hand against Laurent's arm. "We might be related. Mine too! I am very respected in the online genealogy community, so we should have no issues finding out how we're connected. And contact your family there."

Beast murmured yet another string of poisonous words, as if the family reunion somehow hurt his feelings.

Laurent smiled at the unexpected connection he had to this new world. "May I… I mean… the clothes the Oriental lady brought. Hopefully they're more fitting than these?"

Knight stepped away just in time to leave a clean path for Beast, who grabbed Laurent's ear and tugged on it firmly. "What is wrong with you? Don't call her that! She is Japanese-American and King's girlfriend!"

Knight groaned. "Have you lived under a rock? Don't use that word!"

"Oh, oh. I'm sorry." Laurent grabbed the new shirt and held it in front of himself like a shield. "I forgot her name."

Knight leaned over to Beast and whispered something, again leaving Laurent out of the conversation. Laurent sighed and decided to focus on himself instead, since it seemed nothing he said or did was right. At least he was a fast learner. He pulled on the new shirt, which in contrast to the one he got from Beast was verging on too tight. The fabric was strangely stretchy as well, as if it had tiny threads of rubber added to the weave somehow.

"Is this how it's supposed to fit?" he turned to the two men and spread his arms.

Both Knight and Beast looked at him for the longest moment.

"You look fit in that T-shirt," Knight said in the end.

Laurent dared a smile. "And that's good?"

Knight snorted and nudged Beast with his elbow. "Look at that, he's already fishing for compliments."

Laurent felt his face heat. "That's not the case! I simply wanted to know."

"Just finish dressing. You need some more clothes if you're to stay here," Beast said, stepping back.

Laurent pulled his boots off, wary of Hound watching his every move, but as soon as he untied the baggy trousers, Beast pushed at Knight.

"Didn't you want to go piss or something?" Beast groaned.

Knight raised his hands and started toward the bathing room. "Right. Right. Of course."

Beast was silent for a moment, watching his friend until he disappeared from sight. He stepped closer to Laurent and leaned in to speak into his ear. "Look. I know you're hiding something. Maybe you're afraid someone is gonna go after you or whatnot. You need to stay here until I know what's going on, but nothing bad's gonna happen to you. Is that clear?"

Laurent swallowed, surprised by that statement, and he looked up at Beast, who despite towering over him, despite the scary dog, and the grumpy attitude, seemed to be on Laurent's side. And didn`t Laurent need to stay here anyway? He gave a slow nod. At least he wasn't being asked a thousand questions anymore.

Beast stared at him too, on the edge between blur and clarity, where his marked face seemed somehow softened yet sharp enough for Laurent to read his expression. It was an odd moment of silence that had Laurent's cheeks heating for no reason at all.

Knight's voice calling for Beast broke the spell, and Beast looked toward the bathroom. "What?"

"Why are there clothes in your bathtub?"

Laurent touched Beast's forearm, surprised by how strangely textured it was. "Those are mine. I wanted to soak them overnight so that it's easier to clean them later."

Beast stirred, not moving by an inch. "Have you never seen a washing machine?" he asked in an oddly soft voice.

Laurent licked his lips. From the sound of it, he should have. He already liked the sound of it. A machine that would wash clothes, so that the people didn't have to. How marvelous was that? "I have, I have! I just… I wasn't sure if such a machine could deal with blood well. You see, that coat is very dear to me."

Beast rubbed the back of his neck. "When I go to the mall, I could leave it at a dry-cleaners for you, I guess. But it has to dry first."

Laurent wanted to thank him, but a loud ringing, accompanied by a buzzing sound, resonated from Beast.

Beast groaned, as if someone had taken away his wine, and pulled out the same black notebook, which he somehow communicated through with King earlier. Was it a magical device? Nothing would scare Laurent anymore in this strange world that had no limits on bathing water and where light sparked by the press of a finger.

"Yes?" Beast stirred and shifted his weight. "You sure? You're only gonna scare him again."

King's voice resonated from the device, his voice slightly distorted. "Hope my son's treating you well, Laurent. I wanted to apologize again for yesterday. I didn't mean to scare you."

Laurent leaned in closer to Beast's hand and the black device. "Oh, no, Mr. King. I am very well. I even received new clothes from your Japanese-American girlfriend."

King laughed good-naturedly. "Nao? She's a hot one, isn't she? You need to meet the other one. She makes killer Martinis."

So close to Beast, Laurent could smell the citrus scent on him again, although it was not as potent as it had been at night. Instead, the more natural scent of flesh was almost tangible, despite there still being no tang of sweat to be noticed.

"Yes, sir. She was very nice." Also looked like a harlot, but that didn't need to be said. Laurent would keep an open mind about all future-related issues. After all, had Romans not worn different clothes than him? Had Louis XIV not worn a long wig, when a century later, short hair was in fashion? It did not make one time or another more or less moral.

"As far as I understand, you will be staying here for now, so I want you to make yourself feel at home. Beast will take you shopping for any shit you want."

"You... want me to take him shopping?" Beast asked as if he weren't sure he heard King correctly.

"But… I don't have money, Mr. King."

"Don't worry about it. It's just some basics."

Laurent smiled, overwhelmed by this kindness, but the man was a *king* after all. "That is most generous, sir."

Chapter 8 - Laurent

"If your father is King, should you not be called Prince, not Beast?" Laurent asked as they slowly made their way through a world that seemed so different from the one Laurent knew that it felt like another realm, not another time.

They were in a place Beast called *the mall*, and the sheer number of people walking the hallways of this palace of commerce was likely several times greater than the entire population of Brecon in Laurent's day. The strange modern music blasted from every little store within this enormous market hall, creating a cacophony of clashing tunes with an undercurrent of loud voices, laughter, and the background buzzing that seemed like a permanent fixture in 2017. Upon Laurent's complaints of a mild headache caused by all this commotion, Beast offered him pills that swiftly took away all the little aches in his body as well—all that without muddling Laurent's thoughts.

And they hadn't come here on foot either. In the future, people gave up on horsepower and used machines powered by electricity and oil to change location. Laurent had curled up for the drive despite Beast's reassurances that it was all perfectly safe. The thing had made an ungodly noise as if startled, but worst of all, it smelled of fuel and moved so fast Laurent feared the speed itself would choke them to death. No. Even worse was the fact that there were dozens of such carriages—called cars—of all shapes and sizes, and they all moved along smooth black roads that looked like nothing Laurent could compare them to. Highways in hell maybe.

He was glad to be on solid ground, but the experience left him both exhilarated and apprehensive of all the other fears he'd surely have to conquer in this strange new world.

Beast pushed his hands into his pockets as they moved along a large hallway grander and more opulent than any Laurent had ever seen. Glass and expensive colors were everywhere, and the number of items on show seemed to have no limits. Surely, even New York city, even the wealthy cities of the Old World couldn't have boasted such wealth in Laurent's time.

"He's not really a king. It's just how we call him, because he is... the boss of the club. And I am hardly Prince Charming," Beast said, walking alongside Laurent over the floor that has been so perfectly polished Laurent could have seen his reflection in it, were his eyes not so faulty. There were so many people here too, many of them giants, and even some of the women were of a height superior to Laurent's. Some of the members of the fairer sex wore clothes that so clearly had been designed for men, others wore their hair short, and as much as Laurent tried not to judge this place by the standards of his own time, he found himself looking away from the tight fabrics obscenely hugging female thighs.

Intimidated as he had been at the house of the Kings of Hell, Laurent was relieved to see that not all men of 2017 were giants like Beast or his father. Though some had grown around their bellies and became large in their own way. Very large even. There had to be an abundance of food in this world of the future, just like there was unlimited water in the bathroom.

Beast, however, was the tallest man Laurent has seen so far. Broad in the shoulders and with the neck of a bull, he made an impressive picture as he walked through the crowds he so easily dwarfed.

Laurent did have to conclude that what had been a good height for a man in his time, made him short in this one, particularly when compared to the massive bulk of his companion. At 5 foot 7 he didn't stand out the way he was used to. And the clothes, more fitting than the ones given to him yesterday, made him feel extremely unimpressive. The trousers were still loose, revealing that he was too small to fill in the outfit, and he was unsure about the way the soft, fabric shoes he received from Nao squeaked against the polished floor as he walked. From Beast, he also got something he was much less happy about. An ankle shackle of small girth that was to explode and amputate his foot if he tried to run and got farther than a mile away from Beast. Terrible business really, so Laurent tried not to think about it too much. Between the self-propelled carriage and the artificial music, Laurent didn't doubt the threat.

"I guess you would indeed have to try to be more *charming*."

King's newfound kindness was making Laurent slightly more confident about his interactions with Beast, but he was still wary, still testing the waters, because those huge hands could snap him in two.

"I'm called Beast for a reason," Beast grumbled, as if nothing could ever make him feel happy. He walked into one of the stores. Big, so bright it hurt Laurent's eyes, and with clothes arranged on strange metal contraptions.

There were also white faceless figures vaguely shaped like women standing on tables and presenting some of the stock, but for Beast it must have been an everyday sight, because he walked right past them and deeper into the endless hall.

True to his earlier decision, Laurent was trying to simply take everything in and observe how other people acted. So he too paid no mind to the clothed sculptures, and he followed Beast's distinct shape in front of him. With one arm so black he might had dipped it in tar, his height, and his wide shoulders, he was impossible to miss. But when Laurent stayed a few steps behind, he could finally see that on the back of Beast's oversized leather waistcoat, was the symbol of the Kings of Hell MC—a crowned skull.

Two young girls laughed as Laurent passed them, but when he discreetly glanced their way, it became clear that he was not the object of their mockery. Both pairs of eyes followed Beast's towering figure as it moved between the racks of clothes.

"Oh, my God, did you see that?" One of them whispered loudly enough for Laurent to catch it.

He frowned when one of the girls produced a thing similar to the one Beast had used for communication with King and directed it at Beast. The longer Laurent was out of the clubhouse, with all those people around, the more he recognized that even in comparison to people of his own time, Beast stood out from the crowd, and not only due to his superior height. What Laurent wasn't yet sure of was whether people were impressed by Beast, feared him, or were amused by him.

Beast finally stopped when he reached a different room within the store, which seemed to have fewer clothes. Laurent quickly realized what this was when instead of female figures, the two on show here were shaped like males, although Laurent didn't think the styles for both genders differed all that much. Out in the mall most men and women dressed in vaguely the same way - in pantaloons and trousers made of canvas and shirts that were very simple in design but often decorated at the front with letters or colorful designs. He wondered what the Church's opinion was in regard of such immodesty. Then again, who was he to speak, with just a thin piece of cloth to cover his chest. In the cool temperature, the outline of his nipples was peeking from underneath.

"Please, promise you won't walk a mile away from me on purpose," Laurent asked, nervous about the ankle shackle once more. It would be no feat at all, were Beast to use his car.

Beast frowned at him, standing far enough for Laurent to see his overall expression even despite the ink covering his skin. "I won't. Now choose some clothes."

Oh, so this was a kind of used clothes market. He leaned down and smelled one of the sleeves of a shirt. "They have been washed, surely?"

"What? Why?"

"They had been made for someone else, correct? So they were most likely worn by that person in the past." Laurent turned to the racks with clothes and touched the fabrics, trying to understand them better. What pattern would a person contemporary to these times choose? He didn't want to obtain something that he'd find out to be twenty years out of fashion.

Beast crooked his head. "We're in the mall. Everything is new. Where did you get your clothes before?"

"I mean… I had them chosen for me or bought them from people who didn't need them anymore. But I am more than happy to choose any of these. My only worry is that I will not know if they fit me correctly." It was enough that his hair was a right mess after the shampoo and Beast didn't own a brush other than the long-handled one in the bathroom, which he explicitly told Laurent not to use for his hair.

"Are you a Mennonite, or something?" asked Beast very slowly. "You just try them on, and if they fit, you buy them."

Laurent's eyes went wide and he stepped closer to whisper. "In front of other people?"

Beast covered his face with his hands, and Laurent felt embarrassed about upsetting him with so many questions. But what was he to do if he had no idea of the correct order of things?

"You know what, I will choose them for you," Beast said in the end, approaching the first cluster of shirts. He started moving the identical garments over the metal branch they hung on and selected a few before moving on.

It was such a relief to receive this kind of help that Laurent smiled at him. "Thank you. I hate to be a burden, but I would hate even more to choose incorrectly."

Beast took his time to answer but swiftly moved between the models on show. "I— yes. I'll choose something right for you."

It didn't take long for Laurent to be carrying a whole array of items, which he learned he would now be trying on. Having someone to guide him through the process was a relief, especially with his eyesight so poor at close proximity even in the brilliant lights of the store.

Laurent wondered how many people actually lived in the whole town because even this one store was massive and filled with an endless flow of men and women. In the end, Beast guided Laurent to the fitting rooms at the back.

That did not go so smoothly either, because when Beast realized Laurent had no underwear, he told him to wait with trying on the 'jeans' and left him in the large stall, only to come back ten minutes later with three boxes, each containing three pairs of the tiniest drawers Laurent had ever seen. They didn't even reach halfway down his thigh, and hugged his body tightly. He was amused by the colorful designs on them though, which ranged from stripes, to chequers, and even a pattern of trees somehow woven into the fabric or painted on it.

With a pair of those on, he finally pulled on the first jeans while Beast sat on a simple cubical chair in the corner. The fabric of all the pantaloons—or pants as they were now called for short—Beast chose for him was thick and somewhat coarse, but if that was what people wore in 2017, Laurent would gladly fit in. He went through perhaps a dozen pairs, some of which were too tight, some too big, too short, or not fitting well on his hips. But in the end, Beast decided he needed to keep two pairs, one in dark gray and one in black, both extraordinarily tight despite an odd sense of stretchiness to the fabric. The gray ones had holes on the knees, which Laurent objected to, but since Beast said they were considered fashionable, he simply accepted his fate.

It was an odd feeling, to undress in front of Beast. He must have put on perfume before they left the clubhouse, because the stall was filled with the aroma of citrus and musk that was slowly becoming a favorite of Laurent's, as well as a potent distraction. He tried not to look in Beast's direction as he first shed his own clothes and then tried on all the new garments, but he couldn't miss the way his breath quickened when he felt Beast's gaze on him. Nakedness between men had been no reason for fuss in his own time, but being watched like this, with Beast staying completely still and only soft breathing filling the silence, made Laurent's body conscious of the blue eyes following his every move.

He'd had no indication whatsoever that for Beast this was anything but providing help to a lost traveller, but being alone in such an enclosed space made Laurent's thoughts wander. He tried to be graceful as he slowly removed the ugly clothes and made putting on the drawers a slow affair. The fabric was stretchy and pleasantly hugged the curve of his buttocks, as well as his cock and balls, and as he continued, Laurent entertained the thought that Beast enjoyed the view, just for the sake of his own pleasure. Beast was a scary man, but he was also a man of means and position, who could likely have anyone he wanted. Laurent's back covered in goosebumps when he imagined a man like Beast lusting after him. Regardless of how that ended last time, fantasies were harmless, and the only expression of desire Laurent could allow himself.

Wandering from store to store, they also chose several shirts, soft, loose fitting jackets with hoods, and short stockings that did not need to be held by garters. The load to carry had become so heavy that at some point they made a trip to the car to leave the purchased goods, but despite the great number of things they obtained, Beast paid at each store, as if the money spent meant nothing to him. Beast hadn't struck Laurent as someone with vast pockets at first, but as time passed at the mall, Laurent was beginning to think that he'd misjudged the man's station. He wasn't sure how much the items actually cost though, because the prices attached to them were usually too small for Laurent to read.

Even a new pair of black leather boots, similar to the ones Beast himself wore seemed to not be a big expense. And despite people secretly staring at Beast wherever he went, the moment he pulled out his money purse at a store, the attendants smiled widely and thanked him for his custom.

Laurent missed his own elegant clothes, but felt too enthusiastic about fitting in to worry, and eagerly changed into the new items as soon as he had a complete outfit.

"Is the music supposed to be so loud?" Laurent asked when they entered a store that assaulted him with the smell of soaps. It was a strange place, with colorful shelves featuring pictures of heavily painted faces, and some women were even applying the products to their persons in public! But no one paid them any mind, so he chose not to stare either, following Beast into an aisle between shelves filled with all kinds of bottles and jars—all made of the futuristic material that he now knew was called plastic.

In 2017 everything was made out of it. Chairs, cutlery, bottles, even clothes could be plastic! What an ingenious substance that was.

"Okay, choose whatever shampoo you want. You don't need to use a whole bottle each time," Beast told him, staying back.

"Oh." Laurent licked his lips and rocked on his heels, unsure where to start. "What's the one you use? It smells very nice."

Beast was silent for two seconds. "I don't think it would be best for you. I have short hair."

Laurent sighed and after a bit of hesitation, picked up a pink bottle. If this store was like all the others, he was expected to make the choice on his own and pay upon exit. No one would help him make up his mind. "That's a shame. I've never met a man who smells like you."

"What do you mean?" came after yet another pause.

Laurent leaned closer and took a whiff of Beast's smell, briefly closing his eyes when the distinctly masculine aroma made his skin tingle. "It's so… fresh. Like lemons, and something else. Mint maybe?" He forced away the memory of Fane's basement, all incense and rose petals combined with something even more sweet and sickly. The taste of apple seemed to still linger on Laurent's lips.

"That's my cologne. I mean... we could choose one for you later, but pick the basics first, yeah? What does it say on the back of this one?" Beast asked.

Laurent turned around the pink bottle with a sinking feeling in his stomach. The letters were so small he hadn't even realized there was writing there at first. With his heartbeat speeding up in panic, he moved the bottle farther away from his eyes, but with the size of the letters, it was no use.

Why hadn't he taken his magnifying glass? He could have used it when Beast wasn't looking.

"Shampoo… with r-rose?"

They were both silent as Laurent let the sense of shame wash over him, and no amount of bestial music playing in the background could ever distract him from the humiliation.

"You can't read?" asked Beast in the end.

Laurent bit on the inside of his cheek and forced himself to take a few deep breaths to calm down, but it wasn't helping. "I can. Of course I can. It's just this writing. Over there," he pointed to a grand painting on the wall, which showed a lady presenting her bare legs with a smile, "it says 'Smooth like the boys in Paris. Moreau.' And then, 'Now with three razor action'."

"So you can't see well? You're farsighted? Why didn't you tell me you need glasses?" asked Beast in a tone that suggested that he was on the verge of losing patience.

And to think things had been going so well up until now. They'd been chatting, talking about the songs resonating in the stores, about the clothes, about the building. About plastic. Beast had taught him so many new things, and the people around them were an endless source of entertainment. Now though, Beast would realize Laurent was bound to become useless, so there was no point investing time in teaching Laurent anything.

"No, no, I'm fine. I will not be a burden to you, it's a promise. It's only these little letters that cause me so much grief." Laurent only realized he was squeezing the plastic bottle too hard when its cap popped open, and a load of rose-scented goo drizzled out on his hand.

Beast stepped closer. "You're not fine. We should have started with the glasses. Why didn't you just say what you actually need?"

Laurent sighed so deeply he felt like his entire lungs were collapsing. And he had no idea what to do with the broken bottle in his hand. "I usually manage…"

"Why do you have to make this difficult? Everyone knows it's unhealthy to strain your eyes like this." Beast took the bottle out of Laurent's hand and put it back on the shelf before grabbing Laurent's shoulder and pulling him toward the exit.

"It is?" And it's something 'everyone knows'? Laurent glanced up at Beast, not fighting the pull. From the sheer terror of his ailment being found out, a feeling of hope was beginning to bloom. Could spectacles possibly be available to him in this world? Maybe they weren't as expensive as they used to be all the way back in 1805.

The store Beast led him to was very bright, with many small mirrors and rows of spectacles hanging on the walls—black, white, green, red, in any shape one could possibly want! It didn't escape Laurent's attention that attendants in black and white clothes seemed to be assisting the customers, like they would in his own time, but still no one approached him and Beast as they walked up to one of the displays.

"Should I choose something for you again?" Beast asked, picking up one of the pairs.

Laurent raised his hands in frustration, exasperated by how fast this was happening. "I don't know. Maybe. I don't see them well anyway." His shoulders sagged. There. It was out. He was going blind.

The plastic frame slid on his nose, and Beast's patterned face loomed in a blur of unreadable expressions. There was no hope for Laurent if spectacles sold at a store so specialized didn't alter his vision at all. But he said nothing. Many other pairs of glasses followed as they made their way along the wall, with Beast putting pair after pair on Laurent until he decided on one in black that was quite chunky yet light. What did their shape matter though if they did nothing for Laurent's sight?

They approached the shopgirl, who at first seemed to try and run into the back room, but when Beast addressed her by a name, she eventually turned back to face them. It didn't escape Laurent's attention just how very polite and soft-spoken Beast was to all the clerks he interacted with, as if he needed to somehow assure them he was a Beast only by name.

Minutes later, Laurent and Beast were led into a backroom where a lady in a tight skirt that reached to her knees and a white coat waited for them. She was some kind of doctor, Laurent realized, and despite the shock of such a novelty, he chose not to question her expertise. She subjected him to a set of humiliating tests, which included reading letters of various sizes from a picture on the wall, and being examined with a machine that held his head immobile while the female doctor shed bright light into his eyes.

She said many things Laurent didn't understand, and eventually started scolding him for neglecting his eyesight problems. He chose not to argue, although the diagnosis of cataract felt like a blow to the back of the head. His grandfather had suffered of the same ailment, and he'd been completely blind by the age of forty.

The doctor watched him in silence and finally stated, "You are very young, and this is an illness that occurs mostly in older patients."

Laurent could barely comprehend what she was saying as he sunk deeper and deeper into his own body while the dooming diagnosis spiraled him down the drain of grief. It was as if putting a name to his ailment made his fate more real somehow. The doctor explained something about malnourishment being a possible cause in someone his age, but how would that knowledge possibly help him now? His only chance for health was completing the task for the devil.

That was until one word stuck out to him, and he looked into her eyes again, shocked by what he was hearing.

"It's a routine surgery. I can refer you to a specialist who could qualify you for the operation."

"Surgery? On the eyes?" Overcome by panic, Laurent searched for Beast's forearm to grab onto something. He imagined someone cutting into his eye sockets and blood guzzling all over, like when poor Samson Smith lost his eye due to an accident in his father's shop.

The doctor gave him a polite smile. "Oh, don't worry. You wouldn't feel a thing. Millions of such procedures are carried out every year."

Laurent bit his tongue before he repeated the word 'millions' in mindless amazement of a peasant looking at the doors to a cathedral. What if this was part of the freedom the devil promised him? It made so much sense now. He'd been taken to a world where he would be free to make a life for himself. Free of the illness that in 1805 would have reduced his life to that of a beggar.

He took deep breaths to force away the sting of tears in his eyes. His life-long problem would be taken away in a 'routine surgery'. He hadn't even noticed when Beast's rough fingers entwined with his, but he squeezed tightly as soon as he realized it.

"I would like that very much," he uttered to the lady doctor.

She then took him to a special chair that was facing away from Beast and had Laurent look through various lenses that had his heart pounding, because they actually worked. Not all were perfect, but they did improve his vision immensely. In the end, they made a choice between two that were closest to the ideal, and the lady doctor told them to wait for fifteen minutes for the glasses. That was it. Quarter of an hour.

Laurent didn't even want to go anywhere, so they sat down on a bench—a plastic one of course—outside the shop, and he was working hard on staying calm despite the hot and cold flushes raging through his body.

"How much could an operation like that cost?" Laurent looked at Beast, rubbing his hands together nervously. Despite everything being so strange here, if these new times could offer a cure for his eyes, he was set to do everything in his power to stay here and fit in by making himself useful.

Beast shrugged and slowly shifted closer to Laurent. "I don't know. The other doctor will probably tell us."

"I would even work in the mines to gather the funds, if that is needed. You don't understand how long I've struggled with this. And I love reading books so much." He smiled when Beast put his large hand on his knee and squeezed gently, sending unexpected sparks of warmth to his chest and fluttering heart.

"So... weren't you allowed to have glasses before? Why were you so scared of telling me?" asked Beast in his warm, rough voice.

"I don't want to seem useless. I don't want to end up in the streets, blind and destitute. No one would employ me if they knew I am an invalid, and I have no family to support me."

"You do if Knight really is your cousin," said Beast with a soft laugh.

"I doubt that, but I guess it's a notion worth investigating."

"You will not go blind, so it doesn't matter, does it?" asked Beast, keeping his hand on Laurent's leg and gently trailing his thumb over the naked skin on the knee.

The touch made Laurent pay more attention, but he wasn't sure what to make of it. But then again, if ladies walked around with their naked legs on show, should he question the comforting touch? If Beast was doing it in a place so public, then it couldn't be out of the ordinary, even if to him such touch had been illicit and forbidden. Morals and the meaning behind gestures have really changed, and so he needed to make himself stop seeing the touch as a caress, even if it felt so good to be touched by a man in a way that showered his back with imaginary droplets of warm oil.

"I guess it doesn't. Once my eyesight gets better, I will be able to do a great many things. And I learn very fast, so I can surely find a use for myself."

"I'm sure you will. You're very bright, even if strange," Beast said, sounding amused. People stared at them as they passed, and it was making Laurent somewhat uncomfortable, but there was nothing to be done about Beast standing out so much.

The compliment made Laurent glow with joy. If even Beast, who this morning was set on feeding him to his dog, noticed that Laurent had positive qualities, then his prospects for a good life weren't doomed. "I will learn not to be strange."

Beast tapped his foot against the floor and cleared his throat. "I think your glasses should be ready by now. Do you wanna—"

Laurent sprung up. He hadn't even realized that his hands had gotten so sweaty while he waited. "Yes, yes, please, let's go and see!" He snorted at the silly word-game he accidentally formed.

Beast stood up as well, and his towering presence wasn't oppressive anymore. When he touched Laurent's back, it only made Laurent feel taken care of as they strolled into the store and approached the clerk. She accepted the payment from Beast, and gave them a plastic case and a paper with the referral to the eye doctor.

Laurent popped the case open, not even caring that his movements were quick and greedy, as if he were a beggar who hadn't eaten for days and was now up for a feast. His fingers trembled and his heart thudded when he put on the glasses that were of course made of plastic.

He *loved* plastic.

Everything looked crisp, as if his eyes were brand new. As if he'd never been ill. As if he'd never feared complete darkness. He could spot every fibre of Beast's black shirt, but he needed to see more than that and looked up the muscular chest, over the thick, heavily tattooed neck, to the face that was now like a book for him to read, scribbled all over with tiny letters over twisted, mangled skin. And between the rows of black, gray, and the pale color of Beast's flesh, were eyes so bright they took Laurent's breath away. Pale blue, human, and not monstrous at all. Beast's true self was watching him somewhere from beyond the scars, a person deep within, whose ear has not been ripped off, and who just wanted him to be happy with the glasses. There was so much anticipation in that gaze, as if in this moment nothing else mattered to Beast.

Laurent reached up and trailed the writing along Beast`s jaw with his fingers. It was so small, and yet he could see it so well. Only now he realized all the writing over Beast's skin was in Latin. Without thinking, he read a piece of it out loud. "*Midway upon the journey of our life, I found myself within a forest dark. For the straightforward pathway has been lost.*" It was a rough translation of the passage going down Beast's neck, and yet it made him so exhilarated. Under the ink, and the left side of Beast's face, which had more scaring, were features that belonged on a once handsome man. Laurent now understood why people stared, but when he looked into the inquisitive eyes that reflected his gaze, it was hard for him not to smile at the broad-jawed face, the strong nose, and the pronounced cheekbones. He had no hair on the eyebrow arches above his eyes.

Beast licked his lips, seeming nervous as he stared back at Laurent, not moving by an inch. "You speak Latin?" He cleared his throat. "So... you like your glasses?"

"I love them." Laurent couldn't take the tension anymore and wrapped his arms around Beast's waist, hugging him tightly and not caring in the least what the other patrons would say.

Chapter 9 - Beast

Laurent's arms settled around Beast's midsection so firmly there was no way he could break free.

Not that he'd want to.

Watching Laurent briefly close his eyes behind the chunky black frames had Beast's heart beating in a wild rhythm, but as the moment of surprise passed, he put his arms around Laurent too and slowly stroked the boy's head. He had the softest, finest hair Beast had ever touched and smelled of pine so intensely Beast knew that if he buried his face in the wavy locks, he could pretend he was somewhere in the woods, holding a lover.

It's been so long since anyone embraced him like this that he was somewhat awkward about it, a bit unsure whether they should be doing this, but the way Laurent clung to him really did not feel like the brief hugs Knight or his other brothers offered sometimes. It lasted, it was all warmth, and Laurent's head lay firmly against Beast's chest, as if he wished to hand himself over into Beast's protection.

It was yet another surprise after the uninhibited way in which Laurent complimented Beast's own scent, or that firm squeeze of hand in the optometrist's office. No one entwined fingers with people they weren't interested in. Despite Laurent coming from some weird Mennonite sect that didn't allow vision correction, such gestures had a universal significance.

And now Beast, a man who hadn't touched anyone intimately in over ten years, was being hugged in public by a boy so pretty he should have been paid for wearing the clothes they picked up.

Beast stifled the moan of disappointment that formed in his chest when Laurent pulled away, still holding his hands on Beast's sides.

"I see everything," Laurent said with a smile so wide it melted something in Beast and made him wonder if by 'everything' Laurent meant the depths of Beast's soul. He looked to Beast's chest and pulled on the collar of Beast's tank top, making a shiver run down Beast's spine. "*The path to Paradise begins in Hell*," he read and translated the words from Beast's skin.

Read out loud in Laurent's warm, melodic voice, the quote made tiny feet of imaginary ants tap all over Beast's body. "It's... from *Inferno*," he said, embarrassed that it came out so quietly, but it had been so long since anyone showed sincere interest in him that he was having a hard time staying calm. Surely, someone as ill-informed about the world as Laurent couldn't be into him for the patches?

Understanding flashed through Laurent's big brown eyes, and he kept smiling as if he'd just gotten a Happy Meal. "Dante Alighieri's *Inferno*?"

But time wouldn't stand still and wait for Beast to get his fill of the warm touch. Laurent pulled away and started walking around the store with a look of wonder that made everything around seem new and exciting, even though this was just a regular optician's in a run-down mall.

Beast followed Laurent the way Hound always followed him, mesmerized by the wild enthusiasm expressed in each graceful step. Laurent moved with a studied grace of a ballet dancer, his back always straight and his chin up high. It did not help Beast's sanity at all that after watching Laurent in the shower and in the changing room, he had the image of Laurent's naked body etched into his brain so firmly the hoodie covering Laurent's ass couldn't stop Beast's imagination from running wild. Laurent's skin, soft and warm to the touch, was smooth like fine porcelain, but despite the sense that Beast could break it with his clumsy hands, he still wanted to hold the boy tightly against him. He couldn't remember having a sudden crush on someone that would be this strong.

"Yes," he finally answered Laurent's question. It made sense for a member of a religious sect to know of a book about hell.

Laurent's eyesight problems must have been prominent, because he even walked with more vigor. And with this new confidence to his movements, Laurent approached the sales assistant—who had been trying hard not to look at them embracing—and kissed her hand.

"Thank you so much for your hard work. I cannot put into words how much I appreciate these glasses."

The woman's face brightened as soon as she got over the shock, and she slipped her hand away. "You are very welcome. Make sure to come back next week. We will have a new collection of Ray Ban glasses."

Laurent thanked her once more and promised to do so. He returned to Beast with the widest of smiles, and as they left the store, he whispered excitedly. "Did you hear that? They will have glasses all the way from Ray Ban."

Beast swallowed and reached out to touch Laurent's shoulder. It was so warm in his palm that he didn't want to let go until he absolutely had to. "Yes. Yes. I'm sure you could have some shipped even from Japan, if you wanted a particular model."

Laurent was looking around as if he were only now seeing the mall for the first time, and a sense of pride grew in Beast that he was the one to gift Laurent the glasses. *He* would be special to Laurent. He didn't want to get his hopes up too high, but the moment when Laurent looked at him with all the clarity provided by the vision aid, and then hugged him as if the twisted burn scars that permanently altered Beast's naturally handsome features meant nothing, had been transcendent.

"That is beyond exciting." Laurent looked over his shoulder at Beast, but then his attention scattered again when he saw himself in a full-length mirror. "Do I look like an average young man of Maine?"

Beast took a deep breath. He swallowed. He could just outright lie and confirm Laurent's presumptions, but when would another opportunity to give a compliment fall into his lap? He was determined to not let it slip between his fingers.

"No. No, you're very... every girl is making eyes at you when we walk," he said in the end, cursing himself in silence when he realized there was no way to take back the silly words that directed Laurent's attention away from him. Had he forgotten how to flirt? Was that how long it'd been? Yes, it was.

"Are they? You mean in the good sense, I hope?" Laurent walked on with a sly smile on his face that only made him look cuter. Beast would gladly bury his hands under Laurent's T-shirt, carry him back to the H&M fitting room and fuck him there, uncaring if it got him permanently banned from the mall.

He would most likely get arrested, but hearing Laurent moan in his arms would have been worth it. "The best sense. Anyone would be proud to be seen with you."

The blush spilling on Laurent's porcelain-hued face was like powdered rose petals mixed into milk. Beast was not the cheesy type, but Laurent's stunning features begged for such ludicrous comparisons. But when Laurent glanced at yet another mirror in passing, Beast began to wonder if maybe Laurent hadn't been aware of his own beauty at all. With that new knowledge setting in, Beast's company might not be as attractive anymore to a young man who could have anyone he wanted.

"I can't remember walking with so much lightness to my step." Laurent turned around and continued on backwards, as if he didn't want to miss Beast's face when they talked. And Beast let him, intervening only when he noticed Laurent approaching a bench in the middle of the hallway. Using the opportunity given to him, he put his hand on Laurent's shoulder and guided him gently as heat from the slim body that might have been created by an idealist sculptor streamed into his hand. Maybe he could turn this day into a date somehow? Nothing had changed in Laurent's behavior toward him now that he could see the mess that was Beast's face. Maybe in the community he'd grown up in looks were not as crucial in terms of attraction as they were in the real world?

"If you want, we could do something for fun after we're done shopping."

Laurent spun around to once again walk shoulder to shoulder with Beast. Though it was more like shoulder to arm, considering the height difference. And Beast liked that about Laurent too. For a man as strong as Beast, Laurent was so featherweight. He would be so easy to fuck against the wall, those long legs tightly wrapped around Beast's hips. The river of filth going through Beast's mind was changing into a flood by the minute. Oh, the things he could do to Laurent given half the chance… He wouldn't let the boy out of his bed for weeks.

"That sounds marvelous! I would love to do lots of fun things."

Beast weighed Laurent's words in his head. Was the flamboyant use of words a sign that Laurent was gay? He knew all too well that theoretically it was impossible to tell, but… was it really?

"Anything you want to do first? Are you hungry?" Beast asked, never letting Laurent out of sight and already jealous of every pair of eyes that dared to look at him. If it wasn't for Beast's presence, he would likely have been pecked on already.

"Yes, please. I would like to eat, but… after shopping? I can read all the shampoos now. I would like to choose one that's right for my hair."

"Right. Yeah. And you wanted the cologne, and you will need a toothbrush and all that." And Beast would buy condoms and lube. Just in case.

He was not a creep. He just wanted to be prepared.

"Yes, a *toothbrush*, definitely." Laurent nodded eagerly and kept smiling like a maniac, which only made Beast think of a new toothbrush joining his in the cup in his bathroom.

But then Laurent stopped mid-stride, all but gluing himself to the shop window behind which a huge display of flat screen televisions played music videos.

Beast looked at the set in front of Laurent, which showed a vividly-colored clip starring one of the latest pop sensations. It depicted a party full of cotton candy-colored foam, with couples dancing, playing in the pool, and all the other images the entertainment industry pretended happened at all parties. He smiled, glancing at Laurent, who squinted, as if the intense colors were hurting his eyes.

"Where you're from, you didn't have television either?" he guessed, increasingly convinced that Laurent was truly lost and needed help. No one could feign naivety and lack of knowledge about the modern world so perfectly.

Laurent looked back at him in hesitation but shook his head in the end. "No. Nothing like it." He stared at the televisions again, and Beast wondered about the bruises on Laurent's neck and wrist. They'd annoyed him before, but now they were beginning to make ugly black rage overflow in him without an outlet. How could someone have hurt a boy this lovely? But he'd already learned pushing Laurent for too much information at once was no use. Soon enough, he'd get his hands on the person who did this, and there wouldn't be much left for Hound to chew on after Beast was done.

Sooner though, Beast would get his hands on Laurent.

"Oh. Oh my," Laurent whispered, turning Beast's attention back to the screen where in the middle of the pool party two young guys were kissing. Drawn-on hearts flowed from their lips as the two actors pressed closer, their perfectly toned bodies shining with some sort of glitter.

Beast felt his mouth go dry, and he eyed Laurent, suddenly stiff as a piece of dry wood. "Nice, right?" he asked in the end, making himself smile. He just needed a confirmation of Laurent's potential interest. That was all.

When Laurent tapped his fingers against the glass, the camera already focused on something else. "Do you think it's acceptable for two men to kiss that way?" When he looked up at Beast with a tense expression on his face, his eyes seemed even bigger through the glasses.

"Yes," said Beast right away, drilling his gaze into Laurent. "It's... a good thing people can be with whoever they want to be with, isn't it?"

The shy smile on Laurent's lips made Beast's heart skip a beat. *Score*. His initial assumption was correct. He just needed to put in some more effort, and that pretty mouth would be on his cock tonight.

"A very good thing," Laurent said with a deep sigh. "Can I see it again? How do I make the images stop?"

Beast cleared his throat. "Oh, they are here just for display. So that people can decide which of those... picture machines they want to buy. But we have them at home, and if you want to see men kissing men, then you can once we're back." Laurent was also more than welcome to kiss a man. Beast was ready to be the sacrificial lamb for that.

Laurent nodded, finally pulling away from the glass. The traces his hands left on the window had Beast imagining those soft fingers touching him all over. He was sure that even the places on his body that had most nerve damage could take the touch of Laurent's silky skin.

"Where I come from it was punished," he whispered, only confirming Beast's suspicion about some sort of sect. The tactic of not prodding was working then.

Beast nodded to show his understanding. "There are still plenty of places like that, and some idiots don't get it, but it's perfectly legal. I mean... I like men too," Beast said, watching Laurent for any traces of discomfort.

There was heavy breathing, a blush, wide eyes, but no backing away. "Oh," Laurent choked out in the end. Beast bit his lip and stuffed his hands into his pockets as they approached the drugstore again.

"So... I understand. You don't have to be ashamed."

Laurent nodded, but he seemed absentminded. Which likely meant he was actually overanalyzing shit. They returned to the shampoos, where the mood finally became less tense as Laurent started reading the labels one by one.

Beast excused himself to grab the supplies he needed on hand if Laurent were willing to give him a chance. He wondered if Laurent—if something happened—would appreciate flavored lube, or some other fancy stuff, but in the end he picked up the plain one that claimed having no smell, as well as some condoms. It took him more time than it should have to make his choice, but when he returned to the bath product aisle, there was a middle-aged woman with red hair talking lively to Laurent, who just stared at her with a polite smile.

Damn it. Beast shouldn't have left him alone like this.

Like the man on a mission he now was, Beast approached them in quick strides.

Laurent looked up at him, as did the lady, but her smile seemed forced.

"This is my friend, Beast," Laurent introduced him in that ridiculously polite manner. "He's helping me shop. And this is," he pointed to the woman, "Mrs. Avery. She was just telling me about her photography business."

Mrs. Avery eyed Beast and licked her pink lips. "Yes… So, as I was saying, I'd love you to pop into our store some time for a test shoot."

"No," Beast said right away. "He can't."

Laurent stilled, sucking his lips in that distracting way, but then finally spoke when the woman glared at Beast. "Yes, I'm terribly sorry for the inconvenience, but my friend just reminded me I'm already engaged with someone else on that matter."

Mrs. Avery exhaled loudly, as if to signal her disappointment and burden everyone with it. Couldn't she just leave already? "I understand. Keep this in case you change your mind." She passed Laurent a business card, and he took it with a smile, most likely having no idea what she was talking about.

When she finally left, Beast groaned in relief. "That was close. Do you have photography where you're from?"

Laurent's shoulders sagged. "No. Is it a bad thing?"

Beast leaned down to look him in the eyes. "Whoever hurt you could find you through this. She likely didn't mean any harm, but it's tricky business to have pictures taken if you're hiding from someone."

The big brown eyes went wide, and there it was. Fear. Beast wasn't happy to be the one to remind Laurent of potential danger, but Laurent needed to be aware that he wasn't safe when out of Beast's sight. At least that was what Beast was telling himself, because admitting that he wanted to hoard Laurent's attention would have been greedy. But then again, wasn't he allowed to be a bit greedy this one time?

"I understand. No photography." Laurent took a deep breath and ran his fingers over the dressing on his hand.

Beast smiled at him and picked up the basket, which already held some bottles, and sought Laurent's hand with his. His skin itched with heat, and he wouldn't be surprised to be rejected, but Laurent's slim fingers entwined with his huge paw.

Exhilaration exploded deep within Beast's body, and he gave Laurent's hand a gentle squeeze, smiling at him in hope that maybe the mangled skin that was so tight on one side it made all his expressions somewhat lopsided wouldn't make the expression unpleasant to Laurent's eyes. "It's all right. I won't let anyone take you away."

"Because you don't want my foot to explode?" Laurent smiled slightly when they walked to the registers. The playful comment made guilt sting Beast's insides. The ankle cuff was just a tracker.

"That too. But you're so lost. Someone needs to help you, right?" said Beast, deciding not to disclose the truth just yet. He couldn't help but wonder what Laurent really thought of him. Was he honest, or was he looking to gain an advantage?

"I do not turn down any help given, but I wouldn't wish for you to consider me useless. I will quickly learn about everything you want me to know." Laurent had already said this many times, as if he needed to repeat it for some reason.

Truth was that seeing him smile made him useful enough for Beast. When Laurent had appeared last night, Beast had thought he'd be a nuisance to the club and him personally, but now he was overwhelmed by the natural charm Laurent exuded. By the silly, old-fashioned way he spoke, by the French accent, the pretty lips, the soft hair, and weirdly enough, even with rediscovering the world through Laurent's eyes.

Laurent deserved all the best things Beast could give him in gratitude for the attention and interest offered without judgment. And since it was still April, and some days would get cold, Beast decided Laurent needed a leather jacket. And not a cheap one either. Real leather that would allow all that lovely skin to breathe. Seeing Laurent appreciate the quality of craftsmanship in the more upscale store they visited for the purpose melted something that had hardened inside Beast long ago.

Now that Laurent would have something warm to wear, Beast fantasized about taking him for rides on his bike, too. Bringing him to that spot by the lake where Beast used to often bring his hookups back when he still had sex. Back when he could have had any guy he wanted.

Laurent took his time choosing the jacket, asking questions about the buttons, the zippers, the buckles. Even though usually coming to the mall was an in-and-out kind of mission for Beast, Laurent somehow made it enjoyable with his amusingly serious questions.

Could he have those buttons with this jacket? Was plastic better than leather? Did the colors of the jackets signify social status? What brand was considered exquisite? And he actually used the word 'exquisite'.

But Laurent wasn't simply following Beast's lead. Once he gathered all the answers, he chose a soft leather jacket in a pale gray, paler even than his jeans. With pockets inside and out, a side zipper, a fit on the tighter side of things, and silver studs at the shoulders. When he put it on along with the black biker boots they'd purchased earlier, he looked good enough to eat.

Beast couldn't stop looking at him, feeling both amused and tender with the sense of wonder radiating off everything Laurent said. It made the mundane trip to the mall seem so fresh, even the passersby staring couldn't spoil Beast's mood. For once he thought that maybe it wasn't his tattooed face that they were judging, but that they wondered how a guy like him got the pretty ray of sunshine to hold his hand.

On the way to grab some food, they passed a mirror cabinet, a seasonal attraction meant for children, but with Laurent so eager to have a look, they ended up goofing out in front of the mirrors.

Beast couldn't remember having this much fun in ages, and as they approached the nicest restaurant in the mall—a steak place with amazing desserts to seal the deal, holding Laurent's hand made Beast feel like he was just another guy out on a date with a person they liked. He's missed it more than he'd like to admit.

And Laurent wasn't just anyone at that. Beast saw the way the attendant at the store with the jackets made eyes at him while offering a potent mixture of advice and compliments. Yet, Laurent walked out of the store with Beast, the other guy forgotten even though he had a pretty face with no scars or tattoos.

"It smells so nice here," Laurent said, beaming at Beast when they entered the steak house

"I've heard they have very good beef. But if you don't like that, they have all kinds of options," Beast was quick to add as they approached the stand where patrons would wait to be seated. There was a fair amount of people peppered all around the restaurant, but with it being the odd hour between lunch and dinner, it was not too crowded either.

"I'm willing try anything once," Laurent announced, showering Beast with smiles.

Beast committed those words into his memory, to pull them out between the sheets.

The server approaching looked professional and calm from afar, but the closer she got the more Beast could recognize signs of wariness in her eyes. Just typical. But yes, he knew he looked scary, and that was the reason why he was always incredibly polite in stores. He wasn't in the business of making strangers uncomfortable on purpose, but the tools for it had been burned into his flesh even before he added the tattoos.

"Good afternoon. We'd like a table for two," he said and gave her his best grin, the halfway one that didn't pull on the tightened skin of his left cheek too much.

"No problem at all. I will go check if there are any available," she said with a fake smile plastered to her lips and walked off quickly, making Beast's heart sink. Would there be trouble? All he wanted was to treat Laurent to something nice. Yes, he didn't look like most other people. He was tall, maybe even a bit menacing, and he was a member of a biker club, but that didn't mean he'd be gutting someone as soon as they gave him a steak knife.

He wanted to do some small talk with Laurent but couldn't bring himself to speak when a slightly older woman in a pantsuit peeked from behind a column at the back of the restaurant. He smiled at her. She smiled back and ducked behind the divider. Seconds later, the server strolled back their way with an even wider smile on her face. Everything was in order, it seemed. At least until her eyebrows gathered in an expression of studied apology.

"I am very sorry, but we are booked for the day."

The look of disappointment on Laurent's face carved a hole in Beast's heart.

"We have spent all day shopping, with barely any breakfast. Are you certain no space can be found for us? We wouldn't take long," Laurent said.

Beast pressed his lips together and squeezed Laurent's hand as shame and anger mixed into a black, thick, bitter goo choking his throat. "It's fine, Laurent. We had this other place in mind, too. Let's go there," he lied, for the sake of appearances. He would not give these damn bigots the satisfaction of having him beg for a place in their fucking third-rate restaurant!

Laurent didn't protest when the waitress apologized profusely once more. It was all lies. She would sigh in relief as soon as they were out. The one time Beast actually had someone to bring here, and they wouldn't have him?

"Ow! Beast? You're hurting me," Laurent whined, and only then Beast realized he was squeezing Laurent's injured hand far too hard.

He let go and stormed out into the main hallway of the mall. "Sorry. I'm just angry, and I didn't think," he said tightly. If only he could punch something.

"Is it because you wanted steak that much?"

Beast looked down into the eyes that seemed to reflect genuine confusion. As if Laurent was somehow able to look past Beast's otherness and lacked understanding of what just happened. This alone was making Beast's heart beat faster. "No. No. People are just shits anywhere fancy. Let's go somewhere else," he said, already knowing that they wouldn't be eating in. He couldn't risk another humiliation like that with Laurent around.

Laurent followed with a focused expression on that perfect face, and Beast couldn't help but bitterly think that if Laurent went to that restaurant on his own, or with someone else for that matter, he would surely get royal treatment from all the staff.

"Do you like Chinese food?" asked Beast, leading the way to the food court, when he couldn't stand the heavy silence anymore.

"I would gladly try it. Are you upset?"

Beast clenched his jaw, not wanting to reveal just how agitated he was with this situation. "I'm angry. But there is more food available, so it's their loss if we take our business elsewhere."

"Did they assume we have no money?" Laurent asked and stopped right in front of the escalator so abruptly Beast had to jog back down the moving stairs to join him.

It only then occurred to Beast that if Laurent had never seen a TV, he surely had no reference to escalators. "Come on, don't be afraid. It's just another mechanism."

"I'm sorry, I just wasn't sure how to ride those."

A man in an ill-fitting suit pushed Laurent to the side. "Jesus Christ, move."

Beast spun around, grabbed the man's jacket and shoved him back so hard he fell over, dropping his briefcase to the floor. "You forget the magic words?"

The man's eyes went wide, and he started slowly getting up. Beast could see the calculation in his eyes. Should he start a fight with Beast, or should he apologize and piss off, only later swearing under his breath?

"Sorry," Suit mumbled in the end. Wise choice.

"To my friend here, not me. It's him you wanted to shove around," Beast said, still blocking the escalator with his body. There. He'd show Laurent just how safe he was with Beast!

Laurent stroked Beast's forearm, the fully black one, which had been burned much worse than the other. The touch sent shivers all over Beast's body. So tender and familiar. "It's unnecessary, don't worry. I was obstructing the way for this gentleman."

Beast wasn't having it. The fucker *would* apologize. He was so determined and focused on the rude fucker he didn't notice other people approaching.

A pair of strong hands pulled on his other arm. "Sir, I need you to leave the premises," said a tall mall cop. Two more were already on their way, as if Beast were about to start tearing people's limbs off, not simply arguing with another shopper.

Beast stared back at the man, his fists itching for violence. But if he got himself arrested what would happen to Laurent? So he swallowed his anger and raised his hands. "Fine. Fine, I'll go. You can let go of me."

"This way please," the fucking mall cop insisted, and Beast had to bear the guy in the suit flipping him off. If Laurent weren't here, arrest be damned, he'd pull out of the grip and break that coward's hand.

Laurent kept up with their pace, his pretty face marred with worry, which was stressing out Beast even more. "It's a misunderstanding, sir."

"Save it, kid," a security officer who caught up with them grabbed Laurent's arm as if he too needed prodding. "We've seen the whole thing. We knew you two would be trouble."

"Oh, really, what gave you that idea?" hissed Beast, trying to keep Laurent in sight at all times. He knew damn well what, and that was why he always kept calm and polite in public places. But of course, it was he who they suspected of trouble, not frustrated people in nice suits who behaved like cunts.

"The look on your face." A shortie mall cop with a face full of acne followed them with a gloating smile despite not actually being needed. If only they weren't spied on by the eyes of witnesses and cameras, Beast would smash the bastard's teeth in.

At least they were already at the door, and soon enough Beast stepped out into the afternoon sun and stuck his hands into his pockets. Yet another humiliation in front of Laurent. He bet the boy would gladly just go home now.

Once the mall cops were gone, after delivering a lecture about violence in no shape or form being acceptable in the mall, Laurent stood there, red in the face and breathing hard.

Beast swallowed hard, watching him for the longest moment. "Let's just go," he said in the end, feeling completely hopeless about his chances with Laurent after this unlucky display. The condoms would be yet another useless purchase gathering dust somewhere in his bedroom.

"Y-yes," Laurent uttered, but just as Beast turned around to stomp off to the parking lot, Laurent slid his hand into Beast's.

Beast squeezed it with relief so powerful he needed to stand still for a few seconds. Not everything was lost then. He could still make amends. "There is this other place. I go there often, and they are very nice," he said once they sat in the car.

Laurent fastened his seatbelt, just like he'd been taught when they first got into the car in the morning. "Is it normal for so many soldiers to appear from nowhere over the slightest disagreement?"

Beast scowled. "No. You heard it yourself. Those fuckers were just waiting for an excuse," he said, pulling out of the bay.

"At first I thought… I hope you don't mind me saying—that it's your size that is intimidating but today I saw a lot of men much taller than myself. But I saw no man with as many patterns on their skin as you. Is that what scares them?"

Beast howled on the inside and left the parking lot as quickly as possible. Laurent found him intimidating? "They're just stupid fucks, okay? I did nothing wrong. They just didn't want me to be there, that's all."

Laurent nodded and looked out the window. For a moment Beast wanted to ask what he was thinking, but then decided he would rather cool off before potentially finding out there was more about him that Laurent found scary.

At least his favorite Chinese takeout wasn't all that far away, and since he assumed Laurent never had any, he got a few different things to choose from, including a wild card - fried squid.

The sun was setting when Beast stopped the car by a small park and led the way to a newly-built playground, which at this hour was completely deserted. He didn't feel like returning home yet and just allowed himself to enjoy the one-on-one time with Laurent for a bit more. The playground was made mostly of wood and shaped to look somewhat like a castle, with two main structures linked by a bridge, numerous poles for climbing and slides.

He put their food into one of the towers before climbing up the ladder and into the wooden building. It was quite enclosed, so there was a fair chance no one would spot them from afar.

Laurent was right behind him, with that delicious look of amazement once more present on his face. "If there are men as tall as you, is this place for people half your size?"

Beast barked out a laugh and sat with his legs down a broad slide designed to be used by several children at once. "It's for children. Come here," he said, tapping the space next to him.

When Laurent sat down, he was thigh to thigh with Beast. He rubbed his forehead with a deep sigh. "Of course."

Beast pulled out the food and opened the safest bet, a mild curry with chicken, before splitting the wooden chopsticks. He gathered some rice and put it into his mouth to demonstrate.

Laurent followed his example, observing how Beast put the chopsticks in his hand, but he didn't grasp the concept very well. Beast pulled him closer and put the chopsticks into Laurent's hand, first showing him the right movement, then enveloping his hand with his own and showing him how to pull up a large chunk of meat with just enough pressure applied.

Laurent laughed with his mouth full when he finally managed. With the orange sunlight flooding the playground, stuck alone with him in the slide that seemed like a treehouse, Beast felt like a kid again. Not even like the smug twenty year old who had been on top of the world and thought he could seduce anyone he wanted, but his fifteen-year-old self, desperate to work out whether his first major crush was gay or not.

"I've never had anything like it," Laurent said in the end once he swallowed the chicken.

"But do you like it?" insisted Beast, directing Laurent's hand again yet this time making him bring food to Beast's own mouth. The curry tasted somehow even better this way, and he looked deep into Laurent's eyes, searching for the answer he craved.

"I think I do. I need to eat more of it to understand the flavor better." The creases at the sides of Laurent's eyes when he smiled spoke of honesty, and Beast could hardly believe they'd met just yesterday.

"We have plenty. Dig in," Beast said, allowing Laurent to eat on his own despite wanting to touch him all the freaking time. Their knees kissing would have to suffice for now.

"I'll succeed. You just wait," Laurent said, proud like a boy scout when he managed to hold a piece of meat between the chopsticks, and as he leaned closer to feed Beast, he was so focused on his own hand, Beast took the time to ogle Laurent's thighs in the skinny jeans. He felt a bit shitty about it, but back in the store, he'd told Laurent to try on two different pairs of underwear, just to see his ass revealed over and over.

Something fell on his chest and rolled off. Beast realized Laurent had dropped the morsel, and it left a sticky, orange trail of sauce on his chest and stomach. "Oops," he said, pulling out a paper tissue from the bag with food.

"I'm so sorry! I thought I had it." Laurent quickly got a napkin as well and started patting Beast's chest with it. If it was anyone else, Beast would have thought Laurent had done it on purpose, to have an excuse for touching, but Laurent was so different than any of the club hangarounds. So sweet and ridiculously polite.

"It's okay, don't worry," Beast assured him, watching the worried face in the warm light. He'd love to kiss both the beauty spots around

Laurent's lips. "You're still learning. I got us kicked out of the mall, so in terms of fuckups, I don't think you can top me."

Laurent backed off and went silent, as if unsure what to say, so Beast's nerves were already in tatters when he did. "If you knew the ink in your skin would frighten people, then why did you get it?"

Beast flinched and tapped his fingers against the slide. He could tell Laurent a lie, but what would be the point of that? "You see my skin, right? I was in a fire. People stared at me, or pretended I wasn't there because I made them uncomfortable. And then the doctors told me it would stay like this forever. I guess I'd rather have people think I'm scary than pity me," he said with a growing heaviness in his chest.

Laurent nodded, but by the way he took his time to process the words, Beast guessed he was really taking it in. "I once knew an incredibly handsome man. When you looked at his face, his beauty made you assume he was the perfect gentleman. But deep down, in his heart, he held evil you wouldn't comprehend. People are wrong to judge you by your scars."

Beast swallowed, watching Laurent with his pulse drumming in his temples and ears. He didn't expect such understanding. He wasn't the type of man who shared a lot, even with people he was close with, but Laurent was just so otherworldly and different from everyone else Beast knew that it felt natural to speak frankly with him. "Was this the man who injured your wrist?" asked Beast softly.

Laurent backed away slightly, and Beast cursed himself for overstepping. Laurent clearly didn't have amnesia. He was scared of someone, and Beast's need to find out who it was drilled a hole in his stomach.

Laurent nodded and dove his chopsticks into the curry with his shoulders slouched. "Please don't ask me about him. I don't want to remember."

It physically hurt Beast to see the sweet, smiling boy pull back into his shell, as if his fear was so great he wished to just shrink until he became invisible.

Beast put his arm around him, and when Laurent leaned closer, Beast rubbed his cheek against the fine hair on top of Laurent's head. For the first time in so many years, a man was not shying away from his touch. Laurent not only seemed eager for the physical contact but also openly declared that Beast's looks didn't matter. That obviously meant there was a chance for something to develop as long as Beast gave the boy enough breathing room. He would do so.

"How about we try the squid next?" he asked to distract Laurent from the painful memories.

Chapter 10 - Beast

Laurent turned out not to like fried squid at all, but beef wontons were a big hit with him. After the emotional moment, they talked while eating until the sun went down completely. Beast told him what a motorcycle was and promised to take him for a ride at some point. Yet another thing he hadn't done with anyone for years, and already he was willing to take Laurent. Just the thought of Laurent spreading his legs over the bike and pressing his thighs against Beast's had his blood pumping faster.

The closer they were to arriving back at the clubhouse, the more frantic with excitement Beast was getting. He wouldn't show it to Laurent just yet, because he didn't want to get into some weird situation when they were in a public space and he couldn't easily diffuse it. So Beast patiently waited for them to get back into the apartment.

At the clubhouse, everyone was back to their everyday business. He'd already received information about Davy's prognosis being good earlier that day, but no one was in the mood for partying, even though the rubble that had fallen off the ceiling had been removed since the two of them left. The atmosphere was more sombre than usual, and despite some of the guys and hangarounds expressing curiosity in Laurent, introducing them was not on Beast's agenda for the day. Especially not with the skinny jeans Laurent was wearing hugging his round ass so attractively. Beast would lay his claim first, and *then* introduce him, so that there were no doubts as to what Laurent's position was.

"I didn't even see there were numbers yesterday. I thought I'd just press it and it would open," Laurent admitted as he watched Beast use the number pad to unlock the apartment.

Beast let him in first to get another good look at the shape of his back and ass. Despite being small overall, Laurent had a nice width to his shoulders that gave his figure a masculine shape. Beast couldn't wait to see him naked again.

He wasn't sure how to act once the door locked and they were alone in the living room, but Hound saved the day, rushing from his bed and pushing his face against Beast's knees in an affectionate greeting. Knight must have gotten him back here earlier.

Laurent was clearly uncomfortable with Beast's pet, but after some coaxing, he sat on the floor and petted Hound for so long, the beast rolled on his back, wordlessly asking for belly rubs. Laurent gave a pleased laugh, and his brown eyes met Beast's over Hound's wiggling body, causing yet another wave of heat to flow through Beast's entire chest.

Should he shower first after a whole day of being out and about? Then again, he wasn't sure what the protocol of dating was wherever Laurent came from. Besides, wasn't it better to make hay while sun shined?

"So, that was a nice day out, wasn't it?" Beast asked once Hound got fed up with the attention and returned to his bed.

Laurent smiled at him in answer, browsing through the plastic bags they'd deposited on the sofa. "It was the best of days."

A pleasant warmth spread throughout Beast's body, and he stepped closer, smiling at Laurent. This was just the answer he needed to proceed. "Me too. I liked spending time with you."

Laurent sucked in his bottom lip, looking contemplative. "I have to admit that considering the unfortunate circumstances in which we met, I haven't expected for things to go this way, and here I am, one day in this strange new place and already making a friend."

Beast forced himself not to frown. Was this a figure of speech? He would not be put into the 'friend' category! "That's what you call it where you're from?" he asked, approaching Laurent so that they faced one another. The thick scent of the pine shampoo in Laurent's hair was already making him hot. They didn't even need to use the condoms tonight. He'd be fine with just hugging Laurent for now. Preferably naked. Maybe a blowjob.

Laurent stared up at him, staying silent for a while. "Yes, I believe that would be the case."

Beast hesitated, but then reached up and slowly trailed the backs of his fingers over Laurent's jaw. It was quite smooth against the touch, warm and supple as a juicy peach. He leaned in, and with his hands trembling slightly, pressed his lips against that plump, kissable mouth.

He shuddered with glee when Laurent didn't back away, and the visions of pulling all the newly bought clothes off Laurent flooded his mind like seeds of sin. But two seconds later, instead of opening his mouth in invitation, Laurent pulled away, even taking a step back, as if he needed to put physical distance between himself and Beast.

"I… I'm not sure what this is supposed to mean," he choked out.

Beast swallowed and licked the faint trace of Laurent's taste off his lips. He followed Laurent and touched his shoulder. "You said you enjoyed the day with me. We... like each other," he said gesturing between them with one hand.

But Laurent took another step back, dangerously close to the single door that guarded all of Beast's secrets. It should be locked, as it always was, but a tremor of unease danced down Beast's spine. "Yes, but I-I've known you for a single day."

"It's just a kiss," Beast said, pressing his lips together when it dawned on him that the earlier declaration, that people shouldn't judge Beast by his looks, has just been Laurent's way to console him. Be kind to a man so ugly seeing him sometimes made children cry. "You know what, forget it. But if you're not interested, don't fucking cocktease me!"

"Excuse me?" Laurent frowned, not taking his eyes off Beast. "I did what?"

"You were flirting with me all day. You touched me, you were the first one to hold my hand. Do you think this is a game that you can play? That I'll just do anything you want for a scrap of attention? Of course I'm only good for that, no matter what you say!" hissed Beast bitterly and shoved his boot against the sofa so hard the thing moved.

Laurent squinted at him and crossed his arms on his chest while leaning his back against the door. "Is this why you were being kind to me? Should I have not held your hand? I don't understand what the rules are here, but if you thought I was misleading you, know that it was not my intention."

Beast squeezed his hands into fists, unsure how to take that answer. Despite the buzzing anger, he was so deeply disappointed he wished to just reverse everything that had happened earlier. Well, maybe except for getting Laurent the glasses. He needed those, and things had only gone downhill after that anyway. Now that the blinders had fallen off his eyes, he realized just how foolishly he'd deceived himself that someone like him could ever have a chance with someone as beautiful as Laurent. How did he get so consumed by his own lust in one day?

"No, you shouldn't have. And I don't believe you don't know that much. You're lying. Just like you won't tell the truth about your presence here."

"You said men kissing in the television was fine, so I assumed men touching hands was acceptable as well. Why do you have to confuse me this way? Did you think a few long conversations and treats would buy my affection? Maybe buy me a basket of apples next time," the last sentence came out incredibly viciously, and Laurent looked away with a frown, as if he himself wasn't sure how much sense he was making.

"Oh, so now I am the bad guy, huh?" Beast hissed through his teeth, pacing in front of Laurent. His blood was boiling and filling his skull with the angry fumes. "Because I like you and wanted to get you something nice? I would have anyway. We both know I'm fine as a friend, but you don't want to really *be* with any of this?" Beast asked, pulling on the front of his longsleeve. He couldn't bear yet more humiliation, this time delivered by Laurent's own graceful hands.

"You're the one who is making it all about looks. And I think it's because deep down that's all you care about. You've known me for a day, and you want to bed me because of my pretty face. I was thinking today that there is much to admire in you, but I've met men like you before and now I see it. You leave no room for my hesitation. I take one step back and your fury knows no end. You think that just because you have means and position, I will yield to you. You know what? You can take these. I will not be bought." Laurent took off the glasses and pushed them at Beast.

"Put them back on your fucking face," growled Beast as anger reached the boiling point, about to spill out and turn everything to mush. "Take your stuff and get out of my sight."

"Take this shackle off then!" Laurent pointed to his foot, but took back the glasses, which meant his grand gesture had been only for show. Of course, he was greedy to keep everything he got and give not even an inch in return.

Only then it hit Beast what the 'shackle' request meant. Laurent wanted to go farther than a mile away. And where the fuck would he go? He hadn't even known what a car was until earlier today.

"I told you you're only going once you talk—" He stumbled upon words when Laurent's elbow slid over the handle, and the door to the secret room made a sound as if it were budging. "Get away from there. You are not allowed in that room. Ever," Beast said with more aggression that it was strictly necessary. Before Laurent could ask him any questions of his own, he barked, "Until then, go to your room and don't show me your face. I don't wanna see it anymore!"

He couldn't believe his hopes had just got shattered so ruthlessly. What had Laurent been thinking when he'd let Beast hug him? That they'd become platonic besties and exchange friendship bracelets? Beast was a man, and he would not be stuck in eternal blue ball hell. Given half the chance, he'd be fucking Laurent's pert ass right now, and showing the dumb boy how good Beast's cock could feel.

His loss.

Laurent gathered all his bags, the pretty face scrunched into a pout. "Fine!"

Beast faced away from him, trying to catch his breath, which was becoming increasingly difficult as his agitation grew. Each step, each sound of rustling plastic was like a pin pushed into Beast's flesh. He couldn't believe he let himself go like this. That he even for a moment believed a guy like Laurent could have even the slightest interest in him. This humiliation was punishment for listening to his dick.

Laurent ceremoniously walked off to the little corridor where all the other rooms were. Beast couldn't believe he was now stuck with this boy in his apartment. Now Laurent would be shoving himself into Beast's face every day until King was done with him.

The way the little bastard slammed the door was the last fucking straw.

"And stay there," yelled Beast, rushing into the corridor and leaning closer to the hard wood. "You won't leave this room until I say so!"

"I've got glasses, and hundreds of books here! I can stay here forever!" Laurent yelled back like the brat he was.

Beast smashed his fist against the door twice, until the bones in his hand ached so bad he needed to retreat. "You can fuck yourself. Ungrateful cunt."

Beast's mind tormented him with the happiness he could have experienced if only Laurent had been sweet and pliant like he'd been all day and invited Beast between his legs. Was that so much to ask? It would have been fun for Laurent too. And now he was imagining Laurent's face flushed and sweaty, hair sticking to it, lips parting in ecstasy.

He hit the door once more for good measure and walked back to the living room. Hound gave a quiet whine, but Beast gestured for him to stay where he was.

His gaze trailed over the sofa and the single plastic bag that contained a T-shirt he'd bought for himself. It was also where he'd hidden the condoms and lube. Now he just wanted to burn everything.

"Fuck," he screamed out, pacing all around the room until his initial anger evaporated, leaving behind a burning emptiness that could not be filled. Just the day before, simply having a pretty boy around had seemed nice. But now that Beast knew for a fact that Laurent was gay, getting rejected on the first attempt to get laid in years made him want to go back to the sexless life where porn provided the only relief.

And to make matters worse, there was a knock on the main door to his apartment, invading his helpless solitude with cheerful noise. "Yo! Beast! Heard you came back."

Beast sank down to the sofa and rubbed his face in his hands. It took a handful more knocks for him to ask his friend to let himself in. Knight and King were the only people who knew the code unlocking Beast's apartment. No. There was also fucking Laurent now, so Beast needed to change the code. The atmosphere had been so lovely it hadn't occurred to Beast that things could go sour, and he couldn't have Laurent knowing how to leave so easily.

Knight came in with a wide grin on the handsome face that attracted both sexes in equal measure. Beast wondered bitterly if Laurent's morals and convictions would have been as stern if it was Knight who'd tried to get into his pants. He'd probably come up with some stupid excuse after the deed was done, along the lines of, 'Oh, I didn't know sucking cock meant attraction!'.

"Why the long face?" Knight asked, waving some magazines in his hand. He looked around conspicuously and lowered his voice. "Is he around? I've got these gay porn mags. Thought we could leave them lying around to figure out if he's as gay as the words he uses."

Beast shot to his feet, grabbed Knight's shoulder, and led him through the single door leading from his living room to the office where he gathered all the things he needed to keep hidden. With a brief turn of the key Beast always had with him, all secrets were out to be seen.

"He's gay," Beast said as soon as they closed door behind them. There was no decoration here, unless one counted photographs and prints of historical pictures hung all around the walls as decor. "We don't need to check anything. And I don't want him reading porn in my house."

Knight's brows shot up. "O-kay. Since when are you against porn? And how do you know he's gay?" Beast didn't like the glint in Knight's eyes at the last question. Couldn't Beast have one fucking thing to himself? He knew it was shitty to not let Knight make a move if he himself had been rejected, but… seriously? Wasn't there enough flesh on Knight's platter?

Beast bit on his cheeks from the inside, breathing hard and clenching his hand on the edge of the desktop. He didn't want to share his failures, but at the same time, the need to tell his friend that *something* even vaguely sexual happened in his life for once was so strong he fought through his shame.

"He saw men kissing on TV, and he was happy about it being okay. And..."

"That's the proof? I think my plan is better."

Beast groaned. "No. I don't want him getting all fucking excited and coming in here with another guy." Just the thought of it was so humiliating Beast wanted to bash his head against the bare wall behind him.

Knight squinted at Beast, and Beast could see the cogs moving under the messy hair. "...Because you wanna fuck him first."

"Well, it's not gonna happen, is it?"

Knight grinned and leaned against the large corkboard, only to pull away with a hiss when a pin dug into his back. "Why the hell not? He's living here. You've got all the opportunities to butter him up."

Beast snapped, tossing a book off the desk. "I know this because I know he's not interested. He held my fucking hand all day, but the moment I kissed him, he started making up all that stuff about now knowing what it meant. I didn't even use my fucking tongue, and he was fucking *revolted*!"

Knight rubbed his chin. "Oh, man… What a douche. But at least you got to holding hands. Preschool base?" He laughed and poked Beast's arm, but Beast wasn't in the mood for jokes at his expense. Knight cleared his throat. "Maybe you just need to play the long game, you know? Or show him you've got options, get him jealous."

Beast tightened his jaw so hard it made his teeth hurt. "Well, I don't. I have no options. Look at me. What was I thinking trying to get close to a guy like *that*? There's no one interested. Not in me. They'd do me for kicks or for the patches. Would *you* fuck me?"

Knight groaned and shifted his weight. "That's not a fair question. You know you're not my type. You never were. And for the record, I know I'm not yours. It's, like… *ew*. We're practically brothers."

Beast rubbed his face. If it wasn't about Knight in particular, Beast was at the point where he had close to no *type* as long as someone was truly interested in him. The problem was that it wasn't coming his way. He was forever doomed to be someone's thrill, not a person to be seriously interested in. "Yeah. Right."

Knight took a deep breath, eyeing Beast with a concerned look that was making Beast want to kick him out after all. "Sure, we all know that if someone's won the genetic lottery, it's easier for them to get laid, but you're fit, you're tall, you're strong, and you've got a big dick. A guy doesn't need a baby face to get some action. Forget the Amish boy and his whining."

Beast raised his hands, but realizing he didn't know what he wanted to do with them in the first place, he let them drop. "We had a connection. It was a good day. I'm so fucking stupid."

Knight slapped Beast on the arm. "His loss. What's going on with this?" he stepped closer to the desk and pointed to the notes and printouts Beast had gathered in several folders and boxes. Some of them were related to the history of the house, others to the mysterious occult sigil. The one on King's—and Laurent's—nape.

Beast massaged his eyes with his fingers, trying to change his focus. He wasn't a crybaby, and he would not mourn the things he couldn't have. He was a man of action.

"I'm positive the brand on Laurent is the same as the one on King, *and* the one we found under the floor," he said looking at the photograph he and Knight had taken when they first made the discovery. It was years ago, back when Beast was still a promising young man with a dashing smile and clear skin. Back then, some of the floors in the basement had started to rot, and since the club was using those rooms for storage, it was his and Knight's job to replace the old wood with something new.

But under the old planks they found smoothened stone—which must have been the original floor. They found dirt, and even a mouse skeleton, but in the middle of the room was something else altogether. Grooves have been meticulously carved into the stone to form the odd sign written into a double circle of two meters in diameter. And then someone took care to fill the dip in the floor with iron, leaving behind the disturbing sign that Beast's learned by heart since.

Inside the circle was a sixteen-armed star adorned with curious letters on each of the sharp edges and filled with a tangle of signs that vaguely resembled a human skull. It was the same symbol King carried on his nape, and so Beast and Knight made the decision not to inform him of the find. It had all been very weird and pushed Beast to look for answers.

Forbidden books and treatises on the occult helped him and Knight decipher some of the elements on the sigil, but everything pointed to it being an infernal symbol. So what was it doing on King's body? And how did King end up owning a former asylum? The place had been built incorporating an eighteenth century building that used to belong to a famous serial killer and had the very same symbol in the basement. Notably, said serial killer also reportedly had a devil's mark on his nape. There was a connection, but Beast couldn't grasp what it was.

He didn't search for it exactly believing in magic—that would have been ridiculous—but his father was hiding something. Was he a member of a cult? Or was the symbol the sign of an alliance with some gang he didn't want to tell anyone about to keep the money from that connection to himself?

Knight leaned over all the papers and photos laid out on the table. "And I've found nothing about a modern-day Laurent Mercier from La Rochelle. It's kinda freaky actually, because how would he be able to fly under the radar like that? And what kind of connection could a guy like him have to King anyway? It's like an itch I can't scratch."

Beast nodded, tracing the photographs of the symbol that was still hidden in the basement, underneath the new floor. "It's the same sigil. I'm sure of it. He said someone was mistreating him, and he's obviously afraid of being found by that person. Maybe he used to be imprisoned by... a group who uses this as their mark."

"Must be a better kept secret than the Illuminati," Knight said, pulling out a box of chewing gum to have one. "But if pretty boy's been kept somewhere remote, and King has his fingers in it, he'd want to hide it at all cost. He knows no one in the club would stand for human trafficking."

Beast scowled. "That's disgusting. You think King would be dealing with this kind of shit behind our backs?" His father was no angel, but even Beast found it hard to believe that he would engage in that kind of business after establishing a motorcycle club that stood for freedom in all matters, including sex.

Knight wrapped his hands on his nape. "I don't know. I wouldn't accuse him of it, but I'm just throwing it out there. King was furious when he first noticed that symbol on Laurent, and then he's all nice all of a sudden and wants you to take him shopping? But you know what *really* freaked me out? How that brand on Laurent's nape was still hot, but he wasn't in pain at all."

Beast dug his fingers into the flesh of his biceps when he realized that Laurent's neck had still been unnaturally warm when they hugged in the playground. What did that mean? "I wonder if King's is the same."

"It's not like we're gonna go poking at it, but maybe we could ask Nao? Or I could even put up Jordan to hugging him."

Beast nodded, but his thoughts were already drifting off to the findings and thoughts he kept to himself. Knight was his closest friend, but he was mostly interested in the brand because he thought it had significance to the history of the house, and in turn, the history of the Mercier family. He would not understand some of Beast's hopes for it. "Yes, let's do that."

Knight looked down at his phone when it beeped, and he groaned. "Jesus. And there it is. Half an hour like clockwork. That woman's doing my head in. I told her that I'm not fucking anyone behind her back. That if I fuck someone, I'll let her know first. She said she was fine with an open relationship, but I'm not sure anymore if she knows what that means. I've got to go or she's gonna defrost all my food or some shit like that."

Beast nodded, pretending he too felt like the trouble with Jordan was a huge issue in Knight's world of sexual abundance. She was the kind of woman who liked the fantasy of a bad boy and his lifestyle, but didn't appreciate the reality of it. Knight would be better off with someone else, but who was Beast to judge? Knight was a big boy and could make his own decisions.

"Sure, I won't stop you."

"But tell me if you find something new. This has to be the most exciting discovery to happen in the Mercier family tree in *years*." Knight grinned wildly and left Beast to his own devices. Sometimes Beast wondered what the 'genealogy community'—as Knight loved to call it—would think if they found out who Knight was. Beast had definitely never met a biker with a weirder hobby. Then again, who was he to talk about weird hobbies when he was stuck on his own in this room, pulling open the drawer full of his findings on occult practices in the area?

There were stories linked to the symbol under the floor. The symbol Beast now saw on two separate men. A serial killer active in the early nineteenth century reportedly also had one, and whenever references to it appeared on the pages of old journals, letters, or town chronicles, it was always related to unusual events. A sudden acquisition of wealth. Black masses and brutal animal sacrifice in the woods nearby. The birth of octuplets, of which all survived. Never-ending banquets. A mass-hallucination among the patients and staff of the very psychiatric institution that previously occupied the current clubhouse. In the sixties, so many people claimed to have seen the devil within the asylum that the decision to abandon it came suddenly and left the building to rot. Until King purchased it for close to nothing back in the early 2000s.

And curiously enough, all those events were clustered around the property, with each new building constructed in the same spot, re-using the old materials.

How old was the iron-filled sigil under the floor in the cellar? As old as the European colonies, or perhaps even more ancient?

Beast opened his notebook on the one story he kept coming back to. One that was closer to being a fairytale than a historical account, and it wasn't even clear whether it originated in the native legends or has been the product of wild imagination of the first colonists.

The story told of a man who hunted in this area and traded with European ship captains. During one of his hunting trips, a bear mauled him so badly his arm needed to be amputated. The ship captain who wrote about it in his journals, claimed to have seen it with his own eyes. Yet when he came back from England a year later, he met the same man, not only in perfect health but so strikingly handsome one of the ladies traveling with the captain married the man only two days later.

Most fairytales had some kind of moral to it, an ending, and yet this one, just… *was*. The man never told anyone what cured him, and the only thing the captain noted was that the locals said the man made a journey into the woods west from the township of Brecon—which was also the general location of the clubhouse—and came back healed. With his new wife, he moved to live in the same woods. But the story got blurry there. Some versions claimed he started a town of his own, some that he lured in travellers and made blood sacrifices, when another suggested he ate and drank like a monster yet took three more wives and lived to be a hundred years old.

What mattered was that it was a story of a man whose body got crushed, and he found a way to cure himself at a time when most people didn't live into their sixties. And if there was any kind of truth to it, even if it was simply based on science people haven't discovered yet, Beast wanted to find it. He *needed* to find it.

More so with each day he saw his almost sixty-year-old father live a life of drugs, alcohol, and numerous sexual partners yet have barely any wrinkles.

Chapter 11 - Laurent

Laurent lay curled up in the soft comforter that was as light as if it had cotton clouds inside yet kept warmth so well he didn't want to leave from under it despite having been awake for two hours already.

The night before, he'd rummaged through Beast's bookshelves looking for anything that could help him understand the world around him better. Getting to grips with the way people used language, and what connotations words had was crucial if he was to blend in. Even the books themselves, though recognizable for what they were, were different to the ones in his time. Much lighter, made of bright, thin paper and enveloped by cardboard covers that had all kinds of paintings on them.

He also desperately needed a distraction and settled for a book telling the story of a vicious young woman feigning her death to control her husband. He couldn't turn the pages fast enough, and even though many details and words escaped his understanding, he was learning their gist out of context.

But once he turned off the light and lay in his bed with his heart still pounding in his chest, as he recounted the events of the book in his mind, still amazed by how easy it was to read with the new glasses, real life came creeping back to grab him by the throat. The disastrous kiss that followed the most glorious day wouldn't let him sleep.

Laurent should have known Beast would be no better than Fane. He'd shackled his foot and turned into a dragon as soon as Laurent hesitated about accepting Beast's advances. It was for the best. He was drowning in this new world already and didn't need to feel affection for Beast on top of that. No matter how rapidly his heart fluttered when Beast's scarred fingers curled around his or how sturdy his massive arm felt when Beast put it over Laurent's shoulder on the slide. These were all ridiculous trifles to ponder.

Wasn't this exactly the mistake he'd made before? A powerful man showered him with attention and gifts, and already Laurent's heart sparked with excitement, even though it had left him covered in blood last time. He would not be a target again and entangle himself with a man who could snap him like a twig. If Beast reacted with fury when his kiss hasn't been reciprocated, what would he have done if Laurent kissed but wasn't willing to follow through any further? Laurent still remembered how Fane had mocked his nervousness, how he'd called Laurent a flower to pluck.

Laurent flinched when heavy footsteps resonated somewhere behind the door, and he pulled up the comforter, resting the open book on his chest. The man moved just outside of Laurent's room, and when tension reached its limit and made his stomach clench, there was a knock.

Laurent squinted at the door. Hadn't he been told to 'fuck off' just yesterday? He could hardly believe the amount of vile words spilling out of Beast's mouth every time something bothered him, but it seemed that they were more commonly used than in the past. And yet they hurt just as much when hurled at him.

But when the man spoke from behind the door, it was not Beast's voice but King's. "Laurent, are you asleep?"

He put the book away and slid out of bed. Was it appropriate to have King visit when Laurent was in his night clothes? It likely was if King chose to visit him here. "Please, come in," he said, uselessly straightening out his dark green plaid pajama pants.

The door opened, and King's handsome face emerged from behind it. "Why wouldn't you answer at first? Is my son treating you badly?"

Laurent licked his lips, unsure what to say at first. "We might have had a bit of an argument yesterday. He claimed not to want to hear from me, so I chose not to answer the knocking. I meant no disrespect by it, Mr. King."

King's mouth stretched into a smile, and Laurent had to wonder at how healthy his teeth were in comparison to men his age where Laurent has come from. They were so white, and straight, with not even a single one missing! "Just ignore him. He's a sulking troll. Now, come out. I brought you some breakfast from downstairs," he said, opening the door wider.

"That's very kind, sir." Laurent smiled but was still wary of King's strange moods and his change of heart. First he'd tried to choke Laurent, and then had Beast take him shopping. The man either had a twin, or something else was going on that Laurent didn't understand. He wouldn't try to poison Laurent, would he?

He followed King into the living room, where several plates stood on the low table by the sofa, along with two cups of steaming coffee. Laurent's gaze still strayed to the locked door that he'd been explicitly told not to dare approach. The prohibited access only made Laurent's curiosity itch.

"Dig in. I thought the two of us should have a chat in private and talk of our common friend," King said, dropping into a chair across from the sofa. He picked up one of the empty plates and filled with all the goods he came with. There were fried eggs, bacon, tomatoes, pancakes, and sausage, and mushrooms, and bread. The abundance of it in such a simple meal was astounding, although Laurent already knew that the people in this world seemed to want for nothing.

"Knight? Nao? I wouldn't say I'm friends with them just yet, sir." Laurent reached out for a crispy, warm piece of bread and put a fried egg on it, smiling at the sight already. He would not be dragged down into the same mood as Beast's when there was so much this world could offer. One day he would meet a man he could trust, a man who would not abuse him, trick him, or be of a social standing so much higher than Laurent that he could do anything to him.

"No. I mean our horned friend," King said, and the food got stuck in Laurent's mouth as the brand on his neck seemed to flare with heat.

He sank farther into the sofa, watching King with more wariness and suddenly wondering whether Beast would still help him in case of King's attack or if he'd watch on with cruel satisfaction.

King pulled off a black scarf he was wearing, presenting Laurent with an intricate symbol burned on the back of his thick neck. Laurent had taken a good look at his own in the bathrooms at the mall, and he would swear they were identical. But what could that mean?

"Have you… Has he helped you?" Laurent asked in the end.

King smirked and gave Laurent a nod, biting into his bread with a loud groan of pleasure. "Have you met Martina? She cooks so well when she's hungover."

The change of topic threw Laurent off. "I don't believe I've met her, no. But, back to the other issue… What did he help you with?"

King chewed on his food and leaned back, crossing his legs in a relaxed position. "Oh, he's watching over me. But most of all, he told me that you're here for me, so I guess that makes us partners."

Laurent let out a big sigh of relief, and his shoulders sagged. "Yes! Yes, that's right. I've been explicitly told that no harm can come to you. I've been extremely anxious about this, sir, so I'm more than happy to hear we are on the same side."

King waved his hand. "If you have any issues with my son, just tell me, and I'll deal with him. He's pushing so damn hard to move the club, but I can't have that. It would break the terms of my agreement with our friend. We need to make sure he doesn't stir things up with the other club members."

Laurent put all the information he was getting onto tidy shelves in his mind. "Now I understand. I've been sent to make sure he is still here for his next birthday. I understand that is advantageous to you, sir?"

King washed down his food with coffee, squinting slightly. "Laurent, you are adorable when you talk like that. Yes, it will be all done and dusted if we stay here until he's thirty three."

Laurent stuffed his mouth with toast and egg, unsure what to make of the compliment. He was just being polite. "Once that happens, I will be free, but also without an ally in this world. Is there a chance that we could become that when all is settled? I in turn promise to make myself useful."

King spread out in the chair like a medieval king on his throne. "If you do this for me, I will not let you go hungry or poor. That is a promise," he said and reached out his hand over the table.

Laurent was eager to squeeze it. Finally! Maybe the devil was right, and he really had the power necessary to fulfil the task he'd been burdened with. All he had to do was stall Beast's plans for a few months. Being around Beast wouldn't be easy, but Laurent could surely make himself enough of a distraction to make Beast forget other tasks.

The lock clanged, and King pulled back his hand, picking up the mug of coffee just before the door opened and Beast walked in. He stopped mid-stride when he noticed them sitting by the little table. Laurent's eyes went wide when Hound barked, aggressively rushing to stand in front of him, as if he was ready to bite if only his master told him to.

King raised his cup with a wide smile. "Son! I hear you had a little squabble with our dear guest. What could he have possibly done? Just look at him," he said, gesturing at Laurent.

Beast's mouth tightened, and he slowly closed the door behind him. "It would be great if you told me you were about to let yourself into my apartment."

King slurped his coffee loudly. "Technically it's my apartment. This whole property belongs to me."

Laurent picked up his cup as well, anxious the moment Hound came closer with his wide black muzzle and started sniffing Laurent's knee. He wasn't even sure if he should speak to Beast, and when he looked up and caught the blue gaze pinning him to the sofa, he was quick to look back down into the coffee. Now that he could see Beast's face so clearly through the glasses, he was sure Beast was definitely not a 'troll' as his father had called him. Beast was a man of flesh and bone, even if scarred under all the ink. The Latin inscriptions along with the pictures of hell softened Laurent's heart whenever he looked at Beast. Despite yesterday's cruel words, he now knew that the skin in which Beast lived was his personal Inferno, and nothing Laurent did or said could make it any worse.

Hound pressed his nose against Laurent's thigh, peeking at him with curious dark eyes, but pulled back immediately when Beast called him over with a whistle. Beast pulled a flesh-colored bone off a shelf and gave it to the dog, which made a circle in place before running off to its bed in the corner.

"Look, I understand that this house belongs to you, but it's also our clubhouse. We don't know when one of the floors will crumble. There have been no real maintenance works done since the sixties. After forty years of disuse, it does need renovations, whether you like it or not. So we either invest and renovate or find somewhere else," Beast said, walking up to the table with a bottle of a black drink in hand. Laurent cowered under the look Beast gave him.

"That's why we're getting work done in the common room today. You're such a pain in the ass, you know that? I'm paying for it from my own pocket too."

Beast took a few sips and shifted his weight, which made the dark aray shirt with long sleeves cling to his chest. Laurent still remember how soft was the fabric Beast wore yesterday and how hard the muscle underneath. "Get over yourself. Sometimes, hard decisions need to be made. We don't even use most of the building, so why don't you sell it? Why are you so adamant on keeping this particular place?"

King's shoulders went rigid, and he stood up. He wasn't as tall as his son, but Laurent wouldn't dare stand up to him either way. "I don't need to explain myself to you. The building is massive, with potential for expansion, huge rooms to hold parties and concerts in. If you had any imagination, you'd look to the future and see what could become of it if we all work hard!"

Laurent cleared his throat. "I have to admit the whole place is incredibly impr—"

Beast's blue eyes shot toward him, and he pointed his huge index finger at him. "Shut up. This has nothing to do with you!"

King snorted. "Give the boy a break. Seems he's smarter than you if he sees the potential of this property. I'm not going to even start on all the grounds, which could be converted into a recreational area in the future. There's no way I'm getting rid of this place to buy some godawful concrete bunker somewhere."

Beast's jaw clenched. "Whatever. Tell me next time when you come in like a fucking king of the castle."

King shrugged. "Oh, I was going out anyway. You can finish the breakfast. It's delicious. Isn't that right?" he asked Laurent.

"Yes, it's very good. Thank you very much, sir." Laurent nodded quickly, burning under King's scrutiny.

King gave Beast a slap on the back on his way out. "Come down and introduce him once you're done eating. Laurent's our guest, and he'll be staying here for a while, so treat him as such. And stop freaking him out with the dog."

Beast put his arms across his chest, watching Laurent in complete silence until King disappeared behind the door. "Did you suck him off that he's so friendly?" he burst out as soon as they were alone.

Laurent looked up, frozen to his spot on the sofa. "E-excuse me?"

"You heard me," Beast said, approaching in stiff, aggressive steps.

"I… don't understand your meaning," Laurent left his coffee on the table and got up quickly to not be at a disadvantageous position if Beast became violent. He wouldn't admit it, but it had given him a thrill yesterday to see Beast deal with the rude man at the escalator. However, he'd hate to have that kind of force targeted at him. He was sure Beast's strength easily outweighed William Fane's, and Fane had already been an adversary at whose hand Laurent could had died.

Beast barked out a laugh and tightened his fist over an invisible shape. "No? I'll tell you. You take a man's cock, you put it in your mouth, and you suck on it," he explained, bringing his hand closer to his lips and pressing on the inside of his cheek with his tongue, as if something really were inserted.

Laurent's face went aflame. "What a rude insinuation! I am *appalled*!" He turned around to avoid seeing Beast repeat the movement. Even his neck went hot when he thought of Beast—

Laurent stomped off to his room, but he could hear Beast follow. All he could now think of was Beast's lips around a prick, moving up until he kissed the tip. This wasn't good at all.

"Dress in something suitable. If King wants you down with the others, then you're going. You have fifteen minutes," Beast said, standing in the doorway as Laurent stumbled into his room.

Laurent pulled off the sleeveless top he used for sleeping but then stilled, looking back at Beast. "Some privacy, please?"

"*Now* you want privacy? So I'm now banned from even looking at you?"

The question left Laurent more nervous by the second. How was he to answer? It wasn't like Beast hadn't seen him naked before. And yet after the attempted kiss everything felt different. "Weren't you the one to say you didn't want to look at my face?"

An unpleasant smirk twisted Beast's features. "Who says I want to look at your *face*?"

This time even Laurent's ears got hot. To think that Beast had ogled him before when Laurent thought they were just two men whose nakedness had no consequence. He stepped toward Beast and, despite the man's towering size, pushed on his stomach, trying to shove him out of the room. "I am not a piece of meat to be chewed on."

Beast looked at the watch, which was attached to his wrist. "Now it's ten minutes, so better hurry, or I'm going to haul you downstairs in your pajamas."

Laurent huffed in exasperation and backed off from the man-mountain. It was surely not beneath Beast to humiliate him that way in front of other people, if this was the way he acted after being denied pleasures of the flesh.

Laurent stepped away and pulled off the pajama pants, all too aware of the eyes on his backside, and afraid that their presence could make him too excited for polite company. But when he glanced back, just to make sure there was no encroaching danger, Beast wasn't there.

Laurent exhaled deeply, and yet instantly missed the imposing presence. The revelation that Beast was like him, 'gay' as they called it nowadays, had sparked a fire somewhere underneath Laurent's skin that wouldn't stop smoking up his brain, no matter how hard he tried.

With Beast gone, dressing was a quick affair, since all the modern clothes were simple, and easy to put on, to the point of Laurent considering them 'simplistic', but he would fit in at all cost. He took a deep breath and stepped out, feeling much safer in the leather jacket than in the pajama pants that were so tightly fitted they left little to the imagination. Laurent now wondered if that was why Beast chose them.

Beast lay on the sofa with the huge dog spread over his legs. Both their gazes darted to Laurent as soon as he emerged out of the hallway, dressed and with his hair combed with the new hairbrush. Grooming was much easier now that he could actually see himself in the tiny round mirror they purchased at the store.

Hound smacked his jaws lazily and rolled to his back, but Beast gently pushed him off and got up. "Take the tray," he said, gesturing at the leftover food.

Laurent frowned. "Don't you have servants to do that?"

Beast grinned. "I do now. Take the tray."

Laurent pursed his lips and counted the passing seconds to calm himself. He'd escaped that life and was not indentured to follow orders anymore. He couldn't believe that even here he was being ordered around. He fought the itch in his eyes, the memories of a birch rod against his back, and picked up the tray without another word.

"Since King allows you to leave my room, eat in the kitchen. You two left crumbs all over my sofa," Beast said and called Hound over, leading the way to the door.

Laurent walked through the door that Beast opened for him, dying to meet other people so he wasn't stuck with his conflicting feelings for Beast.

Hound followed his master with histhick black tail wagging. The dog kept looking back at Laurent, as if he didn't trust him, but with the sound of music getting louder as the three of them progressed down the corridor. Laurent was glad when they finally came upon a mirror, as there wasn't one in Beast's apartment, and he glanced into the reflection of his whole body to make sure he was indeed presentable.

The surface of the glass was slightly bent though, as if the mirror had an imperfection Laurent couldn't pinpoint. It wasn't that it was misshaped, like the ones in the hall of mirrors they had visited with Beast yesterday, but even with the glasses firmly on his nose, Laurent's reflection was slightly unclear, and dark shadows hid in the corners. Nothing like the clean, smooth surfaces that he'd seen in such big numbers at the mall.

They took a different corridor than last time, but all the passages melted into one big maze in Laurent's mind anyway. All with paint peeling off the walls like skin in the summer and corridors with floors made of dirty-looking tiles. With each room they passed, the sense of unease was growing in Laurent at the sight of fallen chairs and broken bedframes. They were in such contrast to Beast's clean, fresh apartment full of items Laurent could bet were expensive. No wonder Beast didn't want to live here.

But the the closer they came to the noise the more orderly their surroundings became. The corridors, while still vast, changed in shape somewhat, and Laurent's newly proficient sight even noticed crumbled traces of decoration that were of a familiar Grecian style. Was this an old building that was still occupied the same way some European kings lived in old castles back in Laurent's time?

His thoughts flowed freely as he followed Beast down a neat-looking hallway until they faced a grand spiral staircase, partially enclosed by wooden arches that looked like tall castle windows and stood out so completely from the simplicity and crudeness of everything else in the clubhouse that Laurent found himself speeding up to take a closer look.

He faced the circular space the staircase revolved around, and it was as if someone hit the back of his head, emptying his mind until only dull pain remained. In the bright daylight coming through the windows behind Laurent's back, the vicious, disfigured face of a gargoyle stared at Laurent, mocking him with a half-smile. The cutlery and plates jiggled on the tray when Laurent's whole body shook in terror. He stared back into the deep, lifelike eyes of the creature, which has been sculpted with such attention to detail it felt as if it could move any moment now, flying toward the tall ceiling on its spread wings.

It was the very same statue that confused Laurent when he had first entered William Fane's house. And once Laurent knew this much, his gaze inevitably reached behind the monster, to the discolored wooden panels that bore traces of mold yet still hid the secrets of torture and death. Through that hidden door Fane had led him like a lamb for slaughter.

He didn't even realize he'd stopped until Beast spoke to him. "Weird, right? I'm surprised they didn't remove that thing when the hospital was established here. Seeing sculptures like this couldn't have helped the patients," he said, approaching the monstrosity, and he stroked its malformed muzzle.

Laurent's lips twisted into a scowl, but he managed to steady his hands to make the contents of the tray stable despite the nausea rising in his throat. "What is this place?"

Particles of dust danced in the air, creating a quaint atmosphere, yet Laurent's heart raced as if it wished to forcefully pull him out of here and through the nearest door. He'd seen the enormous complex of buildings from the outside twice already, but throughout the past two hundred years the facade must have been modified, because it looked nothing like Fane's mansion. Though to be fair Laurent had only seen it once in the past, and at nighttime at that.

Shivers went down his spine when he glanced at the secret door that had led him to Fane's chamber of horrors, but Beast already nudged him along the corridor.

"Oh, King's owned it since the early 2000s, but it used to be a psychiatric institution before that. That's why there are so many rooms. It's a pain in the ass, if you ask me," he said as they walked past what used to be the main hall at the entrance.

Now that Laurent realized that he'd traveled in time but was in the same place, evidence of it was creeping up on him from every direction. The original doors have been reshaped, but the panel above them still had a wave-like decoration adorned with a relief depicting a garland of flowers. The alcoves in the walls now had little lamps instead of naked statues, but when Laurent looked up, Dionysus's face stared back at him the same way it had when he first entered the house with Fane. The fresco was dark, the paint cracked, and some of the plaster had crumbled and fallen off, leaving blank holes in the painting of the bacchanalia, but it was, without a doubt, the same one.

Something turned in his stomach at the thought that Fane's rotted corpse could still be locked away in that secret cellar. Then again, in two hundred years, someone would have surely found the body. Stabbed, his neck cut open like a gutted fish, and no perpetrator to be found behind a door that locked from the inside, other than a single arm of a faceless victim. Would people have thought the arm itself came alive and delivered justice? Laurent smirked to himself at the thought.

"What's going on? You're coming or not?"

"Sorry, I just..." Laurent sped up to escape Dionysus's prying eyes. "I'm coming." He left the hallway behind and caught up with Beast, suddenly wishing to feel his strong arm around him again.

Words sung by a woman with an oddly deformed voice became clearer, as did the sounds of conversation and the smell of food and coffee. Hound let out a muffled bark through the bone he was still holding between his teeth and rushed down the corridor. Laurent and Beast followed through two pairs of tall doors and a rather large chamber that contained billiard tables and smelled of tobacco as intensely as if a whole party of smokers had just left it.

The next room was the size of a theatre, filled with comfortable-looking seating facing one of the televisions similar to the ones at the mall. This one was huge, almost the size of a billiard table.

The modern age seemed to have frescoes too, but they were crude, done in solid color, dark, and vulgar. As they walked through the television room, naked women gave Laurent lusty grins from pictures on the wall, where they lay on pillows in front of a red-skinned, horned man who was clearly meant to depict the devil, yet had none of the subtlety of the creature's dangerous grace. This one had an enormous prick pushing at the front of his pants and rings attached to his nipples. He gazed upon the women like the personification of infernal lust.

The old Laurent might have looked away, but there was no point in avoiding such lewd depictions after having made a pact with a demon himself.

There was a clear break beyond the tall rooms that must have been the repurposed Fane mansion and the newer structure they entered next. Here, floors were made of something that seemed like a mixture of rubber and plastic and squeaked under the soles of his boots. The architects had provided no adornment to the walls, which made all the rooms and even corridors seem like boxes stacked together for convenience. He saw more of the disturbing frescos, more smooth, shiny pictures of naked bodies and devilish creatures, and the walls were painted a variety of intense colors, the subtlety of reliefs or coving forgotten.

After passing through a narrow corridor they finally entered the room where at least a dozen people sat on sofas, chatted and ate. Just above the doorway Laurent noticed a sentence written in crude lettering.

Abandon all hope, ye who enter here.

Chapter 12 - Laurent

Laurent swallowed at the infernal message above the door as Beast nudged him forward, into a room drowned in red. Paintings of flames and dancing skeletons covered the crimson walls, and sofas of burgundy leather gathered around a low table with the legs of a goat. There were scarlet cupboards in the area likely used for serving food, and the carpet was the color of dark cherries crushed into the floor by heavy boots.

The noise overflowing into all the corridors and chambers of the clubhouse originated here, although Laurent couldn't see any musicians or instruments. The music—a painful concoction of hoarse shouting, banging, and a screech that sounded as if someone were scraping their nails against a chalkboard—was a constant buzz in Laurent's head.

When the people gathered in the chamber noticed him and Beast, some of the conversations died down, and he could sense curious gazes penetrating him without even the pretense of politeness.

"Nothing to see here," said Beast in a tone that suggested he meant the exact opposite. He nodded toward a counter dividing the space from another chamber, which shone with polished metal. "Leave the tray in the kitchen and come back."

Now that Laurent could see everything so clearly, he wasn't all that sure if he wanted to. Most of the men were giants dressed in black, and judging by the clothes of the women, none of them were respectable ladies. Even in comparison to the women Laurent had seen at the mall, the abundance of naked flesh on show here was stifling his voice. Was this a brothel?

Choosing to stay civil and not say anything that could be considered rude, he put the tray on the polished surface by the kitchen, watching Beast walk over to the sofas to be greeted with smiles and pats on the back.

"I'm Martina," a woman with flaming red hair and a thick layer of kohl around the eyes shook Laurent's hand before he could decide if it was an appropriate thing to do. "Did you like the breakfast? I wasn't sure if you're not vegan or something."

Nao, whom Laurent thankfully already met before walked up to them with a smile. "Look at you! Those baggy pants were hiding all that?"

Laurent dared to smile, relieved that at least someone here was shorter than him, even if she was a woman. "Thank you. Beast helped me choose."

Martina's eyebrows shot up. "*Beast* helped you with shopping?"

"I know, right?" Nao asked, casually putting her arm around Martina's waist and picking up a glass of thick juice from the counter. "Ain't he sweet? King never wants to go," she scowled, and Martina rolled her eyes.

"King never wants to do anything that isn't about him being the center of attention. Last time he took me shopping, we split after half an hour, and he spent all that time buying stuff for himself. I ended up waiting for him, and he was late to the movies. Aren't men always complaining that they have to wait for their women? They're just the same as us."

Nao moaned and patted her friend's back. "You should have called me. I wanted to see that film anyway. You know how hot I am for Tom Hardy in pretty much anything."

Only now did it hit Laurent that Nao was King's 'girlfriend', which he'd already worked out meant a kind of common law wife. "Is... I don't mean to be rude, I just wanted to inquire. Is it acceptable for a man to go out with another woman when he already has a girlfriend?"

Martina's face blanked, but then she burst out with laughter and nudged Nao with her elbow. "Oh, my God! You were right! He *is* precious."

Laurent groaned, focusing on the tabletop instead. When would he start getting things right?

Nao waved her hand dismissively. "We're both King's girlfriends, sweetie."

Laurent frowned but decided to leave the question about bigamy to himself.

Nao snickered, leaning back as if Laurent was an artwork to wonder at. "Look at his eyes. He's so confused. Sweet baby, it's all fine. We both agreed to this, so it's not cheating."

Beast's laughter carried across the room and drilled itself into Laurent's ears. It would have been rude to look away from his partners in conversation, but he so very much wanted to know what caused such an outburst of glee in a man so permanently scowling.

"We were waiting for you two with the chili," Martina said and pointed Laurent to a silver metallic box with numbers and symbols on one side. "Put it on for three minutes."

Laurent swallowed, hesitant over what she meant, yet not wanting to seem hopelessly dumb. He nodded and walked up to the box with his heart beating faster by the minute. He would never learn about this future world. There would always be something to surprise him, and make him the outsider.

With his heart in his throat, he pushed the button with the number '3' on it, but when nothing happened, he pressed another, with a red triangle, then one with waves, the '3' again, which only ended up with the number '33' showing up in signs on the display.

He didn't know if he heard Beast's voice first or sensed his presence behind his back, but all of a sudden the mountainous man was there, standing behind Laurent and speaking from above his head as the fresh, citrusy scent of cologne flooded Laurent's senses.

"It's called a microwave. It uses invisible energy to heat food," Beast said and reached past Laurent, touching one of the buttons. The numbers zeroed, but all Laurent could think of was the thick arm worthy of a harbour labourer faintly brushing against his shoulder and the heat of Beast's chest that he could sense even without touch.

Laurent put his hands against the counter on which the 'microwave' stood and swallowed around the uneasiness that formed in his throat from Beast's proximity. "I would have understood it in the end," he whispered, but he was sure he would have never come up with the concept of invisible energy heating food. How could the source of it be invisible? Where did it come from? Why would it be used for three minutes, not five or two?

"Are you really mansplaining a microwave to him?" Martina asked from behind the counter. She was mixing up some sort of drink made of crushed tomatoes and water.

Beast stiffened, and his face twisted. "It's not mansplaining if he's a man. Besides, he knows nothing about anything, so he needs to be warned not to put cutlery inside and shit!"

Laurent rubbed his forehead in frustration. He knew things. He knew Latin and French, and read quickly, and knew how books were printed, and had a keen interest in philosophy, history, and novels. But how was he supposed to convey that in a world with technology on par with magic?

"What is 'mansplaining'?" he asked cautiously, only to have Nao laugh so hard she ended up making a noise reminiscent of pigs.

"Go on, Beast, *explain* that," she said, so amused she had to wipe a tear out of her eye.

Knight came up next to her and grabbed the drink Martina had been making. "What's Beast explaining?"

"Mansplaining and microwaves." Nao grinned, drinking her juice.

Beast clenched his mouth and tapped the microwave a few times, causing the thing to light up on the inside while a white bowl spun around, moved by an invisible force.

"Whoa!" Knight laughed and had some of the tomato drink. "That's like explaining *Inception*."

Nao laughed, and the meaning yet again passed in front of Laurent's nose. For a moment Laurent wanted to ask why cutlery should not be warmed in the microwave, but then he decided against it, since everyone else most likely considered it obvious.

"There will be chili," Laurent tried to change the topic, though he had no idea what chili was.

Knight smiled, and once again Laurent noticed how fine he was, even if his chin was unnecessarily scruffy, and his long hair seemed a tangled mess of wind-combed waves. "Martina's chili? Yes! It's so nice of Beast that he helped you with the microwave, isn't it?"

Laurent looked back at Beast, who stood so close all Laurent could think about was the glorious way he smelled. "Y-yes," he mumbled.

With the bowl and a whole tray of plates made of plastic, they joined the others on the sofas. Laurent tried to keep calm, but there was no denying that all eyes were on him, and when Beast directed him to a backless chair, he was glad that at least he knew what was expected from him.

People descended on the food like hungry seagulls, and since Laurent had already eaten, he kept back to leave the food for everyone else and only accepted a small portion with bread when a young man with short blond hair handed him some.

"Be careful. I don't know if they use such spices where you're from," the man said before offering his hand to Laurent. "I'm Jake. Is it true you're Amish?"

Beast growled with his mouth full. Swallowing, he leaned back in the leather chair and squinted. "Prospect, told you he doesn't want to talk."

"Yeah, just leave it, Prospect," Knight added and shooed the young man away, leaving Laurent to wonder if Jake was some sort of servant. "His name is Laurent Mercier though. So I was gonna ask, are you named after the Laurent Mercier who murdered that serial killer? 'Cause I was looking into it, and I can't work out what branch of the family tree you're from."

The words hit Laurent like a club. "I didn't kill anyone!" he said all too fast, and all too loudly, only drawing more attention to himself. He almost dropped the bread too. If he was to thrive here, he needed to control himself much better.

"Wow, that escalated quickly," said a smooth-shaven young man with very bright hair worn in short spikes. Like Beast, there were patterns all over his body, but they were colorful and bright as the shirt he wore. Despite his words, he didn't seem at all moved, just calmly watched Laurent from above his bowl of chili.

"This is Joker," Beast said, introducing the man. "Don't mind him. He just thinks he's funny."

Joker laughed, shaking his head, which made the rows of rings covering his ear move. He picked up a crumpled piece of paper and tossed it at Beast. "Always dismissed. My heart bleeds."

Knight leaned closer to Laurent and ignored the other two men. "No, I just wanted to know if you aren't a descendant of Laurent Mercier's illegitimate child. He was an indentured servant, so his master wouldn't have let him marry."

Laurent stared, but then a laugh escaped his lips. "Oh, he would not have had time for romance, I assure you."

Knight frowned. "How would you know that?"

How was Laurent to know what was and what wasn't common knowledge, since history has clearly revealed that he was the one who killed Fane? "I… just a guess." He dipped the yellowish bread in the chili, which was some kind of meat and tomato sauce, but when he put it in his mouth and started chewing, his eyes began to water at the sudden assault of spices to his tongue.

"See, I told you it would be too spicy for him," Jake laughed but didn't provide any relief.

Beast pushed a glass of water at Laurent, and he accepted it greedily, downing half of it right away.

"That's why I bought very mild Chinese food," mumbled Beast.

Laurent finished the water, embarrassed by the greedy way he drank but too desperate to stop.

Knight nodded and patted Beast's shoulder. "Yeah, if you're unsure about stuff, just ask Beast, he's your man."

Beast's eyes briefly met Laurent's, but then he looked away and got himself a fresh glass of water, since he'd given his to Laurent.

Laurent put the bowl of chili away and rubbed his lips with a napkin, as other people seemed to do. The low table was a strange choice for eating a meal, but he wouldn't question it.

"Yes, he's been very helpful," Laurent mumbled, and it was a huge understatement. Beast was stirring up so many mixed feelings inside him that he couldn't focus on gathering information that would allow him to influence the man more efficiently.

Joker gave a short laugh. "King knew who to ask to take care of you. Only the most responsible person here. If it was me, you'd have probably gotten my old clothes and cereal to eat."

"It would have been a group effort," said Martina, eyeing Joker with a squint.

"Yeah, yeah! And he's VP now too." Knight pointed to the patch on Beast's leather vest that said 'vice president'.

Laurent shifted in his chair uncomfortably, unsure why Knight felt the need to advertise Beast this way. He couldn't possibly be in love with him, could he?

Jake wiggled on the sofa, watching the patch as if it were the prettiest of brooches, brought in all the way from Italy. "It's been long overdue, Beast."

Beast rubbed the back of his neck, looking surprisingly shy, but the slight quirk to his lips and the relaxed body language told Laurent that it was pride Beast was feeling. Everyone seemed to like and respect him here, despite the physical deformity and tattoos that had made him so unwanted at the mall. Whose opinion on the matter should Laurent trust though?

He just drank some water in silence, straightening up in his chair, to not seem too timid. He was overwhelmed by the sheer number of people, but his confidence grew every time he learned something new, so he wouldn't wish to leave them with a wrong impression of him.

"So, Knight, which Mercier line did you say you were from?" Laurent smiled politely, trying to gauge other people's body language to mirror it, but sitting with his legs spread wide the way Knight was didn't feel appropriate.

A choir of voices gave an exasperated sigh. What did he do wrong this time?

Beast cleared his throat. "Maybe let's not overdo it with the past, all right?"

Knight raised his arms. "Come on! I actually meet someone who's interested and this is what I get?"

Nao laughed. "Then just talk to him about it in private. Everyone's heard about your glorious French 'lineage' at least three times."

"You know what, I know we're not all here, but I wanted to talk to you guys about what happened to Davy and come up with ideas how to stop this from happening again," Beast said, putting down the empty bowl on the table.

"My thoughts? We could just move the parties to a different room," Joker said. "This place is massive. There is more than enough space."

Beast frowned. "And what, jump around the building, constantly move furniture, and lose money on heating of spaces that we don't use?"

At first, Laurent just listened to the argument over the building being in a poor state, and from what Beast was saying, he worked out that someone got hurt by a part of the roof falling on their legs. But what really sparked his attention was the actual argument Beast was making. He wanted to find a new place for the Kings of Hell to move to, just like King had said, and that was precisely what Laurent couldn't allow.

In the middle of an argument, he cleared his throat and managed to intercede. "Well, as a matter of fact I think this place is quite lovely. It has the maturity of good wine." His stomach clenched when everyone stopped talking and looked his way. This was not good at all.

Joker was the one to speak first. "Are you gay or just polite? Because between the French accent and the language, I can't work it out."

"He doesn't live here, so his opinion hardly matters in this discussion," Beast said tensely. "All I want to know is if you'd go to a viewing with me if I found something suitable. Renting out a compound would cost much less than bringing this place back into shape."

Knight groaned. "Love you, man, but I don't want a fucking landlord."

'Love'? Laurent watched on with wide eyes. Was Beast a bigamist like his father, and had been trying to pull Laurent into that sort of scheme? And he didn't know how to answer Joker's question either. Should he admit to it in front of everyone? Beast had said men kissing was fine, and Laurent remembered that in that very same moment, in the crowd of people he'd imagined Beast leaning over him and pressing their lips together. Between William Fane's betrayal and Beast's anger over not being allowed to be free with is touch, Laurent had to confine such things to remain in his mind for now.

Joker spread his arms. "What's there to lose? If it means we can stop talking about it, I'll go see the place. Just find a good one."

Beast exhaled and finally smiled wider. "I know moving out would be a pain, but maybe it would do us some good, too."

"I can't stand this anymore! Am I your spokesperson that I have to deal with all this shit for you?" screeched a female voice, echoing through the corridors and silencing all conversations, which allowed Laurent to notice the rhythmic clicking of heels against the floor.

Knight was on his feet before the woman even came in. "Jordan! What happened?"

A slim woman entered wearing a black dress that reached her knees and misshapen shoes with a very highly elevated, slim heel that made her gait deformed and wiggly. Her golden hair swirled in perfect waves as she tossed her head in a theatrical display of frustration. "I did as you asked and tried to talk to those builders, but one of them kept getting into my personal space and flirting. Why won't you have some other girl fuck them, if that's what it takes? I am done!" she said and spun around, walking off before Knight even reached her.

"Jordan! Wait! Which one of those fuckers was flirting with you?"

"What do you care?" she yelled. "You're here eating fucking chili while I have to deal with club matters for you?"

Laurent took the opportunity offered by the commotion and quickly turned to Beast, unsure who else to ask about the thing that kept prodding at the back of his mind. "Should I curse more?" he whispered.

Beast huffed. "No."

"Should I tell Joker I'm gay?"

"If you want to," Beast said, but he was already getting up when Knight declared he was going to murder someone. "Brother, we don't want any more blood here, not so soon after Davy."

As other people followed out of the room, Laurent would not stay behind, curiosity already getting the best of him. Nao was right behind him.

"This happens at least once a week with Jordan. I wish I'd made popcorn," she said, and Laurent smiled back at the joke he didn't understand, too happy about someone being friendly to him.

"That's her name, right?"

Nao nodded, flinching slightly when Jordan and Knight started screaming at one another so loudly it could break glass. "If you want to know what I think, it would have been better for him if he stopped dating princesses."

"I'm leaving! And I'm not coming back this time," hissed Jordan, stomping away at an agonizingly slow pace because of her shoes.

"Babe, come on," Knight said, following. "Tell me which one was a shit to you and I'll deal with him."

She stopped and crossed her arms on her ample chest, looking back at Knight. "The bald one. He wouldn't give it a rest! I told them they can go. You guys need to hire a more professional crew."

Beast squeezed his hands into fists. "Wait, wait, wait... you told them to what?"

Jordan spread her arms wide. "Yes. If they can't be respectful, they need to go. Say something, honey!" she added, looking at Knight, as if this whole performance was only meant for his attention. And worst of all, it seemed to be working.

Knight looked around his friends in challenge. "Well, I'm not gonna have them disrespect my woman in *our* club!"

Joker groaned. "But we're having Beast's VP party in two fucking weeks! Someone has to mend that piece of roof!"

"Yeah, they're the perfect balance of cheapish and decent quality. They did my parents' house, and that worked out great," Jake said, pushing himself to the front.

"She likely flirted back, too," Nao whispered into Laurent's ear.

Beast approached Knight and Jordan. "Come on, guys. It's likely a misunderstanding."

"He complimented the way I walk!" Jordan hissed. "Stop putting dumb ideas into my man's head. This kind of stuff is not okay!"

Beast rubbed his face. "Knight. Please, we need those repairs done ASAP."

Only now it occurred to Laurent that from what he was gathering, Knight likely wasn't in love with Beast. The relief that thought caused was both pleasant and disconcerting.

Knight pulled Jordan under his arm, and she hugged him tightly. "All I can promise you is that I won't go break his nose now, but I will not beg them to come back."

"Deal. How about you and Jordan go out for drinks, huh?" Beast suggested, clearly just wanting his friend's hysterical girlfriend out of his hair.

Jordan pouted, looking up into Knight's handsome face. "I guess..."

Laurent leaned against a windowsill and looked outside where a group of large men were busy packing some bags into a tall car with no windows in the back. Now he knew why Beast was the 'VP'. He seemed to take charge in all situations. If he was truly set on moving the club into a new place to stay, how could Laurent possibly stand in his way?

"Let's go, babe," Knight put his arm over Jordan's shoulders and pulled her away.

"Beast, how about Laurent talks to them?" Nao asked when the newly reconciled lovebirds disappeared from sight.

Everyone—including Laurent himself—stared at her as if she'd grown a pair of horns, but she grinned in acknowledgement. "I know, but hear me out. Jordan likely insulted them all if they're leaving without a word. And Laurent might not be very good with microwaves, but he is super polite. Maybe it could work?"

Joker shrugged. "I'd pay to watch that."

Laurent shifted his weight uncomfortably, and his whole soul screamed for him to run and hide, but there was no room for hysterics. He needed to prove himself useful if he was to earn the respect of the Kings of Hell.

"If only I was provided with more information, I would gladly attempt such a feat."

Joker snorted. "Aw, man. He's never gonna stop crackin' me up."

Beast looked at Laurent, raising his eyebrows, or rather, opening his eyes wider, because he had no hair above the eyes. Has it been burned away in the fire as well? "Are you sure?"

"Of course he is," Nao said.

Five minutes later, armed with all the details on the issue that he could learn within a short time and all too aware of the eyes on his back following him from the window, Laurent made his way to the men in dirty, baggy clothes.

"Good morning, Mr. Maddock!" Laurent said with a wide smile that hopefully hid just how nervous he was. When travelling in time, couldn't he had been given the average height of a 2017 man? Was that too much to ask?

The three men all looked his way, one even leaning out of the oversized car and watching him approach as if he were a curiosity brought in from faraway lands. Was there something non-contemporary about him after all? Could those men somehow sense it on him?

"That's me," the biggest of them all said. Bald, just a little bit shorter than Beast, and with a belly unflatteringly hanging out of his jeans beneath the tight shirt, Mr. Maddock was a hulking presence in his own right. "What can I do for you?"

"I've been made aware that there has been a misunderstanding in relation to the roof repairs before, and I know how much it means for my friends for the construction works to be done on time. You see, in two weeks, there is a celebration to occur in that same room, which for safety reasons would be impossible, were the roof not repaired until then." He swallowed when the men watched him with more attention. "So, as you can see, this issue is of utmost importance, and I'm sure the lady in question meant no disrespect."

The three men looked at each other, and Laurent stiffened when he noticed one of them hide behind his fingers, as if suppressing laughter. Maddock cleared his throat, eventually looking Laurent's way. "Um. I am sorry dear... sir, but said *Lady* insulted us."

Laurent nodded quickly and touched Mr. Maddock's arm for a second. "Yes, so I have heard. She's had a tough time lately, and she acted out of line, but you have to see she does not represent us all. Not only am I authorised to offer a renegotiation of the financial terms, but I would also like to invite you back for some chili and cornbread to mend the damaged relationship between us. I have tried some just this morning, and it was heaven in my mouth." He smiled widely, and the youngest of the builders laughed again.

"Oh, fuck… Maddock, I just can't. He's been *authorised*."

Maddock gave a little bark, steadied himself, only to roar with laughter so powerfully he had a tear sliding down his cheek within seconds. "Oh, my Lord, this is hilarious! Where did they get you from, kid?"

Laurent didn't let his smile falter. "I… I'm French." Would that suffice?

"To be fair, he hasn't offered us frogs or snails yet, so he is trying to integrate," said the man who hadn't voiced his opinion on the matter yet. "And I could eat some chili…"

Maddock sighed, watching Laurent with a slight squint. "Well, why not. You've got yourself a deal, kid," he said, reaching out his hand to Laurent.

They squeezed hands, with Laurent still in disbelief and his heart beating hard. He'd managed not to mess up! And in an important matter at that! So he wasn't useless in this new world after all. "Please join us then." He pointed to the nearest door.

The men said they'd be upstairs as soon as they got some tools out, and Laurent walked back to the club common room with a sense of triumph. He was greeted with some pats on the back and relayed what happened quickly, but the one person he wanted to impress turned away as soon as Laurent smiled at him.

"Okay, I'm going to join them now and deal with the rest," Beast said, already making his way to the door.

Laurent couldn't bear his achievement being ignored like that and followed him. He managed to catch up with Beast in the corridor, and the feelings inside of him mixed like water and oil that have been abruptly shaken. Beast had so many cruel words for him yesterday, and yet the connection they had forged before seemed like something more than a man trying to win favor with the one he wished to bed.

"Beast?"

Beast stopped in his tracks, his shoulders stiff even before he looked back. "Hmm?"

Laurent swallowed, now unsure what to say. "I… Please remember not to go away farther than a mile…"

Beast groaned. "Your leg won't explode. This cuff is just there so that I know where you are. Okay?"

Laurent entwined his fingers with a sigh, his mind at once blank. So he'd been deceived once more. "Okay," he said, hoping that he was using the word correctly.

Beast stared at him in silence. He licked his lips. And then walked off, leaving Laurent standing in place, disappointed despite this unexpected victory.

"Laurent, you coming?" called out Nao.

He took a few seconds to compose himself and walked back. He smiled at her, and since none of the men seemed to consider the revealing outfits of the women inappropriate, he would try to follow their example. "What else can I help with? Does the chili need more microwaving?"

Chapter 13 - Beast

Two weeks on, Laurent had become a permanent fixture in the Kings of Hell clubhouse. He was everywhere Beast went, now more often than not spending his time out of the room Beast relegated him to, as if knowing that the cuff exploding had been just an empty threat somehow made him feel untouchable. He read books spread out on Beast's sofa in just his tightly fitting pyjamas. He loudly chattered with pretty much everyone, no longer afraid of unfamiliar people. And he more often than not left the damn cabinet in Beast's bathroom open and ready to assault Beast with the sight of his ugly scarred face in the mirror. And yet, knowing that Laurent likely enjoyed looking at his own features Beast couldn't find it in himself to tell him off for it and ended up just shutting the damn cabinet each time.

Because no matter what Beast had said, he still enjoyed looking at the pouty lips, the big brown eyes, and he actually shuddered once when Laurent slipped past him in the corridor and his soft long hair brushed over Beast's arm.

It was hell.

Before, his apartment could get pretty lonely, but now that he had the piece of candy he couldn't suck on, it was a constant distraction. It made focusing on the task of finding a potential new clubhouse close to impossible. Laurent was even slowly making progress with Hound and frequently talked to the dog in French, as if the two of them kept secrets from Beast.

But every time Beast considered throwing him out, assigning Laurent a bigger room in another part of the clubhouse and relieving himself of the bothersome presence, he could never go through with it. At the end of the day, it was nice to have someone other than Hound or Knight sit with him in his fortress of solitude. He even started picking up on how Laurent looked when he was confused, and he kind of enjoyed helping him out with understanding modern concepts. Laurent was fascinated by movies, but Beast wouldn't be taking the lying little shit to the cinema. He'd be too tempted to hold his hand again.

And it would have felt too much like a date anyway.

At first Beast had been so furious and hurt by the earlier rejection that he'd wanted to give Laurent the full-on silent treatment, but he'd failed on day one. They usually didn't talk much, but Laurent had a way of pulling Beast into discussions over the novels he was reading, and he was a freakishly fast bookworm. The talks felt special too, because they only had them when they were alone, as if it was their little secret. It took Beast back to the time when he was still considering leaving for college.

After months in the hospital, Beast had lost all hope for a change in his life. He hated the idea of going to college looking like Deadpool, so his future with the club was sealed. He still did an online course, and King even paid for it, but it wasn't the same.

And yet there was Laurent, discussing Dante Alighieri's *Inferno* with him like they would in a literature class. He loved his brothers to bits, but neither of them shared that passion for reading.

Having someone so inhumanly pretty around him was not only torture but also temptation. Still, he wouldn't dare touch the boy again. His ego was fragile enough after his last attempt.

Nao suggested Laurent was likely a virgin, but Beast didn't want to ask or repeat to Laurent that there was gossip about his sex life behind his back. Still, Laurent's innocence about sex was oddly endearing.

If Laurent found out there was a bet going on about how long it would take for him to get his cherry popped, he'd likely sulk for a month, because he seemed very concerned with people's opinions about him. Beast hoped the bet was off anyway, because he'd given Joker a harsh talking-to about it.

At least Gray was back from his job to New York, which meant all the Kings were finally present, and he could take them to the complex of warehouses and garages he'd found. And the rent was not high for what the property was. Considering that King had taken Nao and Martina on a threeway date, the occasion couldn't have been better.

When he entered his apartment, the place was oddly quiet, even though the tracker device on Laurent indicated this general area. Perhaps he was reading in his room then, since there was no splashing to be heard from the bathroom.

Bathing was one of Laurent's favorite pastimes, and it was driving Beast nuts, but since it meant he'd sometimes get a sneak peek of Laurent submerged in water and foam, he never complained. Beast's mind drifted off to how he'd once walked in on Laurent enjoying one of his long soaks.

Stretched out in the tub, he'd fallen asleep, and Beast ended up watching him for a full five minutes, like the shameless monster that he was. Then Laurent's head tipped into the water, and Beast rushed to him in panic, which only ended up with Laurent screaming out when he woke up and saw the intruder.

That had not been a fun time.

Beast approached the door, wondering whether he should even bother Laurent when he was busy reading or taking a nap, but Laurent was fascinated by cars, and motorcycles, and planes, and this was as good of an opportunity as any to show off his motorbike. Beast itched to be the first one to introduce Laurent to the bitch seat.

He also kind of wished to have Laurent hug him from behind, even if it would end up being yet another torture, and him - a creeper.

He knocked on the door.

"Don't come in!" came in a high-pitched voice.

Beast blinked, startled. "Uh... is something wrong?"

"No, no! It's fine! I'm fine!" He didn't *sound* fine.

Beast stepped back and looked at the door, yet still held his hand on the cold wood, as if its presence could somehow help Laurent with whatever problem he was having. "What's going on?"

"I… nothing."

Beast cleared his throat. "We were heading out for a ride with the guys, and I thought you'd maybe want to go and see the town or something."

The silence just confirmed Beast's suspicions that something was off.

Finally, Laurent spoke. "Will you promise not to laugh at me?"

Oh, so at least it wasn't anything horrible. "I can try not to laugh at you."

"Come in then."

Beast stepped inside the room, which smelled curiously sweet, as if Laurent had eaten chocolate earlier. But when Laurent looked up at him from the bed, Beast froze to the floor, not recognizing him at first. Laurent's wavy hair was up in a bun on top of his head, he was wearing only his plaid pajama pants, and his face was completely black except for his eye sockets and lips. He looked like a reverse panda.

"Uh-huh," was all Beast could produce when faced with that image. It was the last thing he expected to see. Never before had he seen a man using a facial mask. Well, he had, but never in real life. "What's the problem?"

"I can't take it off. Nao gave it to me and said it was great for the skin, and I followed the instructions, but… I don't know what to do." Laurent's shoulders sagged, but the dark pink nipples on show were making it hard for Beast to focus on the matte layer that made Laurent's face freeze in the expression of wonder.

This time, Beast chuckled before he could even think. It was the oddest problem he'd ever heard this side of that guy in his high school who tried to pleasure himself with a vacuum cleaner. "Er... okay? Shouldn't you wash it off?" he asked, approaching Laurent.

"No. The instructions advise to peel it off, but it hurts, and I can't force myself to do it."

"Show me," said Beast, reaching out for the tube. He read the instructions, and Laurent was right. Beast was hardly a specialist when it came to cosmetic products, but he was positive there was no magic to it. And if Nao was so eager to offer Laurent products for women, then maybe she should be supervising the operation instead of leaving Laurent alone with this. The poor guy likely didn't even have an idea that it was not something most men did.

Beast leaned in, watching Laurent's face from up close, and met the brown eyes surrounded by the dry surface of the mask. It looked odd, but nothing to be scared or scream about like men in old comedies did upon walking in on their girlfriends in this state.

"Do you want me to help?"

It took Laurent a while to answer, and he slowly got up, standing close to Beast and looking positively ridiculous. "Maybe."

Beast swallowed when the whiff of cocoa reached him again. Would Laurent's skin taste of chocolate now? "Is it supposed to hurt?" he asked, touching the bits of the thin sheet-like mask peeled off by Laurent's jaw line.

Laurent shifted his weight with a groan. "Nao said it might. But that it was worth it, and it would leave the skin refreshed and supple. I now question if it was worth it, but it's difficult to make a judgment while it's still on me."

Beast grinned and slowly pulled on the elevated bit. The mask was peeling off, but it clung to Laurent's skin as if it intended to melt with him forever. Beast wanted to be that mask. "I heard women have a higher pain threshold because of birth, so maybe they can take it."

Laurent didn't answer, just bit on his lips and squirmed. When Beast pulled on the mask harder, to see if he could get on with it faster, Laurent whined and pressed his palms against Beast's chest, as if to steady himself.

It was difficult not to shiver at the sudden touch, and Beast gently stroked one of Laurent's shoulders. It was so wonderfully soft, as if he'd massaged it with rich oil. "It's okay. I'll try to be gentle."

Laurent took a deep breath, making his cheeks puff up for a moment. "I'm ready." He closed his eyes, but as soon as Beast pulled again, he squeezed them shut tightly, curling his fingers in Beast's T-shirt.

Beast felt like a creep for enjoying this, but Laurent was being so incredibly cute in his helplessness. It took Beast two heartbeats to make up his mind about what to do, and he pulled Laurent close with one arm, cradling him tight against his side. "Easy now," he said, methodically pulling on the mask.

"Shit," Laurent hissed beneath his breath, and it had to be the first time Beast heard him swear. He curled up under Beast's arm, fitting perfectly against Beast's chest. The way he shivered and whimpered so close to Beast was a guilty pleasure Beast wouldn't admit to. And Laurent was half-naked too. If only he were willing to pull down those tight pajama pants, Beast would gladly forget the viewing of the building if he could watch Laurent instead.

Beast was almost regretful when he was done pulling the black film off, because it meant Laurent would soon pull away. Panting as if he'd ran a marathon and rubbing his face, Laurent stood still with his eyes closed for a while longer. Beast couldn't help but envision Laurent panting against his chest for very different reasons, but he didn't move from the spot and didn't try to pull Laurent any closer, simply watching the dark hair that slipped out of the bun, dancing along Laurent's pronounced cheekbones.

He was surreally beautiful, like a creature out of this world, and the worst thing was that faced with this kind of allure only reminded Beast of his own shortcomings in that regard.

Laurent took one more deep breath and opened his eyes, with traces of tears on his long eyelashes. He frowned and shook his head. "The brutality of this treatment is beyond words! But touch how soft it is now!" He grabbed Beast's hand and put it against his own cheek.

Beast hardly suppressed a gasp, frozen in place as he traced the smooth softness that was Laurent's cheek. He must have shaved earlier today to be so completely smooth. The fingers of Beast's other hand danced between Laurent's shoulder blades. He already imagined how the warm skin there tasted, how it would feel against his face.

But then Laurent pulled out of the embrace and the moment was gone. He smiled though, so there was that scrap of affection for Beast to lick up. Laurent rubbed his own cheeks. "Is my skin red?"

Beast nodded, unable to find his voice. He raised his finger, eager to touch the rosy cheeks once again, but stepped away instead. "Don't do it again."

Laurent shook his head. "I won't, I promise. I'm so sorry to have pulled you into this ghastly business."

"It's fine. Maybe just put some cream on it now," Beast said, licking his lips when his gaze trailed over Laurent's softly toned chest. He was short, and yet so perfectly proportioned.

"I have one for that, yes. Thank you so much! I will be ready in no more than ten minutes."

Beast nodded.

Laurent blinked, not moving either. "Your shirt is so intensely soft. What is that fabric?" he asked in the end and pulled down his pajama pants.

Beast kept his eyes on Laurent's face, but that didn't help much, as he was treated to the wonderful image of Laurent's shoulders and neck shifting in the most erotic way possible. Or so he thought. "It's... combed cotton. My nerves got fucked up during the fire, so I don't like rough clothes around the scars," he said in the end. It was a good thing his legs were in a much better shape, or he wouldn't be able to comfortably wear jeans.

Laurent dressed quickly, covering the glorious body with boxer briefs, then jeans and a T-shirt stating 'So many books, so little time'. Then came the leather jacket, and Laurent grabbed his glasses, only reminding Beast that he'd been putting off their visit to the doctor, because he felt like sulking every time he thought about being alone with Laurent outside of the clubhouse.

"Almost done." Laurent started rubbing some cream into his face, but then glanced at Beast. "Do you need to rub the scars with cream? Does it hurt when someone touches you?"

No one touched Beast.

He cleared his throat. It was such a private question it took him aback at first, but hadn't he just removed a facial mask off Laurent's face? It required a degree of intimacy that needed to be reciprocated. "I do. It makes my skin feel better. And some areas are just more sensitive than others, that's all."

"Make sure you never put this mask on it." Laurent shuddered with a scowl and threw out the whole tube into a little box he used for trash. Beast needed to get him an actual trash can. In fact, there were many convenience items missing from Laurent's bedroom, since it had been Beast's storage closet plus an occasional place for Knight to crash. If Laurent was to stay, maybe it was time to get him his own chair, or perhaps a small desk?

"I won't. I'm pretty sure I'd need someone to help me if I did."

Laurent smiled at him and walked out of the room with his hands in his pockets, looking cool and casual, as if he hadn't crashed into Beast's life covered in blood and dressed in historical clothes just two weeks ago. "Well, you know who to call if you make that mistake."

Beast laughed. "Maybe I should borrow that mask after all."

Laurent glanced at him over the shoulder and wiggled his eyebrows, his face still slightly flushed. "Maybe you should."

Beast was still on the fence about this whole thing, unsure whether Laurent flirting back was just a joke, because if it was then the pains of what he'd have to go through definitely wouldn't be worth it.

But when they walked out of the clubhouse and reached the garage where all the other members were waiting for him already, he thought that he'd much rather get closer by riding a bike together.

Laurent looked around, nodding at all the other guys who already sat on their motorcycles. "Are we going on bikeback?"

"Yes. How do you like my big metal horse?" Beast asked, leading the way to a large motorcycle in black and silver, made unique by three vicious dog heads at the front.

Laurent's eyes settled on the steel decoration, and he ran his fingers over the black leather seat. "It's horrific," he said in a way that made it unclear whether Laurent meant it as a compliment or criticism.

Joker laughed, leaning forward on his bike and gently nudged Gray with his foot. Having only recently come back from a dirty job in NYC, Gray was now getting to know Laurent, and so far it seemed to be going smoothly, mostly because Gray was the type of man who took his time to make an opinion. Maybe that was the reason for him going gray, back when he was just twenty one. Old soul and all that.

With the precious stones and jewelry he came back with securely tucked in the hidden safe, Gray was finally allowed to relax, which in his case meant sipping tea and listening to people who were willing to talk around him. Beast felt almost guilty about bothering him already, but despite his quiet nature, Gray cared about the club very deeply and had seemed eager to hear Beast's case.

Beast opened his arms, trying to not be offended by Laurent's statement. "You don't *have to* go."

"No, no! I want to! But… How do I drive it?"

Rev smirked and put on his helmet. "Boy thinks he's gonna drive your bike?"

Beast raised his eyebrows and passed a spare helmet to Laurent. "You don't. You hold on to me while I do the work."

Knight started cackling so loudly Beast wanted to slap the back of his head. "That's what he said."

Laurent zipped up his jacket, giving the bike a wary look. He must have seen guys ride them and take girls on the bitch seat, so it couldn't be that he didn't understand the concept of it. Beast was beginning to suspect that Laurent simply didn't want to be so close to him for a prolonged period of time, and that made him suddenly regret he'd asked Laurent to come along in the first place.

"Just stay if you're not up for it," he said and mounted his bike in a quick, somewhat aggressive movement.

But then he felt a presence behind him, and moments later the slim arms wrapped around him, and a chest pressed against Beast's back.

"Is this okay?" Laurent whispered.

Beast took a deep breath and gave a few instructions for Laurent to be steady on the bike, but his mind was in turmoil. Laurent's arms felt just *so* good. When was the last time someone had ridden with him like this?

Before the accident, when he was still madly in love and wanted to be the only guy in his man's world.

Grim thoughts burned his muscles, and he shook his head, starting the bike. "We're heading out!"

Laurent pulled closer still to Beast and his thighs tensed against Beast's. "Is it supposed to tremble this much?" The question was about the engine, but Beast could only think of the arms shivering around him. The embrace felt burning hot even through the leather, and he needed to steady his voice before answering.

"Just hold on to me. Alright?" he asked and looked back.

Laurent nodded so vigorously his helmet wiggled back and forth. Beast needed to make sure Laurent rode with no one else.

When his foot lifted off the ground, and the motorcycle moved forward, Laurent's whole body seemed to mold to the shape of Beast's back. His helmet dug into Beast's flesh, long fingers clutched at his leathers so frantically it made his stomach twist with pleasure. This would most likely be as close as Beast would ever get to fucking Laurent, so he'd just enjoy it for what it was.

As the bike gained momentum, speeding up along the narrow asphalt road through the woods, fresh air filled Beast's lungs and he could breathe freely for the first time in days. The roar of other machines singing in a choir with his own motorbike was just the melody to soothe him.

Laurent was so still, so motionless behind him that for a moment Beast considered stopping to see if he was all right. But he leaned slightly forward, and Laurent leaned in with him instead of staying stiff, as if they had somehow become one body. The slim arms tightened further when Beast made the bike roar.

The asphalt road was on the empty side even after they all left the grounds belonging to the clubhouse, and they saw barely any cars until they reached the outskirts of Brecon. Laurent was clinging to him so tightly it felt as if he were yet another part of Beast's body. He stopped being so tense too, and it was a pleasant thought that it was Beast who made him feel so secure. Beast kind of missed the close contact already and was looking forward to feeling it again on the way back. He didn't exactly enjoy scaring Laurent, but knowing that right now he was the master of both their lives gave him a thrill.

Beast wondered if he should have taken Laurent after all, considering that otherwise it was only him and his brothers, but at the end of the day it was not an official club run. They were doing this behind King's back, and while all the men declared the viewing would stay between them, he still feared the secrecy could bite him in the ass in the future.

King would have been furious if he knew about Beast organizing this, and he would let them all know, but the Kings of Hell were sensible men. They knew how much renovations would cost in an old building like their current clubhouse. It was only logical to move, even if it required initial investment, since upkeep would be much cheaper and easier than repairs on a grand scale. Hell, considering what had happened to poor Davy, they'd likely have specialists crawling all over the place and testing the quality of the construction, which would drain the club's pockets even before actual repairs began.

Laurent relaxed behind him, his arms resting comfortably against Beast's stomach now, as if the two of them were made for each other despite their difference in size. They sped behind Knight until they reached the ocean and rode along the coast. The wind was just a soft breeze, gently caressing Beast's face with its salty whiff.

They had to slow down when driving through town, and Beast was glad to see Knight leading the cavalcade of bikes down the main street. He could sense Laurent shifting slightly behind him as they moved between small houses with colorful wooden facades and old-fashioned streetlights. Retractable awnings protected passersby from sunlight while they walked past cute stores selling everything from local souvenirs to fresh food.

It was when they drove left, back toward the coast when the street forked in front of a pristinely white church, that Laurent stiffened slightly. In the mirror, Beast saw him frantically look back, and it must have been the old town hall that begged for so much attention. One of the oldest buildings in the area, unchanged since its creation, it was of an odd architectural style. The overall shape of it seemed normal enough, with straight lines and large windows of the Greek revival style, but someone must had considered that too boring. Two little towers have been added on both sides of the facade, barely taller than the roof but topped with domes that resembled those on Russian orthodox churches. The final product remained controversial to this day, but was the pride of the town nevertheless.

In the corner of his eye Beast saw passersby looking at the group of bikers, and pride swelled in his chest when he thought that for the first time in years he was not only riding with his brothers but also had this pretty thing clinging tightly to his back. No one would likely notice or care, but he did, and just thinking about it gave him the right boost of energy needed for the task he'd been preparing himself for all week.

Knight led the way out of town, through the white concrete arch that marked the border of Brecon, and back to the coast where the industrial harbor was located. The complex of warehouses and a block-like office space attached to one of them was separated from the fishy smells of the harbor by almost two miles of woodland and boasted a lovely view of the ocean. The previous tenant, a producer of small tools, had moved production out of the state just months ago, and so the property was in excellent condition, with potential for converting the smaller warehouse into an additional living area. Although in Beast's opinion the existing office building was large enough for their current needs. Especially that the complex also contained lodgings for some of the staff of the previous tenant.

True, moving here would mean downsizing and making use of all available space, but the small warehouse would work very well for recreational use for the club members and their guests while the larger one would be perfect for the big concerts and parties the club sometimes organized for tax purposes. They had other, much more profitable, ways to earn their keep, but even with friends at the local police, a pretense of lawfulness needed to be maintained.

They rode in the warm sun along the solid metal fence and all the way to the open gate. The realtor was already waiting for them, looking professional in her burgundy suit and black pumps.

Beast wouldn't go as far as thinking he had this in the bag, but his heart swelled when he realized that his brothers would get to see the place in the May sunshine instead of the rain that had hung in the air for the past few days. When they parked all their bikes in a semi-circle in front of the realtor, she smiled nervously and took a step back.

Beast waited for Laurent to dismount and got off himself, unzipping his leather jacket and taking off the helmet. One swipe of his hand over the strip of hair on top of his head to make it look neat, and he approached the woman with the friendliest of smiles. At least his teeth were still nice.

"Good afternoon, Mrs. Taube. I hope we're on time," he said, focusing on her only while his brothers joined him one by one.

She smiled a bit too-widely, but nodded. "Right on time. It's me who always likes to be at the property a bit early. I'm happy to see you brought your whole crew with you."

Rev snorted and ran his hand over his bald head. "Let's get this show on the road."

Beast looked back at all the men and smiled. "We are all quite invested. Our current clubhouse is too large for our needs, and this should be a perfect fit. Can you confirm that parties would not be a problem?" he asked while she led them toward the dusky yellow facade of the office space.

Mrs. Taube nodded. "According to our standard contract, the tenant is responsible for the state of the buildings. So long as the property is well maintained, this should not be an issue. As you can see, there are no neighbors, apart from the fish," she said, moving her arm toward the glistening ocean. Beast gave a polite laugh, needing to make a good impression. The Kings of Hell were infamous in their own right, even though they were very careful about maintaining a good relationship with the locals, as per their mutual agreement with the police chief. But that didn't mean they were seen as upstanding citizens either. He knew very well the agency would not be interested in renting to them unless they were losing money on keeping such a large property empty.

"Of course. For some of us, including me, this could be home, so keeping it in good shape is very important."

Mrs. Taube nodded, showing them into an empty hall with a spiral staircase clinging to one of the walls and two tall windows that reached all the way to the ceiling, providing a vast quantity of light and making the large room seem even more spacious.

Laurent looked around with his nose wrinkling slightly and his hands in his pockets. "Would King like this though?" He looked at the sparkly ocean as if it offended him somehow.

Beast frowned, but he quickly turned it around and patted Laurent's shoulder. "That's for him to decide later, when he can come over."

Laurent sighed but trod with the rest of them, lagging at the end as they went through building after building. Beast exerted his social skill muscles on showing Fox an area where his kid could play, telling Gray he could have all of the small building at the end of the property to himself, advertising the area for concerts as a place where Davy's son, Lizzy could have his big breakthrough, and all the while dealing with any questions about living quarters and space for vehicles. He knew all the answers, and to be honest, if the world were fair, he should get half the realtor's cut if all went well. He researched his head off for this, he buttered up the agency with chocolates presented to all the ladies in their office, and he would convince his brothers to put pressure on King.

But best of all was the shape of the property, which Beast himself was also viewing for the first time. No mold on the walls, everything was relatively clean, even if Laurent pointed out several months of disuse left behind a dusty, dry smell. It could be dealt with. Even the half-mouthed comments about the difficulty of moving everything the club owned across town could be somehow turned into a positive. Better environment for the kids when they visited. Lower upkeep cost in the long run. Starting fresh. Wiring that wasn't constantly faulty and a health hazard. That last improvement would free up a lot of Knight's time, as he was the one who dealt with all the electricals.

As they passed room after room, Beast was glad to hear his brothers come up with uses for the space, ideas for putting up extra walls. Laurent on the other hand was a pain in the ass, and despite the exhilarating ride Beast was beginning to regret bringing him with them in the first place.

He was acting like a fucking princess, finding faults in everything, as if he was even the one going to be paying for any of it. He was lucky to have a roof over his head at all. Beast had thought taking him along would serve his cause, that Laurent would be excited to see someplace new and appreciate being included so much that he'd compliment everything. But no.

"Would you have to put bars in all the windows?" Laurent asked with that kissable pout on a face Beast now wanted to smack. He didn't understand the reason for Laurent's behavior, and worst of all, he could see the comments starting to both agitate and rub off on the others, as if any fault in the property was an argument against moving to a different clubhouse.

Laurent had never acted like this before. Since the explosive first day, his relationship with Beast became civil, and really kind of pleasant. Hadn't Beast helped him rip off that fucking face mask just an hour ago? What the hell was his problem now?

When they left the main building, the sun had a slightly warmer hue and started to head lower down in the sky, so they must have spent an hour or two on the viewing, which was a very good sign in Beast's book. The realtor gave him a folder with additional pictures, and he engaged her in pleasant conversation now that she had relaxed after being in their presence for such a long time.

"Does any of you have any questions?" Beast asked, sweeping his gaze over his brothers.

Gray raised his hand and pushed the other into the front pocket of his washed-out jeans. The silver strands looked so odd around his young, handsome face, as if he dyed them on purpose, as was the fashion among some women. "May I use the supervision area above the workshop for my apartment?"

Beast shrugged. A solitary place with no neighbors. A very fitting spot for Gray indeed. "Sure, anyone else?" His chest constricted in anticipation when Laurent raised his hand with that worried look on his face. What the fuck more did he want from the place? A jacuzzi and a private cinema?

"Are there any underground facilities here?" he asked the realtor, who blinked, stilling in surprise for a moment, so Laurent continued. "Our friend King said he was looking to create a dungeon, you see, for sexual practices. So I wanted to inquire in his name if that was a possibility."

Joker started laughing like a maniac, but the dead look on the realtor's face had Beast sweating bullets.

Beast laughed, trying to look as casual as possible before turning to Mrs. Taube. "I'm sorry. He's my cousin from France. Must have misunderstood something. There will be no dungeons, Laurent," he said with a bit more pressure.

The fucker acted dumb, as if he hadn't gotten the hint. Laurent might have grown up in some weird Mennonite cult, but Beast noticed just how quick he picked up on everything, and how he shut up and listened when things were unclear to him, so seeing him act in a way so obstructive was making angry ants crawl all over Beast's arms.

"No, no. King specifically said he wanted a dungeon with shackles, and a cage for a girl to pretend she was his dog. Don't blame the messenger." Laurent crossed his arms on his chest.

"Err… I would have to talk to my manager about that," Mrs. Taube uttered.

Joker kept cackling and patted Laurent's back. "We could add a sex swing while we're at it."

Beast's arms became so stiff his nape started aching, and he looked at the other men, whose reactions ranged from irritation to amusement. His fists itched for something to smash when his gaze stopped on the unpleasantly smug expression on Laurent's face. Beast remembered where he'd seen it last time. On fucking Jordan.

Has he overlooked Laurent's ugly side because of how handsome he was? Just like Knight did with each of his consecutive girlfriends? Laurent looked away as soon as their eyes met, leaving Beast to wonder whether this blatant sabotage had been caused by Laurent and King being unlikely besties, like a baby mink and a lion.

The rest of the viewing went downhill from there, with Mrs. Taube disengaged and clearly trying to abort the whole thing in the politest ways possible.

Beast's mind was growing frantic and boiled over at such speed he could hardly think straight from the sense of betrayal. "I'm sorry, Mrs. Taube. I'll just quickly show something to my cousin. I know where it is," he assured her stiffly and headed for Laurent, not even trying to disguise his mood from the boy.

The hurt look on Laurent's face before Beast even grabbed his arm was like a stab in the guts, but he wouldn't wait for the little snake to twist the blade and led him into the nearest building.

"What is it?" Laurent whined.

"Oh, I wonder. What could be possibly going wrong when I spend two fucking weeks researching places to find the perfect one, only to have you bad-mouth us in front of the realtor?" hissed Beast, squeezing his hand hard on Laurent's shoulder as they walked down the corridor. Only when Beast felt they were far enough that Mrs. Taube wouldn't hear them, did he push Laurent into one of the empty rooms and stalked behind him.

Laurent stumbled, but quickly turned around, backing into a corner. "I only repeated what King said. Shouldn't we be looking for a place that can satisfy everyone's needs?"

"There is no *we*," hissed Beast, pushing at Laurent's chest, just hard enough to make him hit the wall. The boy had nothing on Beast's strength and size, and Beast decided it was time to show it to him explicitly. Electric currents of anger prickled under his skin as he approached Laurent, forcing him against the cold wall before he could duck and run. "You are our guest. You are not a member. I took you with us because I wanted to be nice and show you something on the way. What the fuck is wrong with you?" Beast took a deep breath, steadying himself when he felt his voice was on the edge of breaking slightly from the helplessness of his attraction to Laurent. "How dare you undermine my authority?"

Laurent looked over Beast's arm to the door, as if assessing his chances. "Well, maybe you shouldn't have taken me then, because I don't feel comfortable being disloyal to King. Why is he not here? I won't tell him about this trip if that's your wish, but I don't think it's fair." But despite his defiant gaze, he clung to the wall as if he wanted to melt into it, and his breath sped up like a cornered rat's.

A low growl tore out of Beast's throat as he put one hand over Laurent's mouth and tightened the other around his neck. "Do you have a deathwish? Do you think I'll be your lapdog, just because you have a pretty face? I thought we had an understanding. You live at my apartment, use my water, and eat my food. You barely speak to King, so what is the deal there, huh? You disgust me," hissed Beast and tightened his hand over Laurent's throat.

Laurent whimpered and grabbed Beast's wrist with those slim fingers Beast could crush in his fist if he wanted to. The wide eyes were getting frantic, so Beast hoped he was finally getting his message across. Enough was enough. There would be no more privileges for Laurent in Beast's home, and Beast would watch his back for any signs of manipulative behavior that he might have missed simply because he didn't want to believe so much malice could exist in someone so politely spoken and with a face so innocent.

Dark spots stung the edges of his vision as he leaned over Laurent, watching his skin go from pale to rosy. Closing his eyelids, Beast leaned in and smelled the soft hair. If Laurent chose to be so disloyal, there was no reason for Beast to care for his well-being either. What a joke.

"I don't want you in my home. You will move out. I don't care where to. Ask your beloved King about it. Maybe he'll let you stay with him if you lick his ass long enough," he said in the end and let go, abruptly stepping away.

Laurent started coughing and gasping for air. For a moment he just cowered in the corner like a wounded animal, but as pissed off as Beast was, at least now he knew who was and who wasn't on his side. He was VP of the Kings of Hell because men both feared and respected him, because everyone knew that when push came to shove, Beast didn't take anyone's shit. It was high time for Laurent to learn all about that.

Beast took a deep breath, shifting his weight and rolling his neck over his shoulders when the tension in his back became too much to bear. "Today. You're leaving today. I don't want to speak to you again, is that clear? You ruined everything," hissed Beast in the end before grabbing Laurent's arm and pulling him away from the wall. There was only so much time they could stay behind like this without anyone getting impatient.

Laurent wouldn't meet his eyes, but he must have understood Beast's point, because there was no more whining, no more disrespect, and no more defiant words. How could a kid not even twenty rattle Beast this way? It was about time he stopped torturing himself with Laurent's presence in his apartment.

When they got out into the sun again, Beast couldn't force himself to smile much when he was met with the curious glances of his brothers, and Mrs. Taube's tense gaze.

"I hope all is well?" she asked.

"Absolutely", he said, only then letting go of Laurent. His face ached when Beast forced it into a smile that felt so fake he quickly just dropped any pretense of it. "We will be waiting for an offer."

Mrs. Taube nodded with an expression even faker than Beast's. "Of course. I hope you enjoy the rest of the day."

"In this weather? Of course," said Beast, holding on to the thought that he'd be back on his bike soon, riding it all out of his system.

But seeing Laurent stand next to his bike had Beast's blood boiling yet again. Fucker had another thing coming if he thought Beast would wish for any physical contact after this sabotage.

"Joker, will you take him? I have something to do before I come back to the clubhouse."

The hurt look on Laurent's face had no place there. He wasn't the one who got stabbed in the back.

"Sure." Joker invited Laurent with a gesture to his red Harley.

Laurent sighed deeply, like an anxious puppy, but Beast would not be falling for that act. Laurent was a sly little con artist who still hadn't disclosed much of the information the club wanted from him. Right now, Beast wouldn't even be surprised if Laurent had hurt his own wrist to play the victim and have a free place to stay.

He acknowledged his brothers with a nod and quickly mounted the bike, wishing to just leave and be alone again. Alone in his apartment with just Hound, the only being who would never turn away from him.

Chapter 14 - Laurent

Laurent took a deep breath, assessing his new outfit in the mirror. It's been a week since Beast's outburst at the viewing, and though a part of Laurent had hoped the issue would die down and he would be invited back into Beast's apartment, that had not been the case. So he was stuck in a room containing a mattress, bedding and the few things he owned courtesy of his new friends. He didn't like to be there alone at night because no one else lived nearby and in order to reach the bathroom he had to walk down a dark corridor with no electricity and a mirror that gave him a terrible fright each time he passed it.

Worse yet, he was suddenly deprived of access to books, because as it turned out, none of the other people living at the clubhouse had much interest in literature. So sometimes he traipsed through the building in daytime, wondering about the purposes of some of the items left behind by the people who had occupied those chambers years ago.

Beast hadn't spoken to him once since the horrendous way things had developed at the property they'd been to see, so Laurent didn't dare ask him about more reading material. It would most likely only get him into another argument that he couldn't win.

Beast even got Jake to take off the plastic cuff off Laurent's ankle, as if to signify that he no longer cared where Laurent was, or if he was taken by someone. Laurent was on his own and he detested it with a passion.

No matter how many people enjoyed his company, Beast's rejection stung like a slap to the face despite Laurent knowing that he'd deserved the violence unleashed on him. His attempt at thwarting Beast's plans hadn't been particularly skilful and must had seemed so out of character he was ashamed at hurting the feelings of the man who dedicated so much of his time and attention to make Laurent comfortable in the new place.

He tried to fill the void left by Beast with talking to new people and making himself as useful as humanly possible. Jordan quit some of the administrative tasks she'd been doing for the club, and since there was not much Laurent was good at other than clerical work, he stepped into the maze of information and documents in the office and worked out a system of filing for all the bills. At first it had been a task seemingly unattainable, but Laurent enjoyed the challenge the documents presented.

Nao became his most trusted friend and explained many new things to him, so when the roof of the party room was finally patched up, and the time came to celebrate Beast becoming vice president of the club, Laurent confessed to her that he hoped to attract a gentleman for the purpose of exploring desire. At first she laughed at him, but when he got upset with her mocking, she explained that it was only the way he had put it that was funny.

Yet another little disappointment. Laurent was trying so hard to frame things right, but he couldn't get around all the odd expressions the people of the future used. Some of the words remained the same as in his own time, and yet they were used in different ways, and he feared making his way through the tangle of contemporary words would be no less difficult than learning a new language from the basics.

Nao took him to the same mall he'd visited with Beast weeks before. She chose the same steak restaurant Beast had originally wanted to take him to, and this time getting a table was no trouble at all. The beef indeed tasted great, and the easy availability of sugar for coffee and in desserts pushed Laurent into using more of it than necessary. But the food still left a bitter aftertaste in his mouth when he remembered how upset Beast had been when they were refused the privilege of eating there.

Nao decided that if he wanted to 'get laid', which he worked out meant general sexual activity, then he needed new sexy clothes. It confused him, since he thought the ones Beast helped him choose were very attractive, but he would go with what was required for the venture and put his trust in Nao since she had regular encounters with men.

So there he was, in front of a mirror, unsure if his clothes weren't too obscene to show in public, while music already thudded under his feet. As the honorary guest, Beast was likely already at the party, and Laurent couldn't help but wonder if Beast would like the way he looked tonight.

Nao straightened his hair with a hot iron, and everything Laurent wore clung to his body like second skin. The fabric of his black pants was a bit like thin, soft leather, yet stretched slightly, to accommodate every part of his body. *Every* part. He'd worn fitted breeches in the past, but none that would hug his prick so obscenely. The top-thing she bought for him was even stranger. He tried it on in a shop that sold a whole array of lewd objects, and where Nao herself purchased a short dress made out of rubber to wear at the party.

At first, Laurent wasn't sure how to put the garment on, but then Nao helped him figure it out. It was two long, tight-fitting black sleeves, connected at the back with a strip of fabric with tiny holes in it. This meant his naked chest was on show and his arms hidden, which made no sense at all, but Nao said he looked 'sexy', which seemed to be her keyword for attracting men, so Laurent chose to follow her advice.

He needed to ask for Nao to prepare a dictionary of sorts for his use. Like with Latin, surely memorizing new expressions and words would help him learn them much faster than merely by speaking.

It was almost midnight by the time Nao applied some black face paint around Laurent's eyes, insisting it needed to be smudged to look good on a man, and only then he was allowed to go with her and join the party. From the sound of it, the number of guests was far superior to anything Laurent had seen at the clubhouse so far. The music was louder. And even Nao seemed more excited for the night than she usually was.

That was it. The night Laurent would kiss a man again. Maybe more than kiss, since with so many people around he felt safe enough to try his luck. Someone would help him if the man he chose became aggressive, surely. He'd gotten a second chance at life from the devil. A chance to live freely in a world where he could do as he wished, and he would not waste this opportunity. He would be the master of his own destiny.

An enormous crowd of people he didn't know mingled in the dark space illuminated with red and yellow lights as if this was the pit of hell where all and any sins could take place. The tight outfit made Laurent feel as good as naked, but his nerves eased when he saw that he did in fact blend in, and the alcoholic drink Nao put into his hand helped as well.

Knight was making out with Jordan in the corner by the pool table, and *Beasts of Hell* were playing their devilish music on the stage.

Their singer, Lizzy had frightened Laurent horribly when they first met, but then Laurent learned that the man's reptile eyes were 'contact lenses', and he even took them out when Laurent wouldn't believe something like that existed. Instantly, Laurent wondered if he too could get those invisible glasses, but it turned out that he couldn't wear them because of his condition.

But he didn't want to be greedy if modern medicine allowed him a safe way to improve it and eventually see like a healthy man. Nao assured him he looked very good in the new glasses they chose together, paying with King's money. He wondered if she found it equally difficult to recognize people and discern friends from strangers in the dimly lit room where almost all lights focused on Lizzy, who thrashed on the stage like a man possessed.

Even when he tripped over a cable and dropped to the floor, the crowd only roared with laughter and cheers, as if it was nothing they hadn't expected. For a few moments, Lizzy played his oddly flat guitar lying down and left the other two members of his musical troupe—or 'band' as they were now called—in the spotlight.

All around, people brushed against Laurent when they passed, and he could swear someone actually rubbed their hand against his ass, but the unsolicited touch was gone before he knew who was to blame. It left him with a sense of confusion about his position. Was it his outfit that made someone think he was available for such fondling? And if it was, then shouldn't he invite such touch instead of shying away from it? He did intend to experiment tonight.

Despite his better judgment, his gaze browsed through the tangle of bodies in search of the tallest of men, but the unusual haircut Beast wore was nowhere to be seen. Had he retreated somewhere? Was he getting air outside? Laurent couldn't focus with Nao tugging him through a crowd so vast it seemed larger than the entirety of Brecon's population in Laurent's own time.

The town had changed and grown since then, just as Mayor Lamont had wanted it to. The Orient-inspired town hall was now dwarfed by buildings far grander and more eye catching, and instead of walking on mud and manure, the inhabitants rode machines and gaited over the hard surface that was asphalt.

When the music died down somewhat, King stumbled onto the stage with a microphone in hand, smiling widely and squinting, as always when he drank too much. With Lizzy and his band getting off the stage and no music coming from the box, all attention was on him.

"So many people. I hope no one damages our ceiling again," King said, swaying slightly. In the void left behind by the music, laughter and groans mixed into an odd concoction, and in the corner of his eye, Laurent saw Nao scowling.

"What is he doing…?" Though King's girlfriend, she was surprisingly critical of the man.

"We're all here to celebrate my son becoming vice president of the Kings of Hell motorcycle club." King pulled on one of the lamps so that it pointed toward a spot in the crowd. Beast was seated by a table, with a beer in his hand, looking like the true ruler of the club. He scowled as soon as the light hit his face. "I never thought this day would come," King continued, waiting for the audience to laugh at his joke and only continued when he got what he wanted. "But he's my blood. I suppose he's earned it now that poor Davy retired. You know how it is when no one else wants a job," King said, smiling as if he were one of the comedic actors Laurent has watched with Beast on television.

Beast just raised his beer, but his face remained unchanged, although with the thick layer of drawings and words covering his skin, it was hard to tell any of his expressions at a distance.

The speech continued on into a rant about the perils of having to replace someone irreplaceable, but then King went on to praise his own achievements by suggesting that with him being president, a VP wouldn't have to do that much after all. If felt like the talk would never end, especially when King started drinking another beer midway through the speech. The man was definitely not Laurent's favorite person in the room, especially when drunk.

Still, with the crowd of people also infused with alcohol and enjoying a free party, King got an ovation when he was done.

The spotlight lingered on Beast, who sat next to Jake and Martina by a small corner table and just listened. First, he gazed at his father above the heads of the crowd, but by the end of the spectacle that celebrated him by stating all the reasons why he was a lousy person for his new job, his eyes lowered to look at the glass in his hand. It was all done in jest, it seemed, but with all the jokes being at one person's expense, Laurent considered them insensitive and tactless.

It was painful to listen to King for so long, and Laurent was glad when the music started again. King slid off the stage, waving at them as he made his way through the room with a pearly white smile in place. Nao caught up with him by pushing her slender body through the sweaty bodies. She tugged his head down by the collar and pressed her face against his ear. By the way King flinched, she was likely screaming.

King waved his hand dismissively and patted her ass, but then turned to Laurent, as if he only now noticed his presence. "Come on, boy, I gotta tell you something!" he yelled, loudly enough to be vaguely heard over the aggressive tunes, and Laurent reluctantly followed. King's arm was heavy around his shoulders, and the scents of beer, strong cologne, and tobacco drilled into his nose, leaving behind an unpleasant residue he wasn't sure he would get rid of by the end of the night.

King took a sip from his bottle and then pushed the glass neck into Laurent's face so hard it collided with Laurent's upper teeth through the flesh of his lip. Laurent grabbed it just to stop beer from spilling all over him.

"You look fucking slutty tonight! I like it. Nao took you shopping, eh?" King pulled Laurent into a quieter corner, and the words left Laurent so confused he settled on drinking a bit to excuse his silence.

"That's good, I guess," he said, unsure what the word meant. It sounded positive in context of King's words, even though in his time it would have been used to described someone untidy. "Nao is my best friend here. She really is a wonderful woman."

King snorted. “Yeah, yeah, just a bit of a nag. I tell you, Laurent, women have no sense of humor. So easy to offend them, you know? You’re a smart guy though. How did you like my speech?”

Laurent downed the beer to give himself a few seconds. “It was… a marvel.”

“A marvel! Ha! That’s why I like you Laurent. You always find the right words.” King patted Laurent’s naked back, making Laurent regret the outfit he and Nao had chosen when King’s fingers lingered on his spine. “I’ll let you in on a secret though. You know why it was such a good speech?”

Laurent shook his head.

King leaned down so that only Laurent would hear him. “Because every time Beast gets a punch in the gut, I get a kick like I’m fuckin’ snorting coke. All thanks to our horned friend.”

Laurent blinked, not sure if he heard the words right through the noise, but his stomach was already dropping. “I don’t understand.”

King groaned drunkenly, as if annoyed that his revelation fell on deaf ears. “I get to take his life energy when he’s upset, because all the barriers are down then, and he’s fuckin’ perfect for it, ‘cause he sulks all the time. Whenever he hurts, whenever he bleeds, I get to eat it all up like it’s an open watermelon and I’m dripping in the juices.”

The way he laughed, stumbling to the wall as if he’d just told his best joke, left Laurent stunned with the revelation. It was utterly and absolutely horrific.

“I guess that’s nice, Mr. King,” he muttered despite the tightness in his throat.

King’s blue eyes glinted, and he laughed so rapidly some of the beer in his mouth dribbled down his chin. “He’s so young and strong, and I just gotta know… Did you two fuck? Because since you moved out of his, I’ve been feeling like a newborn. I’m not even going to be hungover after tonight.”

Laurent’s heart sank. So Beast was still upset by what happened a week ago? “N-no. Nothing like that.”

King laughed and patted Laurent’s ass, just like he did to girls. “It’s probably why then. He’s blue-balling like hell. Keep up the good work.”

Laurent groaned and wanted to complain, but King was always the one to choose when he wanted to leave and he did so with the wave of a hand.

Laurent stared after him just long enough to see him pulling a tall, slim woman in black clothes out of the crowd. The woman laughed and gave him a kiss as soon as she saw who it was, and Laurent couldn’t look on anymore. He tried not to judge the depravity he observed around the club every day, as times had clearly changed and so did mores, but he did not want to watch King in any capacity after the things he’d just been told.

Nao didn't care that her man had found another woman for the night and danced by a metal pole in an elevated spot, for everyone to see. Left on his own, Laurent didn't know where to go from here. His gaze kept shifting back to Beast when a heavy arm landed on his shoulders. He hated being so short.

"I am not an armrest," he groaned, but then looked up to find Knight smiling at him widely. He could excuse Knight being intrusive, since the man was so irresistibly charming. Still, he crossed his arms on his chest as the thoughts of King's horrific pact with the devil tumbled in his mind like clothes in a washing machine.

"Aw, I just haven't talked to you in a while. Have you congratulated Beast yet?" Knight asked, moving into the place vacated by King moments ago.

Laurent shifted uncomfortably, still shellshocked by the truth behind King's intentions for Beast. And now he felt like he was an unwilling accomplice to the vile plan. "I… I don't think he would appreciate that."

"You think?" Knight shrugged, looking down at Laurent with a wide smile that made him even more handsome, the messy hair somehow only adding to his roguish charm. "Maybe he's forgiven you already. You were a bit of a douche back at the warehouse, but it's not like you killed anyone."

Laurent's shoulders sagged. "I would very much wish to make it up to him, but I admit I'm somewhat afraid."

The sudden slap on the ass startled Laurent.

"Be a man about it. Go," Knight said, leaning against the wall. It was almost as if he knew something Laurent didn't.

Laurent took a deep breath and started walking toward the little corner table hidden beyond all the sweaty bodies. His new pants were inviting an onslaught of slaps, and he wasn't sure how much he liked that kind of attention.

To avoid touching strangers as much as possible, Laurent moved closer to the wall, effectively circling the room while Nao and another woman both danced by the metal pole together, urged on by a whistling crowd. Nao climbed all the way to the top, only to rest her spine against the rod with her head down and lower her legs, spreading them obscenely. The other woman must have been jealous of all that attention, as she suddenly tore off her shirt, revealing her bosom to everyone gathered.

Laurent was so shocked by the display he walked into somebody. After a profuse apology, he finally reached Beast's table, slowing down as if he were a pauper arriving for an audience with the king. He nervously picked at his sleeve, trying to ignore the feeling of his chest sagging and restricting him from breathing freely.

Beast looked up from above his glass, his eyes narrowing when he took in Laurent's presence. Their gazes met, and it hit Laurent like a bullet just how much he longed for Beast's appreciation. Martina and Jake glared at Laurent too, and the latter actually whistled, but their opinion didn't matter in the face of Beast's frown.

"Okay..." Beast said in an odd tone.

Beast watched Laurent without a word, and yet it felt like there were burning hot fingers rubbing up and down Laurent's body. That, or Beast's gaze was actually flaying him. He didn't know the difference anymore. All he knew was that even fleeting, accidental touches from Beast were what he craved as much as Beast's attention and forgiveness.

"I… I came to congratulate on the promotion to the position of VP," Laurent said in the end, with his heart thudding in his chest so hard he was afraid people could see the evidence of it, since his whole chest was on show.

Beast's mouth narrowed, and he gave a curt nod. Before Laurent could flee in face of such an unenthusiastic reaction, Beast spoke, and each one of his words made Laurent wish he hadn't approached him at all. "What are you wearing? Those clothes aren't you at all. Was everything else you own dirty?"

Laurent licked his lips, looking around, but no help was coming from the other people who just stared, waiting for him to react. "N-Nao helped me choose. And King said they were very slutty."

Jake laughed out loud. "Oh, man… Yeah. They're *very slutty*."

"I think he doesn't know what that means," Martina said, gently patting Laurent's arm.

"Like a prostitute, Laurent," Beast said and took a big swig of his beer. "Nao is lovely but her taste? Questionable."

Martina burst out laughing and hid her face in her hands.

Laurent grew roots into the floor at the shame of it, and he now realized why he'd attracted so many slaps on the ass if that was indeed how he looked to everyone around him. That had not been his intention. His face grew so hot it felt like a lighthouse amongst the sea of people around them.

"She said I look sexy," he tried without much energy, doubting himself more by the second as Beast's blue eyes drilled into his naked chest. Did his clothes really invite men who would pay for pleasure?

Jake have a slow nod. "You do. I'd do you."

Martina laughed even louder and almost choked on an alcoholic drink she was sipping. Beast just stared at Laurent, tapping his fingers against the glass and alternating between keeping his eyes on the beer and glancing at Laurent.

"I do not sell pleasure," Laurent mumbled, defeated beyond belief. So Beast hated how he looked. Beast hated *him*. This had to be the worst night that had ever happened in 2017. No. The worst thing was that Beast was fed upon by his own father, a man who he should trust, and Laurent wasn't allowed to intervene if he didn't want to be spirited away to 1805. Just thinking of it choked the life out of him.

"You sure?" Martina laughed and pulled out a banknote, waving it at him. "I'll give this to you if you show us your lovely ass."

Beast hissed and looked away, as if even the thought of seeing Laurent naked disgusted him to no end.

So much for trying to make amends. Had Knight set him up for this failure on Beast's behalf? "I have to decline," he mumbled and walked off quickly, afraid the sting under his eyelids would intensify if Beast gave him one more hateful glance. He'd come here so proud of his new, sexy outfit, yet now he just wished to disappear into his empty, cold room.

He shouldn't have tried to become something he wasn't. Maybe he just wasn't born to be *sexy*? At least in this day and age, he wasn't a servant bound to a master by a contract that in his time basically meant Mr. Barnave owned him for a fixed period of time.

He found himself a spot in a corner, by a table no one sat at, and hoped to disappear in the shadows despite his skin still scorching from Beast's scrutiny.

He wondered if he should just flee to his room when someone waved his hand in front of Laurent's face. "Are you new here?" asked the man. Just slightly taller than Laurent, he wasn't nearly as intimidating as the bikers, and red-rimmed glasses suggested he was slightly eccentric.

Laurent took a deep breath and held out his hand. "Laurent. I've been around for a while."

The man shook his hand. "Bob." He looked Laurent up and down. "And you look fuckin' sexy."

Laurent dared a smile, assessing the man in a new light.

Chapter 15 - Laurent

Bob turned out to be a fantastic fellow. They soon moved to a quiet corner with piled-up pillows where they talked over drinks that made Laurent's mind slightly fuzzy. He suspected the glasses contained some kind of spirit, only much sweeter than he was used to. Bob even brought him a straw to sip through, and like many of Laurent's favorite things in 2017, it was made of plastic.

With the party spinning around them, with loud music and with the lights so dim, Laurent finally relaxed, enjoying the closeness of a masculine body when Bob pressed against him to whisper into his ear in a way that sent tickling sensations all over Laurent's body.

Could this night perhaps end up in kisses? Bob wasn't dashing like Fane had been, or breathtaking like Beast, but he had a nice smile, he was masculine, made Laurent laugh. What more should he hope for when he was so inexperienced?

"When I saw you from across the room I was shocked you were alone. A guy like you rarely is," Bob said.

Laurent smiled widely. "I don't have much luck in that area. I seem to always say the wrong things."

Bob grinned, leaning even closer, and Laurent stirred in surprise and excitement when Bob rested his cold beer bottle against Laurent's bare stomach. "I can't imagine that. You talk like a prince."

Laurent laughed at the chill and the droplets of water drizzling down his skin. "Maybe they sense I don't really have the right breeding."

"Aw, I think I'm in love now. Your accent sounds so nice," Bob said and leaned in, rubbing his cheek against Laurent's.

"In love with me? That's just plain silly!" But a shiver of pleasure made Laurent's insides flutter.

"You think I'm joking, but I never met anyone like you. I couldn't take my eyes off you since you entered, but I guess I was a bit shy to approach you at first." Bob sighed and slowly put his hand above Laurent's knee.

Instantly, the memory of Beast touching him this way, of the thumb slowly tracing his knee, was like an interference Laurent couldn't get rid of. "You do understand I… don't sell pleasure, right?"

Bob grinned. "What? Why would you say that? I just wanted to ask you to model for me, but the conversation is turning out really great too."

"Because I was told my outfit might suggest I am of loose morals. But I'm happy that you don't see it to be so. How would I model for you? Do you want to paint me?"

"Like one of my French girls." Bob laughed and Laurent joined in, but he wasn't sure why it was so funny. He did want to oblige though, and he assumed that the joke had something to do with his accent.

"That sounds exciting."

Bob licked his lips, watching him with a dark glint in his eyes. Laurent's skin itched for closeness, and he dared a glance at Bob's lips.

"So, would you like to model for pictures? We could do a trial in one of the rooms available to guests."

Laurent cocked his head. "You have all you need for with you?" Maybe in the future easels and paints expanded from tiny objects? He'd watched so many movies in the last weeks, asked his friends so many questions, and yet so much still escaped his grasp.

"All of it," Bob said and slowly pulled himself up before offering his hand to Laurent.

Hesitantly, Laurent slipped his fingers into the clammy palm. "I would love to see more of your work." He entwined their fingers with his heart in his throat from the stress of it all. Since the first time he'd made an attempt to bed a man, every romantic interaction had been a disaster. Could this one possibly break the bad spell? Bob seemed genuinely nice and non-threatening. Besides, he was an artist, a sensitive soul by definition.

Bob stroked Laurent's hair with his other hand and pulled him toward the doors Laurent knew led to a whole array of rooms with just mattresses in them. Earlier that day, he'd helped make them presentable, because the party guests were free to use them.

"Will you have enough light in there?" he asked in case Bob actually wanted to paint, though he was positive they would kiss instead, and who knew what else would happen once passion arose.

"I think we might just get to know each other better first. It will allow me to capture your personality better once I start painting."

Laurent smiled to himself and squeezed Bob's hand, increasingly nervous as they walked out into the empty corridor where music was only a dull sound. "I would like that."

Once the doors shut behind them, the sense of apprehension curled around Laurent's insides, giving him an unexplainable urge to run. But he couldn't just run from his true needs forever. He couldn't just wait. He was a man in this new world where men could freely be together, and he needed to reach out for the things he wanted, not expect them to fall into his lap.

The doors opened again so rapidly they smacked against the wall. Bob glanced over his shoulder, squeezing Laurent's hand.

Beast was approaching in rapid strides, his face as tense and marred with cruelty as it had been a week ago when he had grabbed Laurent by the throat. What had Laurent done wrong though? Had Beast been waiting for Laurent to leave the dancing hall to punish Laurent for daring to speak to him after being explicitly told not to?

"Where are you taking him, huh?" Beast growled, showing his teeth in a snarl reminiscent of Hound. The massive, tattooed hand landed on Bob's shoulder with such finality Bob seemed to melt under it.

"I… Is this a problem?" Bob raised his eyebrows. "I was just—"

Laurent grabbed Beast's wrist. "He was just going to paint me. There's nothing questionable going on."

"Paint you?" Beast practically spat it out like a dirty word and shook Bob, who let go of Laurent's hand and curled his shoulders.

"Beast, come on. I'm not doing anything illegal."

Laurent nodded quickly, eager to protect his new friend from the sudden threat. "Yes, he said he'll paint me like his French girls. I guess that would mean I'd be the first French boy he paints. No wonder he wants to do the initial sketches already."

He smiled at Bob.

Bob didn't smile back, his face briefly twitching before Beast's huge fist collided with it so hard Bob crashed into the nearest wall and slid to the floor with blood spurting over the gray tiles. He screamed out, clutching his nose with one hand and raising the other in an attempt to protect himself. "No, please! It's a misunderstanding, I swear!"

"No!" Laurent yelled in panic and grabbed Beast's arm. "Stop! What are you doing? How dare you!"

Beast hunched his shoulders, glaring at Laurent with his lips pressed so tightly together they were pale. "Go on, tell him what you do!" He roughly pulled out of Laurent's grasp and grabbed Bob's wrist, dragging him over the floor.

Bob shrieked, curling into a ball, as if he expected Beast to kick him. "I didn't do anything!"

Laurent tried to stand between them but Beast pushed him away with ease. "Stop tormenting this poor man! All he wanted to do was to get to know me better! Is that such a sin?"

"Know you better?" Beast hissed, widening his eyes at Laurent. "This man doesn't paint. He takes naked pictures of people and puts them up for everyone to see. That's how he makes money!"

Laurent took a step back, unsure what to believe. "Is that true?" he whispered, looking down at Bob, whose nose bled all over the floor.

Bob put one hand up, holding the other to his nose. "I'm sorry I misjudged things. I can just go!"

Beast punched the wall so hard his fist left a dent, and Bob screamed out, shielding his head. "You are banned from here. Try to come back, and I will personally break your arms, you piece of shit! *Paint him like your French girls*... what a joke!"

Laurent took another step back, farther into the shadows, so deeply embarrassed it physically hurt. And the worst thing was that Bob wouldn't have even had to come up with lies to win Laurent's favor. Laurent would have considered being intimate with the man anyway. Now the very thought of it repulsed him. Was it his fate to be deceived by everyone he chose to open up to?

Bob scrambled to his feet, having to hold himself up with the help of the wall. "Sure, sure! I'm going! No need to get violent." He laughed nervously and a bubble of blood burst at his nostril.

Beast snapped his fingers, and it was enough to send Bob out through the door without even a glance at Laurent.

They were alone again, with Laurent's back hugging the wall, Beast's hulking presence filling the walkway with stiff muscle and deep gasps, and the muted noise that people in 2017 called music.

Beast licked his lips and spared Laurent a brief glance. "He didn't give you any strange things to eat, did he? Are you feeling weak?"

Laurent shook his head quickly, still confused why Beast would even follow him in the first place if he despised Laurent so much. "It must have been my outfit that gave him the wrong impression," he said weakly, backing out even farther. He was dying to be alone, to take off the clothes and rub off the paint from his eyes. This night was a disaster.

Beast pushed his hands into his pockets and opened his mouth, making no sound when a man and a woman stumbled into the corridor locked in an aggressive kiss. Laurent and Beast watched them try two doors before one gave, and the couple rushed into the room.

Beast cleared his throat. "He must have noticed you don't know what he was talking about. He just wanted to use you because you're naive," he said in the end.

The dam that was holding in Laurent's frustration gave and he spread his arms. "I'm not naive! I'm trying so hard to make the best of this situation, and yet I'm sure this will not be the last mistake I make. Why do you have to flaunt just how much you know everything better than I? So my clothes are 'slutty', and I've misjudged Bob's intentions. I will know better next time."

"Laurent. This isn't a game. This is your life. You can't just jump into things. Your past life didn't prepare you for any of this." Beast licked his lips, stepping closer.

Laurent stood his ground, releasing a heavy sigh of exasperation. "How am I to learn? I've been wanting to touch a man this way for so long, and every attempt ends in disaster!"

Beast's Adam's apple rolled up and down his neck, and he briefly looked to the floor. "A week ago, I thought we'd become friends. Why did you make a fool out of me in front of everyone?"

Laurent's misery would know no end. The man Laurent had treated with malice for his own gain rescued him once again. He couldn't possibly tell Beast the truth, and yet no matter how much he hated what he'd done at the viewing, there was no alternative. Laurent couldn't allow Beast to change living quarters until his next birthday. Was there a half-truth he could say? One that wasn't his motivation yet described his feelings?

"If we moved, I feared we wouldn't live together anymore," he said, looking to the bloodstained tiles under his feet. The words communicated the sorrow he felt every day at being banished from Beast's apartment. He didn't even realize how deep it was until now. There were plenty of other men around the clubhouse, many more conventionally attractive, but neither of them was Beast. Neither of them had the oddly rough voice or muscles strong enough to hide the softness of the heart beating in Beast's chest. He would have gone with Bob, because he wanted to finally feel how it was to be with a man, yet in the past week he'd been regretful about rejecting Beast in the first place every day. Bob could have never been a replacement for the man Laurent really desired. The man Laurent would allow to be hurt by King for several more months in order to save his own skin.

He was scum, not worthy of Beast, and yet selfish enough to long for it all the same.

Beast was very quiet. "If you like me, why didn't you say anything?" he asked in the end.

Laurent rubbed his eyes, only seconds later realizing the black paint had now gotten all over his hands. "You said you despise me."

"You didn't want to kiss me and told me you wanted to just be friends."

Laurent looked up at him and dared a step forward to the big man whose fist dripped with another's blood. "You have power, property, and position. How can we be on equal footing? I had known you for less than a day back then, and I hadn't even outright rejected you. I hesitated and you got furious. It made me wonder what you would do were I to allow a kiss yet refuse other… things."

Beast swallowed and then rapidly pointed at the drops of blood on the floor. His face was so tense it looked as if it might tear at the seams any minute. "You didn't know him either."

"I don't live with him. My well-being doesn't depend on him. He has no authority over me. And he's… not as big and strong as you are."

Beast's shoulders dropped even lower, and his face twitched. "I'm sorry I scared you."

Laurent was about to speak when the couple from before burst out of the room, laughing loudly as the woman adjusted her bra.

"That was... quick," said Beast, watching them until they disappeared from sight again, but at the same time he very slowly reached out his hand to Laurent. The inside of his palm was burnt too, the twisted skin not covered by tattoos and naked in a tangle of pink and white. Laurent wanted to kiss it until the skin became soft from the constant touch.

Laurent swallowed and spoke only when the couple closed the doors behind them. "But what will it mean if I do hold your hand?" His heart was already screaming *yes* to his fingers entwining with Beast's.

Beast took a deep breath that made his massive chest expand under the black shirt. "That maybe you'd like... to try out some of the things you want to do with a man... with me."

Laurent's throat was tight, and he slid his hand into Beast's before he actually thought it through. He wanted to be in Beast's good graces so badly it hurt every bit of his being. He hadn't even realized just how much he craved Beast's touch.

Something changed in Beast's eyes. The bright blue irises have gone softer as they met Laurent's gaze. Beast pulled him closer, leading him down the corridor and away from the noise, away from the rooms where people escaped to do lewd things with strangers. Beast's fingers were warm and inviting, as gentle as they had been back at the mall.

They walked into a long corridor illuminated by a single yellow bulb.

Beast led the way into one of the rooms and closed the door with a soft thud. The sound sent the tiniest of ants crawling down Laurent's spine, and an unsettling sensation curled up in the pit of his stomach. Not knowing the contemporary rules of courting could have yet again put him in the most disastrous of positions. What if Beast demanded things Laurent wasn't ready for? He had been willing to take the risk with Fane, and that ended with blood on Laurent's hands.

He was so nervous, so focused on the man before him he didn't even bother to look for a light switch or check whether there was a bed nearby. All he knew was that Beast was big, and warm, and smelled like no other man alive—both in the past and present.

"What if I change my mind? What if I decide to back out?" Laurent asked quickly, not letting go of Beast's hand. "What if I want to experiment with things you do not wish to do with me?"

Beast stepped closer, trapping Laurent between the wall and his chest. He sighed, and with his face turned away from the windows, Laurent couldn't see his features well, even with the glasses on.

"If you're here with me... I'm assuming you don't think I'm completely revolting. I'm sure we can work out a middle ground."

Laurent's heart started thudding desperately hard, and it wouldn't stop. He made an attempt to control his breathing more, but each inhale smelled of Beast, and the rich yet fresh scent was making Laurent dizzy with lust.

"Revolting?" he asked, somewhat confused. Beast was definitely not traditionally handsome with the inked lines and patterns all over his body, with the scars marring even his face, but all Laurent wanted to do was to gently trace them with his fingers and get to know each one. There was nothing disgusting about the imperfections. "Your whole presence makes my heart jump. You tower over me in every way, to the point where I fear we can never be equal, and that anything I do with you will end in disastrous conflict."

Beast exhaled, and then slowly, very slowly got to his knees in front of Laurent. His large palms moved down Laurent's bare chest, cupping his pectoral muscles, only to caress his stomach and rest on his hips.

Laurent couldn't breathe.

Beast looked up, his eyes pale in the faint light from outside when he raised his head to look up at Laurent. "Is this less scary?" he whispered.

Laurent could hardly swallow, trembling from head to toe, like a kitten in the rain. One thing was for sure, Beast was no longer towering over him. Too bad now Laurent had no idea what was expected of him. "That… That's a-agreeable." What a stupid thing to say! Why couldn't he say something witty, or filled with lust? Why was he at a loss of words when many times he imagined the things he could say to a man when in an intimate situation?

Beast exhaled, and there was a faint shudder to his voice when he leaned forward and rubbed his face against Laurent's bare stomach. But it was when Beast's mouth opened against Laurent's navel and teased him with warm air that Laurent moaned, melting against the wall.

"Oh, dear God in heaven," Laurent whispered, looking down at the muscular man kneeling before him as if Laurent was worthy of worship. Beast wasn't charming like Knight, or alluring like Fane, but he was beautiful in his own right. His appeal lay in the tightly packed muscle, in the lines of his body, and in the way he exuded confidence when he touched Laurent. Everything about Beast was filling Laurent's prick at an impressive speed, making his head spin with the sensation of heat spiraling down his body.

Beast's laughter teased the sensitive skin around Laurent's navel, but then came the tongue, warm, wet, and wonderful as it painted burning lines all over. For a moment, Laurent was completely certain the touch would leave behind traces, a mark that would forever remind Laurent of this moment, of Beast's tattooed shoulders looking silvery in the moonlight.

"Is there… something I should do?" Laurent asked, moving his trembling fingers over the lines on Beast's arm. The muscle there was like steel. Never had Laurent met a man resembling an ancient warrior in stature as much as Beast did. But when he squeezed his fingers harder, the wide shoulders tensed under his touch, beckoning Laurent to be gentler, to understand the unusual nature of Beast's skin.

Beast gasped and slid his tongue into Laurent's belly button before pressing a wet kiss to the skin. "What do you want to do?" he asked in a raspy, uneven voice as he lowered himself farther, moving his lips and nose to the front of Laurent's tight pants where Laurent's prick was already straining against the fabric.

"Everything, I want to do everything," Laurent mumbled fervently, unable to resist watching the square-jawed face at his crotch. Beast suddenly seemed more handsome than Knight and Fane combined. Could anyone ever be compared to the beauty of a man so eager to give one pleasure?

Beast licked his lips and grinned at him, slowly moving his large hands up and down Laurent's thighs. "You remember what sucking someone off means?"

Oh, he did. No matter how much the explanation had embarrassed him at the time, it had implanted itself in his mind like a rock could in a shoe, always there yet impossible to find when one wanted to get rid of it. He nodded vigorously, and had to push back the hair that fell on his face. "I'm sorry that of all nights, it's this one that I am dressed in a way that displeases you so much."

Beast looked up when his fingers moved over the front of Laurent's pants and squeezed him gently. Any blood that was still left behind in Laurent's head momentarily trickled down, filling his cock so rapidly he feared he'd soil the new clothes with his seed.

"It's not... like that. They just don't fit you. You look so very sexy in the things you wear every day," whispered Beast, pulling on the waistband of Laurent's tight pants.

"I do?" Laurent's chest kept rising and falling rapidly when his erection was revealed, bobbing so close to Beast's face as if it longed to kiss him. The sight was beyond arousing yet so obscene. Never before had a man seen him in this state, let alone touched him.

Beast grunted, like a dog about to claim his bone. "Y-yes," he whispered with a slight tremble to his voice. He ran his fingers over the length of Laurent's cock, gently teasing the underside with his thumb.

Laurent's toes curled, and he pushed his hips forward, unable to resist the touch. He felt so exposed, so vulnerable to abuse of trust. Beast had been right. He was easy to trick. The thoughts of Fane's apple-tasting kisses had his stomach in a twist, and he needed to force himself to get back to the present where he shared a growing intimacy with Beast. He could only hope Beast was getting as much pleasure from this as he was, because were he in Beast's shoes, he was pretty certain he would be on the verge of release.

Beast traced the fingers of his other hand up the inside of Laurent's thigh, gently teasing until they reached Laurent's balls and closed around them. It felt as if he were tugging on a thread deep inside Laurent's prick just before touching the cockhead with his lips.

Laurent now wished he'd found the light switch, but pleasure illuminated every last stream of thought in his mind, making them flow quicker and deliver lust all over his body. He bit down on the side of his fist to stifle a moan, all too overwhelmed by the lips travelling up and down his prick. Never had he imagined that this would be something Beast was willing to do for him.

But Beast was on his knees, breathing hard and practically groaning with pleasure as he played with Laurent's prick, sucking on it and teasing the whole length with his warm, slick tongue. His mouth was pure heaven, so unbearably hot and sweet at the same time that Laurent was already starting to feel sparks of lightning in his toes.

He wouldn't last much longer with Beast toying with his balls, running his other hand over Laurent's hip, giving sounds of delight as if he were the one being indulged. Sensation stormed inside Laurent quicker by the moment, and he had to lean forward and steady himself against Beast's shoulders, wary not to squeeze them too hard. Every time Beast sucked harder, a moan escaped Laurent's lips, and every teasing touch to the intimate parts of his body had him trembling with the upcoming release.

Pleasure toppled over Laurent like a hot wave and buried him in the sweetness of Beast's mouth. Beast greedily squeezed Laurent's buttocks, sucking him all the way in, only to withdraw slightly the moment Laurent's prick spasmed, releasing sperm from his balls.

Beast swallowed loudly, his whole body moving like a wild animal's in heat as he took in Laurent's seed with no complaint whatsoever. Laurent leaned against him, slightly easing the grip that he'd tightened on Beast's shoulders when he realized he could be hurting him in his pleasure. But he couldn't stop panting, shattered by the experience of sharing the peak of his lust with another man. A towering mountain of a man with thick muscles, big hands, and eyes that could pierce right into his soul.

He'd been lying to himself about considering this experience with men other than Beast.

Beast was still breathing hard when he released Laurent's cock with one last kiss to the head and slowly moved his body up, trailing wet, greedy kisses up Laurent's bare chest, neck, all the way to Laurent's mouth.

With Laurent's knees soft and trembling, he dared steady himself against Beast's chest and opened his lips to the kiss, too mindless to worry about potential consequences. He was still floating on the waves of his release and when Beast pressed on with his tongue with increasing ferocity, Laurent was eager to give in. Even the erect prick suddenly pushing against his stomach couldn't scare him. If anything, he shuddered with the desire to touch it.

There was a bitter undertone to the kiss, but the soft glide of Beast's tongue, which slowly yet insistently licked its way into the depths of Laurent's mouth, was already pulling on strings of latent arousal and making him want to just give into anything Beast might possibly ask of him.

Beast's breath was coming in sharp gasps, his skin trembling as if he were cold and longed to bury himself in Laurent's warmth. Laurent let his hands glide to Beast's sides, and then around him, holding him close. He was so overwhelmed his mind didn't function with its usual sharpness, so he followed his instinct and slid his fingers under Beast's vest and just kept them there, indulging in the forbidden skin to skin contact with a man.

And not any man at that. A beast.

Chapter 16 - Beast

The kiss was explosive. As if Beast was fourteen again and kissing a boy for the first time. Tiny, invisible people danced all over his skin, drumming their feet in the fast rhythm of the red rivers that were about to overflow with adrenaline and arousal. It was a mating dance, and he pushed at Laurent, cradling the smooth face in his palms for the deepest, sweetest of kisses. His thirst had no end, as if his body needed to sate itself after ten years of drought, so he licked, and nipped, and sucked, sharing the saltiness of sperm and the sweet aroma of Laurent's warm mouth.

Laurent had never been more beautiful than he was now, frantic and flushed even after he came. His palms were pressed flat to the skin of Beast's back, but it was the way he kept pulling Beast down for kisses that was most enticing. Beast wasn't just a means to an end, Laurent wasn't a horny guy looking for a mouth to suck him. He wanted to hug and kiss in a way Beast forgot was even possible.

Beast whimpered with emotion and nuzzled Laurent's cheek, breathing in the scent of his shampoo. He didn't want this to end yet. He wanted to see Laurent naked and cover each and every inch of his body with kisses. Now that Laurent knew how it felt to be with Beast, maybe he wouldn't change his mind on the way home. "Okay?"

Laurent nodded frantically, pulling his hands away only to pull up his pants. "Yes. So good. Thank you. Shall I…?" His eyes were searching Beast's face for an answer when he pressed his fingers against Beast's cock, which was still trapped in his jeans. The vision of Laurent sucking on his dick exploded in Beast's mind like a supernova. Would he be looking up, cheeks rosy from arousal, or would he keep his eyes closed, embarrassed to meet Beast's gaze? Would he want to swallow or just jerk Beast off until he sprayed his cum all over the graceful hand? There were so many options, and Beast wanted to see them all come to life.

"I... not yet," whispered Beast, gently pulling Laurent's hand away, because his touch was clouding the rational part of Beast's mind. "Let's go home."

Laurent nodded and entwined their fingers before Beast even attempted it. He raised Beast's hand to his lips and kissed his knuckles. "I would like that very much."

Beast stared at him, barely breathing as the soft, kissable lips brushed against his hand, as if the ugly scars were of no importance. He smiled, standing taller as he caressed Laurent's cheek with his other hand and pushed back his long, unruly hair. It was straight as Nao's tonight, and he liked it so much better in its natural state.

They stood motionless for several seconds until Beast realized it was up to him to make the next move. He pulled Laurent out of the room and into the dark corridor, toward the bright lights of the hallway that would lead them to Beast's own apartment.

Even the distorted mirror they passed on the way couldn't bother Beast tonight. The only mirror he now needed was the one in Laurent's eyes. They walked in silence, with Laurent looking up at him every now and again, and he finally slid his arm around Beast's back. It was adorable just how hesitant he was. As if there was anything he could possibly do to have Beast back off.

He fit so well under Beast's arm with his graceful shoulders and warm skin that smelled of cocoa butter and some kind of musky perfume. Despite numerous attempts to, Beast didn't dare speak either, and so they both walked in silence, away from the noise of the party and toward the privacy of Beast's apartment. Since Hound was locked in his pen outside for the night, there would be no one to disturb their intimacy, and the anticipation built by the long walk was drilling holes in Beast's skull.

"Are you sure you want to leave your party?" Laurent whispered in the end once they passed the last turn on the way to the apartment.

Beast looked down at the pretty face, and he knew without a doubt that he'd be willing to give up parties for a year to tumble between the sheets with Laurent a single time.

"You're kidding, right? You think I'd rather drink beer and listen to Lizzy's moaning on stage than be alone with you?" asked Beast, squeezing Laurent tighter against him. The smile slowly stretching Laurent's mouth made Beast's heart beat faster, and as they approached the door that would finally grant them all the privacy they needed, his muscles tensed from the pressure to do this right. He knew Laurent liked him, but he could still decide he didn't want to go any further with this. He could want to fuck someone else in a matter of days, and what would Beast do then?

He dismissed those nagging thoughts and just focused on the joyous feeling of warmth in his chest, on the pink nipples he saw every time he looked down at Laurent, and the way Laurent watched him, as if Beast held all the answers. He would not spoil this for himself. Not now. He would take everything he could and enjoy it while it lasted.

"It's not every day that you officially become the vice president of the Kings of Hell." Laurent smiled, pressing against Beast's side when they stopped for Beast to enter the code to his door.

Beast chuckled, slightly embarrassed that he sounded so giddy, but he was with Laurent, so maybe it wouldn't be taken the wrong way. "I think I already got the best surprise I could have," he said, pulling Laurent into the dark living room. He didn't bother searching for the light switch, because he knew his home by heart. He immediately turned toward the corridor that would lead them to the master bedroom. His dick was so hard it almost felt sore, but he would wait and make this night count.

Laurent smiled at him in the darkness, following his lead as if there was no one else he'd rather be with. Beast could recall in all the vivid detail how Laurent's cock tasted, how it throbbed against his tongue and palate, and how desperate to come Laurent had been just minutes ago. At his age, Beast had already fucked too many guys to count, and yet for Laurent it was all a fresh start, which in turn made Beast feel as if he was doing something completely new.

He opened his bedroom and switched on the small lights behind the black wooden headboard instead of the main lamp, for a more intimate atmosphere. He briefly wondered if he should offer Laurent something to drink, but he figured it would have been odd, and formal, and in truth he just wanted to get rid of the tight clothes that were so incompatible with Laurent's personality.

Thank God he always kept his home tidy, and he'd recently changed the sheets to a soft black set that would be such an exquisite contrast to Laurent's pale, wonderful skin. He closed the door and looked up, only to stiffen at the sight presented to him.

Laurent stared at the old-timey clothes hung on the door of the wardrobe so that Beast could look at them from the bed. He stepped closer and ran his fingers over the sleeve of the blue tailcoat. "You got it cleaned..."

Beast felt suddenly breathless and unsure what to say. He'd been so exhilarated over getting his hands on Laurent that he'd forgotten all about the clothes. He'd meant to return them to Laurent after he picked them up, he really did, but without Laurent here to fill Beast's house with conversation, it was the only thing he had left of him. As pathetic as that was, he'd just wanted the imagined closeness to last a little bit longer.

"Yes. I... forgot to give them back to you."

Laurent ran his fingers over the pretty enameled brooch in the lapel of the jacket. "I worried it was lost," he said so softly that the tight sexy clothes looked even more out of place on him than before.

"No, no. Sorry I didn't tell you. I kept the brooch here, just in case. Is it antique?" asked Beast, trying to cover his restlessness. Straightforward questions should do the trick.

Laurent finally turned around, looking up into Beast's eyes. "It was a gift from my mother. I'm sorry to be spoiling the mood. It doesn't matter. I'm just happy to have it back." He smiled yet seemed to be waiting for Beast's move.

Beast sank down to sit on the edge of his bed and reached out for Laurent. The sadness at the very edge of Laurent's voice was drilling its way through Beast's body, making it flush with the need to know everything about Laurent and his past, to be closer to him, to be everything to him. "No, tell me. I want to know."

"She… My parents gave me up when I was still a young boy, but it's fine, really. I'm a grown man now, I can fend for myself." He came closer and straddled Beast's lap, wrapping his arms around Beast's neck.

Beast gasped when Laurent rubbed against the cock straining his jeans, even if just slightly. The contact made his head spin, and he moved his fingers up and down the bare spine uncovered by Laurent's obscene clothes. "Don't act so brave. Give me space to help you out," he said with a brief chuckle.

Laurent smiled at him and pushed closer, first to reach for another kiss. A gentle one this time, all soft lips and barely-there touches. "It's thanks to you that I have glasses, Beast. You've helped me out plenty."

Beast slowly rolled them over, keeping Laurent close to him with both hands so that he wouldn't just drop to the mattress but be softly lowered onto it, with all the care Beast wanted to invest into this... thing that was developing between him and Laurent. "Did they leave you with the strange people you stayed with? You don't keep in touch with them, do you?"

Laurent shook his head, but he was becoming tense, alert. Like every other time when the topic of his past came up. Beast wondered whether Laurent had been sexually abused by his keepers, but considering his drive for new sexual experiences, Beast hoped that wasn't the case.

"No. I gave up on that long ago."

It was such a sad statement Beast felt compelled to just hold Laurent for a moment, brushing his lips against Laurent's forehead to express his sympathy. "I'm sorry. I lost my mother. I know it must have been difficult," he whispered.

The attentive brown gaze bore into him instantly. "What happened to her?" Laurent asked, distracting Beast with the touch of his fingers and the legs wrapping around Beast's hips as if he were pulling Beast inside his body already.

Beast swallowed, bracing himself above the pliant body and pressing his forehead to Laurent's. They were so very close he could almost feel the touch of invisible hands on his cock, but he caught Laurent's gaze and kept it. "Her car exploded. I pulled her out, but she died." It was as if every single scar on his body was proof of his failure, and he closed his eyes, burying his face in Laurent's neck, so soft, hot, and tender to the touch.

And Laurent was there to sooth every bit of Beast's pain. "Oh, Beast… I'm so sorry. Is that how you got burned?" The soft fingers danced over the arm Beast had gotten tattooed solid black because of all the scarring.

Beast nodded, swallowing the warmth of Laurent's scent and hugging him tighter. That was the worst of it all—no matter how hard he'd tried, he still couldn't save her. Sometimes, he felt that had his mother lived, the pain that resulted from the accident would have been more bearable somehow. It would have had a purpose. Instead, the deformity was just a particularly painful entry in the journal of Beast's life.

"It's okay."

Laurent kissed Beast's cheek, in the sensitive spot right under the eye. "Why did her car explode? Are they dangerous?"

Beast shook his head. "No. We were in conflict with this gang. They planted a bomb and killed her."

Laurent nodded slowly, but Beast wasn't sure how much of it he understood. What really mattered was that he listened. After the attack, the Kings of Hell made the rival gang pay in blood, but that couldn't bring Beast's mother back to life or make him handsome again.

"Can I… see more?" Laurent asked, gently pulling at the back of Beast's cut.

Beast swallowed but gave Laurent a nod and kneeled, slowly sliding off first the vest, and then the black T-shirt he wore underneath. His chest was covered in thick scar tissue and tattooed into a warped image of Lucifer's fall. Would Laurent recognize the image?

Laurent ran his fingers over it, so perfect with his lips slightly parted and hair forming a halo around his face. His breath quickened, but Beast wasn't sure if that was a good sign or not. "Did it hurt to get the pictures to remain on your skin?"

"A bit. Depending on the place," Beast said, pulling on the stretchy fabric of Laurent's barely-existing top. He wanted this thing off him quick.

Laurent bit back a smile and arched up to brush his fingers over Beast's nipple. "What about here?" He struggled with the garment that was basically only sleeves but finally pulled it off, revealing his slender arms.

Beast licked his lips, gasping at the touch. "Harder," he said and moved his own fingers lower, to the waistband of Laurent's pants. He couldn't believe that he had someone so beautiful, so wonderful in his bed. And not only did Laurent take pleasure from him, but wanted to touch Beast as well.

"Like this?" Laurent gasped and pressed his palm to Beast's pec, moving the other one down the side of Beast's chest that had less scarring, and onto his stomach. He lowered his legs around Beast, spread out like a platter of delicacies for Beast to sample.

Beast smiled, taking Laurent's hand and rubbing it against his nipple until it stiffened from the continuous touch. "No. Like this. Feels good."

Laurent laughed nervously, but let Beast guide his hand. The sight was so sweet Beast could lick Laurent all over. He couldn't recall ever being in bed with someone this innocent. Because despite his declarations of maturity, Laurent was the most unspoilt person Beast knew. So utterly different than the life he and his brothers led as members of Kings of Hell MC, and yet somehow Laurent fit in as if he was meant to be here to offset all the bloodshed and violence.

"Can I see more of you?" Beast asked, not wanting to frighten Laurent. He swirled his fingertips down Laurent's stomach and rubbed his knuckles against his groin. The moan it got him already told Beast what the answer would be.

Laurent playfully pushed at Beast's stomach. "You've already seen it all. Me? Left starving for even a hint of flesh."

Beast laughed. "Okay, I will go first then. Is that what you want?" he asked and pulled Laurent's hand to the front of his pants. Just the closeness of Laurent's fingers caused his skin to explode with sensation.

Laurent nodded eagerly, his breath going raspy before he even pulled down the zipper, and Beast's chest thudded with a sense of pride that this beautiful creature was so excited to see his entire body. Not just because Beast was the only man available, or because Laurent was a patch-slut. No, Laurent was trembling all over as he pulled Beast's jeans lower along with his underwear, and he wouldn't give it a rest until all of Beast's cock was revealed.

Laurent actually moaned at just the sight of it.

Beast grinned, looking down at his dick, tattooed with dragon scales. It was old ink, from before his accident, and he was ecstatic to have someone see it again. Without thinking, he pulled Laurent's hand to it and made his fingers slide up and down, moving the foreskin so it would slide over the head, sparking sensation that exploded all the way in Beast's skull. He imagined Laurent lowering himself to suck on his cock, and it created such a strong reaction in him, clear fluid beaded at the slit, about to drizzle down Laurent's fingers.

"It's… I… oh, and there's ink on it," Laurent uttered, completely mesmerized.

Beast never cared much before if his partners had a lot of experience or if they didn't, but having such a fresh, ripe peach in his bed, ready to be bitten into for the first time, was giving him shivers. He was now the only man Laurent had touched this way. He could already imagine lying down between Laurent's eagerly spread legs, showing him how it felt to get fucked well… So many things Beast could do with Laurent to make him forget all his other options.

"Yes. It's smooth, isn't it? Not like the rest of me," Beast whispered, letting go of Laurent to allow him to explore. "You can touch my balls next. Gently."

Laurent's rounded nose twitched like a bunny's, but all of the boy's attention was on Beast's cock, just like it should be. Laurent slid his hand between Beast's thighs, his chest rising and falling rapidly. "It's… big too. Like all of you," he whispered.

"Do you like it?" asked Beast, trying not to smile too widely, because he knew that it might seem predatory with his overall looks. He slowly rocked his cock in Laurent's hand, flinching in pleasure when Laurent tightened his fingers around it.

"Yes. It's… the most magnificent one I've ever seen." Laurent's face was as red as a tomato, but those soft fingers moved up and down Beast's cock, as if in slow motion.

"How many have you seen?" whispered Beast, moving in time to Laurent's caresses. He praised his own self control, because he would be coming already otherwise.

Laurent stalled, and Beast already missed the caresses to his balls and dick. "It's a trick question."

"Is it?" Beast asked and leaned in to kiss Laurent on the mouth, to make him understand that with Beast he was free to speak his mind.

"Yes. If I say 'many' it would be a lie, and if I say 'a few' it would make my compliment of less value."

"I just want to know who you ogled in secret." Beast laughed and stepped off the bed, eager to get the rest of his clothes off. It went quickly enough, and with the socks landing on the floor as well, he was ready to fulfil any fantasy Laurent might have. The way Laurent had claimed he wanted to do 'everything' was still a firm presence in his mind, but he knew it has likely been just a figure of speech. And he didn't care either way. Just being able to touch Laurent in an intimate way was making him ecstatic.

The way Laurent's eyes kept following Beast was a pleasure in itself. "A few people. But none as well… built. And none when aroused." He sat on the bed in all his half-naked glory, as if unaware just how hungry his flesh was making Beast. Laurent's cock was clearly back for seconds too.

"It's time for you to show yourself to me again," Beast said and tugged on the black fabric clinging to Laurent's calf. Without waiting for an answer, he pulled on Laurent's hips, twisting them so that he ended up on all fours and facing away from Beast. The black pants hugged his ass in a way that made Beast salivate with the sheer hunger to see it revealed.

Laurent looked over his shoulder, wide-eyed but not protesting. The little tease even spread his legs slightly, as if inviting Beast between them already. His earlier words only confirmed Beast's assumption that Laurent had never shared any intimacy with a man. Beast would be the first to get a taste of him, and he would savor every bite.

He exhaled, completely mesmerized by the beauty of Laurent's naked back, so unspoiled, so pale, with toned muscle softened by shadows all the way to the waistband. Beast rubbed his hand up and down Laurent's back before sliding it to the pert buttocks while his gaze remained focused on the handsome face, searching for traces of discomfort or protest. "What do you want?" he whispered before slowly rolling the tight fabric down along with the black underwear to reveal supple flesh.

Laurent's breath became so heavy Beast was dying to kiss him just to feel it, but the perfect ass distracted him too much. He'd seen it before, but not like this. Not when he was allowed to touch. "I… I want to…"

"Hmm?" Beast hummed, revealing all of Laurent's ass and thighs before pulling the garment all the way off.

Laurent was completely naked then, so vulnerable and beautiful in the enticing position Beast moved him into. He was like a juicy fruit about to spill all over Beast's fingers.

"I'm sorry. I'm not sure," Laurent choked out, glancing back at Beast over and over. "I want to be close. I want to touch you."

"And what if I do this?" Beast whispered, lowering his chest to Laurent's back, which made his cock fit right into the valley between Laurent's buttocks. The touch sent liquid fire down Beast's body, and he aggressively sucked on Laurent's shoulder, hugging the slim, wonderful body tight against his.

"Oh… oh! This feels good. Your— It's so exciting." Laurent's whimper was like the sweetest music to Beast's ears. He could play Laurent like this all night, just to hear moan after moan. Laurent's back shivered prominently against Beast's chest, and knowing that he was the cause of Laurent's state made his skin static with electricity.

"So is yours," whispered Beast, languidly moving his palm down Laurent's stomach and teasing his cockhead with fleeting touch. He grinned at the way Laurent arched under him, squeezing Beast's cock between their bodies so deliciously Beast thought for a moment that he was about to come between the open buttocks.

Laurent moaned and fell to his elbows, the dark hair sliding down his shoulder. It gave Beast so much satisfaction to see him lose control. It only made him imagine how Laurent would sound once Beast actually fucked him, that tight body squeezing around Beast's dick and milking it. Laurent wasn't exactly passive, but definitely pliant with his spread legs, doing as asked and following Beast's lead.

Laurent pushed into Beast's hand, rocking back and forth like a feline in heat, and his dick was rock hard again. Of course it was. This was the first time he was in bed with a guy. And as long as Laurent stayed the night, they'd do it all over again in the morning. He pushed his ass against Beast's groin, but Beast had other plans. He pulled away slightly, only to push Laurent's ass higher up and slide his cock between the lovely thighs.

Laurent's balls dragged over Beast's dick, and he groaned with pleasure, smiling when he looked down between Laurent's buttocks, at the pink ring of his hole. He couldn't rush things too much with Laurent being so inexperienced, but one day he would slide his dick between the peachy halves.

Trailing his hand up Laurent's spine again, he buried it in the thick, wavy hair, making Laurent look back at him. At the same time, he moved his fingertip around the pucker, his dick so heavy and pulsing that for a moment he itched to ignore his worries and convince Laurent to go all the way. The boy would surely not protest, but the idea of exploiting his innocence after protecting him from a predator earlier didn't sit well with Beast. He was not that kind of man. He cared for Laurent and he wanted to let him explore less invasive activities first. He would be patient and tease Laurent until he was addicted to Beast's body and the pleasures it could give him.

Laurent's eyes went a bit wider at the intimate touch, and the tension was obvious in his shoulders, but he didn't protest. Was he scared to? Did he want to go with whatever his more experienced partner saw fit? Or did he want to be touched there but was nervous?

"No? How about this?" Beast whispered, leaning down and licking the sensitive flesh with the tip of his tongue. It cost him the pressure against his cock but the rush of doing this exciting yet somehow illicit thing to sweet Laurent was making his head pulse with pleasure. The valley between Laurent's buttocks provided him with the perfect view of the pretty face that immediately flushed so dark it became almost purple.

"Oh, good God!" Laurent watched him so intensely his neck would surely hurt tomorrow from twisting back. "Is… is that a thing people do? I don't even know anymore what is hell and what is heaven."

Beast laughed and flipped Laurent over. He himself slid his knees to the floor so rapidly it made them hurt, but that was a small price to pay for getting his face buried between Laurent's open thighs. He pulled him to the very edge of the bed and sucked on the soft skin of his sac, tasting the fresh sweat and arousal as he trailed lower, intent of having his fill of the boy.

"You taste good," he said, digging the tip of his tongue against the tightly squeezed pucker.

Seeing Laurent's toes curl and twitch at the edge of the bed made Beast forget about the scars on his body. If he could make this beautiful boy spasm and lose his mind, he was good enough. The legs in front of him opened wider, and it was all the invitation he needed to alternate between drilling his tongue against the twitching hole and licking up the soft balls, then gliding all the way to the underside of Laurent's dripping cock. He wanted Laurent incoherent, moaning, and on legs so soft he wasn't able to stand.

The salty musk of Laurent's body was just the nectar Beast craved. The fulfilment of years when he wouldn't approach anyone online for fear of being just a novelty, and without anyone who would be worthy of pursuing in real life. Laurent was the answer to his most secret needs, pliant and wonderful, and trusting in a way that made Beast wish to cherish him, even if his mind was filled with the dirtiest of thoughts.

Greedy like a wolf at the end of winter, he devoured Laurent's flesh, taking his young cock all the way into his throat. After years of celibacy, he managed to only choke a few times. He sucked on Laurent's balls and played them in his hand. He kissed, bit, and sucked on Laurent's trembling thighs. He spread his buttocks wide and ate Laurent's ass with so much dedication the hole softened to him within minutes. With his tongue deep inside the tight channel, with the tip teasing the wrinkled flesh, he imagined burying his cock in Laurent's ass and fucking it until Beast came, filling Laurent's hole with his cum. They would look at one another, and Laurent would then understand that no other man could ever give him the things Beast could.

He was so immersed in the mixture of fantasy and reality that the first spurt of seed splashed over his cheek before he could suck the cock back into his mouth.

He'd only drank Laurent twice so far and already he felt addicted to his taste.

The boy panted and squirmed so beautifully, grasping at the sheets and moaning without shame. His thighs were still trembling when he finished, but considering the dazed look in his eyes, he wasn't all there yet. What were his fantasies and thoughts? Did he also dream about how Beast's cock would feel between his buttocks instead of his tongue?

Fired up, Beast jumped on the bed, caging Laurent with his body. Unable to keep still with his balls aching and cock hard, he pulled his teeth over Laurent's neck, massaging the flesh in his mouth and sucking on it.

Laurent's thighs closed around his sides and it was the sweetest embrace. "You're too good to me," he whispered between one whimper and another, and his fingers started tracing the lumpy skin of Beast's shoulder.

Beast was so horny at this point he barely registered the words. "N-no... I want to. You're so wonderful. So sweet," he murmured, rolling his hips against Laurent and moaning when his dick rubbed against Laurent's stomach.

Laurent wrapped one of his arms around Beast's neck and kissed what was left of his left ear, but it was hard to worry about how Laurent perceived him when the soft, skilful fingers dove between their bodies and reached Beast's painfully erect cock. "And you're inhumanly patient."

Beast groaned and found his lips, pushing his arms under Laurent's back to close him in a tight embrace of hot, sweaty bodies. He shut his eyes, floating on the rapids of lust as Laurent's hand worked his cock, using the precum as lubrication. Any capacity for thought was evaporating from Beast's brain, and he just pushed on, riding the tight fist until it milked him dry.

He was still panting after his brain-melting orgasm when the thought of his cum all over Laurent's hand and stomach gave one more pang of arousal to his empty balls. Only now he truly knew how much he missed sex. How much he missed having someone in his bed but also being cherished and appreciated not just as a great leader within the club, a good friend, and a responsible man, but as a lover worth touching and kissing. By allowing him so close, Laurent replaced a piece within Beast that'd been broken for so many years.

"I did it!" Laurent exclaimed joyfully, as if with his looks it was a challenge to make a man come.

Beast laughed, hugging the slim body tightly against him. Unable to hold himself up as energy drained out of him rapidly, he rolled off Laurent and dropped to the mattress next to him, completely and utterly spent. "It's a miracle I didn't finish faster..."

Laurent rolled over to his stomach to look at Beast when they talked, and it was yet another spark of glee for Beast. His new lover didn't shy away from looking at him. Flushing furiously, Laurent covered the lower part of his face with both hands. "That thing you did with your tongue?" he whispered. "I really do know nothing about anything."

Beast burst out with laughter and pulled Laurent closer, grinning widely. "Oh, which one of the things I did with my tongue?" he asked, pressing a soft kiss to Laurent's lips. He couldn't stop himself from smelling the warm skin again. The boy's scent was even more intense now, even sexier.

Laurent laughed and hid his face in the crook of Beast's neck. "I'm still all… tingly down there." Laurent pulled Beast's hand to his ass, and that gesture of invitation made Beast groan with need to make Laurent come all over again.

"I want to do *everything* to you down there," he declared, staring at Laurent in wonderment. He couldn't believe this just happened. He made such a lovely boy come, not once but twice. And he wasn't done pleasing him yet either.

His heart soared when it turned out Laurent was thinking along the same lines. "Can we do things again in the morning?"

Chapter 17 - Laurent

Beast's cock was a thing of beauty, and the ink on it only enhanced the effect it had on Laurent. Not that Laurent could see it when half of it was buried in his mouth.

He'd woken up pressed tightly against Beast's chest, and for a moment he'd thought he was still dreaming, but then Beast gave his thigh a little pinch and Laurent was definitely not asleep.

As the master of his own destiny, he'd dipped his head under the covers, and the rest was history. The throbbing flesh in his mouth was about to release its juices, and Laurent would eagerly swallow them all, listening to the glorious sound of Beast's groans above.

Beast's thighs trembled on both sides of his head. Unmarked by scars and hairy, they squeezed and tickled Laurent's bare skin each time he sucked harder or twisted his lips around the girth in his mouth. Before coming here, he'd never even considered putting his mouth on another man's prick, but Beast's whole body had such a nice, clean scent, with just a bit of tang from last night's sweat that he physically longed to return the favor and offer his lips in return for the care shown to him last night.

Seeing such a big, powerful man lose control bit by bit, to have the strong body struggle for breath because of Laurent's doing, was such a treat he wanted this to last longer, regardless of the slight ache in his jaw.

Beast slid his hand into Laurent's hair when the first spasms of release hit his body, and he kept Laurent's head in place as the tangy, slightly bitter-tasting sperm filled Laurent's mouth. He wanted everything Beast could give him, but crossing the line he'd put between them before yesterday had Laurent frantic with thoughts of what it all meant and how their friendship would change. He had no frame of reference to help him on this new journey, but at least Beast was there to hold his hand.

After Beast's prick did its last twitch in Laurent's mouth, Laurent slowly pulled away and put his cheek on the strong, muscular stomach he'd yearned to touch for so long, only to conclude it wasn't enough and proceed to kissing the stiff muscle and scarred skin that made for such a beautiful landscape.

It felt as if he'd transcended to another plane of existence where desire was free to be expressed and where he was allowed to offer his devotion however he wished to.

Beast was breathing hard, and every time he took a deep inhale of air, Laurent's head was pushed up, only to sink down when Beast exhaled. Strong hands stroked Laurent's hair, playing with the strands so very gently. There was nothing clumsy or brutish about the caresses, and Laurent felt himself smiling as he nuzzled the scarred skin on Beast's upper stomach.

"How was it?" asked Beast in the end.

Laurent snorted and crawled up from under the covers, resting on top of Beast. "I loved it. How was it for you? I know it might have been a bit too forward, but I don't know if there is such a thing at this point. I have a newfound joy in your body. and I wish I could never leave this bed."

Beast stared at him for several seconds, gently brushing his fingers along Laurent's jaw, but then smiled so wide it pulled on the scarred skin on the half of his face that had been burned worse, making his expression adorably crooked and roguish. Even his eyes were smiling, a brilliant blue softened by the faint lines around them. Laurent had never seen Beast so happy.

"Well, there's no reason to be coy with a lover. It's good to communicate," Beast said in the end before rolling them over, only to press a kiss to Laurent's temple.

Laurent gasped, suddenly trapped under Beast's impressive weight. It was glorious to lie naked under a man. Under Beast. Everything they'd done yesterday was like a dream full of surprises and exciting, obscene things Laurent never even imagined. Yet when Beast made them come to life, all at once they seemed the fulfilment of all Laurent's desires and hopes.

And if they were to communicate, he might as well say what he thought. "I like to be under you." Laurent wrapped his arms around Beast's neck and pulled him down for a kiss.

Beast's breath caught, and he cradled Laurent's head in the crook of his elbow, making him feel almost impossibly safe from any and all harm. "And I like you under me."

Laurent angled his face to kiss Beast's neck. The scars weren't the prettiest of sights, but there was something extremely intimate about being allowed to touch them that Laurent wanted to cherish Beast's body all the more. Even the most gruesome one—the hole and twisted flesh that remained of Beast's left ear—did not disgust Laurent in any way. He simply felt bad that Beast had had to go through so much suffering and had not even managed to save his mother.

"I'm afraid I have to go pee though. Or is that too forward?"

Beast broke into laughter and gave Laurent a brief hug before releasing him. "No. Go on and then come back to me before I'm bored of waiting."

Laurent rolled out of bed with as much dignity as he could muster, since he knew he was being shamelessly ogled. He stretched in front of the window to prolong the moment.

"I am already getting used to this. You might need to cut me off if you want to get rid of me," Beast said, laughing.

Laurent walked to the door backwards, just so that he could watch Beast for a bit longer. Stretched out and smiling, his wonderful lover was a sight Laurent would gladly have etched to the back of his eyelids. "It would leave me wounded," he said in the end and wouldn't let Beast answer, walking out. But the moment he closed the door and spun around to rush for the bathroom, he faced Knight, who stood at the end of the corridor, staring at him with a smirk.

Laurent stilled, feeling needles of embarrassment prickling at his skin.

"Hello. I was wondering if I shouldn't come back later. Lucky me you two are done," Knight said.

Laurent took half a breath to assess the situation and fled back into the bedroom, pressing his back against the door and staring at Beast, still trying to process what just happened.

Beast frowned. "What's wrong?" he asked, rolling off the bed and approaching him in quick strides.

Laurent hid his face in his hands with a groan. Back in more innocent times he used to not be much bothered by another man seeing him naked, but his opinions on the matter changed since he found out he was not an aberration and many more men shared his proclivities. "Knight is here," he said flatly.

Beast shut his eyes and took a deep breath. "Do you want to talk to him or stay here?"

Laurent rubbed his face, all too aware that the paint around his eyes was an utter mess. "It's fine. I just need my pants." He gave himself two more seconds to gather his thoughts, and then picked up his clothes and dressed. Beast in turn seemed to not care about Knight seeing his nakedness.

"Won't you…?"

Beast growled. "If he thinks it's fine to listen to me having sex in my own house, then he can deal with seeing my dick. Come," he said, offering Laurent his hand.

"But I don't want him to see it," Laurent whispered and wrapped his arms around Beast's waist. The man was so big it was giving him shivers.

Beast grinned. "We're like brothers. He's seen me naked a million times. No reason to be jealous."

Laurent sighed deeply, but grabbed Beast's hand in the end and followed him into the corridor. Knight waved at them from the sofa, grinning like a madman. He wiggled his eyebrows. "I'm glad to see you two have made up."

"You could have left a note, you dirty spy," Beast said, pulling Laurent closer and embracing him with one arm.

Laurent bit his lips so as not to smile too widely. Yes, Knight. We had sex yesterday. And today. And it was amazing.

Knight grinned. "I'm not a spy! I actually came over 'cause I noticed Laurent was missing, and I figured you'd like to know. But looks like that mystery's solved."

Beast pulled his teeth over his bottom lip and played with Laurent's hair. "Yeah, we needed to talk some things out."

"I bet there was a lot of talking involved," Knight said with a straight face. Beast opened his mouth to answer, but Knight raised both his hands and continued. "I'm not trying to be a shit. You know I love you, man. Good for you. Good to see you finally unblocked."

Laurent wrapped his arms around Beast's waist, so unbearably comforted by the protection the heavy arm offered. Everything he was anxious about seemed to disappear when they touched this way.

"What about me?" Laurent demanded. "Good for me too."

Knight burst out laughing but offered an apologetic gesture when Beast made a face at him. "I know, I know. You have to teach him everything you know. It's just too cute. Did this guy hide under a rock all this time? What do you say, Laurent? How has nobody snatched you for themselves before, with a face like that?"

Laurent smirked, even though the memory of Fane soured his good mood. "They tried. But it is I who decides who to welcome in my bed," he said, but it fell a bit flat, because he didn't actually own a bed.

Beast petted the top of his head while Knight looked between them in amusement. "Good choice then. Anyway, I'll be off and leave you two lovebirds to it."

Beast grunted. "Knight, can this stay between the three of us for now?"

Laurent paid attention to the words, unsure if they actually bothered him or if they were a relief. He wasn't exactly sure how to navigate the minefield of social interactions and what the time spent with Beast in bed actually meant, so it was for the better if he could take his time. Hasn't freedom been what he wanted from his pact with the devil in the first place? He wanted to never again be bound to someone.

Knight nodded. "Sure, no problem. It's all just good fun as long as everyone's happy." The last sentence seemed to be somehow aimed at Laurent, as if it was a question.

"Yes!" Laurent was quick to say. "I would rather take time figuring things out without people asking questions. Especially if that's what Beast wants, too."

Knight gave a deep sigh and ran his fingers through his hair. "Oh, man. I wish Jordan was like you."

Beast put his hand on Laurent's nape. "You know my opinion, brother. But it's your woman and your choices."

Knight slowly retreated to the door. "You know, I'm starting to agree with you. I hate it when people can't make up their goddamn mind."

Laurent considered if he should say anything, but his tongue itched, and it wasn't like Knight could get violent when Laurent was under Beast's arm, under his protection. "You have to excuse me, but isn't it you who engages in dirty deeds with other people? Both men and women…"

Knight rolled his eyes. "Yeah, but she knows that we're not exclusive. Come on. *She* can't make up her mind if she's fine with that or not. No one can tell me to do something I never agreed on."

Laurent nodded slowly, trying to organize the information in his mind. He'd noticed that the relationships between people in the club were nothing like what he knew from his time, so he tried to take everything as it came.

Beast let go of Laurent and came up to a cupboard. He poured himself some juice and shrugged. "That's the problem, isn't it? She likes the idea of a guy like you but still tries to change you. Maybe that's her fantasy? Domesticating you."

Knight snorted. "Fuck knows. She's got another think coming if you're right. Anyway, I'm off. Take good care of my friend," he said, winking Laurent's way.

Laurent felt himself blush a bit and leaned against the edge of the sofa, left to his own thoughts and the glorious sight of Beast's strong, naked body. "I would never try to domesticate you." He hoped to have understood the connotations of the phrase correctly. Knight's anger seemed to be about Jordan trying to tie him down, and it reminded him of Mr. Barnave and having to always do as he was told, never being free to decide about the things that mattered.

Beast's gaze swiped over Laurent, and for once he wasn't sure whether he'd said the right thing after all. Knight tapped his fingers against the door and opened it, disappearing from sight after a word of goodbye and leaving Laurent and Beast in a void of silence.

Laurent brushed his hair over his shoulder. "Did I misunderstand the meaning of the word? The context is of not chaining someone to yourself, is it not? And I have noticed that liberty is the biggest value for all Kings of Hell."

"Well, I can't tell you what you're supposed to want for yourself," Beast said somewhat sharply.

Laurent paused, giving it some thought. "I believe nothing is as valuable as freedom." He glanced to the door that Beast always kept locked. Knight was allowed in there. Would Laurent now be too? He didn't dare ask just yet.

Beast downed a whole glass of juice. "I'm hungry. Do you want to go out and have breakfast somewhere?"

Laurent nodded. Preparations took much longer than usual, because showering turned out to be much more pleasurable together. Then the paint on Laurent's eyes wouldn't come off, so he made a detour to Nao's, which also provided him the chance to stop in his own room and change into fresh clothes that Beast would like so much better.

It was fine for him to take a bit of time, because Beast wanted to go feed Hound anyway, but the truth about last night's events tickled at the back of Laurent's throat when he spoke to Nao. She was very curious whether he managed to find a partner, but he tried to tell as few lies as possible.

Once he was done with his errands and went downstairs in search of Beast, he felt thoroughly refreshed and like himself again in the clothes Beast had chosen for him the first time they went shopping together. Laurent did pin his priceless brooch to the lapel of his leather jacket though, and he was happy to find it suited this new modern style just fine.

He was halfway to the billiard room when an old man stumbled into the corridor, cutting off his way. It took Laurent several seconds to realize that the mass of matted gray hair and the curled shoulders belonged to none other than King, who'd sported bright golden hair just last evening.

Martina followed him out, dressed in last night's clothes and with traces of makeup on her cheeks. Her hair was a bit of a mess, but despite the copious amount of alcohol she consumed at every party, she did not seem in a shape nearly as bad as King was.

"Please, you can just dye it. Lots of men do that," Martina cooed, stepping back when her man moaned, rubbing his forehead. "Are you gonna be sick again? Do you want some mint tea? Coffee?" she tried, but King dismissed all her efforts with rude, rapid gestures.

Martina eventually noticed Laurent and sighed, crossing her arms under her breasts. "It's fine. He had a bit too much to drink last night."

Only then did it occur to King that he was being watched, and pale, wild eyes spat poison at Laurent from behind the silvery, tangled mane. "You. Come here, you little fucker."

Martina approached, trying to calm him down, but after a few dismissive words, she must have had enough and rushed the other way, barefoot and with high heels in hand.

King didn't even move like a human being anymore, stumbling against the wall like a wounded wolf that had lost too much blood. Laurent didn't dare move when he approached, hunched over like the most pitiful drunks of Brecon in Laurent's time. In 2017 wives weren't keen on helping their men at all cost. Martina was technically not King's wife, but it still seemed to Laurent that she was, by common law at least.

"Get in," King urged, pushing Laurent into the open room, which reeked of liquor and sweat.

Laurent smiled nervously. He'd seen the men sometimes call each other 'fucker' and laugh about it, but the tone of King's words didn't make it seem like he was in a playful mood. "How can I help, Mr. King?"

"*Mr. King*, my ass," King hissed and pushed at Laurent so hard he almost landed on the dirty mattress covered only by a sheet that was halfway on the floor anyway. "Look at me. What have you done?" he asked, pushing back to reveal an earthy complexion and dull, blotchy eyes.

He looked like a badly aged man.

"I?" Laurent stumbled away, assessing his chances in case he needed to run. He was wary not to let King approach him close enough to be at arm's length. "Are you just tired after too much drink, sir?"

King gritted his teeth, ferocious like a sickly wolf out for food. "Don't you fucking play dumb, little boy. I'm drained. I don't feel like myself. It's like the connection I share with my son has been cut. Do you want to starve me out before he turns thirty three?"

Laurent licked his lips, hiding the sense of satisfaction at King not being able to steal from Beast. The guilt that accompanied him last night evaporated in the sense of achievement when he realized that he unknowingly aided his lover in getting back at his secret tormentor. "What happens when he turns thirty three, sir? And I don't understand how your current condition is my fault."

King massaged his temples and suddenly looked up. It was as if a bulb had suddenly lit up in his head, shedding a new light on everything. "Did you fuck him?"

Laurent stilled, and his face went hot. He quickly pulled at the collar of his T-shirt but it wouldn't hide the love bites on his neck. "Excuse me?"

"You did, didn't you?" whispered King, suddenly dashing at Laurent and pushing him down on the mattress with surprising force. Putrid spirit-infused breath blew into Laurent's face, choking him. "I knew it. This has never happened since his accident. I was never so... drained. You need to break things up, right now."

Laurent swallowed. "I… I need to keep him here until his birthday. That is my job to do, and he is so determined that I have to grasp at any means necessary." What he had to grasp really was King's trust in him, because he was beginning to understand that there was something he was missing about King's pact. All Laurent knew was that in exchange for keeping the Kings of Hell here, King could somehow obtain Beast's life force, and that this effect was amplified when Beast suffered. Would King's pact end when Beast turned thirty three? "Once I am free of my obligation, I will leave him immediately. If I find another way to distract him, I will do that as well, but he is very set on convincing everyone to move."

King hissed through his teeth and raised his hand, as if intending to strike Laurent, but in the end he spun around and started pacing with his head in his hands. "Fuck. Fuck, fuck. He is working behind my back, isn't he? Are the others supporting him?"

"The others are… not entirely against the idea." Laurent quickly stood up from the mattress, eager to once again be out of reach. He hated what King was doing to Beast with all his heart, but he would not give voice to those thoughts when it was much more advantageous to have the man believe Laurent was on his side. This way, once Laurent fulfilled the terms of his own pact, in just a few months' time, he could expose the man for what he was, or at least encourage Beast to leave this place behind. "But last night convinced me that if I stay in Beast's good graces, I will be able to influence him on the issue very easily."

King swallowed, watching him from under the bushy gray eyebrows. Laurent had heard of men turning gray overnight if sorrow struck, but it was the first time he'd actually seen the truth behind those anecdotes. Well, there was Gray as well, but this again was something others told him of. Seeing the dashing, golden god that King used to be only hours prior turned into a man who looked his age gave Laurent shudders.

"So what, you fuck my son to distract him? Is that what you want to say? Is he thinking of leaving the club before August 29th?"

If King needed Beast here for his birthday, he wouldn't actually hurt him until then… would he? But then again, Laurent couldn't encourage Beast to leave yet. He needed to think about himself and the life he was offered in exchange of fulfilling a contract that only lasted for a few months. He refused to go back to a life of servitude and poverty, and even worse, to a blood-soaked bedroom with Fane's cooling body. In 2017, he would work hard until he saved up for his eye surgery, and he would earn his own money.

Since he was twelve years old, he'd always had to depend on himself only. He was lucky that Mr. Barnave wasn't a cruel master, because some servants he'd known had been far less fortunate, but the man still worked him all day, every day. No matter how sweet Beast's kisses were, Laurent had to rely on himself when considering his future. Beast would be the addition to make his heart flutter and his body writhe in pleasure, but everything needed to be done on Laurent's terms, and he would not compromise on that matter.

"Yes, he is. But if you leave it in my hands, I will make sure nothing changes for the next four months." It was even less than that now, and once August was over, Laurent would be free to pursue an independent life in 2017, with Beast at his side on whatever terms they decided on. "He likes me a lot."

King spat on the floor, and Laurent tried not to squirm at the sight. King didn't look much like a king anymore in sweaty clothes and so sleep-deprived. He stumbled at the wall and dropped to his haunches. "Of course he does. He just got laid for the first time in ten fucking years. Maybe this energy high of his will pass once he gets used to fucking again. No, that's right. It should be fine. We need to keep him here at all cost."

Laurent rubbed his neck, uncomfortable with the way King spoke of his and Beast's intimacy. It was a delight to be cherished, not a disposable event. And yet, it still gave Laurent a tingle of satisfaction to think that all the carnal pleasures they shared had Beast so elated King wasn't able to drain any of his youthful vigor.

"I'm sure that things will ease in the matter, sir," Laurent said, even though he hoped King would forever remain estranged from Beast's life force, and end up shriveled like a prune. A man who abused his son so ruthlessly deserved no compassion. To think that even last night, during Beast's celebratory party, King had found ways to bring Beast down, just to feast on his vitality.

King nodded and rubbed his face. "Okay. Continue, but don't overdo it. I'm not gonna go vegan in order to survive until then, you hear me? Keep him just pleased enough. Be mean every day, just a little bit. It helps if you say something about him being a bother, or about the scars. This makes his mood drop, even if the actual words are innocent and can be excused, you get me?"

Laurent despised the advice with all his heart. "Absolutely, sir. I understand. Being close to him will allow me many opportunities. But please, you need to make sure you don't reveal to anyone that you know of me and him. He might want to back out, and that would only make matters worse in terms of keeping him here." Laurent's whole chest hurt so much he wanted to retch. King was evil on par with Fane to torture his own son this way for years for no other reason but his own gain.

King licked his lips and nodded. "Fine. But I'll be watching you. Better not get all sentimental over him."

Laurent shook his head, and decided to reveal something about himself to ease King's mind. "No, sir. I am here to obtain freedom, and I will do everything in my power to get that. The blood you saw on me that first night is testament to my conviction." He hoped it sounded ominous enough to get King off his back.

King watched him for several moments before dragging himself back to his feet. "Good. Keep that in mind, because if you breach your contract and the devil doesn't rip you apart, I will." He blinked, touching the door with a contemplative expression on his face. "Oh, and on the eve of his birthday, I could fuck you and make sure he finds out. That would make him really lose it." With that, King opened the door and walked out, leaving Laurent numb. What in all hells was that last suggestion? King hadn't even asked if that was something Laurent wanted to partake in.

He didn't.

He plopped down on the mattress but jutted back to his feet when he felt something sticky touch his hand. He never expected the feat asked of him by the demon to be an easy one. He'd anticipated he'd have to fight for his life, or walk through a world full of peril, but he could have never predicted the emotional turmoil that had already caused him so much grief.

He didn't get the peace to clear his mind before venturing outside to find Beast, with King cursing loudly somewhere in the corridor. The carefree laughter that came next made all of Laurent's skin explode with tangible memories of last night. He stood up immediately and approached the open door.

"Is that a new fashion statement?" asked Beast. "Gray can pull it off only because he's twenty six. It doesn't really compliment someone your age."

Laurent looked out into the hallway to see King violently push at Beast's chest. "Who are you to criticize anyone's looks?" he hissed, but someone else's laughter down the corridor seemed aimed at him anyway.

Laurent rushed out of the smelly chamber, eager to lead Beast away from King as fast as possible. "Ready," he announced with a wide smile.

The blue eyes brightened, making Laurent's whole body ache for touch, and Beast crooked his head to indicate the direction of the main exit. "Sorry, King, I'm taking Laurent to see the eye doctor. Maybe ask Nao what to do about your hair. There is probably some coconut oil and cinnamon treatment for it," he said, walking a thin line between mockery and advice. Nao liked natural cosmetics, so he might have as well been serious.

King snarled like a wild animal and left the room, slamming the door behind him. As soon as he was gone, all the people in the room—with a notable exception of Gray—erupted with laughter and chatter. But Laurent and Beast wouldn't be staying. Only when they were alone did Laurent remember what Beast had said.

"Eye doctor? Weren't we going out for breakfast?"

Beast shrugged and walked through the billiard room, which was now occupied by Rev and Fox, who played in the company of scantily-clad women. "Yes, but we should go to the eye doctor next. I called the clinic, and an appointment opened up for today, because someone couldn't make it."

"I… um… when did you manage to do that? I mean, King paid me a bit of money for sorting out the documents that Jordan messed up, but I doubt I have collected enough for the surgery." His heart drummed as they walked into the garage.

Beast stretched as they approached his big bike, with the scary-looking hounds at the front. "Oh, you were taking a bit long, so I thought I'd make myself useful. And don't worry about the money. I've got this," he said, looking at Laurent with such warmth it was enough to melt the frost of unease around Laurent's mistrustful heart.

He squeezed Beast's hand after making sure no one was around to see it. "I don't know if I can accept an offer this generous. I've already taken so much from you." And wasn't he supposed to fend for himself? Find independence? Why did it feel so good to be cared for then? For someone to freely offer protection and affection?

Beast shrugged, also glancing in all directions before rubbing Laurent's hands with his big, warm palms. "You should accept it. I promise this isn't... a transaction, or anything like that. I just really want you to be healthy again."

Laurent buried his face between Beast's pecs, unable to explain just how much it meant to him. The only reason Mr. Barnave ever wanted Laurent healthy was to have him useful. There had never been anyone who cared for Laurent's well-being just for the sake of it. Maybe his grandmother.

"Thank you," he whispered against the soft fabric of Beast's longsleeve and sighed in relief when the thick arms embraced him in return.

Chapter 18 - Beast

"Do you think he just saw my last name somewhere and that's why he used it? Because there is seriously no record of a Laurent Mercier," Knight said, his voice like the buzz of a fly by Beast's ear. After three glorious weeks of having Laurent fall asleep in his arms, for all he cared, Laurent could have fallen from the heavens just for him. And he was here to stay, if Beast had any say in it.

He exhaled, trying to keep his cool, because otherwise he'd lose to Knight again. Slowly, he leaned over the pool table and arched his body, watching the balls and mentally planning their trajectories before finally making one precise hit. The white ball rolled over the table, knocking into a blue one. Beast's breath caught when he watched the ball first crash onto the edge, and then run across the surface, all the way to the hole in the corner. He exhaled loudly when it fell in.

"Beast, are you even listening to me?" Knight asked, and Beast wasn't even sure if his friend really wanted to know the answer to those endless history questions or if he wanted to distract Beast.

"You're overthinking it. He can't be from here. How would he have found out about you? It must be a coincidence. There have to be other families with the same surname as yours," he said, seeking another ball to approach, and he fought the smile widening on his face on its own when he thought back to when they'd come here with Laurent the other night and he taught his boy all about how to play pool. Laurent's back had fit so well against Beast's chest…

"Well, okay, there are, but if I knew his lineage, I could track who he descends from, and that could give us some answers," Knight insisted, frowning as he leaned over the pool table. He lowered his voice. "I get it, all you care about now is fucking his brains out, but what if he's involved in something that will come back to bite us all in the ass?"

Beast missed his mark and hissed in exasperation when the white ball only grazed his chosen ball, spinning off and almost falling into a hole itself. "He's just a boy. What could he possibly do to us? Someone just dropped him off here, and that's that," he said sharply. He didn't want to discuss this anymore. Laurent had many issues and his past was an enigma, but he was intelligent, and eager to learn, and so sweet Beast wanted to be with him all the time.

In the first week after Laurent's surgery, he needed a lot of care despite the healing process going smoothly. He'd been released on the day of the operation and has been doing very well after the initial shock of his vision turning blue before his eye got used to its new state. Beast was more than happy to provide him with all the care he needed, applying medicine to Laurent's healing eye several times a day and reading to him, so that he wouldn't be too bored. It'd been weeks since, and Laurent was slowly preparing for the final surgery—on his other eye. This was what Beast needed to occupy himself with, not some genealogy bullshit.

Knight glanced to the small radio they had playing on the windowsill when it started buzzing strangely. "Fucking hell! Does this always have to happen in this place?" He groaned and walked up to it. "I heard you're going to a job tomorrow with Joker and Gray. You sure you guys don't need more backup?"

"No, you know big groups draw too much attention. I don't want any shit happening during this run. The cargo is too valuable," Beast said, watching his friend scoot down by the socket. He didn't tell Laurent about the long trip yet, unwilling to worry his boy about something that had to be done anyway.

Knight examined the socket as if he were a nose and eye doctor checking on someone's sinuses, but got back to the pool table, walking around it to find a good position. "Well, at least if our dear partner coughs up a decent sum of money, we could have a look at repairing some of the plumbing downstairs. The wall in the basement is so damp I'm sure we have a leak somewhere. Don't give me that look! I know you wanna move, but it's not gonna happen overnight, so let's work with what we've got here."

Beast exhaled. His knowledge of electricity ended on flipping switches in the fuse box and trying not to touch electricals with damp hands. "You know, with fewer people in the house, maybe you could look into the cables? Switch the power off in parts of the building, or something?"

Knight leaned on the cue stick. "Sure. I could have Laurent move somewhere else for as long as you're away and have a good look at the wiring in your apartment. It drives me nuts that even in the most recently renovated parts of the building the electricity is still unstable."

Beast scowled. "Nah, I'm fine. Any problems in my apartment are just temporary. No need to stress him out. He's been through a lot already," he said, watching the colorful dots on the green background of the table. "By the way, if we could have anything and everything in that new clubhouse, what would you think is most important?" he asked.

The last property viewing had only gone downhill after Laurent lied to the realtor, but the longer Beast was with the boy, the more he understood that maybe his approach hadn't been all that great. The moment he actually asked Laurent what was up, things between them smoothed out. There was no reason for this to be any different. If he showed interest in what his brothers wanted, they would treat the matter more personally.

Knight rubbed his permanently scruffy chin, for a long time saying nothing. "If—don't laugh—if we had classy bathrooms, with like mirrors and stuff, we'd get more chicks through the doors."

Beast stared at him, momentarily startled. "Oh, okay. Yeah, we might think of that. Have a place where hangarounds could put on additional layers of face paint," he said, chuckling when Knight pretended to toss the cue stick at him.

"It works. Jordan would totally love that kind of shit. She'd bring her friends over then, because as of right now all of them think the place is foul."

Beast groaned. Lately, even Jordan's name gave him a shudder. That woman wasn't worthy of Knight's attention, so it was particularly uncomfortable to see Knight stressing over her opinions. "Yeah, if that's gonna keep you happy."

Knight smirked and pointed to his crotch. "When she's happy, I'm happy."

Beast wasn't *happy* to hear that. Now that he had Laurent in his life, it was somehow easier to judge Jordan too. Not all pretty people needed to be complete and utter wastes of space. Despite his model-worthy appearance, Laurent remained a modest, sweet guy, who always had smiles for Beast. Being with him changed so much. It was as if Beast was slowly re-learning how to live. No matter how much he respected and loved his brothers, they couldn't give him the sense of completion he experienced when Laurent approved of him. It was a completely different kind of relationship, and not just because it involved sex—as glorious as it was—but because for the first time in so many years Beast could express a part of himself that remained locked away for too long.

Knight pointed a finger at Beast with a grin. "I know that smile. Someone's dick's getting a lot of attention." He wiggled his eyebrows, but a dash of footsteps and voices from the main room made Beast attentive as well. It was time to ask more people what they wanted from a future clubhouse.

"Yeah, well, I won't deny it. The other Mr. Mercier is giving me a lot of attention," he said, leaving the cue stick in the stand.

They both went for the door, and Knight slapped Beast's arm, not knowing it was a particularly sore spot when it came to the burned nerve endings. Beast had to take a deep breath to ignore it.

"Don't talk about him like that, or it's gonna feel like you're fucking my little brother."

Beast snorted. "I don't know. Maybe he is. Any long-lost relatives?" he teased as they entered the common room with its red walls. The low buzz of the sound system being adjusted meant Lizzy was at it again. He sat on the edge of the stage with a notebook, while the band's bass player worked on the electronics.

"Ew. You're suggesting I've had incestuous thoughts."

Beast raised his finger at Knight. "No."

Knight laughed out loud, looking like he had no care in the world when he waved at Fox and Joker who sat on the sofa rolling joints. Fortunately for everyone, the topic died the moment they both spotted Laurent.

He sat curled up in a leather armchair, reading a book in the glow of the spotlight. The moment his eyes shot up and met Beast's gaze, the wide smile that bloomed on the handsome face made Beast's heart skip a beat.

For a moment, he was so focused on Laurent's eyes that he almost walked into the coffee table, but fortunately reason came back quickly enough, and he adjusted his steps, taking a seat in a chair. "What's the book?" he asked, reaching out to the table and picking up a small bottle of Coke from a tray of drinks.

Laurent showed him the cover which had a lightning bolt hitting a kite. "It's a book on the history of electricity. Knight's promised to show me some basics in practice once I'm done with it."

Beast squinted at Knight. "Yes to that." Knight would never be disloyal and try to snatch Laurent for himself, but after such a long time alone, even the slightest possibility of losing Laurent to someone else felt like encroaching danger.

Knight spread his arms with a groan. "I'll be showing him how to connect some cables, not checking out his socket."

Joker spat some of the beer he was drinking back into the bottle, laughing so loudly Beast wanted to smack him. And worst of all, Laurent glanced their way, clearly confused and not getting the subtext of Knight's joke. Well, fuck. At least Joker and Fox were straight unless completely drunk.

"I'm just saying."

Laurent put away his book. "I learned how to cook popcorn today. Would you like to see?" He smiled and already got up from the seat.

Beast watched him move, quick-footed and graceful like a gazelle. The skinny jeans made Laurent's buttocks look so fine Beast wished to just pull them down and eat Laurent's ass. Were he drunk enough in the dark, perhaps he might have not even cared if people watched it happen.

If he could justify it, he'd stop leaving his room and just fuck Laurent around the clock. He wasn't pushing for anal, too happy with what he was getting so far but considering how much Laurent enjoyed rimming, Beast was sure sooner or later he'd get to slide his dick into that tight pink hole. Better yet, he wanted Laurent to ask him for it.

The sound of the microwave humming in the background distracted him so much he didn't notice someone approaching. A slap to the shoulder made him hiss, and pulled him out of pleasant thoughts so rapidly he wanted to punch the culprit.

"Arms on show today?" King asked and plopped his ass in the armchair Laurent had just vacated. "I hope you always put sunscreen on? You know, for the scars."

Beast forced his hands to stay open and gave King a tight smile. He didn't want to think of the scars on his body when Laurent was here, and he definitely didn't want to be constantly pricked by King's words. They were polite enough and wouldn't seem vicious to the average bystander, but Beast could recognize each and every passive-aggressive note behind them. "I don't need a nanny."

Fox put his feet on the table. "That's right. He's over thirty. If he burns, it's his problem."

King rolled his eyes and opened himself a beer. "Not if it's me who will then have to listen to him moaning about it."

Another fucking empty statement, because Beast never moaned to King about shit like that. And it'd been dark for a while anyway, so sun wouldn't be an issue until morning.

The sound of the microwave humming in the background distracted him. He had many other reasons to *moan* lately, and it made him unreasonably giddy that King had no idea. In fact, King probably thought Beast was chaste as a monk, jerking off each night and watching a rom-com when he felt particularly lonely.

Well, that might have been the case some weeks ago, but now Beast had someone who made his life infinitely better, and he didn't need two girlfriends or a line of hangarounds sucking his dick at parties to prove his masculinity.

"No, he's the kind who suffers in silence," Joker said, making a face and stiffening his arms to imitate someone whose skin was so burnt from the sun they didn't want to move.

This kind of stuff could only be funny to someone who never really experienced similar injuries, but Beast didn't want to spoil everyone's mood because of the things he was much more sensitive to. It was high time to change the topic.

"Joker, if you could have anything in a clubhouse, what would you want?"

"An adult indoor playground," Joker said without even a second's hesitation, leaving everyone silent.

Beast cleared his throat. "Okay. What about you, Fox?"

Fox didn't get to state his opinion, because King's eyes pierced him like two sharp blades. "What is this about? Are you planning to renovate one of the rooms?" he asked tightly, and Beast met his eyes without a flinch.

"The electricity is fucked again."

"Well, maybe Knight should check on it. Again."

Anger bubbled up in Beast's chest. "What is that supposed to mean? It's not his fault this fucking building is shit!"

Knight groaned and leaned back on the sofa with his arms wrapped on his chest. "Sorry, King, but I'm doing my best here, and it always goes to shit in the end. There could be rats eating through cables, dampness in the walls, and all that stuff that's out of my control."

King spread his arms. "Then let's get some fucking cats in here! Doesn't even Disneyworld do that?"

Joker snorted. "This place is no Disneyworld."

Laurent came over with a big smile, and it was as if the sun itself descended into Beast's arms. "I cooked the popcorn." He put a deliciously smelling bowl full of the stuff on the coffee table, but hesitated when he noticed that King had taken his place while he was away. The confusion on the sweet, handsome face made Beast worry that Laurent would just leave to read somewhere else.

Beast briefly swiped his gaze over King's tense jaw and the crow's feet that had deepened recently. He would show the bastard things were looking up for him while King got as gray as a dove. A boost of heat pushed through his fingers, and he pulled Laurent into his lap.

Laurent laughed nervously, but grabbed Beast's arm for support. "Oh," was all he had in him to say when he settled on Beast's thigh, clenching his fingers on the back of Beast's tank top.

Even the girls hanging out in the kitchen looked their way, drawn by the astonished silence.

Joker squinted. "What am I looking at? Is this a rom-com moment?"

Beast licked his lips, for a moment feeling his throat tighten. He never really declared his sexual orientation to his brothers. They'd seen him fuck around with pretty much every type of person, and when Beast had a steady boyfriend one time, he hadn't revealed the depth of their relationship to anyone but Knight. His face flushed slightly, but he met Laurent's eyes and petted the top of his head, slowly giving him a smile.

"Maybe," he said, not even looking away from the warm brown gaze that communicated so much when Laurent was too breathless to talk.

And in a moment that made his heart soar, it was Laurent who leaned forward and gave him a little peck on the lips.

Fox whistled. "That's new."

Joker glanced at Knight. "Guess someone else is working on that socket," he whispered in a purposefully loud way.

Beast kicked him in the shin and pulled Laurent closer, moving his hand over the bare arm, that broke out in goose bumps under his touch. "It's been going on for some time now. I guess it's time to go public. What do you think, Laurent?" he asked, tracing Laurent's chin with his thumb.

Nao drifted from the kitchen all too quickly, and now Beast felt he was the spectacle over which everyone would be eating popcorn. For once, he didn't mind.

"I guess there isn't anything illegal about this, right?" Laurent asked with a shy smile.

Joker slapped his own thigh. "Oh, man! That guy always cracks me up."

Nao smiled and leaned over the back of the chair, massaging King's stiffened shoulders. "So, are you boyfriends?"

Laurent quickly shook his head, making Beast's heart sink. "We are not boys. We are manfriends."

Beast blinked, joining in reflexively when Joker burst out laughing. But he didn't want to put Laurent to shame, so he squeezed his hand and nodded. "Yes, we are manfriends."

King was silent as he let Nao touch him, and despite wanting to see him experience even the smallest defeat, Beast didn't really wish to play a game here. So instead, he focused on Laurent and everyone else, just pretending his father wasn't there. Laurent's fingers played over Beast's nape, and the warm popcorn tasted like victory.

There. A guy like him could have Laurent. A handsome, young sweetie with lips that were anyone's dream. Beast navigated the conversation back to what Fox was looking for in a clubhouse, but then Laurent whispered into his ear, tickling him with the soft hair.

"Can we talk in private?"

Beast's blood turned into hardened resin, radiating sudden worry all over his body. He breathed in the pine scent of Laurent's shampoo and pressed his lips to his fragrant skin, just enjoying the softness of the baby hair close to Laurent's ear. Despite the pleasant warmth that felt so natural to Beast, the timing of Laurent's request felt off, and the blackest of thoughts descended on Beast like a flock of harpies. Could it be that Laurent only went with Beast's earlier declaration because he didn't want to embarrass Beast in front of everyone? Leaving things ambiguous had seemed to serve them both. And for him, it'd been yet another way to make himself believe the thing he shared with Laurent could last. That maybe it could turn into a real relationship someday, but now his whole body was aching from the stress of keeping up a stoic facade for the benefit of the man who never promised him anything.

But Beast wasn't a coward. He'd always faced head-on all the things life threw at him, so this time as well, he gently pushed Laurent off his lap and stood up.

"It's kinda late. Talk to you guys tomorrow." He grabbed Laurent's hand, and Laurent squeezed back, so at least there was that.

They walked the short corridor to the billiards room, and Beast closed the door behind them, forcing his shoulders to relax. A bit of the weight lifted from his heart when Laurent smiled at him. Maybe the thing he wanted to tell Beast wasn't something that would ultimately crush his heart.

"I was thinking…"

Beast took a deep breath, watching Laurent in silence and still holding his hand. Holding? No, Laurent flinched and looked at the hand that Beast unknowingly squeezed a bit too hard.

"That we could maybe expand on… on the things we do together? I know you're busy trying to look for this new place and all that, but I hoped you'd have time…" The brown eyes watched him with so much intensity Beast couldn't look away. He didn't even understand what the question was about, and yet Laurent seemed so happy it was like a siren's call, beckoning him into the warm arms regardless what else lay ahead.

"Expand on... other things," muttered Beast, physically unable to look away from Laurent.

Laurent licked his lips, making Beast instantly focus on them. "Well… With the expertise you've proven in the bedroom so far, I'm certain you know there are other… *things* we could do, right?"

Beast's head spun with images of Laurent spread out under him, and his soft, wonderful ass taking his cock. The long hair on the pillow, Laurent's hands grabbing at Beast's flesh. He saw it all in the innocent expression on Laurent's face, and his brain fried in liquid lust. "There are *so* many things," he said in a low voice, suddenly realizing that maybe Laurent's hesitation whenever Beast suggested progressing their sex life to something more intense could have been the result of him not feeling secure in their relationship. It was so obvious now, Beast wanted to knock himself on the head. He hadn't wanted for it to be common knowledge in the first place, because he worried Laurent would soon walk out on him, leaving him to everyone's pity, but maybe he'd misread the boy's intentions completely.

Laurent leaned in for a hug, and Beast wished to lock the doors, lift him to the pool table, and fuck him right here, even if that would put them at risk of being overheard. The invitation between Laurent's legs throbbed in

Beast's mind like a presence with its own consciousness, and he found it difficult to think of anything else. He loved watching Laurent's come-face. Beautifully flushed, uninhibited in that moment of pleasure, lips trembling, eyes closing. He couldn't wait to see it when his dick was embedded in that tight body.

"Will you show me?"

Beast had no idea what the previous conversation has even been about. He just moved the back of his hand down Laurent's chest, all the way to his crotch, and leaned in, watching Laurent's pupils dilate. "Do you want me to penetrate you?" he asked, just to make sure this wasn't yet another instance of miscommunication, like many before.

Laurent seemed shy about it, hid his face in Beast's chest, but said, "yes."

Beast exhaled, watching the tangle of soft hair pressed between his pecs. As much as he wanted to just throw all worry out the window and do it here, on the pool table, with everyone else listening to how amazing their sex life was, he didn't want anything to spoil the moment. Laurent would be stressed if he knew they could be interrupted, and that would inevitably spoil the experience for him.

"Okay. Let's go home."

Laurent looked up with a small smile and stood on his toes, but still had to pull on Beast's tank top so that their lips could meet. This never got old. Beast grinned into the kiss and hugged Laurent, but the explosive arousal simmering beneath his skin and the sudden urge to just push Laurent against the wall and rub his stiffening cock against the boy had Beast moving.

The walk to the apartment felt like an eternity, even if it couldn't have lasted more than three minutes. Beast's cock got stiff enough to be uncomfortable in the confines of his underwear and jeans, and the moment when he could carelessly open the zipper and have Laurent touch him couldn't come soon enough. With Laurent, even handjobs were exciting.

They didn't talk on the way, and when the right door appeared down the hall, Beast wished he could just teleport himself inside, a thought that became even more pervasive when he put in the wrong code and needed to do it again while his brain fried.

Laurent dispersed the tension with a short laugh, and he slid his fingers under the back of Beast's tank top. "Did you forget it? Are we stranded here?" He punctuated the questions with a kiss to Beast's arm, and Beast couldn't want his dick in Laurent more than now.

"No, I just... I just... oh, there," Beast said triumphantly when the door unlocked, letting them in.

Beast kicked the door shut and picked up Laurent, pulling him close so rapidly he staggered back at the door. It was dark outside, but the cool glow of the moon played in Laurent's dark hair, gorgeously framing his flushing cheeks.

Laurent yelped, but wrapped his arms around Beast's neck in an instant. He was so ridiculously compact. Beast wouldn't tell him that, since Laurent complained sometimes about his height, but Beast thought it was one of the things that made him cute. When Laurent wrapped his legs around Beast's waist and let himself be lifted, Beast's mind already provided the image of Laurent's back against the wall, the pliant body taking Beast's cock. But he would be a good boy. He would wait until they stumbled into bed. He would give Laurent the most amazing first time and make him so, so addicted to fucking.

Beast growled and rolled Laurent against the wall, just for a kiss, a nip, a sniff of the warm skin behind Laurent's ear. He sucked in the sensitive flesh, gently biting and rocking his hips against Laurent.

The boy let out a soft moan, tightening his thighs as if in an attempt to give Beast a taste of things to come. When Beast pulled away, it was only to take Laurent into the bedroom where the sheets were still in disarray after their morning sex. Laurent's soft fingertips teased the back of Beast's head as if silently urging him to hurry and bury himself in his body already.

Beast moaned and put one knee on the mattress before safely lowering Laurent as well. He pulled his palms over the lovely, well-shaped thighs and back up, to open the tight pants and let Laurent's body breathe. "I want you naked. Completely naked."

"Oh… okay." Laurent nodded, slightly tense, but it was understandable that he was a bit anxious about this.

Beast licked his lips, resting his hands on both sides of Laurent's head. "Don't be nervous. I know what I'm doing. Just relax," he said, slipping his fingers under Laurent's T-shirt and drawing indistinctive shapes on his warm skin.

Laurent gave him a quick kiss on the lips and pulled off his top, revealing all the flesh Beast was so eager to lick up and down. "Will you stop if I ask?"

Beast sighed and leaned in. He rubbed his face against Laurent's stiff stomach and licked his way up. "Of course I will. Just relax. It feels good," he said softly, pulling his teeth over Laurent's nipple and opening his own jeans at the same time. The relief of pressure lifting from his dick made him shudder with anticipation.

Laurent's heartbeat was frantic, and Beast could clearly feel it when he put his cheek against the smooth chest of his lover. The heat of the beautiful body would soon welcome his cock, and Beast was determined to give just as much as he took. Could they possibly avoid using rubbers? Laurent was a virgin and Beast himself hadn't had sex for years before

Laurent, so he knew his STD status. The thought of filling Laurent's ass with cum made Beast moan against the silky skin.

He licked his lips and pulled on Laurent's jeans, tugging them down with a sense of *déjà vu*. His first time bottoming hadn't been exactly amazing, but he'd been too drunk to care. This would be different. He had all the tools to make Laurent feel utterly amazing, to make this moment profound and special for him. "Do you want to go bare?" he asked, petting Laurent's naked legs. There was no surprise in seeing Laurent's cock fully hard as well.

Laurent watched Beast as the rest of his clothes landed on the floor. "Bare? Are we not *bare*?" The big brown eyes were full of innocence. Of course the pure soul didn't know what rubbers were for.

Beast swallowed, pulling Laurent's hand closer and into his open jeans. Seeing his eyes cloud when his fingertips brushed Beast's rock-hard cock was poetry. "Do you want me to put a rubber sheath over my dick when it goes into you?"

Laurent let out a bark of a laugh. "Why on earth would I want such a thing?"

Beast's stomach twisted with pleasure, and he rocked his hips against the warm hand, enjoying its touch on his throbbing shaft. "Well... some people don't want cum inside their bodies. Or... so that a woman doesn't get pregnant, or so that people don't get diseases from each other." The moment those words left his mouth, he wanted to reverse the whole thing, but it was impossible. Things had been said, and he could only label this moment as educational, even if not particularly sexy.

"Oh." Laurent's gaze drifted off. "N-no. I want all of it," he whispered in the end, squeezing his soft palm over Beast's cock.

Beast smiled, touching his forehead to Laurent's and briefly shutting his eyes to just feel the touch and smell his skin. "Me too. I want to feel you without anything between us. No barriers. Just you and me," he whispered, pulling Laurent's other hand to his pants and directing it so that it would be Laurent who undressed him.

Laurent stole another breathless kiss and didn't waste time pulling Beast's jeans and underwear all the way down to his knees, his other hand still caressing Beast's cock. Beast could hardly remember the last time he felt so fully accepted. It was as if his scars meant nothing to Laurent, and maybe they really didn't. Maybe it really was all in Beast's head.

Beast rolled off Laurent only briefly, to get rid of his pants and socks, and then pushed between Laurent's thighs, rocking his hips against Laurent's balls and cock while they kissed. There were so many positions in which he could fuck a man Laurent's size with ease, but tonight he needed to think of the most comfortable one. They'd have all the time in the world to experiment once Laurent knew what felt good for him and what didn't.

There was something so pure about Laurent despite the occult brand on his nape. When he wrapped his arms around Beast's neck and they kissed, it was hard to imagine him doing any wrong, even if Beast knew Laurent wasn't exactly incapable of being mean if he wanted to. It was as if this wholesome beauty was the compensation for all the years Beast had spent in the body that used to be his personal hell.

Beast smiled at Laurent, rolling them both closer to the edge of the bed, so that he could reach for the lube. They were using it for some of the other things they did in bed, so at least he knew he wouldn't be surprising Laurent with the cool touch of the gel. Kissing Laurent again, Beast rubbed his whole body against his lover, never looking away, even then the touch made his cock twitch from pleasure. He needed to keep cool and come at an appropriate time. Even if his enjoyment were to be spoiled by having to keep himself in check, Laurent's pleasure came first tonight.

Flipping Laurent over was a quick affair, and Beast pushed against him, moaning when the head of his cock briefly traced Laurent's anus before pushing up and emerging between his buttocks. Beast lifted his body slightly, just to see that magnificent view again.

Laurent whimpered, and the sound only made Beast's cock twitch even as his brain translated what Laurent said next.

"Can we stop?"

It took Beast much longer than necessary to process the question. He cleared his throat, suddenly feeling his balls ache. "W-why?"

Laurent arched his shoulders, which only made Beast fantasize about holding onto them as he drove his dick into the tight hole.

"I just don't want to anymore. I'm sorry."

Beast stared at him. Arousal was slowly turning into a dull pain that throbbed around his cock, as if someone clamped something tightly around the base. "Did I do something?" he whispered, at loss and trying not to sound disappointed, even though he was. He was. It was Laurent who told him he wanted this.

He'd confirmed he wanted penetration.

He'd confirmed he wanted to go bare.

Beast knew he had to back off, but his whole body flooded with such bitter resentment he wasn't sure what to do about it.

"N-no," Laurent muttered, wriggling out from under Beast, which only agitated Beast's cock more. "But you said we could stop…"

Beast took a deep breath, squeezing his hands on the comforter. He didn't understand any of this. Just moments ago, Laurent was eager as a puppy, so what had happened? "It was your idea," he said in an unpleasantly dull voice.

Laurent rolled around and curled his legs up, watching Beast as if he were an exhibit at the zoo. "I know. But it's okay to change my mind, isn't it?" he asked softly, as if he wasn't driving a knife into Beast's balls.

Beast took a deep breath. Of course it was fine to change one's mind. Of course it was, but he couldn't help feeling that there was something deeply artificial about the whole situation. It didn't seem like Laurent hated what they've just been doing, or that something got him scared. He seemed calm and completely fine, like someone who decided to switch movies after the first fifteen minutes, because the current one wasn't as much fun as they'd expected.

"So you're not in the mood anymore?" Beast asked, looking at Laurent's stiff cock. Maybe there was still a way to salvage the moment. Maybe they could just settle into their usual fare, and the uncomfortable mood would go away.

Laurent licked his lips and shook his head, pulling the comforter over his lower body, as if to signal he was off limits.

The fuck was this bullshit?

Beast exhaled, trying to reason with himself. "Is there anything you want to tell me?"

"Are you okay with not doing anything after all?"

"What do you want me to say?" hissed Beast and rolled off the bed, pacing through the dark room, hands tightly interwoven at the back of his neck. He could hardly breathe, and right now all he wanted was to leave and go for a ride, but with Laurent behaving so strangely, he didn't want to leave him alone either.

There was something odd about the way Laurent's eyes followed him in the darkness, the side of his face illuminated blue by a lamp outside. "I want you to say it's okay," he whispered. "I need to know you will stop if I ask."

Beast stood still and did a double-take of Laurent, suddenly so choked up he thought he would just storm out, to be as far away from Laurent as possible. "What are you saying? That this was some kind of fucked-up test?" he asked in the end.

The way Laurent curled his shoulders instead of instantly denying the accusation, made Beast's stomach clench and his erection deflate as if someone had kicked him in the nuts. "How am I to otherwise be sure? Sometimes you think you know a man well, only to find out he is not the gentleman you expected him to be."

Beast pushed his palms to the back of his head, breathing hard through the pain in his chest from the sheer sense of betrayal. "What's wrong with you? We've been together for weeks now, and I've never done anything you didn't want. This isn't a game. You can't play me and test me for no reason!"

Words pushed their way out of him one after another, until he didn't have any air left in his lungs anymore and leaned against the windowsill to recuperate. "Fuck. I'm so stupid."

"No, Beast…"

He heard Laurent getting off the bed behind his back, and he couldn't believe he'd thought of Laurent in terms of 'innocence' just minutes ago when the boy had been manipulating him all along. The soft footsteps on the wooden floor beckoned him to just accept the touch, pretend this never happened and again just stop asking questions, but the shock of this revelation had him despise the idea of being touched at all.

Beast gestured at Laurent, wordlessly telling him to back away. "This is so fucked up. I thought we had a good thing going. I didn't even pry into your past, like you wanted," he said bitterly, squeezing his other hand on the windowsill.

Laurent looked to his feet, and the worst thing was that the deceptive beauty of his body and face were still there to taunt Beast. "I'm sorry. I just… I've met a man before who made me trust him." Laurent was gasping as if it was him who'd been wronged here. "And he used to be caring, and even bought me gifts, and then he—"

"He what?" hissed Beast, uncertain whether he even wanted to believe anything Laurent said. It hurt to know how little trust Laurent had in him, but maybe at least he would get a scrap that would somehow justify the stupidity of Laurent's actions.

Laurent curled his shoulders, and his hair fell down on them, obscuring his face. "H-he wanted to force himself on me. And he hit me. And I killed him," he said the last bit in a higher, breathless pitch, making Beast stall as he tried to process what he was hearing, only to have Laurent go on. "I grabbed a pair of scissors, and I stabbed them into his throat, and there was blood all over both of us." His whole body shook like a leaf in the wind.

Beast was by him before he could even think. He pushed Laurent on the bed and kneeled in front of him, squeezing both his hands as the moonlight revealed the dampness hiding in the big brown eyes.

"Was that his blood? When I found you?" Beast asked, horrified by what he'd just heard. He was still agitated by the way Laurent got about dealing with his trauma, but now at least he understood. He wanted to understand. "Where did you leave the body? Is it somewhere in the clubhouse?" asked Beast, feeling his stomach sink. Was it possible that there was a rotting corpse hidden somewhere in the vast building or nearby, and no one has found it yet? They needed to get rid of it, because he wouldn't have Laurent taken away from him.

Laurent nodded with a loud sniff, squeezing Beast's hands in return. "It's long gone. Do you understand? I killed William Fane. My name is Laurent Mercier."

Chapter 19 - Beast

Beast stared at Laurent in silence, his brain desperately trying to process what he'd just heard. The slender hands were so warm, so alive in his, and yet cold apprehension stabbed at Beast's back like thousands of needles. He took a deep breath, trying to calm down, but it seemed impossible. How was he to deal with this? Could this possibly be a joke? A way for Laurent to diffuse the animosity he created by playing with Beast's feelings?

But no, Laurent's eyes were damp with unshed tears, and his knees trembled as if he'd been assaulted not months but minutes ago. Whatever hid in Laurent's head, it was real for him, and that scared Beast into silence. Has he missed the signs of a problem much deeper than Laurent's naiveté about the world? Was this actually a mental issue, which he'd just ignored because Laurent was so lovely Beast couldn't resist him?

Had he slept with someone who was somehow mentally unstable and couldn't truly make their own choices? It chilled him to the bone to even think of that. He wasn't that kind of man. Maybe not an innocent, but he would never knowingly use anyone's disadvantage like this. Then again, hadn't there been so many red flags that he'd chosen to just dismiss, without pursuing answers?

"William Fane?" asked Beast, and he couldn't even recognize his own voice when it sounded so weak, so faint.

And yet the way Laurent looked at him, with so much hope for understanding, made Beast's heart sink. "Yes. The one Knight spoke of. I thought he was charming, and attractive, but then he invited me to his home and—I had no choice. I didn't want to die as his prisoner."

Beast swallowed hard, torn between calling Laurent out on the lie and actually getting some information out of him. His stomach felt queasier with each word falling out of that lovely mouth. Maybe they'd all been in the wrong about not asking questions? It seemed completely probable now that there was a family somewhere, looking for their lost relative, and instead of coming forward about an amnesiac young man turning up with blood all over him, they'd just swept everything under the rug. True, that was what Kings of Hell usually did when trouble arose, but hadn't Laurent's arrival been an occurrence worth looking into?

"And how did you meet him? Where is your family?"

"I... They're in France. But not anymore, of course. They're long gone. I needed to tell someone. To tell *you*. If we are to trust each other, you need to know this." Laurent barely even blinked, and his whole face was a tense mask.

The body was likely still hidden somewhere, because Beast would have heard of a man murdered in the area, had he been found. Whatever happened, it had left its mark on Laurent, making him believe in things that belonged in fiction.

Very gently, Beast squeezed Laurent's hands and looked into his eyes. "I understand this must be hard for you. Do any other odd things happen? Do you hear voices or see things that shouldn't be there?" he asked, sick to his stomach that maybe Laurent has been out of his mind all along, and he had just overlooked it. What did that say about him?

Laurent took his time answering the question, which made Beast instantly wonder whether he was searching his mind for an answer, or trying to hide something. "Have you never noticed there's something wrong with the mirrors in this building?"

Beast swallowed hard. The mirrors always appeared dusky in the clubhouse, but everyone knew this. Still, he nodded, wanting to know what was hiding inside Laurent's skull.

"The devil came through one to me after I killed Fane," Laurent said slowly.

Beast choked up. "The devil came to you. Through a mirror."

"You don't believe me," Laurent said quietly and his shoulders sagged.

At least Laurent recognized that much. Then again, Laurent was suspiciously good with people for someone with mental problems, so maybe it wasn't that he had amnesia or didn't understand what happened. Maybe he was simply a compulsive liar. Maybe he's been manipulating Beast the same way he manipulated his feelings tonight to test him. "Would you?"

"Do we not trust each other?" The sweetly worded question couldn't be more insidious after what Laurent had put Beast through in the last half an hour.

"You clearly don't trust me. Why would I trust you?" hissed Beast but didn't let go of Laurent's hands.

"I'm just trying to navigate this whole new world. Do you not understand how hard it is for me? I went to see Fane with a heart as light as clouds, and when we kissed it was as if the sun came out, but when everything started happening too fast and I wanted to back out, he wouldn't let me. He tried to collar me. He shackled my wrist." Laurent pulled his hand up, as if to remind Beast of the scar on it. "I couldn't see well, I was so frightened, and when I thought I was only dealing with an angry, slighted man, I came upon a rotting arm that he kept in a trunk. I've never been more terrified in my life."

Beast swallowed, calculating in his head. Maybe there was a grain of truth in the warped reality of Laurent's story. Laurent had been covered in blood when he arrived. He had been scared, and his body had borne signs of assault, but Fane? Had Laurent somehow dealt with his trauma by imagining he was someone else? "So you traveled in time. You killed a serial killer, and you have absolutely no one looking for you?"

Laurent huffed, as if it were he who had reasons to be frustrated. "How else do you want me to prove it? Are the clothes I arrived in not enough? I could tell you more of how people lived in my time, but I don't know what is common knowledge and what isn't."

Beast swallowed. The lady at the dry cleaners had told him Laurent's clothes were a fantastic recreation of a historical outfit, but that proved nothing. He might as well have been a re-enactor. "I don't know, Laurent. Maybe you can't. Maybe I should have taken you to see a doctor instead of trying to date you."

"But you *have* taken me to one. And even though I was so frightened, you were with me through it all. I'm trying to be as honest with you as I can be."

Beast swallowed, looking at him with tension pulling at his muscles. He wanted to believe every word, because otherwise the whirlwind relationship that had made him happier than he'd been in years would turn out to be a sham. "I don't know... something about Fane maybe? Like, did he tell you what he did with the bodies?" Worst case scenario, if the whole Laurent Mercier fantasy had any basis in truth, maybe Laurent would take him to the body of the man he'd killed.

Laurent sat up straighter. "Have they not been found? He is a known murderer, is he not?"

"They found two bodies buried in the cellar, but he had kept souvenirs from many other men who disappeared around that time. Almost thirty, but the location of other bodies remains a mystery."

"I… I know where he buried Marcel Knowles. The one whose arm he… kept." Laurent's face scrunched with disgust, as if he could smell the rotting flesh. "He was a baker, and a good man."

Beast exhaled, watching Laurent in silence. "I know nothing of an arm. Where would that guy be buried then?" he asked, trying to keep his cool despite the anger simmering beneath skin. And the worst thing was that he didn't know whether his feelings were justifiable or not, because if Laurent honestly believed all this then how was he to blame for his conduct?

"There is a large rock nearby the old well, not far from the building. I know it's still there. When I came to meet Fane, the ground next to it had been recently disturbed. Now I believe it's where he must have buried the poor man."

Beast knew the rock. Maybe if he proved to Laurent that the whole thing had happened in his head, Laurent would be able to confront the truth. If he had enough strength in him not to break the shovel in sheer helpless anger.

"So if we go there and dig, we will find bones, is that right? Can you promise me this?"

"If, as you say, they have never been found, then… yes, I believe we will find the bones. Will you believe me then?"

Beast counted to ten in his mind. "And if we don't find them, will you either tell me the truth or go to a psychiatrist with me?"

Laurent picked on a few hairs on Beast's forearm and nodded.

Beast huffed, sitting on his haunches, somewhat helpless. Then what now? Was he to really just get a shovel and dig? He could ask the others for help, but that would have put Laurent in a horrible position.

"This is insane."

Laurent stood up, and picked up his clothes. "Maybe it is. I never thought this kind of witchcraft possible, and yet here I am!"

Beast got to his feet and stormed to the pile of clothes left behind after the most disappointing sexual encounter of his entire life. "Sure. Fine. Let's dig."

Laurent was rapidly putting on the outfit, as if *he* had the right to be angry. "And I hate that so many people call me 'kid'. In my time, I was considered a grown man, able to fend for himself. And tall."

"Well, now you're a kid. And short. And fucking mean and manipulative. Just face it," Beast said, pulling up his jeans.

Laurent pursed his lips and threw Beast a stormy glance. "At least I don't spew curse words all the time," he spat, but it fell flat, and he had to know this. Swearing was hardly an issue when put on the scales opposite all the things Laurent was throwing at Beast. Laurent pulled on his hoodie and zipped it up as if he were readying for war.

Beast shook his head. "Should have thought about it before getting into my bed if I offend your ears so much." With that, Beast put on his boots and stormed for the open door of the bedroom.

The 'tap tap tap' of Laurent's feet behind him followed. Beast couldn't believe they were about to go dig in the ground in the middle of the night. If they found the body of the 'Fane' who Laurent killed, it would sure as hell be a rotting mess, not bones.

The supplies closet offered high-beam flashlights and shovels, so they took what they needed and walked off toward the lone rock, picking up Hound from his pen on the way. The dog was ecstatic about the unexpected walk and led the way, enjoying himself as if he hadn't noticed the sour atmosphere.

Beast just wanted to get this over with. He was so angry he didn't even want to talk anymore, constantly reminded that either he could only be of interest to someone who wasn't in their right mind, or he'd been lied to for weeks.

Laurent turned the beam of the flashlight to a spot by the rock. "It's here," he mumbled. "Unless the rock was moved, but it's too large, so I doubt it, and it's still aligned with the well. Beast… I don't know. Maybe we should leave the body in peace?"

Beast's chest tightened, and he flung the shovel like a pike, stabbing it into the ground. "Oh, so you don't want to deliver proof after all? What are you going to tell me next? That you've come from the dark side of the Moon?"

He noticed with irritation that Hound approached Laurent and sat by his feet, as if taking *his* side!

"Fuck you!" Laurent hissed and stuck his shovel into the ground as well. He rarely swore this way, and it gave Beast a sense of dark satisfaction. Laurent was not such an innocent after all.

"Now we're getting somewhere. I've been through too much shit in my life to just accept this. I won't be played with, no matter how sweet or handsome you are." He deserved respect too, and he could hardly muster any for himself right now.

But Laurent didn't answer, digging with that annoyed pout on his face even when rain started drizzling from the sky. He just pulled on his hood, digging the shovel into the wet ground time and time again. Their flashlights gave just enough illumination to provide lighting adequate for a horror movie, and the smell of damp ground that usually made Beast want to take a deep breath seemed to be choking him now.

At least they were hidden beyond the trees, which made it unlikely for anyone to notice them from the house. Still, the drizzle covered every inch of Beast's bare skin, making the joints in his hands stiffen with cold and clouding his eyes with the rain smacking his face whenever the wind changed direction. But he wouldn't give up, no matter how uncomfortable all this was.

Beast had no idea how long they've been digging by the time Hound decided it all wasn't worth it and went off to hide beneath a tree, but Beast couldn't just put off this task until tomorrow. Without definite proof, he wouldn't be able to even look into the treacherously pretty eyes.

Bitterness was choking him as he worked, sneaking its way into his bones and muddling any positive thoughts he had left. He didn't want to discover that there was nothing sinister hidden here, but he still dug despite the ache in his muscles and the cold that made him shudder more violently with each passing moment. He should have grabbed a rain coat.

He glanced toward Laurent, who worked just as tirelessly, grunting when he pushed the shovel into the ground with force, and despite the resentment growing its roots in Beast's heart, he still worried about Laurent catching a cold as a result of this.

Three feet into digging, and neither of them said a thing, neither suggested giving up. Beast could blame Laurent's stubborn nature, but he wasn't any better himself. He rammed the shovel into the ground, ignoring the cold mud that clung to his shoes and the downpour that soaked through his clothes, making him shiver as if he were naked. It felt like he was digging his own grave.

"Wait. I think I see something." Laurent pushed Beast aside and forced him to pull the shovel away.

Beast sighed, leaning against the tool and watching Laurent dive his pretty hands into the wet dirt. He was so tired. All he wanted was to take a long bath and go to sleep. And tonight, he didn't even want Laurent in his bed anymore.

Laurent was like a worm in the ground, frantically pushing through mud with his fingers. Was he seeing things in the slush but was unable to reach them because they didn't exist?

"All hells! I can't see well with all this rain. Can you come down and have a look?"

"Sure," Bast said, resigned to his fate and just plain sad. He didn't know where to go from here. Asking Laurent to bring the flashlight closer, he dug his hands into the chilly mud and touched a branch. In the hole that kept being disturbed by wet dirt rolling down into the pit it was impossible to tell what was really hiding under their feet, but as he pulled and the piece didn't outright crumble like a stray piece of wood should have in this climate, his mind did a backflip and made him freeze as pieces of a puzzle slotted into place.

No. This couldn't be right.

It couldn't be.

But Laurent had been so certain of this particular spot. As if he really *knew,* not just suspected what could be hidden beyond the rock.

Frantic, Beast swiped his hands over the smooth surface, uncovering the pale, elongated shape. It was sinewy from dirt, but when he closed his hand around it and pulled once more, the bone emerged, splashing his face with dirt.

Beast felt his blood pulsing all over his body, even in his throat, and very slowly, he looked back at Laurent.

"Should we keep on digging?" Laurent whispered, rubbing layers of mud away and revealing more of the skeleton that Beast could suddenly see. After discovering a single bone, the shapes of the bumps in the dig were clear as day, with the slope of the skull looming just left of Laurent's boot. The boy was swiping the water and mud off the bones, his glasses not only wet but also foggy. Beast was beginning to realize that even after the surgery, the unmarked grave was likely only a blur for him.

All of a sudden, Beast wanted to take Laurent far away from this horror.

He dropped the bone and pulled him back, closing the smaller body in his arms. "No. No," he said, frantically wondering if another member of the club hadn't buried someone out here. But no, they wouldn't have. They wouldn't have hidden a body so close to home, not on the property.

He closed his arms tighter around Laurent, breathing so heavily the hyperventilatory rush was starting to get to his head. "Laurent...you're not insane."

Laurent's arms slid around him immediately, and just as expected, Laurent's hoodie was so utterly soaked it could provide no warmth. "Is it Marcel's body?" he whispered shakily, kneeling with Beast in the shallow grave over mud-covered bones.

Beast put his chin and exhaled, unexpectedly moved by the discovery. He had seen men die, but this was something completely different, which came with its own set of questions. "It is a body. You were right." Slowly, the weight behind this truth sank into Beast's flesh, and he pushed Laurent away to look at him, wet glasses, hair sticking to his cheeks, and all. "Is the... is the brand on your neck...?"

"The devil left it on me. He saw what I did, and he granted my wish. I wanted to live in a world where I could be free to support myself, free to love a man. And he brought me here."

"To me," Beast said, slowly moving his hands down Laurent's arms, completely out of his depth.

"I know how it sounds." Laurent sniffed against Beast's chest. "I really do, but this house, this land belongs to infernal creatures, and he can do here as he pleases. Isn't the brand on my nape evidence as well?"

"My father has one, too," Beast whispered, glancing back to the body. They couldn't just leave it uncovered until morning. "Do you know why? Did he also travel in time?"

Laurent went still but eventually looked up at Beast, his face both wet and muddy, eyes barely visible through the glasses. "No. But he does something for the devil. I don't know what it is exactly, but it has something to do with the house."

Beast swallowed hard, gently petting Laurent's hair. "I'm sorry. I—this is just so unbelievable," he uttered, watching Laurent in a new light altogether. He had gathered legends and gossip about magic and strange things that happened in the area, and yet when the truth had been given to him on a platter, he refused to believe Laurent. He'd been an idiot.

This was what he's been searching for all along.

Laurent pulled off his glasses and put them in his pocket, shivering all over. It was time to leave this shallow hole filled with mud and bones. "I know. I was never one to be superstitious. I didn't seek this out either. I killed Fane in that house, and the devil appeared on his own. He spilled out of the mirror, like steaming tar. I was so frightened, yet I wanted to live."

"I know, baby, I know," Beast said, hesitating. He wanted Laurent away from this rain, but the hidden grave couldn't just be left like this. He excused himself briefly and covered the skeleton with some of the dirt before whistling at Hound and pulling Laurent close again.

The way home was long and miserable. Beast was so caught up in his own thoughts that he couldn't summon words of comfort. His head spun with the newfound knowledge that his father wasn't a member of some kind of cult. He'd made an actual, literal, pact with the devil. This was insane, and yet the body that had been hidden away for the last two hundred years was proof enough. This was real. The demons were real, and so it meant that magic was real too.

If Beast met the devil, he could ask him to grant his wish too. He could have his old self back. He could live like a normal person again. He might have been seeking out all information about strange events around the house for years, but it only now occurred to him that he'd never truly believed any of them to be true accounts. They were just threads that he clutched at for an illusion of hope that had been apparently within his grasp.

When they reached Beast's apartment, they were both dripping mud and water all over, but Beast itched to see the sigil on the back of Laurent's body again, to call Knight as fast as possible and analyze in a new light all the evidence he'd gathered in his office. Right now, even Laurent's earlier fucked-up trust test didn't matter as much.

Laurent was lost, and afraid of a world that was so new to him. It was a miracle Laurent fared as well as he did. All of a sudden he didn't seem funny and naive, but really brave and a quick learner with the way he grasped concepts that had to be as foreign to him as magic was for Beast.

Hound's dirty paws left mud stains all over the living room, but Beast couldn't find it in him to care. As soon as they entered, he pushed the soaked clothes off Laurent and quickly shed his own. Despite the heat that he now felt in the air contrasting with his freezing wet skin, he and Laurent were still shivering and needed to deal with the cold as fast as possible.

Laurent's teeth clattered when they walked into the shower stall together. Hot water was surely as much a relief for him as it was for Beast. They stood close, and Beast couldn't stop thinking of what the boy had been through. Laurent wasn't even twenty yet, and Fane had been in his thirties when Laurent Mercier had killed him. It was hard to see the boy in front of him as the mysterious man from history, and yet there he was, in the flesh, with the pretty long hair, handsome face, and slender fingers Beast couldn't imagine committing an act of violence. Was it violence though if it was self-defense?

If Laurent's words were true, for him, the attack had only occurred over two months ago.

"You should have told me. We should be honest with each other if we're to be together. Not about the time travel. I'm talking of the abuse. I'd have handled things differently if I'd known," Beast said in the end as he washed the shampoo out of Laurent's hair. He was glad to see color coming back even to Laurent's fingers, but he still touched them, just to make sure they were indeed warm.

Laurent nodded with a deep sigh when Beast ran his fingers over the devil's brand on his nape. "Fane told me he kept that man, Marcel, in his basement for months. I knew I had to do something. I have never been more terrified in my life. How could such evil exist?"

Beast swallowed hard and slowly leaned in, kissing Laurent's lips, eager to show him it would be okay from now on. "He's not here anymore. It's just you and me, and I will protect you. I promise."

Laurent's lips showed a hint of a smile, and it sent such relief through Beast's body that he finally felt ready to deal with Knight, the research, and looking for answers.

Laurent wasn't insane and still wanted to be with Beast. This was all that mattered.

Beast kissed Laurent again and switched off the shower, energized and feeling better with each passing second. "Good. You should sleep it off. I need to get Knight, and we'll see what to do about Marcel."

Chapter 20 - Laurent

Beast's scent clinging to the puffy comforter and pillows was the only consolation Laurent had left. Tucked away in the soft cocoon in the middle of the bed, Laurent listened to the steady tap of rain against the window. He flinched when the wind howled, tossing droplets of water against the building, but he was just being overly sensitive after the horror of this night.

He was warm. He was safe. Yet so utterly lonely.

Why was it Knight that Beast was so eager to discuss his findings with? Why was Laurent not allowed into the secret room when not so long ago Beast had claimed they should be honest with each other?

Laurent couldn't believe how a perfectly good evening had turned into such a disaster. He'd first pulled Beast away from conversations about the house, simply because thwarting such plans was his job, but then the spur-of-the moment decision to distract Beast by suggesting expanding their bedroom repertoire turned into an unstoppable avalanche of regrets.

At first, he had thought the test of Beast's patience a sound idea. One that would once and for all provide the sense of safety and trust Laurent needed to fully give his body to Beast and enjoy their lovemaking without even a hint of fear. Nothing went as planned once he put his idea into motion. In his dumb head, he'd only taken his own anxiety into account, completely forgetting how his actions would affect his strong but loving Beast.

So then he *had* to explain to Beast why it was that he was so rattled. One thing led to another, and here Laurent was. Alone, even if with hope in his heart that Beast did believe him. He seemed sincere when asking questions, not suspicious like he had been at first.

Laurent just wished to be included more. He wished he was allowed to be with Beast and Knight, not tossed away the moment Beast found something more important to think about. Now that Beast knew of the time travel, Laurent itched to talk with him of things that he'd been forced to keep secret so far. And yet Beast wasn't there for him, too busy with the new discovery.

Outside the bedroom, a door clicked, and loud male voices spilled out, making Laurent lift his head off the pillow and glance toward the entrance. He soon recognized that Beast and Knight must have left the room where Laurent wasn't allowed.

It was a thorn in his side.

Laurent slid out of bed and walked up to the door with his feet bare, putting on his glasses on the way. The chill that greeted him beyond the heat of the comforter gave him goose bumps, but he was too eager to hear what was being said to care.

He put his ear against the door.

Knight sounded agitated. "This is history, Beast. We need to have someone preserve those bones for future generations."

"We can't call the authorities now. Gray and Rev recently came back from the run, and we have too much cargo in the clubhouse to risk it. This needs to stay quiet for now. Those bones aren't going anywhere," Beast said, and Laurent heard the familiar clinking of glass.

'Cargo' was another secret Beast would only tell Laurent vague lies about before changing the subject, but Laurent wasn't an idiot. He knew that some of the sources of income of the Kings of Hell were shady at best. Men left only to come back a few days later with small packages that everyone treated with such reverence they might have been holy objects. It seemed some of the women knew what was really going on but pretended not to, so he followed their example and avoided the topic.

If only ignoring secrets was as easy when it came to the secret room, which hid something of personal value to Laurent's lover.

Knight let out a groan of frustration. "So the Count is still allowed to make his stupid and unproven claims about Fane and his methods of killing, and I'm supposed to just sit on my hands and listen to his ranty YouTube videos—"

"What the fuck, Knight? What do you care what some dude says on the internet? He's yet another conspiracy theorist."

"He's tarnishing the memory of my ancestors! Do you know that one of his theories is that Laurent was a male prostitute who was in on Fane's scheme, and the murder was caused by an argument over money?"

Beast remained silent before giving a grumpy sigh. "We both know it's not true. And it's not like I'm saying this should be kept under wraps forever, but we need to take into account that a body might attract feds, and we'd have to tiptoe around them until they confirm the age of the corpse. Isn't the club more important?"

Laurent was still processing the fact that some unknown man was making up lewd things about him when Knight responded, clearly unhappy.

"I guess. We can arrange a reveal with historians and all that once you're back from the next trip and we have nothing to hide."

Beast was going somewhere? This was the first time Laurent was hearing about it.

"We'd also need to talk to the others, and we both know King's not gonna like it. If you want to stop creepy serial killer fans from writing Fane/Laurent fanfiction, maybe you should come up with a case for King to agree to this, because he never really listens to me."

"Laurent Mercier deserves better," Knight said, but his voice drifted off, and after another click of doors, Laurent realized Beast and Knight must have left the apartment.

He looked out into the corridor to make sure, but they were in fact gone. For how long? The door to Beast's secretive room had been left open, and Laurent's heart skipped a beat. His feet moved before his brain could even make a decision.

Hound opened his eyes, pricking his ears in curiosity, but he didn't move from the bed, likely too sleepy to worry about human matters. Laurent swallowed and faced the secretive chamber where no one but Beast and Knight were allowed. It was always locked, but this time the key was sticking out beneath the door handle, and the door itself was not even shut.

Heat flushed Laurent's chest as he slowly approached and peeked inside, only to see complete darkness. There were either no windows or very thick curtains in there. He patted the wall on the side from the door, where light switches usually were, and as expected, all he needed to do was press on one to illuminate the room.

All at once, notes and pictures assaulted Laurent from the walls. Book pages were connected to newspaper clippings, some pinned together with drawings, and stacks of folders lay on the desk next to two cans of Coke, the dark, fizzy drink Laurent despised.

He shuddered when photos of several satanic sigils, including one carved in a stone floor, assaulted him so unexpectedly he grabbed at the back of his neck where the protruding lines burned at his fingertips. Behind the door stood a whole bookshelf of literature and folders marked by phrases such as "occult activity", "satanism", "Brecon 18th C", but it was too much to take in at once, so Laurent swiped his gaze over the cluttered desk with piles of open notebooks and drawings on top.

Above it, pinned to a corkboard, was a large, somewhat faded photograph of a handsome young man with a squarish jaw and blond hair that tickled his bare shoulders. Laurent was instantly drawn to it and adjusted his glasses as he walked up to it and squinted at the sense of familiarity the portrait gave him. It took him a while to realize why he felt like this, but another photograph of the same man on Beast's motorcycle made him realize who the stranger was.

The colours faded somewhat, but Laurent would recognize the blue eyes anywhere. The face itself had been completely transformed by scars and tattoos, so much so that it made the man difficult to identify as Laurent's lover, but upon close inspection it became clear that his bone structure was the same.

Would Beast have been the same man he was today if not for the accident that killed his mother? Would he even be 'Beast'? It only now hit Laurent that he didn't know what Beast's real name was. How sad was it that a man who could be so tender, such a good friend was only known as a monster.

He exhaled, letting himself watch the roguish smile for a few more seconds before tearing his attention away to look at the open notebook in the middle of the table. Unlike some of the other items, it wasn't even slightly dusty, and the writing inside didn't look like Beast's either. He leaned in, sensing a stab of heat in his chest when he realized it was a family tree of the Mercier family, with Travis's—or Knight's—name circled in red at the very bottom.

Laurent quickly traced it with his finger, all the way up to… Adolphe, his brother.

He blinked when he saw his own name gently crossed out with a pencil. His own branch had been cut off like a rotting part of a tree, whereas his brother's thrived for generations, all the way to 2017, to Knight and seven of his siblings, none of whom Laurent had seen around the club despite those people having families of their own according to the tree.

He started flipping the pages of the notebook, trying to hurry in case Beast and Knight came back, but his mind was going in circles about this room. The truth about his past had been here all along. With research and books about the devil, about other places where the sigil has been found, and never had Beast as much as mentioned things that so clearly could provide an insight into Laurent's situation.

There were all kinds of things about the Mercier family in the notebook, which was even divided into chapters where Knight has meticulously put in dates, places, as well as anecdotes and trivia. Laurent Mercier had an entire section dedicated to him.

It contained a copy from an old register, which listed him as Mr. Barnave's indentured servant, a note about him being a murderer, and an account written by the local priest, whom Laurent remembered speaking to only weeks ago. A physical description of him was there as well, colored by prejudice and accusing him of having dealings with the devil himself. His unusually long hair was pictured as proof of Laurent's association with witchcraft. What struck him most though was the way he was portrayed, almost matter-of-factly. A killer. A sly thief who wanted to steal from the good Mr. Fane—who at the time the note had been written clearly hadn't been yet exposed as a murderer. It speculated that Laurent had wanted to make a run for it with Fane's rings, which must had been taken by a dishonest servant before the body was actually reported missing to the authorities.

Near the end of the chapter he also saw photographs of items associated with the killing of Fane—among them, the thick collar that had Laurent shrinking on the inside with the memories. Attached was also a photograph of an object from the local museum—a bullet described as likely fake. The real one had been apparently taken out of a different man's body around the time of Laurent Mercier's execution.

Laurent's stomach clenched at the shame of it all. He was confused by all the mentions of the devil, but a few paragraphs later, he realized that it was because Fane himself had been found with the devil's sigil on his nape. It all came together in Laurent's mind. Fane's murderous schemes had to be him doing the devil's bidding. But of course it was Laurent, his killer, who got all the blame.

The next page screamed at him with brightly colored streaks underlying elements of text. It took him several seconds to understand that they were all reports about the murder and the trial that followed.

He'd been found.

He'd been in the cellar when the servants broke down the door.

He'd been taken to jail and put on trial.

So... how was he here?

His breath caught when yet another quote was followed by Knight noting that Laurent Mercier had been sentenced to hang. On the following page, names of his three siblings were mentioned at the very top. They arrived in Brecon three years after the murder of William Fane, expecting to find their brother thriving but were confronted with his crime instead. They didn't even have a gravesite to pay their respects at, presumably because Laurent's body had been buried in an unmarked grave.

And yet, he was here. He didn't understand. Was he a living soul, and the devil left his body back in 1805?

He rubbed his eyes in panic when tears fell on the notebook. His siblings, his family had come to him after all those years, and he had no idea. They hadn't abandoned him after all. He squeezed his hands on the edge of the desk, staring at the scribbled notes and pieces of paper with someone else's writing, completely overwhelmed by the storm raging in his chest.

As if suddenly, beyond the confusion and the terrifying process of reading about his own death, a ray of light was penetrating Laurent's soul.

He still had family. He even had a living family member who was interested in his life. He wasn't alone in the world.

"What are you doing here?"

Laurent turned around in panic, too overwhelmed by his findings to even form a coherent lie. What was he to say? He had obviously sneaked in here despite numerous warnings not to. "I…"

Beast stared at him, his hand squeezing the door handle tightly. He took deep breaths, as if in hope it would help him somehow keep his cool when even the tendons in his neck were visibly shifting. He was a bull about to charge. "What? You what?" he snapped.

Laurent took a step back, bumping into the desk. "I'm dead," he whispered. "And you knew this. How could you not tell me?"

Knight hovered behind Beast, but Laurent's focus was only on his beloved.

Beast hit the wall, leaning forward with both his hands resting on the doorframe. "It's been over two hundred years, Laurent. And you're here, so you're obviously not dead. And stop turning this around, because I told you to never come in here. I don't want you to look at any of this," he said and rapidly pulled on Laurent's hand, taking him out of the small room.

Laurent bit back the yelp that tried to escape his lips. Out in the living room, he got a clear look at Knight. "I had family come to me years later. Why am I not in there with you, trying to understand it all?" He pointed to the room in frustration. Most of the notes and clippings in there weren't fresh. Beast has been working on this for years, and didn't find it appropriate to tell Laurent even though Laurent was wearing the devil's brand on his body!

Beast swallowed hard, his arms so stiff it almost looked painful. "You're one to talk. This is personal. How dare you break my trust like this? Haven't you put me through enough for one night?"

Knight sighed and looked to his feet, as if he wanted to pretend he didn't see what was going on.

"Why are you researching this? What do you know?" Laurent demanded breathlessly, unwilling to let go or apologize. He was being treated beyond unfairly. What if he could still die? Get sucked back into the past when the time came? "Is there anything about the dead Laurent having the brand?" he asked Knight, hoping his own family would be more cooperative.

Knight cleared his throat. "Yes. That's why some people think he was in on it with Fane. That they were both part of a satanic cult."

"I don't need to tell you about every second of my life," hissed Beast. "I can't believe you played me the second time on the same fucking night!"

Laurent shifted his weight from one foot to the other, uncomfortable with the way Beast was gripping his wrist. "*I* told you everything!" he lashed out, feeling guilty beyond belief the moment the treacherous words left his mouth. But lying was a matter of survival. He couldn't tell Beast all there was to know about his pact with the devil, or even the things he knew about King's pact. If Beast knew, he would most likely leave this place and Laurent behind.

And Laurent couldn't have that. There were still over two months to go until Laurent was free to live in this world, and only after his deal was finalized could he come clean to Beast about it.

And he would. Even if it meant Beast abandoning him, Laurent promised himself he'd be truthful.

But not now. Not yet.

Beast spread his arms. "And what, am I supposed to just gut myself for you, about all my thoughts? Do you want to know what my favorite color was in school, too? It doesn't work that way. You can't force people to give up their secrets like this. This is getting more fucked-up by the minute."

Laurent glanced at Knight, but the man shook his head.

"You don't expect me to support you in this against my best friend, do you?" Knight arched an eyebrow.

"Fine!" Laurent managed to pull out of Beast's grasp, but it took so much force he stumbled against the sofa. "I'm sorry I've encroached on your privacy," he hissed with no regret at all.

Beast clenched his jaw and stuffed his hands into his pockets so rapidly as if he wanted to rip them. "Go to sleep."

Laurent swallowed and looked between the two men. "Goodnight," he said in the end and turned around.

He would be sleeping in his old room tonight.

Chapter 21 - Beast

Beast was roused by a soft knock on the door followed by a loud whine and a banging that could have only been caused by Hound's tail slapping against the floor. He groaned, rolling to his back and forcing himself to sit up, still groggy after going to sleep when it was already getting bright outside.

"Come in."

The door slid open slowly, and Laurent, the traitor, came in with a wary look on his face and a tray of food in his hands. After yesterday's outburst, the sight was enough to make Beast raise his eyebrows. The anger after having his privacy breached was still a burning presence in his body and awoke the moment he cast his eyes on Laurent's pretty yet deceptive face.

"So, I… made breakfast," Laurent said and sat on the edge of the bed. He put the tray between them, showcasing a steaming cup of coffee and toasted Poptarts with pink icing. "Your favorite, right?"

Beast looked at the treat and couldn't help but be amused. He wordlessly commanded Hound to not jump on the bed when two front paws rested on the edge of the mattress. "Let me guess, you cooked them yourself?"

Laurent smiled and pushed his hair behind his ear. "Well, yes. You remember? You told me to toast them, not eat them straight out of the bag."

Beast pulled himself up and leaned against the pillows, watching the meager offerings. He supposed that if this was meant as some kind of bribe to make him less angry then Laurent must have tried his best. "To what do I owe the honor?" he grumbled in the end, not really certain what to think of this. He couldn't be appeased like a dog, with a morsel of meat thrown his way.

Laurent licked his lips, squirming under the scrutiny. "I wanted to apologize," he mumbled without looking into Beast's eyes. "I was angry yesterday, but I had a lot of time to think at night. I found it hard to fall asleep without you after all that's happened, and… I came to the conclusion that you were right to lose patience after all that we'd already gone through earlier that day."

That was new.

While Laurent wasn't entirely bratty, some of his behaviors were hard to swallow, particularly the kind he expressed the day before. Beast had imagined Laurent would be nice and submissive until Beast's anger evaporated, but an actual apology was the last thing Beast learned to expect from the boy. "It was not a good evening."

Laurent nudged the plate closer to Beast. "I was frantic with the findings, but after giving it some thought, I realized you didn't exactly have that much time to focus on what to tell me once you found out who I really was. I should have been just grateful that you believed me."

Beast exhaled, rubbing his face and trying to ignore the sugary aroma of the Poptarts and the caffeine that seemed to already worm its way into his system, before he could even have a sip.

"And?"

Laurent sighed and wrapped his arms around himself. "I'm sorry I went into your secret room." This time he was getting grumpy, and the familiar pout was back in place—a token of just how begrudging that last apology was.

Beast scowled. "What's with that face? Didn't I allow you to keep your secrets? Why did you think it was okay to just help yourself to mine?" hissed Beast, instantly getting agitated all over again. "I didn't want you to see any of that. And you just burst in there as if you had any right to my thoughts or my past."

Laurent's shoulders sagged, and the pout was gone. "You're right, I don't. My curiosity and nerves are no excuse for my conduct."

Beast licked his lips, squeezing the comforter in his fists. Should he stop being upset, just because Laurent was sorry? He wasn't sure he could do that just yet, but at least it sweetened the bitter pill he'd been forced to gulp down last night. "I'm glad you understand."

"Did you find anything yesterday that you *would* like to share with me?"

That was a surprise. An actual question, and Beast instantly felt sorry for speaking in such a vicious tone. Reluctantly, he picked up a Poptart and had a bite. "Well, I found out magic is real, and I'm still shellshocked."

Laurent smiled, but wouldn't look up, moving his feet up and resting his heels on the edge of the mattress. "There's a lot we don't understand about it. But you're right that maybe I shouldn't have panicked the way I had. I'm clearly still alive, so I couldn't have died in the past."

"Maybe there's two versions of history, and in one, you're here," Beast said, reaching out to touch Laurent's hand. It was warm and smooth from the hand cream he kept using, and Beast rather liked its touch.

The fingers quickly squeezed Beast's hand, and it soothed Beast's heart to see Laurent so invested in him that he'd come to apologize instead of sulking and playing the prince.

"That must be it. What's most important to me is that I'm not alone in this, and last night… I felt very lonely without you."

Beast sensed an odd, hollow sensation spreading through his chest. Suddenly he remembered the way Laurent had looked at him in the shower last night when Beast told him to go to sleep, as if their findings didn't concern him at all. "I'm sorry about yesterday, too. I wouldn't have found the body without you. Even if I wanted to talk to Knight about all this, I shouldn't have just pushed you aside."

When Laurent finally looked up at Beast, it was such a relief Beast had another bite of the Poptart. "We all make mistakes, right?"

Beast gave a sharp laugh, relieved to see that Laurent honestly wanted to make up. "Yes. Is there something you can tell me about my father's pact?" he asked, wondering whether Laurent had noticed the old pictures of him in the office. Whether he even recognized the handsome guy in them as the same man Beast now was.

"There is much I don't understand myself. King has been very vague, and I keep trying to stay in his good graces so that he tells me more."

"What about yours? What did the devil want from you in return?" asked Beast, downing the coffee in a few gulps. It suddenly occurred to him that the request might have been something terrible, and he choked on the beverage, remembering all the stories that featured demons stealing people's souls.

"I… It's still to come, but I'm not allowed to tell anyone what the exact thing is. I will be free of it in due time. It's a minor thing, really. I believe that the devil's powers are limited in respect to what he can offer, and I am just a cog in his scheme. He even suggested he is not the devil of the *Bible*, so maybe he's another type of monster entirely."

Beast exhaled and put down the cup in favor of holding Laurent's hand. "So your soul is still yours? And you will stay here?"

Laurent crawled over the bed until he was close enough to pull Beast's arm over his shoulders. "I will, as long as I fulfil my duties to him."

Beast licked his lips, his body immediately relaxing when Laurent's heat slotted into place against him. "Is it something horrible?"

Laurent kissed the scarred skin of Beast's forearm. "No. But King cannot die until it's done, so no matter how much you hate him, please keep him safe."

Beast laughed, but the request still made him uneasy. "Why would I want to hurt him? He's my prez. I mean... he is a dick, but we're family. I wouldn't."

"Good," was all Laurent had for him.

Beast cleared his throat and ate some more of the Poptart while watching Laurent's handsome profile with hope slowly settling in his chest. "Can you call him? The devil, I mean."

Laurent pressed closer to Beast's body. "Why would you want that?"

Beast exhaled, pulling Laurent closer, and the memory of his old face, of all the things he missed out on for the last twelve years, flooded his mind along with that story about a man getting back his lost limb. "There are things I want."

Laurent pressed his palm against Beast's chest. "Is there no other way to get them? You never know what the devil might want in return, and… it could change you. Contact with this *creature* is best avoided."

Beast's heart beat faster against Laurent's palm, and when they looked at one another, Beast knew one thing: he *wanted* the creature to change him. He wanted to be a man people didn't turn away from, and who wouldn't look odd next to Laurent when the two of them were out together. The name of Beast had become almost synonymous with him, but he still mourned the loss of his old self. "No, I can't. I need those things. I need them. That's why I collected all those notes in the office. I just never really believed I'd succeed."

Laurent kissed Beast underneath the jaw. His lips were so soft and his touch so tender it almost physically ached to be such a monster next to him. If only Beast could become the man he should have been all along, Laurent would never leave him. He didn't even need to live life as he used to, fucking around and hooking up with new people all the time. He'd changed since then, both in looks and on the inside. But no one ever saw his true self, only the scars, visible no matter how much ink he'd covered them with.

"I could try. For you. But I haven't contacted him since I appeared here."

Beast leaned closer, sensing heat spread throughout his body. His hands were so ugly against Laurent's smooth, graceful ones. "Can you do it now? Please."

And yet, Laurent still leaned down and gave Beast's knuckles a kiss before getting up. "Let's go to a mirror."

"A mirror?" asked Beast but already rolled out of bed, briefly wondering if he shouldn't wear something more formal than black pajamas, but he decided infernal beings likely didn't care about such earthly issues.

The sole thought made him choke out a laugh. Was it possible? Would he finally get what he'd been seeking?

In truth, Laurent's story was still difficult to believe, even if Beast has chosen not to doubt him. Getting to experience the supernatural himself, would give him the evidence he needed.

Laurent seemed distant, but he was most likely just tense. "Yes, he came to me through a mirror, and I believe every mirror in this house could be a doorway for him."

Beast's breath caught when he remembered the never-ending frustration dusky mirrors caused in the house. "Is he... looking at us through them?" he asked, squeezing Laurent's hand on the way out the door.

"I think so." Laurent's nose wrinkled when he frowned. "But I never think about it much when I wash my face or brush my hair. I don't think he… The whole house is his domain, and I believe he knows of everything that goes on in it anyway."

Beast licked his lips, suddenly uncomfortable. A being not of this world witnessed his and Laurent's intimacy, and Laurent didn't even care? "Okay. That doesn't bother you?" he asked but followed Laurent to the only room in the apartment that contained a mirror. The bathroom.

Laurent groaned. "Whatever this devil is, he's not a peeping tom. I doubt he thinks the way we do. Would it bother you if the trees were watching you?"

Bright light illuminated the modern bathroom, and the muddy residue on the tiles reminded Beast that they'd discovered a grave last night.

"The trees don't have eyes," grumbled Beast, curling his shoulders and psyching himself for... something. He had no idea what to expect so he tried to just calm down and be as open-minded as possible. Still, he flinched when Laurent opened the little cupboard, revealing the mirror image of them both in the sickly white light of the lamp above. The brightness only stressed the discoloration of Beast's skin.

Laurent glanced up at him. "How do you know?"

The question gave Beast a nasty shudder, and he focused on the mirror instead. Despite the bright light, the glass seemed dimmed at the edges.

Laurent cleared his throat and stood on his toes to reach it over the sink. He rubbed his hand over the surface, giving Beast a nervous look. "I'm not sure how to go about it, so please bear with me."

What if Laurent had found out about the skeleton buried on the property in some other way and this was an elaborate scheme after all? But why would anyone go through this much trouble? Hadn't Beast decided to believe Laurent? He should stick with that decision and stop overthinking every single detail.

Beast shifted his weight, watching Laurent's shoulder blades shift under the T-shirt he was wearing. His ass pushed back slightly when Laurent leaned over the sink to gently knock on the reflective surface.

A shudder passed through Beast's body, but it came from beneath his feet, like a deep base during a particularly loud gig. There was a whiff of a breeze, as if there was an open window in the bathroom, and just like that, the door slammed shut.

Failing electricity, he could still explain, since the wiring was shit in the building, but this was weird.

Laurent glanced over his shoulder but kept his hand on the mirror. "I would like us to speak," he said after another pause, and the lamp Beast had just thought about started blinking as if it were a shivering animal, afraid of what was to come.

He took a deep breath, but the air was so dry it left his throat feeling like parchment. The base thumped again. And again, and this time, cracks opened in the tiles behind like ice over a lake. Beast stared at it, not quite sure if he was hallucinating or if it was real. An unsettling sensation curled in his stomach, and when he saw smoke come from where Laurent's hand met the mirror, he almost pulled him back.

With a loud crack, the lamp died, leaving them in a darkness unnaturally thick during the day. There should have been sunlight coming through the tiny gaps around the door, but there was nothing.

Nothing beyond the sickly reddish glow of the mirror.

A part of Beast didn't believe any of this would happen even when they came here, and yet here he was, having to admit that the fantastical events Laurent told him about were all too real.

The water that had been dripping from the sink before, turned pink, but then a deeper, darker color Beast didn't want to believe possible.

Laurent backed into him, watching the mirror as it became duskier, smoke building up on the other side of it as if it was not their reflection, but a screen into another world altogether. A part of Beast regretted asking this of Laurent, worried he could get hurt, so he quickly wrapped his arms around Laurent, pulling the boy close.

He stiffened when a high-pitched screech that couldn't have originated in a human's throat tore through the small room. It sounded wrong, an artificial sound like nothing he'd ever heard before. Beast's embrace tightened around Laurent, and he wasn't even certain if he was holding on in hope of protecting Laurent or because his body was helplessly battling its fight-or-flight response. The rusty-looking mirror hypnotized him, drew in his gaze, and if he looked closely enough, there was something he could spot in the surface that no longer resembled their faces.

The screech came again, sending trembles down his arms, and for the briefest moment it felt as if ghostly claws trailed down his spine under his clothes.

And then, a voice came, loud and clear, even if it sounded like the product of a crazed electronica artist rather than something that could be produced by vocal cords. It had a metallic quality to it, as if the throat that made the voice was rusty steel and old wood.

"I don't need you."

It was a simple statement, but before Beast could react, the ghost of long fingers appeared in the mirror, long claws ripping through glass and leaving behind five long scars running throughout the surface.

Beast screamed out and pushed Laurent away, hitting the mirror with his fist. The glass gave in, crumbling under his touch, but then the door opened, and as the daylight came in, it revealed nothing but cracks on the mirror and walls. There was no inhuman presence to be seen.

With one more blink, the lamp came back on.

There was no blood in the sink.

No smoke in the air.

And yet, the broken mirror, the tiles, were proof that Beast hadn't imagined this.

Laurent cowered in the corner by the shower. "I guess he didn't want to speak."

Beast looked at him, slowly removing his aching hand from the mirror and letting it rest next to the sink. His chest throbbed with the rapid heartbeat within, and his hand with the pain of impact.

The devil didn't want him. It simply didn't think he was worthy of its time. A dull sense of anguish coursed through Beast, closing him in. He didn't want to talk to anyone or see anyone.

Did the thing think Beast had nothing to offer? That a boy like Laurent was worthy of its attention more than him?

Beast had to leave, to not spill his resentment out on Laurent who had only done as he was asked. It wasn't Laurent's fault.

"Y-your hand…?" Laurent stepped closer, but Beast only growled in answer. He was an injured animal, and he would lick his wounds on his own.

"It's fine," he said, without even looking back at the boy, and stormed out of the bathroom, heading straight for the door out of the apartment. Even Hound's whimper wouldn't stop him.

Chapter 22 - Laurent

Beast had been gone for a week now. Laurent had been stunned at first when he found out Beast had left without as much as a goodbye. That after all they'd been through, he went off with Joker and Gray to do some vague 'job' in New York, and as much as Laurent understood that it was something Beast had to do, it still hurt to be left behind without an explanation.

At least he had Hound, who'd stopped being scary a while back, and Beast's scent in the bed that felt much too big for him now. He agonized over the events in the bathroom, wondering if he should have called the devil in the first place every time he looked at the broken mirror.

What could he do other than wait though? He read yet more books, made himself useful in any ways possible, spent time around the Kings of Hell, their women, other hangarounds. He worked hard on fitting in and yet wasn't even close to achieving that goal, but the more time he dedicated to learning the ways of modern people, the more he felt that there was a place for him in 2017, even if he was considered eccentric. People here seemed to have a tolerance for oddness far exceeding that of Laurent's own time.

On Sunday morning, he was torn between anticipation and anger. It was the day when Beast was supposed to come back from his run, and considering that Laurent had had no communication from him for an entire week, he didn't even know how to greet his manfriend—or as Nao told him, boyfriend, which was apparently used with no regards to age.

He couldn't just accept Beast leaving without saying goodbye. Not after he'd walked out on him after the devil refused to grant Beast an audience. It was hardly Laurent's fault, and it hurt him deeply that Beast seemed to have put the blame on him. After so many days without having heard Beast's voice, Laurent was starting to think that he was the only one feeling the loss.

Unsure whether he had appetite at all yet knowing he should eat something, he hovered aimlessly around the kitchen. Most people who hung around the clubhouse were out, some spending time with their families, which left Laurent stranded. He considered preparing a snack to welcome Beast home, but that only made him feel pathetic. He could cook things that only needed heating, but after watching Martina work her magic and make the most elaborate meals from scratch, he knew his skills in the that department were severely lacking.

Was food really the only nice thing he could do for Beast? His lover most definitely enjoyed the carnal side of whatever one would call their relationship, but it made Laurent uncomfortable to think that lust might be the only thing he was good for. The need to satisfy him became more prominent every time Laurent thought of the vile way King was using Beast, but he kept telling himself that it would only last until Beast's birthday. Telling him now would cost Laurent his life.

The itch to consume sugar hit Laurent almost immediately, so he scooted down to pull some cookies out of the bottom shelf of the kitchen island.

Loud laughter resonated in the room nearby, followed by the sound of bodies crashing against metal. The female voice sounded like Jordan, Knight's girlfriend, who never even awarded Laurent with a single sentence spoken directly to him. He didn't like her very much, and neither did Beast, although Laurent's man never voiced that sentiment.

"Oh, Babe, show me," said Knight in a low, raspy voice that instantly put Laurent on high alert.

Oh, no.

Laurent froze when he realized what was happening. A soft thud and a jangle of glass over the coffee table suggested Knight and Jordan had gone for the sofa. Laurent fought a battle of wills with himself, wondering whether he should announce his presence somehow but then moans and the sound of slapping of flesh against flesh began.

Public sex in the clubhouse was an occurrence that never failed to make him uncomfortable, no matter how many times he stumbled upon couples engaged in such illicit encounters. Maybe if he just stayed quiet by the cupboards for long enough, Knight and Jordan would eventually go away.

A loud slap accompanied Jordan's moan and rattling. Which sounded as if something knocked against the coffee table. "Go on, pull up that dress for me. Show me your ass now, or I won't allow you come today."

Laurent covered his face, too embarrassed for words. Was this going to take long? Maybe he should come out and excuse himself after all? Or try to crawl to the door when they weren't looking? What a disaster.

"No!" Jordan whimpered after another slap. "I want your cock now. Give it to me, come on."

"Yeah, you want it in your pussy?"—an even louder whack—"Or in your ass, you naughty girl? Huh? Tell me, or I'll just fuck your mouth and leave you like this."

Laurent's ears were bleeding, but covering them was no use, because Knight and Jordan were too loud anyway, consumed by lust even though they'd argued just last night.

"You beast!" she laughed, and Laurent's face scrunched at the notion of calling someone other than *his* Beast… well, a beast. "I'll take that thick cock however you like it," she lowered her voice but Laurent could still hear it.

Then, both were silent for the briefest moment before Jordan gave a shriek so loud Laurent almost rushed from behind the counter to help her, but a thumping of boots kept him frozen in place.

"You sneaky fucker," Knight hissed. "Don't you dare, I see where you are!"

"What the fuck! Doesn't he understand people's need for privacy?" cried Jordan as if she hadn't just been loudly proclaiming her carnal needs in a place that was called a *common* room for good reason. If she so wanted privacy, she should have taken Knight somewhere else, especially since Knight wasn't necessarily shy about having sex in public - something Laurent had accidentally found out when he walked in on Knight getting a blowjob from a guy in one of the corridors. Knight had actually *winked* at him then!

"I'm sorry Knight!" Jake yelled, his voice coming from somewhere outside. "I was just passing! I didn't mean to look."

How did Laurent get himself into this mess? All he wanted was some cookies.

Laurent peeked out from behind the counter right on time to see Knight haul Jake into the room through the window. Jake screamed out when he landed on the floor with a dull thud. The buckle of Knights open belt jingled when he stood over Jake, pulling the prospect up by the cut. Laurent would not swap places with Jake now. Knight was rarely unkind to Laurent, but despite his handsome face, he was a force to be reckoned with when angered.

And he was easily angered.

Knight punched Jake in the face so hard Laurent gasped and covered his mouth to dull the sound of it.

"You think you can perv on my girl, you bastard?" Knight yelled, with his fist balled and aimed at Jake, who desperately grasped at his own face.

Oh, no. Did this mean Laurent would also be the recipient of violence, were he found? Sure, Laurent was Beast's boyfriend, and Beast was Knight's best friend, but maybe it wouldn't matter in the heat of the moment? Knight was an impulsive man, always eager for a fight the same way he seemed always eager for sex.

"No! That's not it!" Jake grasped at Knight's wrist when Knight pulled on Jake's leather vest, hauling him over the floor, all the way to where Jordan was sitting with her skirt pulled back down.

"What is then? You better fuckin' apologize for being a creeper!" Knight's face was flushed, his long hair in disarray even more than usual, and his thick forearms were filled with tension as if ready to unleash fury.

"I'm sorry, Jordan," Jake groaned, "but you know I'm gay," he finished flatly.

Knight just watched him for a few seconds, but then burst out laughing and harshly patted Jake's cheek. "You perv! Just gotta ask me if you wanna see my dick."

"Knight!" Jordan growled at him.

Knight rolled his eyes and turned around to face her, with poor Jake cuddled up under his powerful arm. "What? He's not even a girl, and I gave up on all the girls for you. See? I'm making a fucking effort. What compromise have you made for me?" he said, pulling out a pack of tissues, which he handed Jake. The poor guy quickly pulled one out to deal with his bleeding nose.

Jordan crossed her arms on her chest, which was never a good sign. "Are you fucking kidding me? I put up with knowing you're fucking guys, I put up with listening to your bullshit about finding some old skeleton, and you cancelling our date tonight because you'd rather go look at some bones? That dude's been dead two hundred years! He can wait!"

Jake shifted uncomfortably. "I… I should go," he mumbled, pulling away from Knight.

Knight crossed his arms and moved his gaze from Jordan to Jake in such a demonstrative manner it had to be on purpose. "Prospect, meet me in the billiard room in three hours. Be there."

A silly grin bloomed on Jake's face but he yelped when Jordan got up and viciously smacked his head. "Don't you dare be there!" she yelled.

"He doesn't answer to you. He's our prospect, he listens to me and the other members. You are only a girlfriend," Knight said, pointing his finger at her.

In any other circumstances, Laurent would mentally support Jordan, but she was such a horrible human being overall that he ended up cheering for Jake, who'd get what he wanted later today.

Jake quickly took his leave while Jordan tapped her heels against the floor in helpless fury.

"I am so sick of the indignity of it all!" She pushed at Knight's chest, and the way it didn't seem to affect Knight at all reminded Laurent of the frustration he sometimes felt when arguing with Beast. "I am a fucking princess, and you treat me like dirt! I deserve so much better! You should be grateful that you have a girl like me, so unlike all the skanks that hang around here. And what do I get in return? You're more interested in some great-great-great-great uncle of yours than your woman's needs."

Knight's shoulders relaxed, but he squinted at her. "Did you just call my friends skanks? *And* call yourself a princess? Where are the cameras?" he asked, mockingly looking around. Fortunately, he wasn't being truly inquisitive or he'd have spotted Laurent.

"Hell yes I did!" She raised her finger in the air with a snarl. "And you better stop disrespecting me if you ever want a taste of this again." She pushed her breasts up with her hands in front of his face.

Knight just stared at her. "Wow. You're such a bitch. You've got a pretty face and gold jewelry that you bought on credit, and that makes you think you're all that much better than everyone else here? Nao is a much better fuck than you. Maybe you should take some classes. You're fucking welcome," he said, stepping away before she could hit him with her tiny bag. "Tell me one thing that makes you oh-so-different from those other 'skanks' that I don't consider just showing you out right this moment."

"How can you say that? We've been through so much together, and now you're like this? Deep down you know I'm much better than all those lowlives, but you're just being nice."

Laurent backed out behind the cupboard and put his face in his hands. He would never be free to leave here, and he most definitely didn't want to listen to the embarrassing exchange.

Knight gave a loud sigh. "Yeah, and you're disillusioning me every fucking day of the week. I have stuff to do beyond coddling you, and if you don't want me fucking anyone else, you're barking up the wrong tree. I told you that at the very beginning."

There was a long silence. "Okay, Knight, sweetie, but if we're to be together you've got to give me attention," she said in the voice of a petulant child. "You can't go off to look at some stupid skeleton with Beast when we were supposed to go on a date. Is he more important than me?"

"Listen, woman, those aren't *bones*. Those are the remains of a man murdered by William Fane, if you even know in that tiny brain of yours who I'm talking about. If you can be two fucking hours late because you needed to change your fucking nails in the last minute, I'm gonna dig up a grave, and take fucking notes, and do with my brothers whatever the hell I choose too!"

This time, Knight sounded seriously angered.

"Fine!" she screeched. "You go jerk off with your buddies over William what's-his-name, and I'll go find myself another boyfriend. One who actually treats me right!"

"Perfect. Start getting on someone else's nerves. I'm curious who you can get with that temper."

"Anyone I want! You're such a dick!"

By the sound of the heels clicking rapidly on the floor, Laurent figured Jordan really was leaving this time. Which was good because Knight usually followed her in such situations, and Laurent would finally be able to flee.

But the door slammed, and heavy footsteps were quickly moving toward the kitchen.

"Fucking cunt," Knight muttered, "doesn't even know who Fane is."

Laurent curled his arms, trying to be as tiny as possible, and kept still when Knight's long legs strolled to the fridge. He stopped in front of it, and Laurent felt the heat of his gaze.

"Fucking Christ. What are you doing here? Since when are you into listening to straight sex?" Still, Knight opened the fridge and pulled out a can of beer.

"I'm sorry! I wasn't! I was just getting cookies, and then it all escalated. I wanted to leave," Laurent whined.

Knight sighed, leaning his back against the fridge and opened the can before taking several sips at once. "Can you believe her? Thinks she's so much better than everyone else, and what can she do apart from doing her hair and makeup?"

Laurent took a deep breath and opened his packet of cookies in resignation. He'd been too afraid to have the wrapper crinkle loudly before. "A partner should provide something of value," he mumbled, trying to figure out what he could possibly offer a man like Beast.

"I know, right?" Knight asked, gesturing toward the door that Jordan just exited through. "Can't believe I was putting up with this shit for so long. What is wrong with me that I keep dating those stuck-up bitches?"

Laurent got himself off the floor and leaned against the counter of the kitchen island. "Do you love her?"

The question seemed to have thrown Knight off guard, and he shrugged, watching his toes. "I thought I did. She was so charming in the beginning, and was agreeable, and said she liked me the way I was, and then she started changing. Every day she came with a new demand. And it's always like that. I'm done with relationships."

"I… think Beast might still be angry with me. Do you think it's why he doesn't talk to me?"

"Do you have a phone?" Knight had a sip of beer with his eyebrows raised.

Laurent stuffed his mouth with another cookie, feeling so pathetically needy. Hadn't he wished for independence all his life? How was it possible that another person's silence could rattle him so much? He didn't even notice when Beast became a figure of such importance for him. "He calls *you*."

Knight gulped the beer loudly, watching Laurent for a prolonged moment. "He did ask how you're doing."

Laurent's heart skipped a beat, and he stepped closer. "And what did you say?"

Knight put down the empty can and helped himself to Laurent's cookies. "That you seem fine. Why? Aren't you okay overall?"

"I miss him," Laurent whispered. "He left so abruptly. And right after *the discovery*."

Knight sighed, chewing on the cookie. "Well, you know, his trip's been scheduled for a while. That's the way things are in the club. Sometimes, he won't be there. Just distract yourself with something else. We could go back to the family tree, so you could help me with previous generations of the Merciers."

That did make Laurent smile. Knight was so dedicated to preserving their family's history it made Laurent warm all over. Despite the passing of time, a descendant in 2017 cared to find out more about the past generations and honor their memory. "I would love to find out more. What about Beast though? What about his family tree?"

Knight shrugged. "King's family is Finnish and German originally. His mom was Russian and Irish. But I don't think he's that interested in the past. You'd have to ask him if you want to know more."

"And the two of you? Have you…? I mean… is there a past I should know of?" Knight laughed. "Nah. We don't really mix this way. He's like a brother to me. We jerked off together a few times as kids, but that's that. Don't worry, I'm not taking your man, great uncle Laurent."

Laurent groaned in embarrassment. Knight could be so patronizing sometimes. "How did you two meet then?"

"School. There's no magic to it, to be honest. We pretty much grew up together."

"And at school, was Beast making many acquaintances with men?"

Knight could be a goldmine of knowledge if only Laurent was careful with the way he mined the ore.

Knight grinned and poked Laurent. "You're jealous, aren't you?" he said, but when Laurent vigorously denied the accusation, Knight just went on. "He started out with girls, at his dad's club. And then he started fucking guys too and decided that he enjoyed that so much more."

"And then he was too badly hurt in the fire to… pursue that?"

Knight's face stiffened, and he licked his lips, briefly looking away from Laurent. "He had a man when that happened. And that was a real thing, not a bit of fucking around. Beast *loved* that guy. He had still been a prospect and even considered giving up on club membership for him, because that asshole wanted to move to Hollywood. But then the accident happened, and Beast was just... uh. We didn't know if he'd even make it.

"So two weeks pass, and Beast is out of intensive care, right? Everything seemed to go well, and this dickhead comes to Beast and tells him he can't cope. That it's gonna take ages until they can be like a couple again, and that Beast likely won't ever be the same man he was. Told Beast he needed to understand how hard it was for him, as if it was him to lose his mom and have his health permanently damaged. He had all those dreams, and Beast just didn't fit in anymore. Too ugly to take to the red carpet, and helping him out would take too much time. People are always like that. They want everything to go smooth, to be easy. And then they bail on people they're supposed to care for," Knight finished, visibly agitated.

Laurent absorbed all the information as if it was air he needed for breathing, but the story was so unbearably sad he still felt needles prickle his lungs. "That is vile. If you love someone, you stay by their side." It was a story from the past, and yet every time Laurent repeated it in his mind, he got angrier about it. He wouldn't call himself a violent person, but he would gladly punch that man.

Knight sighed. "Yeah. It fucking went downhill after that. The breakup destroyed Beast. He had no energy for sex at first, but then he just didn't seek it out. Not that he didn't have people propositioning him, but he just got burned so bad that he kept away. Until you came," he said, frowning at Laurent, as if he were trying to somehow read Laurent's thoughts.

Laurent smiled to himself, feeling warm all over. "In all fairness, he does look quite intimidating at first glance."

"But he's a good guy, isn't he?"

"He's… rough around the edges," Laurent said, but his smile was widening on its own at the memory of all the things Beast knew how to do in bed.

"I know we're family, but I've known him longer. I will be watching," Knight said with a smile, but there was an undertone to his voice that told Laurent he wasn't entirely joking.

"As long as you're not watching in the bedroom." Laurent felt bold, but he could feel a flush crawling up his neck the moment he said it. Fortunately for him, some kind of commotion and the roaring sound of motorcycles barged in through the window.

Laurent rushed over there to see what was happening outside. Was it Beast? Finally back from whatever he was doing?

"There they are," Knight said, stuffing one more cookie into his mouth and padding to the nearest exit.

The riders would all be at the garage, and Laurent followed Knight's lead with his heart beating faster. Despite the lack of contact, he still wanted to see Beast. And he would scold him about not giving a single sign of life throughout the week, but that would only happen in due time. Once he was sure Beast had missed him too.

He knew something was off before they even reached the garages. Gray was shouting something about getting a doctor, and even Joker kept serious as he relayed how they got chased close to state border. Laurent was too busy searching for Beast to listen.

He barged into the garages and froze the moment he saw Beast, without his helmet, sitting on his bike and breathing far too laboriously. A trickle of blood dripped from under the sleeve of his leather jacket, slowly pooling on the hard, cement floor.

Laurent ran the last few steps.

Joker grabbed him hard by the arm and pulled him away while Gray shouted something over the phone. It was the first time Laurent saw the stoic, fair-haired biker so agitated. There weren't many of them here, but everyone seemed frantic, except for Beast, who was getting paler by the minute.

Beast glared at Joker. "It's fine."

"It's not, you're bleeding. What's wrong?" Laurent grabbed Beast's clean hand as soon as Joker let go of him. His breathing was getting frantic. "Should I help you take off the jacket?"

"Leave 'im be, kid!" Joker hissed, only agitating Laurent further.

"I'm not a child!" he yelled back.

"It's just a flesh wound," Beast said despite the sweat beading on his forehead as if he'd been sprayed by a sprinkler. He pulled Laurent closer from his uninjured side as soon as he got off the bike.

"Oh shit, is Beast okay?" Jake asked, rushing closer as soon as he entered the garage.

"He'll be fine. Take the cargo," Knight told him, pointing to several saddlebags, some of which were already on the floor. With everyone else losing their minds—understandably—it was Knight who took charge of the situation, and despite it seeming unfeeling of him on the surface, Laurent was glad that it allowed everyone else think of Beast's well-being.

Jake gave Beast a worried look, but quickly did as he was told.

"Doc's gonna be here in five to ten minutes. Get Beast inside. On a tall table. Or on the stage even," Gray said.

Despite waving his hand dismissively, Beast still settled a lot of his weight on Laurent when he got off the bike.

He groaned, scowling as he made careful, short steps toward the door while the other club members rushed around, gathering the bags and communicating in clipped sentences. Laurent heard King's name mentioned but didn't think much of it, completely focused on Beast's touch and weight.

He was so big and warm, somehow warmer than usual, and the tremble in his arm was so noticeable Laurent had to fight his own panicked shivering.

"How have you been?" asked Beast after several seconds of silence, as if everything about this situation was perfectly normal.

The sudden thought of losing Beast struck Laurent speechless, and hardly because it would have also meant Laurent failed his mission and would go back to the horror that awaited him in the past.

"I… it doesn't matter."

Gray followed them while still on the phone. "Talk to him, keep him occupied," and with those words he turned in some other direction, leaving Laurent to help Beast up the stairs under Knight's watchful eye.

"Good. I've been good. Reading a lot. Knight showed me some tricks with electricity." Laurent's heart was thudding as hard as if it was him who was wounded.

Beast gave him a weak smile, flinching when Laurent didn't notice that the door was too narrow for both of them and Beast ended up walking his injured arm into the doorframe. He hissed loudly, stiffening against Laurent, but then pushed inside, clearly intent on getting somewhere where he could rest. "I knew you two would have fun together."

"Yes, Knight is very kind to me." Laurent sighed deeply, more careful now that they walked down the corridor toward the common room. "And Hound goes on walks with me. And… I've missed you," he added in the end. All his plans of being standoffish and waiting for Beast to apologize about the way he had left went out the window as soon as Laurent saw blood.

Beast glanced at him, smiling again, as if he didn't care for pain as long as Laurent declared his affections so plainly. They finally reached the kitchen, and Knight quickly pulled everything off the counter before ducking to grab some bleach from the cupboard. The cleaning liquid smelled horribly, but cleanliness was apparently more important to keeping wounds in a good state than anything else. And considering how many old people there were in 2017, Laurent was certain modern medicine was right about a great many things.

"I have something for you," Beast said and looked down. "Inner pocket of my cut."

Laurent took a deep breath. He wanted to say it didn't matter right now. That he didn't need any gifts, but since Beast thought it important enough, Laurent reached into the pocket.

"You didn't have to," he still said, finding an elongated item made of plastic. He licked his lips, looking up into the pale face. Beast remembered how much he liked the material, but what could it be?"

He pulled out the item, and it caused a tightly spun cable to fall out to the floor. He didn't know what the item was at first, but it was dark blue and pretty, with a small screen and a keyboard similar to the one on the TV remote control.

"So that we can stay in touch when I'm away," Beast said.

Knight snorted. "You got him an old person's phone?"

Laurent gasped and hugged the cell phone to his chest with tears itching his eyes. "I love it."

"He doesn't need a smartphone," Beast said and leaned in to press a kiss to the top of Laurent's head, leaning against the cleaned counter. "Messages and calls will be enough."

Laurent gently rubbed the front of Beast's body. "And you will teach me how to use it?"

"That's why I got it for you," Beast said patiently and grunted, pushing his body at Laurent's. It became clear that with the one healthy arm busy keeping his weight up, he didn't have the means to properly hug Laurent.

Laurent was quick to help him with that and wrapped his arms around Beast's waist.

"Be careful, lovebird," Knight said, watching Beast like a hawk.

"What happened?" Laurent asked and kissed Beast's pec.

Beast's chest rose when he took a deep breath, his heart, healthy and beating fast despite the wound, was music to Laurent's ears. "Trouble during the run, but we dealt with it. Those people likely won't be a problem anymore," he said, briefly looking at Knight before glancing back at Laurent. "This is a secret, Laurent, but we move certain valuables for a friend of ours. And sometimes, people want to get those valuables off us."

Laurent nodded, looking between Beast and Knight, since this was clearly a point of tension. "If anything, you know I can keep a secret," he said, glad that he was finally considered trustworthy enough to be told even that scrap of information. "And that is what brings the Kings of Hell money?"

Beast nodded. "That's what we do. It's profitable enough and allows us to live how we choose. But Laurent, no one can know."

Laurent squeezed Beast's healthy hand. "There is always a price to pay for living a life of freedom. I for one, understand that clearly. There is no greater value. I will stand by you."

Beast met his gaze with a wider smile and eventually rested his chin on top of Laurent's head, practically curling up around him. The sensation was so pleasant Laurent closed his eyes and simply enjoyed it until someone's footsteps alarmed him into looking back. A middle-aged man hurried their way with a large bag, and he looked so odd in the clubhouse in a dress shirt and pants made of soft cloth rather than denim, that Laurent immediately realized it was the doctor. He watched Knight help Beast strip his top half and lie down on the counter, but grabbed the healthy hand as soon as he felt it wouldn't disturb the process.

The wound was in fact shallow, but the way it bled all over made it hard for Laurent to breathe calmly. The doctor carried on with the work of closing the injury with thread, and it was Beast who ended up trying to distract Laurent than the other way around.

Knight was assisting with setting up the phone, since Laurent didn't want to let go of Beast's hand.

"There is a list of all the people you could call in case of emergency, or if you just want to bug them for any reason," Beast said with a sneer when the doctor must have hurt him with the needle.

Laurent squeezed Beast's hand harder, reading through the list, increasingly frantic. "Why is your name not on there?"

"There is. The one where I put 1 at the front, so that it's on top."

Laurent immediately searched for it, breathless at the importance of it.

1Kai.

"Kai..." he whispered, longing to say it out loud for the first time. Beast had given Laurent his name. "Thank you." He squeezed Beast's fingers once more.

Chapter 23 - Beast

Two weeks after the shootout that left Beast with a hole in his arm he was feeling much better. With Laurent rushing to his aid even at times when it wasn't necessary, he managed to recuperate very quickly. If only his mind were in as good of a shape as his body.

The encounter with the... devil—demon, creature, or whatever else he could call it—had left scars on not only his walls and mirror. The sense of helpless anger coursed through Beast's veins and sat on his chest at night, waking him up with its weight.

He was worthless to the devil.

Any normal man wouldn't have thought much of it. If anything, they'd likely be happy about their nature being so uninteresting to a being that could twist their life, but Beast longed for nothing more than having his life twisted out of its current shape. To have a power beyond that of even the best doctors to take away all the pain reflected in his flesh, to make him a man Laurent wouldn't ultimately start being embarrassed of. Spending most of his time in the clubhouse, where everyone was used to Beast, Laurent couldn't see yet how much Beast stuck out like a sore thumb. The more television Laurent watched and the more he went out, the more he would realize that his relationship with Beast was a trap. That he could have a different life, with a different man, who could take him into any restaurant and wasn't constantly at risk of being gaped at.

The walls of the old building of the clubhouse were becoming so oppressive that as soon as July came along, Beast was dying to get out and forget all the eyes watching him from mirrors, and all the shadows that now seemed longer than they actually should be. The little things like failing electricity and strange echoing in small rooms were unnerving even if he now knew the reason behind them.

Beast wished to get away from it all, even if just for a few days, and he was happy to find out Laurent was eager for that too when Beast proposed a camping trip. Their bags were ready, the weather was warm, and Hound followed Beast excitedly, knowing he would soon get his own backpack too.

"Don't worry, we have enough food so that you don't have to hunt, you lazy bum," Beast told his dog, caressing the top of his head. Hound yelped, turning his muzzle up to look at his master before jumping and spinning around, as if he expected it to be playtime.

Beast exhaled, smiling at his pet. "You will be tired soon enough, I promise," he said, walking along the wall and toward the garages. Hound left him when he noticed something between the trees, but Beast knew the dog would come when called, so he just went on, approaching the garage where the pickup truck was already waiting for him with Laurent. He slowed down when bits of harsh-sounding conversation reached his ears.

"Whatever you're doing, ease the fuck on it. I'm not even joking anymore. Do what you've got to do, but stop interfering with me!" King snarled, making Beast stop in his tracks. The anger-tinted voice was coming from inside the garage.

"I'm not interfering. We all have our part to play," Laurent answered.

King's growl sounded so menacing, Beast came closer and took a peek inside, at the two men facing one another next to the pickup truck.

King leaned against the wall, squinting as if daylight were hurting his eyes. Gray hair obscured some of his face, but he was as pale as he has been after every party in the recent weeks. The bottle of an electrolyte drink completed the picture of misery, and yet next to Laurent's slender form, King was a menacing giant, no matter what state he was in at a given moment.

"You're enjoying this far too much," hissed King, stepping into Laurent's personal space like he always did when he tried to intimidate someone.

"That isn't any of your business." Laurent stood his ground, but he didn't manage to for long, because King grabbed Laurent by the throat and slammed him against the cement wall of the garage.

Beast saw red, and he charged at King, grabbing him by the neck and pulling up so hard he could swear he could hear bones crack. There wasn't even a moment's hesitation between the attack on Laurent and Beast's reaction. He wished he really had the horns of a bull so he could spear them through King's pathetic hungover body.

"Let him go," he hissed through his teeth, barely stopping himself from lifting King off the ground.

King choked, staring at Beast as if he saw a ghost, but let go of Laurent, even if the gesture was full of reluctance. Laurent stepped away quickly, massaging his neck and breathing hard.

Only then did Beast let go of King, spinning him away so hard his bottle landed on the floor and spilled all over. Beast exhaled, looking down at his hands. He hadn't meant to be so forceful, but maybe his anger got the best of him. "What the hell are you doing? He's mine."

"Is he?" growled King and Beast licked his lips, glancing at Laurent. There was no property vest on him, and that void suddenly made Beast itch.

Laurent stepped closer and cleared his throat. "There's no need for this. All is well. Mr. King and I had a misunderstanding."

King squinted at Laurent and even that made Beast itch to punch his own father. "Yeah, you can call it that."

Beast bit on the inside of his cheek. "Don't touch him. If you have any issues with Laurent's behavior, you should bring them to me."

Because Laurent was under Beast's protection now. He wasn't wearing a property vest yet, but he would soon, so that no one dared as much as brush against him without Beast's permission. It gave Beast a pleasant tingle in his stomach to even think of a patch on Laurent's back pronouncing to the whole world that the beautiful young man wearing it was Beast's.

"I will next time, so fuckin' watch it," King said to Laurent, but at least he didn't touch him. He bumped into Beast's shoulder on the way out. Beast watched his hunched form until it disappeared inside the building and only then his body relaxed.

He glanced at Laurent, instantly worried again when he saw how pale his face was. "What was that about?"

Laurent gave a deep sigh. "It's nothing. He just doesn't like when things don't go exactly his way. Is Hound ready?" He smiled at Beast.

Beast frowned, and a heavy sensation settled on his chest. "It's about the... you know what, isn't it?"

From the way Laurent shifted in place uncomfortably, Beast knew what the answer to that was. "We don't always see eye to eye on the issue."

"And you won't tell me?"

"I can't. Please, let's just go."

Beast exhaled, squeezing his hands into fists as his head filled with an unpleasant pulsing. He whistled loudly and walked away from Laurent, tossing his backpack into the bed of the pickup truck.

Laurent walked over to the other side and took the passenger seat. How long would this last? How long would Laurent be in some conflict with King about which Beast wasn't even allowed to know of?

At least Hound would never lie to him, just as happy to see Beast as ever when he ran up to him with a bark.

*

With the dog safe in a cage at the back, they drove off to the forest where Beast frequently spent his days off, away from people to stare at him, with just a compass and his furry friend, who'd never judged him based on looks.

And yet, the voracious need to spend time alone in the wild with Laurent dissipated, leaving Beast with silence in the cab and an emptiness in his chest.

He hated that his lover kept some major secret from him, hidden in plain sight and yet inaccessible. If at least Beast didn't know the secret was there, he wouldn't feel that their relationship was somehow fractured on the inside.

Beast was now aware of much more than before. He'd been coming to terms with the fact that he was dating a time traveler who had a pact with the devil, but it was difficult to even consider it simply dating, since they lived together. Yet the details of one of the biggest parts of Laurent's life were still off limits to him.

Then again, maybe this trip, away from the club and with only each other to talk to, would open up Laurent's mouth about the things Beast so desperately craved to know. How was he to make plans, know how to act, if this vital piece of the puzzle was missing? Especially that it was one apparently worthy of violence.

They hardly spoke on the way, and then, once they left behind the pickup and went along the trail, the uncomfortable silence became even more noticeable, because the beauty of nature wasn't enough of an excuse to keep their mouths shut. Beast couldn't bring himself to stop thinking about the encounter in the garage. Even during a midday stop, when they ate their lunch at the bank of a picturesque river, Beast's brain was occupied with the demon living under the same roof as them and the matters this being chose to entrust to King and Laurent.

The trip was about getting away from it all, and yet it seemed that the farther they went into the woods, the harder it was to forget that fucking house.

"Have you planned where we will camp?" Laurent asked with a subtle smile, which had been a constant along the way. He'd been making an effort to communicate and be pleasant, but Beast couldn't get himself to forget the sour note on which it started.

"Not really. We'll just get off the track and choose a place. At the lake, maybe?" Beast suggested, annoyed that even his throat felt tight despite it being several hours now. He was burning on the inside, and the greenery that was supposed to be soothing only brought him more misery.

The world had made a false promise to him. He was here with a man whose presence brought so much joy into his life, and yet the truth about him was constantly denied to Beast. It almost felt like the good days could end at any moment, with Laurent gone before he could have his second eye surgery.

So Beast tried to calm down, smell the earth, and the fresh plants. He tried enjoying the wind in his hair and religiously re-applied sun lotion to the bits of skin that weren't covered by clothes. He threw sticks to Hound and tried to discuss neutral topics. Nothing worked. It was as if his mind got stuck in a whirlwind centered around King's and Laurent's secrets, and he couldn't find a way out.

"I always used to like walking, but I don't think I've ever been on a trip like this." Laurent pulled on Beast's shirt to make him stop, and took deep breaths. He was flushed, with his nose pink from the sun, but he still smiled at Beast. "You take long strides."

"Yes," said Beast and dug into his pocket before handing Laurent the sun cream. "You're gonna get burned."

Laurent applied the cream to his face, but without a mirror, he left streaks of it all over. "I was thinking about the misery of the trip I made from France as a child, and how I would now be able to do the same, flying in the sky in less than a day." He stood closer to the edge of a cliff overlooking a dark sea. "Isn't it a wonderful world now?"

Beast swallowed hard, watching the wind play with Laurent's long hair. The breeze tangled the strands with invisible fingers and made Beast irrationally jealous. With Hound rolling in a thatch of grass, the moment really felt like they were the only two people alive, and yet the secret Laurent was holding from Beast was a thorn in his side.

"It can be very grim. There's war. And people are dying somewhere from hunger. But it is nice here."

Laurent groaned and turned around to face Beast. He held his hair up to air his sweaty back, but that only reminded Beast of the brand on his nape. "Beast! Don't make it all so dreary. How about we camp here? I want to smell the ocean when I wake up." Even with the streaks of cream on his face and his nose wrinkled, Laurent was so handsome Beast could eat him up like he was a Poptart. The kind with pink icing.

He swallowed and shook his head. "I don't want Hound to be so close to a cliff when we sleep. Let's go to the lake."

Laurent's shoulders sagged. "Oh. I hadn't thought of that." The sunny energy was gone, and he started walking down the hill. At least the brand was once again obscured by his hair.

They started the slow descent toward the lake, heading into a valley that soon opened between them when the light was slowly dwindling. "Do you want to go back someday? To the place where you were born?" asked

Beast, remembering what Laurent said when he was looking out into the ocean.

Laurent looked over his shoulder, taking his time to answer. "Yes. I would like that. Knight's showed me pictures, but that's not the same, is it?"

Beast shook his head, and it suddenly dawned on him that he would likely have trouble traveling into another country looking the way he did. The reality of not being able to fulfil yet another of Laurent's wishes clung to him like a layer of burnt skin, and he hardly spoke until they reached the pleasant, secluded spot by the water where he'd camped once before.

It was painfully beautiful, with grass so green it seemed unreal, and mountains emerging from behind the woods on the other side of the lake. The orange and purple glow of the sunset caressed their peaks, and fluffy clouds trailed over the sky just above. When Beast tossed his backpack to the grass, he caught a glimpse of the reflection of the lovely skyline before Hound rushed into the water to greedily quench his thirst.

"Can I help with the tent?" Laurent asked, running his hands over Beast's back.

Beast stiffened, not expecting the touch. He looked over his shoulder, briefly settling his eyes on the lovely face only to see the familiar need for attention that he'd seen reflected in Laurent's eyes all day. With the sun quickly descending down the colorful sky, it wouldn't have been unreasonable to ask for help, and yet in this moment Beast wished he were alone, not having to face the man who kept so many secrets from him.

Still, he agreed and with Laurent following Beast's instructions, the tent was up before it got completely dark. With Hound already at his canned dinner, Beast rushed between the trees to collect some firewood.

But he wouldn't get the time alone, because Laurent followed him like a puppy. His hair was up in a bun, because it kept getting caught in everything before, and the bared nape once again reminded Beast of the brand on Laurent. The same one his father had, and yet one *he* was deemed unworthy of getting by whatever that demon was.

"I should only get dry ones, right?" Laurent asked, picking up a large branch.

"Yes," said Beast curtly.

He knew he wasn't being entirely fair to Laurent, but the situation he'd witnessed earlier was proof that something was definitely amiss, and that the stakes were against Laurent. How was he to protect him from King without being at Laurent's side at all times? It wasn't possible. And the fact that an inhuman being had its sharp claws invisibly clasped around Laurent's neck wasn't helping either. He had the notion that he himself could bear such a weight perfectly well, but Laurent's shoulders were too fine, he was too sweet to deal with a monstrosity from another world. Beast didn't want him touched by the hellfire or marked by a brand that looked so perverse on the porcelain skin.

No matter how much Beast craved being alone for a while, when Laurent stopped gathering branches in the same area, Beast was instantly on edge. How was he not to worry when it was getting darker by the minute? What if Laurent lost his glasses? Maybe if Beast got Hound to follow Laurent everywhere, it would be safer?

When heavy clouds gathered above and obscured the moon, a different kind of menacing thought crawled into Beast's heart. What if for some reason it had been Laurent's mission to seduce Beast? Wasn't it entirely possible that Laurent had been chosen for his beauty? Then again, Laurent wasn't always agreeable. They'd argued in the past, and wouldn't someone trying to entice him have made sure Beast was always getting what he wanted?

When the light became so sparse it was starting to strain his eyes, it suddenly dawned on Beast that Laurent's vision was far worse than his, and he looked around, trying to spot the familiar figure between the trees. He called out Laurent's name.

"I'm at the camp!" Laurent yelled from afar.

Beast exhaled and carefully made his way back, watching the gray sky above the mountains. The clouds became thicker too, but he didn't think of it much when he spotted Laurent sitting with Hound, hands running up and down the dog's belly as the beast rolled, grunting with glee at every touch.

Beast stood still, just watching the two of them in front of the tent, next to a stack of wood that would become the campfire.

Laurent took his time but finally looked up at Beast. "Are you angry with me?"

"No," grumbled Beast without thinking, finally depositing the wood he collected along with Laurent's. He wasn't even sure whether he was lying or not. Maybe it was just that he was angry despite knowing that he didn't want to be so. Why did all of this have to be so convoluted when this trip was about keeping things simple?

Laurent frowned. "Okay then." He got up, giving Hound a few more pats on the belly, and… walked away.

Electricity went down Beast's whole body. He followed, as if led on a leash. "Where are you going?"

"For a walk." Laurent didn't turn around, leaving Beast to simmer in his own frustration.

"You're not going on a walk on your own. It's dark. You're gonna get lost in the woods," Beast hissed, running up to him. He wanted to grab Laurent's arm and forcefully lead him back to the camp but found that he couldn't. Why was he so angry anyway if he'd longed to be alone for most of the day? Unconsciously, Laurent merely wanted to give Beast what he wanted.

"I've got a flashlight." As if to annoy Beast more, Laurent turned it on aimed the beam at Beast's face.

Beast flinched, shielding his eyes when the beam fell on him as if he were a monster in the woods tracing Laurent's footsteps to take him to his lair. All Laurent needed was a red hood to complete the picture.

Laurent started walking again, and his boots crunched against the dirt and stones. "I'll be back later."

Beast's heart pounded, but he followed Laurent without a word, a slender figure between the shadowy trees. With the long, wavy hair and walking with such grace, he could have been some kind of spirit natural to this region. Instead, he was the prey of a beast, who couldn't even keep him content.

Laurent walked on for a while, but then slowed down. He turned around so abruptly Beast had to step back to stay out of the beam of the flashlight.

"I can hear you. This is beyond unfair. You barely talked to me all day. This trip was your idea, and now *I* don't get to be alone?"

"I wasn't hiding," Beast said before slowly dropping the hand he used to shield his eyes from the bright glow. "Am I not scary enough in the dark without the surprise?" he asked, not looking into Laurent's eyes. He understood his anger perfectly, yet his own resentment was still there, burning holes in his heart.

"You're not scary at all!" Laurent circled him and started walking back to the camp. Faster this time, but it wasn't hard to keep up with him.

"No?" asked Beast, finally moving to walk arm in arm. "Am I less scary than King?"

Laurent glared at him. "I'm not as easy to frighten as you might think."

"I bet. You made an agreement with a monster from hell."

"I did. And I will see it through whatever it takes, because I won't be the Laurent Mercier who got sentenced to hang. I killed Fane in self-defense!"

Beast grabbed Laurent's shoulder, stopping him from going any further. The trees around them cast long shadows, locking them in a bubble that smelled of fungi and fresh air. With the flashlight as the only source of light, Laurent's face was sculpted by darkness and light. Beast swallowed, studying the one eye he could see well. It looked back at him, inquisitive yet bearing no trace of fear whatsoever.

"This secret... it feels like a wall between us. I see you, but I can't really touch you. I keep thinking what this is about, especially after today, because whatever it is you're doing, King doesn't like it. I can't have him attack you."

Laurent glanced toward their tent not far away. "You can't always know everything. Weren't you the one to say that we have to be allowed to keep our secrets? I promise that I will tell you the truth one day, but right now, I cannot. I'm handling King."

"Are you? Because it didn't look like you were. He's been a loose cannon lately, so who knows how he's gonna react when he gets high next time?" Beast said, pulling on Laurent's shoulders to make their eyes meet.

All it got Beast was a groan. "I don't know. I take it one day at a time."

Beast exhaled, unclenching his hands to just let them rest on the well-formed shoulders. As if this conversation weren't going bad enough, a drop of rain fell on Beast's head. After a whole day of pushing Laurent away, the urgent need to touch him now came as a surprise, but since Laurent had come into Beast's life, there were many things he didn't quite understand about the way he felt.

"Can you promise me at least that you're not gonna leave? That you'll stay?" he asked, leaning closer and glancing into Laurent's eyes as his hands climbed up Laurent's neck to cup his face. Did he even need to finish the sentence and say *with me*, or was his meaning clear enough? He could overlook anything and forgive all if Laurent never left. If only he could be there, proving to Beast every day that he was worthy of someone so lovely.

Laurent finally focused all of his attention on Beast, and he put his slender hand over Beast's, cuddling up his cheek to Beast's palm as the rain started getting more intense. "To stay in this time, I need to do my duty. I will do everything I can to do so. But there is something I can tell you. The closer we are, the closer we get, the more intense our… lovemaking gets," Laurent's cheek became hotter against Beast's palm, "the angrier King will be, and the better off you will be for it. And I hoped this trip could bring us closer still. Away from everyone's scrutiny. No tests, no lies, just you and me."

Beast gave a shuddery sigh, so completely engrossed in watching Laurent in the sharp glow of the flashlight he barely noticed that fat droplets of water were trailing down the shaved sides of his head and under his collar. The dampness made Laurent's own face shine as if it were covered in morning dew, brown hair not yet flat from the downpour, eyes shining at Beast as if he were the last man left in the world. Or at least the only one that mattered.

Beast would protect Laurent at all cost.

"Just you and me," he repeated, overwhelmed by the realization just how much of a pain he'd been throughout the day to this beautiful creature who only tried to get through to him.

Laurent pulled on the collar of Beast's T-shirt to pull him down into a kiss, and it was as if he were pulling on Beast's heart instead, with a thread attached to Laurent's little finger.

"I'm soaking through," Laurent said with a smile once their lips finally parted, the kiss tasting of bubblegum and rain.

Beast grinned and pulled Laurent close, unwilling to let go despite the embrace making their walk back to the tent more awkward. "I know just the way to make you warm," he whispered against Laurent's hair, walking him to the campsite, only to be greeted by a yellowish glow in Hound's eyes when the light fell on him. The dog didn't seem to mind the rain much, but when he saw his humans, he gently rose to all fours and stretched before making a circle around them, as if needing to make sure the whole pack was back together.

Laurent petted Hound's head, but then rushed for the tent. "Our wood's getting soaked, but I guess we wouldn't be making a fire anyway."

Beast knew that with Laurent in it, this would be the coziest tent he'd ever stayed in.

"Oh, we will definitely be making a fire," Beast said, grinning uncontrollably. There was a place for Hound in the annex of the tent, so he ordered the dog to stay and crawled into the dome-shaped room where they previously made their beds. The rain tapped on the roof, but in here they were safe from the cold, and once Beast closed the zippered opening, the flashlight guided him right back to Laurent, who was putting his glasses back in their case.

They kissed.

The constant tapping of raindrops against the tent was like background music to their heated touch. Laurent's lips were so soft and pliant when it came to kisses, always reminding Beast of how eagerly Laurent took cock into that warm mouth.

The way Laurent had spoken of 'lovemaking', and 'no tests' had Beast almost sure that it was an invitation for the kind of fuck that Laurent had denied Beast in the past. This would have been clearer if Laurent weren't such a prude when it came to swearing. Funnily enough, Laurent was definitely not coy when it came to sex within the boundaries they'd established.

Beast hoped to expand those boundaries tonight.

Laurent pulled on Beast's clothes, kissing him more intensely and wrapping his legs around Beast's thighs.

The heat of his body was still distant under the clothes, but Beast wanted to amend that as soon as possible. Peeling the wet layers off Laurent was not even a chore. Each inch of bare flesh was a welcome sight in the shaky beam from the flashlight, and Beast rubbed his face against the damp skin, wondering how incredible it was to sense the burning heat beneath a layer of cool rainwater. He enclosed Laurent's nipple in his mouth, rapidly pulling Laurent's hips closer to his own when the boy groaned at the sensation.

"I love being all alone with you like this," Laurent whispered, as if afraid to disturb the quiet night outside. His fingers trailed Beast's back until they reached the hem of Beast's T-shirt. Laurent pulled on it to get it over Beast's head.

Beast rubbed his palms up and down Laurent's slender arms, eventually clasping their hands together as the initially soft kiss turned more urgent. "I wish you never leave my side."

"Pretty easy when you know I have nowhere to go, and that you are my whole world." Laurent teased Beast with a lick to his cheek, rocking his hips under Beast.

Beast brushed their noses together and lowered himself to rub their bodies where they were still covered by denim. He groaned when his own stiffening cock pressed against Laurent's. It was a simple pleasure, and it felt like the most natural thing in the world. "What if you could go anywhere you wanted?" he asked, unable to keep the question in despite knowing how needy it was. His longing for Laurent's approval was growing with each day they spent together, and it wasn't just because of Laurent's beauty, or because he was the only one to look at Beast as if he were any other man. Laurent could truly see the man Beast was on the inside.

Laurent groaned in response. "Beast... Can you feel how excited I am? You're the only man I trust like this. You could offer me a visit to La Rochelle, and I'd still rather be in this tent." He spread his legs under Beast, as if to emphasize his point.

Beast's breath caught, and he showered the soft ivory neck with kisses. Beast had never been a romantic, and yet there was something about Laurent that made him wish he knew how to write poetry that would do justice to his lover. "I am going to take you to La Rochelle someday. It's a promise."

"And I am going to show you tonight just how much I want you," Laurent whispered into Beast's ear, wrapping his legs around Beast's hips and rocking his hard-on against Beast's stomach again and again. "Because I really do. I want to know how it feels to have you inside me."

The shiver those words caused went all the way to Beast's balls, robbing him of coherent thoughts. He opened Laurent's jeans and tugged them down his well-shaped legs. Laurent told him he used to walk everywhere back in his time, and the exercise had given his body a shape that asked for worship. With Laurent's remaining clothes tossed aside, Beast leaned over him, hungrily touching every bit of skin. His hand cast delicious shadows over the smooth flesh, and he took his time watching his fingers trail over the back of Laurent's thigh and up the curve of his ass.

"Tell me. How do you want it to happen?" he asked, eager for even the tiniest bit of knowledge when it came to Laurent's expectations. The last thing he wanted was to disappoint his sensitivities, because clearly Laurent had been reluctant about going all the way so far.

"I… I want you to take the lead," Laurent uttered, and his eyes were full of trust Beast would never dare break. "I'm not certain of the details of how we should proceed. But… I liked that first time in bed with you, when you seemed to know how to do everything. Things I haven't even known possible turned into unexpected pleasure with you." Laurent trailed his hands over the patches of scars on Beast's shoulders, not minding the texture at all. If anything, he seemed to explore with delight.

Beast hummed, smiling at Laurent and finally pushing down his own pants, without ever breaking eye contact. With his forehead resting against Laurent's, he got naked quickly and spread his body over Laurent's, allowing him to feel its greater weight and gently rubbing his cock against Laurent's stomach. He wanted to speak, but words escaped him yet again when he met Laurent's loving, warm gaze. Nothing he could say would be appropriate, because his mind was going down to the gutter at the thought of 'taking the lead'.

Fuck yes, he could do that.

He could take the lead all night long. He'd be the first man to show Laurent how pleasurable it can be to take a cock deep inside. So far Laurent had proven himself as a very pliant lover, so Beast could only hope getting fucked would be up his street as well.

Laurent left a gentle kiss on Beast's jaw, only feeding the fantasy of breaking into all that innocence until Laurent was flushed, panting, and begging for more.

"It's… big." Laurent laughed nervously, rubbing himself against Beast's dick.

"It is," Beast said, pulling his hips back slightly and, with the help of his hand, pushing it between Laurent's thighs so that he could sense the girth and length minutes before that thick prick would slide into the tight heat of his body. "Imagine how it will feel inside you," he said with a kiss to Laurent's chin.

The gasp it got Beast was music to his ears. The past weeks with Laurent had been a fuck-fest in itself, one that Beast had deeply missed when he was away with Gray and Joker, but he hadn't actually penetrated a man in twelve years. The prospect of doing that with Laurent was making his muscles tingle with anticipation. That virginal hole would be so tight on his cock, Laurent's moans would be raspy and drenched with lust. Beast had fantasized about it many times when rimming that pink pucker.

Laurent squeezed his thighs over Beast's cock, clinging to Beast tightly. "I've thought about it."

Beast pulled his teeth over Laurent's lip and made a hard push with his cock, rubbing the head against the sensitive flesh between Laurent's ass and balls. He rose, straightening his arms to look down as he thrust several times, with only a bit of spit and precum for lubrication. The friction of it was making his head spin, and he stopped, lying back on top of Laurent to pull him closer, embracing the smaller body so hard he could feel the rapid pounding of Laurent's heart against his ribcage. Or was it his own? He didn't know anymore.

"Yes. The way they did it in the movies we watched together?" Beast had introduced Laurent to porn. Nothing super hardcore, and mostly clips depicting the kind of stuff they were already doing anyway, but he played a nice film with anal sex as well, quietly watching Laurent's reaction to the couple depicted on the screen. Was this what Laurent had in mind now?

Laurent wouldn't meet his gaze, but his touch on Beast's skin was constant, as if he couldn't get enough. "Yes. And sometimes I saw people have sex in the clubhouse, and I imagined how it would be to have you do that with me. I… I feel like I give up all of myself to you when you take over, and I keep wanting more of that feeling."

Beast licked his lip, watching Laurent in silence. The rain has become more rapid, now drumming above their heads like a force urging him into action. He reached over Laurent and tugged his backpack closer. He'd put lube in one of the easily reachable pockets—just in case—and was so glad he didn't have to ruin the atmosphere by tossing everything out of the main compartment. With the tube in hand, he rolled them both over, so that he and Laurent lay on their sides facing one another.

The smooth glide of Laurent's mane over Beast's naked arm was a pleasure in its own right, but his heart wanted to see Laurent every step of the way. He cradled the warm head in the crook of his arm and urged Laurent's lips to open with his tongue, trailing his fingers down the curve of his spine, teasing and grabbing gently until his hand rested on Laurent's buttock. It was round and fit so well in Beast's hand he grinned against Laurent's lips.

Laurent's cock twitched when Beast dipped the tips of his fingers between his ass cheeks. The skin on Laurent's arms was covered in goose bumps, and Laurent's kisses only became more desperate.

Beast didn't want to rush things, since he'd waited so long for this already, but his stiff cock was making exercising patience much harder. All he wanted was to see his dick dip between those juicy round halves until it disappeared inside of Laurent's body over and over again. He didn't even realize when the fantasy led him to circling Laurent's pucker with his fingertip. Laurent moaned into Beast's lips and arched against him in the most exquisite way.

Trailing warm kisses down Laurent's neck and onto his arm, he pulled on Laurent's knee, bringing it to rest on Beast's hip so that his hole would be exposed. Beast groaned, rubbing his cheek against Laurent's damp hair and moved his hips for good measure, until his long prick settled between Laurent's thighs again, comfortably resting against the heat of Laurent's sac. He pushed their bodies closer, squeezing Laurent's cock in between, hard enough to tease yet with not enough pressure to make his lover come prematurely. That would only happen once Beast was inside. With a devilish smile tugging at his mouth, he pushed the tube into Laurent's hand. "Squeeze some on my hand."

Laurent's face was already getting that glorious flush that always made Beast want to get Laurent to suck him. Laurent's obedience had Beast growing harder. Every lick of his lips, every uncertain glance into Beast's eyes had him feeling like this was special and binding Laurent to him the same way Beast was already tangled up in Laurent.

"Is this enough?" Laurent whispered, pushing his cock against Beast's body.

Beast rubbed his forehead against Laurent's and lapped at his half-open lips. They were warm, and sweet, and he wanted to do nothing else but kiss them all day long. "A little bit more, so I can push into you real easy."

Laurent shivered at the words, and the wolf inside of Beast awakened completely. He'd eat his beautiful boy alive until Laurent was gasping and panting to be devoured. He began the process by biting into Laurent's lips with a groan as Laurent squeezed more lube onto Beast's fingers. The cock pressing into Beast was hot and throbbing, but would get no more attention until Beast decided so.

With so much slick gel in his palm, the glide of Beast's fingers into the crack between Laurent's buttocks was a smooth, languid affair that had them both groaning for entirely different reasons. Laurent's eyes shut, and he gave a low moan, hiding his face in the crook of Beast's neck as Beast explored the sensitive skin with his digits, moving them up and down, almost all the way along the perineum, then back across the hole itself, which twitched violently when one of his fingertips rolled over it. The soft folds around Laurent's anus were a thing of beauty on their own, and Beast took his time swirling his fingers over them, not quite trying to open Laurent's body yet.

It was odd how despite the urgency burning in his balls all but commanding him to roll Laurent over and take him at last, another part of him wanted this to go on forever, until his careful touch had Laurent so hot, so pliant he'd beg for it. The slender body shivered with anticipation, suddenly humping against Beast when he finally dipped half of his index finger into Laurent's ass. It felt smooth and slick around his digit, almost like oiled-up silk, and beckoned him closer.

Laurent wrapped his arms around Beast's neck, hugging him tightly and kissing the side of Beast's head, as if he really found the badly damaged skin and missing ear of no importance. Each time Laurent moved against Beast had his ass sliding back and forth, deliciously stirring around the finger. Laurent seemed so restless Beast smiled at the thought that he'd soon be pinned down and taking whatever Beast chose to give him.

Even now, Beast was horny around Laurent all the time, making up for the missing years, but he remembered what a mess of buzzing hormones he'd been at Laurent's age. If only Laurent ended up enjoying this kind of fuck, he'd be begging Beast for more in no time.

"Even your fingers are big," Laurent whimpered, clinging to Beast.

"That's why I need to push them in first," Beast said, moving his hips in tune with the way he gently thrust inside Laurent with his index finger. His cock received just enough stimulation from this to make Beast's head burn with heat and his balls draw closer to his body. When Laurent's anus easily accepted two digits at once, Beast kept them still, nipping on his lover's trembling lips with growing urgency. "But I really need to be inside you soon. I've been imagining this so many times."

"You have?" Laurent gasped, as if it wasn't obvious that he was the object of Beast's constant lust. The way he kept fidgeting on the fingers made Beast's cock throb at the fantasy of how the same motion would feel around it.

Laurent's arms held Beast with surprising strength, but it was the slight drizzle of precum from Laurent's cock, gliding down Beast's stomach that gave him a surge of satisfaction.

He gave Laurent one last aggressive kiss before pulling away and moving Laurent to all fours. He kneeled behind him, rubbing the perfect back with one hand while his eyes focused on the glistening wetness of lube all around Laurent's pliant hole, which dilated and narrowed slightly as the boyish body arched in front of Beast, moving against Beast's hand like a cat in heat.

"You have no idea. All I can think of is leaving my cum inside you."

The tent was getting damp with their heavy breaths, but Beast didn't mind. It felt like they were locked in a cocoon together. Laurent looked over his shoulder and pulled his long hair over the other, giving Beast a great view of the flushed face and the glistening eyes in the faint yellow light from the flashlight that has rolled over in the sleeping bags.

"I… I've wanted that too," Laurent uttered in a whisper, and Beast could think of few things that would be as sweet to hear. And if the words weren't lovely enough, Laurent lowered himself to his elbows, spreading his thighs a bit more, which created a picture so erotic Beast had to grab the base of his cock to keep himself from coming on the spot.

His beautiful Laurent was so open to him, so ready, his ass on show, his hole all slippery and available with the way Laurent spread his legs.

Laurent's beauty stunned Beast so deeply he needed to consciously start breathing again. He applied some more lube to his cock while massaging Laurent's anus with his thumb, slowly and gently. He liked to imagine it as the kind of touch that would ultimately make Laurent go completely soft on the inside once Beast finally entered him.

"That's right. I want no one else this way," he whispered, moving his hips closer and rubbing the cockhead up and down the slick hole, letting it glide down all the way to Laurent's ass, only to grab it at the base again and nudge at the opening over and over.

The sharp moans he got from Laurent in return were pure bliss. That was what Laurent needed to remember. That no one would ever give him pleasure the way Beast could.

Beast smirked at the thought that with Laurent so short, he'd easily be able to kiss his lips even from behind once their bodies connected.

"Go on, I want to feel it. I need to know," Laurent said breathlessly, looking back again despite his shoulders trembling.

Beast wasn't sure if he should stare more at the perfectly angelic face, or the pert round ass that he couldn't wait to see wrap around his dick. Even just having his cockhead nestled between Laurent's buttocks was such a fucking turn-on that he could hardly think.

Without considering it much, he put his dick against Laurent's hole and pushed, carefully watching the lovely features even as pleasure triggered explosions in his head and clouded the edges of his vision.

The tight ring of muscle clamped down on his dick right under the cockhead and this time it was him making an incoherent groan. He thought he knew what to expect, but time must have made him forget just how good it felt to push into that channel of muscle.

Laurent arched his back, and Beast wanted to kiss each beauty spot on the pale skin. Laurent's head dipped lower between the shoulders and he pushed it against the sleeping bag, just as restless as he was before.

Beast looked down, at his cock halfway buried between the lovely globes of Laurent's ass, but with Laurent having gone so quiet, he gently slid his hands all the way to Laurent's buttocks, breathing slowly to distract himself from the mind-numbing sensation around his dick. "Laurent?"

"Y-yes?" came the muffled voice from behind the mass of wavy hair. Laurent's thighs trembled, and he stirred his hips every now and then, as if teasing Beast's cock on purpose.

Not being a teenager anymore came with the perk of being able to hold in his excitement that bit longer, but Beast was still on such a high he hardly remembered what exactly he wanted to ask. "You fine?" he whispered in the end, rubbing Laurent's back in slow circles.

"I'm a… a bit overwhelmed." Laurent pulled his head up and looked back, his full lips trembling. "But I still want it all. Your hands all over me."

His eyelids were halfway down, which made his eyes barely visible from beneath of the long dark eyelashes. Beast could hardly recall seeing anything sexier than those 'fuck-me' eyes.

Beast licked his lips and pushed in, assured that Laurent wasn't in pain, but this wonderful ass was still so tight that by the time Beast's pubic bone pressed against the soft buttocks, he was panting so hard ne needed to think of something else for a few seconds, or he'd come before delivering what he'd promised. "Oh, baby, you feel so damn good. You have no idea," Beast whispered, smoothing his palms up Laurent's sides.

His lover's body was so pliant to touch, so hot and strong despite its size. Beast trailed his hands all the way to Laurent's chest, pressing them against stiff nipples, then rubbing the puckered flesh slowly until he had Laurent moaning and stirring. Beast's cock loved every little movement Laurent made, and it felt as though they really had become one.

Laurent held himself up on one elbow, but raised his other hand to entwine his fingers with Beast's. "You have all of me," he whispered.

Beast gave a low whimper and leaned over Laurent, covering him with his body, for comfort, for heat, and the closeness that both of them so desperately needed. He pushed his fingers into Laurent's hair, and used it to turn Laurent's face toward him, for a deep sensual kiss that sent electricity down his limbs and into his balls. The pressure around his cock was so wonderful he wanted to just ride Laurent all night in that languid rhythm that allowed them both to be free with their touch.

The tapping of water against the tent became steadier now, a white noise to cut them off from anything else in the world as Beast moved back and forth, dragging his cockhead over Laurent's prostate.

What Beast loved so much about kissing as he pushed his cock in and out at a steady pace was that each of his moves caused a moan, a whimper, a gasp that Beast could directly feel on his mouth. Laurent's fingers tightened on the sleeping bag every time Beast penetrated him deeply.

As the pace at which Beast thrust his hips quickened, once Laurent even bit Beast's lip when Beast pulled out only to slam back in all the way to his balls. He loved the way Laurent's hole fit so snugly around him, as if inviting him to come already and leave all his spunk inside of that gorgeous body.

He could have made the penetration deeper if he simply kneeled behind Laurent, and he wasn't opposed to doing so in the future, but right now he just wanted to be close. As close as possible, with Laurent's breath teasing his lips in between kisses, his hair tickling Beast's flesh, the nimble body moving to the rhythm of Beast's thrusts, to meet them halfway, so beautifully needy and burning with lust.

Beast bit on Laurent's ear, pulling on it gently as he moved his fingers down the tense stomach, toward Laurent's cock, which he could hear slapping against Laurent's belly over and over. Not knowing how long he'd last, Beast needed to make Laurent come as well, feel his cum drizzle between his own greedy fingers.

As soon as he touched Laurent's cock, the smaller body bucked against him. Laurent arched his ass higher, pushing onto Beast's cock and swallowing all of it in one push.

"Please, yes!" Laurent exclaimed, needy and dragging his fingers over the sleeping bag. The begging made Beast's cock swell inside the hot, throbbing body, and for a moment his mind became fuzzy.

He'd give his pretty boy all he wanted and more.

"Like this?" Beast licked up the nape covered in a brand that had given Beast so much grief. But the sigil was now a part of Laurent, a part of what had brought the boy here. To him.

He sped up the thrusts of his hips, pushing into Laurent's ass at a rapid pace. His hand moved over Laurent's prick at the same speed, making him buck against Beast time and time again. He needed to remember this, because it was so fucking hot he to see Laurent jerking on his dick like that, he was sure he'd come—

The wanton sound of Laurent's moans mixed with the heat of spunk drizzling through Beast's fingers created a sensation so powerful that between that and the glorious spasms of muscles around Beast's dick, it was unclear which made his brain go white with pleasure.

He curled up around Laurent, holding onto him with frantic devotion, his lips hard against the pulsing artery in Laurent's neck as they spasmed together, eventually collapsing on their sides, still very much connected, still in each other's arms even as their bodies slowly cooled, minds soothed by the steady tapping of rain above their heads.

Beast pressed his cheek against Laurent's, swirling his fingertips over Laurent's reddened chest as they lay in silence, unbothered by anyone and anything. With Hound guarding their peace, nothing could put an end to the glorious afterglow that put to rest over a decade of Beast's inadequacy. If Laurent wanted him this way, if Laurent loved him back, then who was he to question that decision? Why would he not let Laurent shower him with all this affection?

When Laurent pulled Beast's hand up to his lips and kissed the knuckles, Beast could both cry at the way his heart clenched, and get horny over the fact that there was cum on that hand.

This mixture of tenderness and sexual attraction was like nothing he ever felt before. Only now, with Laurent for comparison, he could see there had been much more physical attraction than love in the relationship that broke his heart all those years ago.

The realization felt as if Laurent had pulled out a thorn that had been stuck in Beast's heart since forever.

Chapter 24 - Laurent

Laurent didn't like Lizzy's band, *Beasts of Hell* all that much. They made an ungodly racket, made obvious mistakes as they played, but despite those faults, everyone else seemed to consider the music great, so Laurent politely went along with it and didn't voice his opinions. Beast's birthday was in under two weeks now, and it meant that he was soon to be free of the pact.

Free to pursue an independent life in 2017. There was no doubt in his mind that the Kings of Hell Motorcycle Club would be a big part of his future, so if most of the Kings and their friends liked metal music, he wouldn't complain about it too much. Was there a kind of music named after plastic? He assumed he would like that so much better. But despite the noise leaving his ears numb each time metal was played, he wanted to be a part of it all, even if only because Beast was the VP of the club and Laurent revolved around him like the Earth did around the Sun.

There was a big party planned for mid-September, and so several local musical troupes came to present their work to the Kings of Hell in hope of being employed for that evening. Laurent knew almost nothing about the strange musical culture of 2017, but there was a sense of urgency in all the new people who came to present their skills. Beast told him nearby Portland was a place where many different bands could find admirers, but locally, the clubhouse was a prominent venue, famous for its wild banquets, although during events that were accessible to outsiders. sex in the open was considered less acceptable. Tonight though, members and hangarounds could relax in familiar company.

Knight certainly made good use of the open atmosphere. Since the breakup with Jordan, he was at it every evening, shamelessly naked in a large bed that was only partially obscured from view by a velvet curtain.

Three more people had joined him long ago, and Laurent did his very best not to look at the obscenity of it all. He tried not to judge, since he himself was involved in acts someone else could call indecent, but Knight's lack of modesty was something else altogether. Knight never spoke of Jordan anymore, as if the few months they'd shared didn't matter to him at all. She only came over once, to retrieve some of her belongings from the clubhouse, and even that visit ended up in a massive argument, which for once hadn't been defused with sex.

Laurent had never liked Jordan much, and apart from hurtful words spewed by both parties, there hadn't been any violence between the former couple, but the whole break-up made Laurent a bit uneasy. If Knight had been in a relationship with Jordan for months, only to part as if they'd never shared a bond, could that be Laurent's future as well? He only worried about it on melancholic evenings when Beast was away because when they were together, everything else ceased to matter. His man was a mountain both in the physical and spiritual sense, his stature as large as his convictions were unshakeable.

In the last month, their intense and frequent lovemaking seemed to have created an unbreakable bond between them. Never in his life had Laurent thought he could let his guard down this much around another man.

Still, was it wise of Laurent to tie himself to Beast's future in a way so inseparable? Regardless of the sense that Beast was a trustworthy person, Laurent knew that no ties were resistant to wear and tear. There was so much he still needed to learn, and the last thing he wanted was to end up like some of the mistresses of wealthy men in his time. Used and thrown away with their hearts broken. He didn't believe that would be the case with him and Beast—because Beast had a genuine heart and would likely not just toss Laurent out to the streets if he fell out of love—but Laurent knew he needed to think of his future and was slowly saving money whenever he received payment for any tasks he performed for the club. Knowing that the stash was growing made his sleep better.

With yet another group of musicians done with their cacophonic songs, Lizzy and his band, who were here in the role of experts, started whispering to each other in the silence left behind once the music died down. Laurent was glad, because the electric guitar had been particularly cruel to his ears in the hands of the scrawny boy who played it moments before.

A group of young women took the stage next, each one in tattered clothes that belonged on beggar prostitutes, not young ladies. They all wore men's boots that seemed far too big on them, and the one who approached the microphone without an instrument at all had one side of her dress sliding off her shoulder, completely uncovering her underwear, which in these modern times was particularly sparse.

"What's that sneer, Laurent?" Nao laughed, sipping her beer next to him. "You don't like 'em?"

"No! No! I must have drifted off."

Nao chuckled, putting an arm around Laurent's shoulder. To be fair, her clothes were even skimpier than the singer's and consisted only of a pair of denim shorts that uncovered half of her buttocks, and a blouse that barely hid her chest.

The woman behind the percussion set was gently nudging the metal plates used for making particularly disturbing sounds when Fox's bellowing tore through the air at such high volume it might have even been heard with a band playing. "Prospect, get your ass here. And bring a bucket!"

Laurent looked away from the stage to see what was going on. Jake ran through the door moments later, standing straight in front of Fox, as if he were saluting, and the bucket—a rifle. "Yes, sir?" The furrowed brow on the handsome young face spoke of the kind of focus he'd need for arithmetics, not a task that required a bucket.

Fox stepped back, revealing a young woman hunched over the floor and shaking so badly Laurent's first reaction was to offer his help. Only then did he notice the puddle of vomit between her hands, and the sudden sense of nausea made him look back to Jake, who gave a curt nod, eager like a young soldier for the praise of his general.

"Clean the sick and help Thalia. Take her somewhere where she can sleep it off. Then come back. Knight asked for you."

That last sentence made Jake nod frantically. "Yes, Fox! Sir. I'm on it!" He looked toward the curtain and bed with the kind of devotion Hound sometimes expressed for Beast. It was… unsettling.

"Better make it quick!" Knight laughed, pulling the curtain aside to reveal his naked body, with a motionless girl draped over his legs. He poked his tongue at the inside of his cheek in the same lewd fashion Beast had once showed Laurent.

"Yes, I will!" Jake turned around on his heel, probably to get a mop and water.

Knight leaned back, immediately assaulted by a pair of bright red lips as a topless woman climbed into his lap and pressed her large, naked breasts against his chest.

Laurent had never liked the way Jake was treated by the club members, even if he seemed to never complain. Beast had explained to Laurent that 'prospecting' was something most of the club members had gone through, and that it was a transitional period before becoming a part of the inner circle of the club. That didn't change the fact that the practice of prospecting reminded Laurent of his servitude with Mr. Barnave. He'd never again submit himself to such an arrangement if he could avoid it.

Lizzy's voice coming from the speakers turned most people's attention back to the stage. In light distorted by sweet-smelling smoke from special weed-packed cigarettes Beast forbade Laurent to accept, his bright yellow contact lenses made Lizzy look like yet another creature of the underworld. Despite enjoying the stage so much, Lizzy seemed quite tame when he spoke, clearing his throat before presenting the young women as Hellcats. The music the band produced right after did sound like a bag of cats tossed into the river Styx, but Laurent was getting used to it and just had some more wine to dull his senses somewhat.

His eyes wandered, and across the room he spotted Beast. The handsome profile was prominent above the crowd that barely reached Beast's shoulders, his hair had been styled with particular care earlier, his clothes so fresh Laurent couldn't stop himself from burying his face in Beast's chest before they left the apartment. Purple light cast dark shadows on his face, as if the words scribbled all over melted, creating pools of ink in the creases.

To others, Beast might not be the dashing suitor one would fall for at the snap of fingers, but Laurent saw everything Beast represented. The strength that gave Laurent a thrill when Beast carried him to the bedroom. The emotional depth of the Dante quotes in Latin sprinkled all over Beast's body. The tenderness of hands that looked as if they were made only to mete out violence.

Laurent wasn't going blind anymore and he'd seen enough of the world to know that out of the two of them he would be the one considered conventionally attractive. But it was Beast who held Laurent's hand throughout the operation on his other eye, and it was Beast who explained this new world to him.

Because of Beast's kindness, strangers could think that Laurent looked past Beast's exterior, that he was somehow generous with his affection to someone who others called a beast. But apart from all the gentle traits in Beast's personality, Laurent wasn't simply wishing to remain in his care. In fact, he was also greedy for touch and selfish about having all of Beast to himself. He was not doing Beast a favor by being with him, because it was Beast who made Laurent's body spasm and shiver. He took their lovemaking to a point where Laurent was too overwhelmed by pleasure to remember propriety and shamelessly gave in to the crude, animalistic *fucking*.

Such, such good fucking.

So when his eyes met Beast's, all that mattered was that the two of them knew what they meant to each other.

Beast grinned so widely it made his burnt face look somewhat asymmetrical, but it was yet another quirk of his appearance that Laurent had learnt to love about his man. Like any other supposed imperfection, it was a part of him, and made him seem somehow even more handsome.

Beast patted the man he'd been talking to on the back and made his way through the herd of drunk people who danced to the horrendous music. He never looked away from Laurent as he swam toward him through the purple sea of heads.

Modern people didn't know how to properly dance, it seemed, but with Beast Laurent would gladly just move around to the rhythm, because it would feel good to be close.

A strong shove to his back sent Laurent closer to Beast, and when he looked back, Nao, who now embraced a youngish guy with a red beard, gestured for Laurent to go.

Laurent stood on his toes to get a kiss from Beast. "Late," he said, but didn't mind really. He'd had fun with Nao, pointing out who had the worst costume.

Beast leaned down so that his lips brushed against Laurent's ear, and he needed to actually scream to be heard over the ungodly racket. "Needed to deal with something. I'm all yours now," he said, and his large hands slid to Laurent's hips, pulling him closer, and then between the other people, who danced in groups or in pairs.

A woman nearby was bent over and rubbed her buttocks against the crotch of the man standing behind her. Laurent wouldn't have been comfortable dancing like that, not with everyone watching, but he didn't even have to ask Beast whether he'd want such a thing or not.

Sometimes, it really felt like they could communicate without words, and when Beast rested one palm on Laurent's back and pulled his fingers down Laurent's arm, they both moved slowly, to a rhythm only they could hear.

Laurent wrapped his arms around Beast's waist, marvelling at what a sturdy presence Beast was. "I still never know how to dance to these modern melodies," he said and put his cheek on Beast's chest.

"Just ignore it. This is much better," Beast yelled at Laurent while they languidly rolled over the floor, hugging one another as if this was the most natural thing in the world. Throughout his time here Laurent learned that not all people in 2017 were as accepting of two men being together as he'd hoped, but that didn't seem important when the people who actually mattered were completely fine with his desires. The world was changing at a slower pace than he'd initially imagined, but maybe it was really Beast that he'd been meant to meet? Even with the noise attacking them from all sides, he could hear the firm heartbeat against his ear and delight in it.

Maybe the whole thing with King sucking vitality out of his beloved was about to be over on Beast's birthday, and that was the point of keeping

Beast here. So that the devil could make good on his promise. Laurent couldn't wait to come clean about it all.

To think that back in 1805, his dreams had been so modest. To find a man who he could be with somehow, to have a means of supporting himself despite his failing eyesight, to be free of his servitude to Mr. Barnave. And now? He had so much more. He lived in a world where his affection for a man was acceptable. Where the man he chose cared for him deeply, where his eyes had been healed, and where he was making a modest income.

He kissed Beast's bicep discreetly, and it got him a sweet smile in return. But with Beast pulling Laurent toward the newly-freed sitting space in the corner, Laurent didn't object. If they weren't dancing in tune with the music anyway, they might as well give up for now and delight in the intimacy of a dance to decent music, which was still attainable on special plastic disks. Later. Another time.

But as they walked off the dance floor and past Nao, who was now deeply involved with her redhead's mouth despite still being King's girlfriend, Laurent inevitably looked for her man, worried he might not like this very much. True, Nao seemed to have many partners and didn't try to hide it, but King was the kind of man who'd smile at you in one minute and punch your nose in in the next.

Fortunately, King was busy talking about something to Martina by the set of steps leading to the stage, but with the way he grabbed her arm, the conversation looked more like an argument. Laurent stopped Beast, pointing with his head to the beginnings of violence.

Martina's face was visibly red even under the usual thick layer of makeup, and she shoved at King with an unhappy expression.

Beast's chest sagged, and he slid his hand to Laurent's, leading him closer while the four girls thrashed on stage, jumping around and screaming into microphones, because their performance could hardly be called singing. Laurent really did his best not to judge, but it was close to impossible sometimes.

Laurent's stomach sank when King twisted his hand in Martina's red mane and tugged on it so brutally the pain expressed on her face couldn't be just for show. Beast sped up, pushing apart people as he walked up to the stage, just in time for the act to end. Lizzy said a few words to conclude the performance, but he couldn't mute other voices, which resonated loud and clear in the void left behind by music.

"What the hell are you doing? Let go of her," hissed Beast, grabbing his father's wrist.

"I'm doing whatever I think is appropriate when my fucking girlfriend is pissing me off on purpose!" King stood his ground, but even he was shorter than Beast.

"I just wanted to sing a song with Lizzy's band," Martina whined, already in tears.

Laurent's heart sank at the sight.

Beast looked between the two, a big frown marring his forehead. "Is that it? You're yanking at her because she wants to sing a song with Lizzy? What's your problem?"

King snarled but let go of Martina, who pulled back her hair and rubbed the wetness off her cheeks, smudging the black tint all over.

"I don't want her to perform. Should have actually asked me. She wouldn't have been embarrassed then," he said, as if that was the answer to the actual problem.

"I wanted to surprise you!" Martina looked to her toes with her lips trembling.

"Should've fuckin' given me a surprise blowjob then. You looking for a new boyfriend or something, that you have to advertize yourself like a cow?"

Laurent wished to get closer and give King a piece of his mind, which with Beast for backup wasn't even that risky, but he knew better. King was a tyrant, and would find a way to get back at Laurent sooner or later. It was better if he stayed out of it.

Martina pulled out of King's grip and shoved at his chest. "You're such an asshole!"

"What's wrong with singing? You're fine with them having sex with other people, so why not that?" hissed Beast, spreading his big arms.

King snorted. "Because if she gets too much into it, it will distract her. And I want here here, not on tour, or trying her luck in fucking Portland!"

He scowled when Martina poured a whole glass of water into his face, tossed the container to the floor, and ran off, leaving the two of them with King, who rolled his eyes, as if he were the reasonable one here.

"See? A property of the club but can't even show respect when it's needed."

Laurent took a few steps toward the door, considering going after Martina, but he wasn't as close to her as he was with Nao. He didn't want to pry. It left them all standing there uncomfortably, with no music to kill the silence, and only the awkward sound of skin slapping against skin coming from behind the curtain where Knight was having sex with someone.

Lizzy went to the middle of the stage and looked around, briefly skirting his yellow gaze over Laurent. "Okay. So it seems one contestant isn't participating after all. As for the bands, we will need a few days to make up our minds, but you are all invited to stay for the party and have fun."

King grinned widely and walked into the bright light, so that he'd too be visible. As if on cue, Lizzy pointed his hand toward him. "King's orders!"

The clapping to that was somewhat flaccid, but when King added that he was bringing up a free keg of beer, everyone cheered with more enthusiasm.

Lizzy's eyes settled on Beast, and he smiled widely, even sticking out his split tongue that never failed to give Laurent the shivers. "Ah, one more thing. I've heard someone prepared something special for their boy tonight, and I bet everyone will want to see that."

Laurent glanced around, unsure who Lizzy might be talking about, but then, the light around him became brighter, and he caught Beast frowning at the stage, somewhat tense. Lizzy didn't seem to worry much about the murderous stare and sent Beast a kiss before moving back to his bandmates.

The room became much quieter, and Laurent could actually hear people shushing each other when Beast slowly turned his massive body to face Laurent. The pale light made the imperfections of his skin stand out more, but his blue gaze was so soft Laurent wanted to cuddle up to his lover and stay in his arms.

Beast cleared his throat and reached inside his cut where a black packet was attached with straps. Slowly, he looked into Laurent's eyes, and the tension around them was so obvious Laurent could sense people's stares licking at his skin.

"Oh." Laurent's breath caught in his throat. "Um… what is it?" he asked as he accepted the neatly folded bundle of soft black leather. He wasn't comfortable being the center of everyone's attention.

Beast licked his lips, just as unsure about everyone watching as he was. "This is for you. I had it made to fit your taste."

Laurent slowly unfolded the leather, realizing it was a vest, very much like the ones worn by bikers and their women, but with a shorter front and two tails in the back. It bore resemblance to the style of coat worn in Laurent's own time, but adapted to modern fashion sense, and with tails that wouldn't be long enough to get into the wheels of a motorbike during a ride.

He smiled and held it up, but the wave of tenderness going through him went cold when he turned the vest around and saw the well known patches.

Kings of Hell MC.

An intricate skull in a crown.

Property of Beast.

Laurent's mind galloped as if a gunshot exploded nearby.

"W-what is this?" Laurent said in a hushed voice, already balking at the word 'Property'. He'd made a pact with the devil, and escaped through time two hundred years to not be anyone's property.

Martina was also a property, and now she couldn't even perform a song on stage without her man's permission. Why would Beast offer him this? Was his intention to also exert such control over Laurent? To make him perform services like Jake and enforce his authority over Laurent whenever they didn't see eye to eye? Had their time together only been an opportunity to woo Laurent before the real relationship began? On Beast's terms?

Beast exhaled and pushed back his hair, watching Laurent intensely. "This is so that everyone knows you belong to me."

"So this means I will *belong* to you?"

The pressure of the decision scrunched Laurent's lungs. He felt like everyone was waiting for his answer, and each whisper was like a prying hand. Nao with the bearded man, King, Lizzy… Panic began clutching at Laurent's limbs and wouldn't let go.

Beast nodded, stepping closer and almost reaching out, as if he wanted to put shackles on Laurent's hands already, despite the soft, pleasant expression on his face. "Yes."

Laurent thought back to Marcel, who spent the final months of his life as the *property* of William Fane. He stepped closer to Beast, increasingly shaken.

"Forever?" he asked in a weak voice, gripping the vest as if it were a noose the hangman expected him to put around his neck himself.

Beast's shoulders relaxed, and he leaned closer, as if he couldn't stop himself from touching Laurent. This time, the soft glide of his fingers burned.

"Forever."

Laurent licked his lips and gently pushed the vest at Beast, trying to make this as discreet of a scene as possible. "I can't take it, Beast." His fingers trembled, and his heart ached, but he would not be a slave, even to love.

Beast's hands twitched, and the garment fell to the floor. He quickly ducked to pick it up and twisted the fine leather into a messy ball, as if he wanted to make it invisible.

King's voice came like from another dimension as Laurent watched Beast take a step away from him with an expression that was impossible to read under the scars and letters.

"Figured, he'd be the property of the club, just like the girls."

Laurent's eyes went wide, and he exploded with all the pent-up anger. "I am nobody's *property*! I live however I choose!"

King broke out into laughter that was weakly echoed before the music suddenly erupted from the speakers with such force Laurent felt physically punched by it.

Beast was even farther away now, briefly meeting Laurent's gaze, only to push through the crowd and away from him. Laurent had to make amends somehow, yet his heart ached at idea of Beast wanting to trap him. He didn't need to. Laurent was his out of free will, and he couldn't allow for that choice to be taken away from him.

He rushed through the crowd toward the door at the back where Beast disappeared. Everything inside of him burned as if he'd swallowed sulphur and was set alight from the inside.

He rushed past two girls who laughed so hard they were practically falling over, but he didn't really care for their well being right then. He pushed past the door and dove into the bright corridor, which resonated with loud moans coming from behind a door nearby. Beast was nowhere to be seen, but as Laurent wondered what to do next, the door swung behind him, slapping his ass.

"Ow! Watch it!" he hissed, but faced with King, he took a wary step back. The wide smile on King's face had a sinister quality to it, and when King stepped closer, Laurent backed away until he hit the wall.

"That was a good job. There I was, thinking you turned against me, but I suppose each of us has terms they can't speak of. That big swig of grief was fucking excellent, I feel five years younger already," he said, and in the bright light Laurent noticed King's pupils were so wide they made his eyes appear much darker than they were. He looked like some of the people who took speed at parties. As if he was so high on the energy he couldn't control himself anymore.

The firm, warm hand grabbed Laurent's wrist and pulled it to the hard bulge at the front of King's jeans. The obscene gesture shocked Laurent so deeply he didn't pull away immediately, eyes locked with King's, who stroked Laurent's head with mock-gentleness. "It got me fucking hard, you know. Can't even imagine how it's gonna feel when I finally have all of him."

"All… of him…?" Laurent found it in him to rip his hand away, his mind a sizzling mess of conflicting thoughts.

King sighed, leaning his elbow against the wall and keeping his face so close to Laurent's it was impossible not to smell the liquor on his breath. There was a vitality to him now. His eyes shone with a victorious gleam when he smiled, intimidating Laurent with his broad shoulders and superior height.

"Yes. The day he becomes 33, the devil will give me all of him. I will be strong like a young man, and this hair"—he pulled on a gray strand and scowled at it—"will likely turn blond again. Fuck, I'm so fed up of being an aging geezer."

It took Laurent several breathless heartbeats to catch up with what King was saying, but maybe it was because he didn't really want to accept the truth behind the words? Of course his task for the devil couldn't have been simple. How had he not anticipated this?

He was numb, yet still forced a smile for King, to not seem like the enemy. "You will have his life, and his wish to move will no longer be a problem," Laurent said, wanting his statement to be false, yet deep down knowing it was true even before King nodded.

King gave a sharp, drunken laugh and patted Laurent's cheeks, as if he were making a patronizing gesture toward a child. "Who'd have thought you're so smart? Don't you worry, Laurent. I will take good care of you once he's out of the picture."

The way King's thumb pushed at Laurent's lip made bile rise in his throat. Disgust was so visceral in his body despite King's handsome features, that there was no other way but to pull away.

He gave King a trembling smile, just to feign his agreement, but then walked off down the corridor despite his legs being made out of lead, and his heart weighing him down like an anchor.

He'd been sent here to kill Beast.

Chapter 25 - Laurent

Laurent could swear he'd been walking the endless corridors forever. The thumping of the loud music in the party room became dull as he went farther away from the walls that over two hundred years ago had contained Fane's home. The newer additions to the structure built by subsequent owners of the property were bleak, simplistic in their form, with many walls shedding plaster, whole corridors and rooms disused and cold despite it being summer.

After searching for Beast in their apartment, the garage, and other places where Laurent could have expected him to be, he simply went on, examining each empty room full of broken furniture. The silhouette of the narrow building sandwiched between the two long wings of the former hospital and connected to them with skywalks loomed beyond the window, cold and empty like Laurent's own chest.

He couldn't believe he'd been so stupid as to not push King for an answer about his pact earlier. He never assumed a father would sentence his son to death.

Laurent ran his fingers along the damp wall, walking without a purpose and with not much hope to find Beast anymore. He hadn't spent much time exploring the complex that made the clubhouse, but this particular area seemed familiar somehow.

Even now when he could see so well, the estate was no less of a maze than it had been. Just like the pact he'd made with the devil, the corridors were made to trap him. Give him no way out no matter how long he looked for doors.

At 33, as long as Beast was within these walls, he would die, his life force an unwilling sacrifice on the altar of King's greed and selfishness.

If King died before that, Laurent would be taken back to Fane's still-warm body.

If Laurent told Beast about the details of his pact, he would be taken back.

If Laurent killed King, he would be taken back.

If Laurent made sure Beast wasn't there for his birthday, he would be taken back.

If Beast died, King wouldn't even be the only one at fault. Laurent would share the blame in equal measure.

He hugged himself, fighting tears as he searched for an answer in the dark and dusty corridors. No wonder this infernal building belonged to the devil, because it had the power to completely drain him of hope. If there was a hell, he was already in it.

The dull sound of wheels screeching over a dusty floor caught his attention, pulling him out of his own head. He swallowed when he spotted Martina marching toward him—hair in a mess, and traces of black tears staining her cheeks—tugging behind her two large wheeled travel cases.

"M-Martina? Are you all right? Have you seen Beast?" Laurent asked, noticing the bruise blooming on her forearm.

She curled her shoulders, as if expecting aggression coming her way, but she shook her head. "No. I haven't." She then took in Laurent's appearance and added, "You look like shit."

Laurent rubbed his face. Martina never minced her words. "I'm just tired. I'm sorry about what happened back there with King. I'd love to hear you sing one day."

She stalled, just staring at him before her tense face softened into a smile. "I will send you an invitation. And you know what? I'm happy King behaved like an asshole. They all seem so cool at first, but all they do is chew through you and control your life. All of them, no exception. I can't believe I wasted so many years of my life on a biker."

Laurent took a step back, and her words slapped him in the face. She'd known King for years and this was her ultimate conclusion. King treated her as his property, which was exactly what Laurent wanted to avoid in his own life. And yet here he was, looking for Beast like a lovesick puppy.

"You're leaving?"

Martina glanced at her two cases. "Like you can see, after five years with King, that's all I have. Not a very good deal, but hey, I'm still young enough to find a man who will treat me with the respect I deserve. There comes a moment when you need to put yourself first, no matter how much you love someone."

With that, she turned around and continued her walk down the corridor, emanating determination Laurent had never seen in her before. It made his mood sour further when he thought back to the moment when Beast put him on the spot, demanding an impossible choice of him. Why couldn't things just stay the way they were?

He continued his search in growing frustration, unable to stop the pounding of thoughts in his head from drumming a rhythm for a funeral procession.

Laurent stopped in front of an old dusty mirror in one of the corridors and rubbed it. "It's not fair! I wasn't told what keeping Beast here meant!"

The mirror thumped, the sound drawing him closer while at the same time making his body hair bristle. The surface slowly changed color, the orange tint traveling from under the frame, all the way to the middle, burning Laurent's face with heat.

The creature was merely a shadow at first, but the longer Laurent stared into his own reflection, the more he saw the demon rather than his own face. The large, symmetrical eyes burned in the tar-black face, singling Laurent out and making his feet freeze to the floor.

"It matters not to you what happens once your agreement with me is completed. Do what I asked, and you will have a chance for a happy life. That is what we agreed on," the demon said in a raspy voice that sounded as if it was produced by the embodiment of gravel.

Laurent punched the walls next to the mirror. "How can I ever have a happy life after this? How can I possibly live with myself knowing I sentenced to death the one person I care for so much? This wager is unreasonable!"

The creature watched him. "This is none of my concern. I did not make you care for the Beast, and now it is up to you whether you want to stay here or go back to your old life."

The surface of the mirror trembled, creating concentric circles, as if the devil had plunged one of its claws into the glass and turned it into water.

In the frame, Laurent saw his own face again, but it was not his reflection. In the vision, he sat on Fane's bed, still in his old clothes, which were stained brown by old blood. Fane lay facedown at his feet, a motionless tangle of limbs dressed in expensive silks and fine wool.

A few quick heartbeats later, the Laurent in the mirror raised his gaze toward the edge of the frame, then shielded his head with one arm when men spilled inside, slamming their fists down on him. The scene then changed to the same men dragging him up the stairs and then down the corridor, with Laurent's own body so lifeless from the beating he couldn't walk anymore and face so swollen it was barely recognizable.

"Your choice," said the creature in an emotionless voice.

"But—"

"You better hurry, Laurent, if you want to fulfil your obligations."

The image in the mirror faded, revealing one Laurent didn't understand at first. A floor covered with the same symbol as the one of his nape. A shadow obscured it partially, but it was only as the picture revealed itself further that Laurent realized it was none other than Beast pacing around the room. He came into view, only to disappear again. His mouth opened wide, into a voiceless scream, and he dragged blood-stained fingers down his face, leaving behind the red residue.

"What is this?" Laurent didn't even blink, petrified to the bone.

"He wants to forge a pact of his own. One to keep you as his forever. But I don't need him."

"I don't understand!" Laurent cried. "Where is he?"

A shadowy figure came into view in the mirror, looking straight at Laurent. Straight into his soul. Fane. William Fane was in the same room as Beast, menacingly watching everything from a corner. He wore an outfit identical to the one from the night he died, and even without being in the same place Laurent was getting sick from the phantom smell of perfume, and yet Beast acted as though he were on his own

"What is he doing there?" Laurent hit the wall in helpless fury.

"He? That is his place of eternal unrest. You know where that is, Laurent."

The surface trembled, and out of the ripples emerged Laurent's own face, staring back at him in horror.

Fane's cellar. That was where he used to murder his victims, so why the hell would Beast have chosen it in the first place?

And yet, each time he thought about Beast, the demon's words came back to him to dim all tender feelings. He couldn't believe Beast would be trying to entrap him in such a vile manner. It was almost—almost—what Fane had done to all the poor souls, to poor Marcel whose hand Fane spared for some perverse reason. It had all been about control over another, and now it was Beast who wished to bind Laurent to him, regardless of Laurent's own wishes.

Even with this knowledge, Laurent's feet started moving, and he rushed along the corridor, toward the part of the building that he'd always avoided. He couldn't have Beast bleed out. Partly because it hurt to even think about Beast being wounded, and partly because if Beast died tonight, a horrible death awaited Laurent on the other side of the mirror, in a past he wished to never go back to.

It would have been easiest to simply pass through the rooms where the party was still going strong, but Laurent didn't wish to see anyone—least of all King—and so he used a small corridor that must have been formerly used by servants. It was eerily quiet when he approached the staircase that would lead him into the abyss that was the cellar, almost as if the old walls magically dulled the loud base and the aggressive rumble of electric guitars.

Laurent stood in front of the old staircase. Were he to walk up, he'd enter King's own quarters, but the steps hiding beyond the secret door behind the gargoyle's back were like a black hole, and despite his best attempts, he didn't manage to switch on the light with any of the buttons on the nearby walls. If he wished to go down there and assist Beast, he would have to forget fear and just dive in.

Each careful step he took brought him closer to Fane's soul, trapped somewhere in these rooms. Could a ghost hurt him? Could it wrap its translucent fingers around Laurent's neck and squeeze until Laurent could no longer breathe?

With only the moonlight behind his back illuminating the steps, he still noticed that something was different about the cellar. Were there fewer rooms than there had been in 1805? Was the corridor shorter? Or had it just seemed longer in the past because everything in Fane's house had been so grand?

Step, by painful step, he was getting closer to the chamber Fane had taken him to that fateful night. He breathed in the dusty, somewhat damp air of the corridor that hadn't been touched for decades.

The entrance at the end was closed, and no sounds came from beyond the door, but a thin line of brightness just above the floor made Laurent breathe faster. He approached, hesitating for just a moment before he pressed down the handle and opened the door.

The smell of mold and fresh blood filled Laurent with nausea, but he stepped into the room, eyes drawn to the red smears visible in the faint light of a flashlight placed on the mantelpiece. The room was empty, with just a few boxes and metal barrels grouped in the corner. A section of the floor had been removed, uncovering the symbol underneath, which made a cold shudder run down Laurent's spine.

His heart might have stopped for a moment when he noticed the dark silhouette curled up in the one of the corners, and he frantically swiped his gaze along all the walls in search of the deceptively handsome face of a ghost.

Fane was gone, but Beast looked up, and his face twisted when he spotted Laurent, but he remained seated on his haunches.

Laurent didn't know what to say to the man he used to think only had Laurent's best interest in mind. Had Laurent missed warning signs as he slowly entrapped himself by waking up in Beast's arms every single day? And even if Beast's plans weren't nearly as sinister as Fane's had been, it still stung to be treated like livestock, as if Laurent couldn't be trusted to stay true to Beast of his own will and needed a chain around his neck.

Worst of all, despite knowing of Beast's desire to keep Laurent at all cost, the thought of living without him cracked Laurent's heart open. How could he smile, kiss him, and enjoy their remaining days when he was selling

Beast's life in exchange for his own? He could already hear the clock ticking away the days until August 29th.

11 days.

Beast stared at the bare wall, as if it were covered with gold paint and mosaics. The smear of red on his face was like barbarian war paint, but even in the white light of the flashlight, Beast seemed overly pale under his tattoos. How much blood had he lost?

"I see you, my beast," Laurent said with all the tenderness overflowing in his heart.

Beast took a deep breath, so loud it echoed between the empty walls. "Yours? You rejected me. What do you want now?"

Laurent stepped into the room, choked by the sickly smell. Couldn't all clocks just stop ticking in his heart, as if reminding Laurent of the future that was too terrifying to consider? "I need my freedom. That does not mean I want to change what is between us."

Beast shot to his feet, clutching the vest in one hand as he approached Laurent in long, menacing strides. Now that he stretched in the light, Laurent could see the glimmer of parallel cuts on the tattooed forearms. They weren't bleeding anymore at least. "Freedom to do what? Fuck around if someone better comes along?"

Laurent shrank in the face of such anger but didn't back down. "Freedom to do whatever I wish." It came out hoarse, as if he was already being infected from the inside by the choice he hadn't even made. He looked at the man in front of him. It hadn't been that long since they met in the dusty corridor upstairs, yet already Laurent couldn't cope with the thought of Beast not being around. His mind was falling down an endless well where only pain and suffering awaited.

"How about I help with your cuts?" Laurent tried to touch Beast's forearm, but Beast made an abrupt turn, pacing between the wall and the disused fireplace like a lion Laurent has seen during a trip to the zoo earlier this summer. With his shoulders set and head lowered, Beast marched around his cage as if it could somehow unload the angry energy buzzing inside him. Maybe death at his hands would be better than having to choose between hanging from a noose and sentencing the man… he loved to die.

With no answer, Laurent tried again. "Beast, what were you doing here?"

Beast tossed the vest he had made for Laurent to the floor and grabbed Laurent's cheeks. The stench of blood overflowed Laurent's senses, but he didn't dare look away from the intensity in Beast's gaze. "I need him. I need him to give me something"

Laurent flinched, because he didn't need to be told this anger was meant for him. He was the 'something' Beast wanted to be granted by the devil, and Laurent couldn't bear hearing it, yet wouldn't step away from

Beast either. The urge to be close was visceral even when he sensed sticky blood on his cheeks.

"What if you can't have it? What if the devil won't grant it?" Laurent asked, even though his own goals were in contradiction to Beast's. He would never again be anyone's possession. Not Mr. Barnave's, not Fane's, not even Beast's.

Beast licked his lips, leaning over Laurent with fire burning in his blue eyes. "I won't rest until it's mine," he said, pushing his bloodstained fingers into Laurent's hair.

Laurent stepped closer, so desperately needing to find a way out that would allow them both to stay together. "What can you possibly need so much? You have the club, friends, a good position. We live together in your home. We care for each other. But we are both free men, you have to allow me that." When he reached out for Beast's arm, his lover stepped back, and it stung so much Laurent quickly pulled his hand back as well.

Beast clenched and opened his hands so stiffly it looked as if his fingers might break. "You're gonna run the moment someone else catches your eye, and you don't want to commit because you fear retaliation. Admit it."

Laurent rubbed his face, frustrated that this was what he had to deal with on top of what he'd found out from King and what the devil showed him. "I will not! But I will also not be your *property*. I refuse to."

"Why? Why not? If you're mine, nobody touches you. And I *need* you to be mine." A muscle by Beast's jaw pulsed as he gritted his teeth, his eyes pinning Laurent in place.

The words both hurt and soothed Laurent. Beast was desperate for him, maybe even felt the same way Laurent did. But what was Laurent to do with that? How was he to hand over his life when he'd fought so hard to get out of servitude. Did it even matter if in eleven days he would ultimately have to make a choice between himself and Beast?

The notion of Beast dying made Laurent's eyes ache with unshed tears yet again. He thought back to the conversation he'd had with Martina and wondered whether she would have still put herself first if King's life were at stake?

Beast didn't understand what it meant to live as somebody's property. Even if Mr. Barnave had been a good master, who provided Laurent with a few coins now and again, gave him a decent place to sleep, every day Laurent had lived knowing that his life wasn't his own, and that in the eyes of the law, Barnave could beat him like a dog.

Beast swallowed, watching him, equally silent. It was as if a wall has been erected between them and neither of them knew how to break through. Standing over the devil's symbol etched into the floor only reminded Laurent of the pact. This was where he'd killed Fane, and this was where he would come back to if he failed at his task.

In the end, it was Beast who spoke first. "What *do* you want then?"

Laurent rushed the few steps to Beast and hugged him tightly despite Beast flinching as if Laurent's touch revolted him. "I want to be close."

Beast took several deep breaths, for the longest moment avoiding Laurent's eyes as if they could infect him with consumption. But then he grabbed Laurent's forearm and moved his hands up, all the way to Laurent's shoulders. "Close."

"Nothing's changed between us, Beast." Laurent took a deep breath through his mouth to avoid crying. The impossible choice was choking him, and he couldn't share his despair with the one person who mattered most. Could he choose between Beast and himself? Wasn't Beast attempting just that by trying any means possible to trap Laurent at his side?

Would a life at Beast's side be a trap?

Was an invisible cage not still a cage?

And why was he even considering those questions if the agreement with the devil made any kind of future together unattainable?

Beast's mouth crooked into the most insincere of smiles, and he blinked. "Sure. Whatever you say." But before Laurent could answer, Beast pushed him back until Laurent was standing flat against the wall. With his face buried in the folds of Beast's T-shirt, he listened to the rapid heartbeat just inches away from his ears. The large hands moved down to Laurent's chest.

"That you want?"

Laurent gave a trembly gasp and nodded, even though he could feel Beast's actions coming from a place of anger. Couldn't closeness soothe his doubts, though? Maybe he could forget his pact with the devil for just a few precious moments. Maybe they could mend what they'd broken. What *he'd* broken.

"Yes," he whispered, placing his hands over Beast's. Slowly. Afraid Beast would change his mind after all.

Beast gave a shuddery exhale, pushing his enormous body against Laurent and pressing him against the wall. He moved his hands to Laurent's hips as he pressed his nose and mouth to the top of Laurent's head, breathing loudly.

Laurent wasn't sure if he felt trapped, or protected from the whole world, encased in the most precious cage. Words had already failed him tonight, so he kissed Beast's chest through the fabric instead.

The hands on his hips tightened, and Beast pressed their heads tighter together. He shifted his weight and moved his leg, lifting it between Laurent's thighs. He didn't have to ask, Laurent would spread his thighs for

Beast like he already had so many times. Deep down, he *was* Beast's. Body and soul.

Laurent slowly rocked against Beast's thigh, just like when they were dancing. But at a more languid pace, dreaming of forgetting himself in the motion. He was ready to take all of Beast's rage. He deserved it.

The low rumble of Beast's voice might as well have been thunder. It rained shudders down Laurent's back, and as the leg between Laurent's thighs found its rhythm, each brush and rub became charged with electricity. Beast pushed one of his hands under Laurent's T-shirt, greedily massaging his flesh, as if he were worried he'd never get to do this again.

How would Laurent possibly live with not being touched this way? Could a man actually die of despair? Would his heart stop? Clench and then turn to stone?

Laurent focused his whole being on just this moment in time. On the harsh way Beast ran his hands all over his chest and back, on the heat Beast radiated, and on the way his thigh insistently pressed against Laurent's cock. The slower things were, the more time he had for thoughts.

Thoughts he despised.

Laurent needed faster, needed break-neck speed to consume him.

He rocked his hips quicker, and let his hands climb up Beast's chest. Beast grunted, rolling his cheek against Laurent's temple. It was as if Laurent's eagerness had given Beast permission to go further, and he instantly opened Laurent's fly, aggressively pushing down his jeans. He didn't say anything, just kept his face close enough for Laurent to hear his rapid breathing but not to actually see him.

Laurent wasn't sure why he would need his pants off completely, but when Beast pushed them down, he didn't question it, and rushed to slip off his sneakers. Even as he did so, he was already unbuckling Beast's belt, aching to communicate without words in that way only two bodies could.

There were no words between them, and he prayed they hadn't lost the ability to talk to each other despite his rejection wounding Beast so badly. Their breathing was loud in the empty room, crawling up the walls as they rubbed against one another, touching each other's cocks in a frantic rhythm that left them both hungry for more.

Laurent dared to look up, trying not to think about the dirt he was standing on bare-footed. Instead, the thick prick in his hand occupied his mind. "How do you want me?" he whispered, with his heart rattling. Was this a good enough way to show Beast that he was willing to give himself over into his care? Would anything ever be enough again?

Beast pulled back slightly, and it was the first time Laurent could look into his eyes since they'd started touching. His mouth was thin and tense, eyes searching, as if Beast expected Laurent to strike him, not love him. It only lasted a moment, with Beast quickly leaning forward, his mouth wide open and hot on the side of Laurent's neck, eating at his jawline, biting, pulling, and sucking. Beast grabbed Laurent's hand and squeezed the lube into it before tossing the small tube away.

"Get me ready," he whispered through his teeth.

Breath caught in Laurent's throat, and he slid his hand over Beast's cock in rapid moves. Everything about this moment in a dirty room where he stood only in the short modern shirt was so crude, and yet all his efforts were set on forgetting what King had told him. If only for one more evening.

He nudged Beast's chest with his forehead, eager to take whatever he'd be given. Beast's cock was so hot in his hand, as if there was no invisible noose about to slide on one of their necks, and they were about to give into their desires like they always did.

Beast's cock throbbed in his hand, and he let go, already putting his arms around Beast. The big, strong body smelled of the cologne that had amazed Laurent so much on their first meeting. It tensed, hunching slightly and then Laurent flew up, carried by two firm arms. Braced against the wall, he could barely breathe from the shock until Beast directed Laurent where to put his legs.

Another testament to Beast's inhuman strength. Laurent wrapped his arms around Beast's neck, and his legs around Beast's hips, and he could already feel Beast's erect prick nudging between his buttocks. He hugged Beast tightly, unwilling to let go even if Beast held him steadily anyway. His heart was frantic, his skin going hot and cold.

Laurent's lips ached for a kiss even more than his body ached for Beast's cock, but their eyes met only briefly before Beast buried his face in Laurent's neck. There was an urgency to his movements as he reached down and, crushing Laurent against the wall, pushed in with his cock. A low moan escaped his lips, vibrating against Laurent's throat as the thick girth sank in at a steady pace.

Laurent's toes curled, and he whimpered at the intense feeling of being penetrated so rapidly. His whole body tensing wasn't of help, but he held on to Beast even more firmly. He wished they could both just melt together and become a chimera, leaving the devil unable to take either of them alone.

A choked sob left his mouth, and he bit down on Beast's shoulder, his whole body trembling as the thick cock moved in him slowly.

Beast's muscles trembled, as if despite their strength, Laurent were a burden difficult to carry. The familiar texture of scarred skin felt so right in the crook of Laurent's neck, and when Beast pushed all the way into Laurent, curling him up against the wall, the big hands moved all the way to Laurent's ass, digging into his buttocks as if they were dough for him to knead.

Beast growled and bit so hard it was walking the fine line separating pleasure from pain, but when he moved, Laurent couldn't even speak anymore, reduced to raspy whimpers each time the trembling body of his lover dragged him up and down the wall with his powerful thrusts. He now wished he didn't have the T-shirt on so that his back could feel the pain from rubbing against the crumbling plaster or a rusty nail, there to punish him for his pact with the devil.

In the bright glow of the flashlight, Laurent could read the writing going down Beast's neck. The opening verse of Dante's "Inferno".

Midway upon the journey of our life, I found myself within a forest dark. For the straightforward pathway has been lost.

Oh how true that was. He'd ventured onto the path the devil had set out for him so full of hope, only to find out that nothing was the way it seemed. Beast's thrusts were rough, punishing, but Laurent took it all, hugging Beast tightly and hoping he wasn't choking his beloved. He kissed the words inked into Beast's skin, and a helpless sob left his throat despite him willing it away.

Beast stilled, taking a few deep breaths before leaning back, away from the tight grip of Laurent's arms. "Did I hurt you?" Beast whispered, his blue eyes pale as they stared back at Laurent. He was flushed, and his nostrils flared as he looked back with an expression so raw it was making Laurent's heart bleed.

Laurent wished to hide his trembling lips against Beast's neck, but it was no use. Maybe at least the shadows obscured his face, because he feared everything was written on it in the same way Beast had his pain inked over his. That Beast would see Laurent was the Judas sent to betray him.

"No," he uttered, but it came out somehow broken. "It's just intense… I want everything from you." He hated his choice of words as soon as they were out of his mouth. Would that be his path? Would he take everything away from Beast and leave nothing but charred bones? He was no better than King.

Beast licked his lips, breathing slower, and despite his hard dick throbbing inside Laurent, Beast wasn't in a hurry anymore. He leaned closer, pressing Laurent harder against the wall and moving his warm palm up his ribs. Their lips met in a languid movement that was so delicate it would have left butterfly wings unscathed.

He nodded, suddenly deepening the kiss and pulling away from the wall. Laurent shrieked, clutching to Beast's steady frame as gravity pulled him down in a struggle between Beast's own strength. The world spun in a cloud of dust as Beast got to his knees, still holding Laurent close, his dick still buried deep in Laurent's ass, and then Laurent was flat on the dirty floor, with Beast leaning over him.

Laurent curled his knees closer to his chest, ready to have Beast rip his chest open if that was his wish. He couldn't care less about the dirt rubbing into the back of his T-shirt. The need for Beast to be with him in the moment was so visceral he couldn't breathe.

He answered the hungry kiss with equal passion, exploring Beast's hot mouth and unwilling to think of death. Beast's whole body was hot as an ember, exuding vitality that King had no right to take away.

He went right back to fucking Laurent too, and the way he moved, the sounds he made, were drilling their way through Laurent's mind and driving away all coherent thought. The truth about his pact dispersed in the closeness, in the discomfort of dirt digging into his skin, in the beastly way his lover moved over him. Their tongues danced together faster with each passing moment, until Laurent was so utterly brainless with pleasure he didn't notice Beast was about to come. The explosion of heat inside him, and the rapid thrusts that sent him over the floor with their strength suddenly made him open his eyes and look at the handsome, tattooed face relaxed in absolute bliss.

It was the least Laurent could give him.

Laurent reached between their bodies and stroked his own cock. All it took was just a few times for him to come with a moan muffled by Beast's lips. He never stopped jerking under his lover, tense as a string until his release passed, leaving him completely boneless.

"Could the dust just cover us, so that we never have to leave this room?" he whispered, still panting yet already flooded with waves of sorrow.

His release was fake.

It was worthless if he couldn't truly share his heart with Beast.

11 days.

Chapter 26 - Beast

Beast's thighs trembled around Laurent's head, and he choked on a moan, forcing his eyes to open, just so that he could see the lovely flush across Laurent's face. Their gazes met, briefly, and when Laurent hollowed his cheeks around Beast's cockhead while gently rolling his balls in the slender hand, Beast came.

Pleasure streamed through him like hot waves, and he went completely limp in the sheets, barely capable of even petting the fluff at the back of Laurent's skull. He slid his fingers down to Laurent's shoulder and tugged on it, still unable to speak. Laurent crawled up his body and lay in Beast's arms. They fit together so perfectly that sometimes Beast thought that his arm was shaped this exact way so that it would comfortably curl around Laurent.

It'd been over a week since Laurent rejected Beast's property vest, and Beast's feelings on the matter had calmed down somewhat. He accepted Laurent's decision, he promised himself not to make things weird, and tried to act as if nothing happened. But the truth was that it had, and the events of that evening had left a hole in the middle of Beast's chest, which grew more sore with each day, as if instead of healing it became infected.

King was making a big deal of Beast's birthday and had everyone keep quiet about the party that surely was to come. At the same time, nothing seemed to have been done in terms of preparation in the clubhouse, which led Beast to believe his father had chosen a different venue for some reason. It was nice for someone to put effort into this celebration, but in truth all Beast wanted was to spend time with his brothers, with Laurent. Maybe that at least would take his mind off the failed attempt at talking to the devil. If only he had something of value to offer the fucking monster, he'd get his looks back, his old self, and he wouldn't have to worry that Laurent would eventually leave.

Laurent's smile was so pretty Beast could hardly believe he was holding such a beautiful creature in his arms. "What would you like to do for your birthday? I know it's tomorrow, but I want to make one more day about us only. I want it to be the best day."

Beast swallowed, surprised by the proposition. Laurent has been oddly sweet and compliant since that fateful party, almost as if he felt guilty about being unable to commit. Beast did his best to be positive about this, but he couldn't help but wonder if this wasn't a cheating-husband-bringing-flowers kind of situation.

Maybe not yet, not this year, but sometime in the future Laurent intended to leave him, and when that time came, Beast knew he'd have to let him go. That was the reality of it, and he couldn't change it. All he could do was try not to be brooding, to not disturb the harmony of their relationship while it lasted, but keeping a positive attitude was bullshit. He still hurt every night, every time he didn't have anything to keep his mind busy.

Maybe it was Laurent's age that was the issue? Where Beast knew he could spend the rest of his life with Laurent, Laurent had barely started living. He was probably still assessing what he could and couldn't do in a whole new world. What kind of people were out there for him to meet?. What kind of men?

He nuzzled Laurent's forehead and pulled him closer, wishing he could memorize each body hair. "That would be nice," he said, wondering if it had been King's idea. If he and the guys wanted to prepare a surprise for Beast, they would want him out of the clubhouse.

"Is there something new we could do? Or something you loved when you were a child?" Laurent trailed his fingers over the image of a falling Lucifer on Beast's chest.

Beast licked his lips and brought Laurent's hand to his lips, watching him in silence while his stomach twisted. Laurent said he wanted this to be Beast's day, but there was nothing Beast wanted more than to indulge his boyfriend. There was something so joyful about Laurent's excitement each time he saw something new that his past life could have never offered him, that Beast would gladly just see him having fun all day.

"What about a water park? They have slides, and fake waves, and pineapple ice cream."

That had Laurent perking up like a kitten. "Oh, that sounds splendid! And we could catch the last of this summer's sun. How are waves made? And ice cream. I would love some ice cream." He kissed Beast on the lips. "Are many things there made out of plastic?"

Beast laughed, suddenly relaxed. He combed his fingers through Laurent's hair and kissed him gently. "I'm sure there are many things made of plastic. Like chairs. And I don't know about the waves, but I'm sure we could ask someone who works there."

Laurent lay his whole body on top of Beast's and made the next kiss last longer. If Beast closed his eyes, he could just about believe that Laurent would be in his life forever.

When Laurent pulled away, his eyes were so full of tenderness it made Beast self-conscious.

"Let's go, and see where this day takes us," he finished off without a smile, and that brief expression made Beast's eyebrows rise, but Laurent was on his feet before Beast could ask if everything was okay.

*

It was Saturday, and so the parking lot by the water park was packed, but luckily one could always find just enough space for a motorbike. Beast carried their towels and swimming gear in a backpack as they approached the gate, already listening to the tropical-themed music and shrieking kids as they walked along the fence. Laurent stopped for a moment and looked between the steel elements, at all the fun that was awaiting them. Beast would wear his wetsuit in order to protect his body from the sun and keep the most offensive tattoos out of sight in a place so filled with little kids, but he'd enjoy swimming and watching Laurent use the slides.

He used to come here with his ex a lot. Back before the bastard left him.

"Should we hold hands? Or is it inappropriate in this area?" Laurent asked when they walked up to the ticket office.

Beast hesitated, not sure whether he wanted to risk the staff to immediately label them. Maybe it would be for the better to just stay neutral until they emerged from the changing rooms? "You never know what people will think. It's complicated," he said as they stood in the line of about ten people.

He kept his eyes on Laurent, but when two small boys wouldn't stop staring at him from their parents' arms, he smiled at them, disappointed when they looked away rather than grin back.

He got so lost in thoughts that he didn't even notice Laurent buying their tickets. He had his wallet out, and it was incredibly sweet that he wanted to spend the tiny bit of money he'd earned on something for Beast.

"Excuse me? Why not?" Laurent asked, trying to shove the money at the woman behind the window.

Beast frowned and leaned down to look at her. "Is there a problem?" he asked, looking at the young brunette behind the cash register. She gave him a fake smile, and a cold weight was already gathering at the pit of Beast's stomach. *Not today...*

"Could you please wait at the end of the line? Someone will be with you shortly," she said, and Beast straightened his back, grabbing Laurent's hand without even looking his way.

"Come."

Laurent squeezed it back, and they went where they were asked to. A sinking feeling had Beast already regretful about the idea of coming here. People were such shits. Couldn't he go to a water park with his boyfriend on his fucking birthday? But if he blew up about it, he'd surely get arrested, and that would be even worse for Laurent.

They stood by the railing at the end of the line, and it didn't take long for a flustered manager to arrive. He was an older man with a gray combover and a bit of a pot belly. He was sweating profusely into his blue button-up shirt.

"Good afternoon, I heard there was a problem."

Laurent spread one arm to the side, not letting go of Beast's hand. "I have enough money, and the lady wouldn't sell us tickets."

Beast cleared his throat, briefly glancing at the way their fingers interlaced, and he felt a warmth spreading through his chest at the sight. "It's such a nice day. We wanted to have a day out at the waterpark. I used to come here a lot when I was younger," he said with a pleasant smile. There was still hope as long as they remained polite.

The manager licked his lips, staring at the multitude of tattoos visible on Beast's uncovered skin. "I'm sorry, but we do not allow tattoos depicting religiously divisive material, or swear words," he said in the end.

Laurent stood on his toes, as if he craved to seem taller. "Oh, no, you don't understand. Kai thought about that. He brought his wetsuit, and we will not cause any trouble, sir, I assure you."

The manager shifted his weight, watching them for a prolonged moment. "Does it cover your neck?"

Beast swallowed, imagining the red devil tattooed over his throat move. "No," he said in the end. "But I'm sure no one will notice. It—"

"What about the tattoos on your face? People associate those with gangs, and I can't afford to have customers worry for their children," the manager said, seemingly emboldened by Beast's calm demeanor.

"It's just book quotes."

"Doesn't matter. This is my final decision. I'm sorry."

Laurent pulled his hand out of Beast's grip and stepped forward as if he could possibly intimidate anyone with his height and cute face. "This is beyond unreasonable. We are just trying to have a good time. It's Kai's birthday celebration. Can one exception not be made?"

"That is not an option."

The man's frown was telling Beast they should back off, or they'd have security on their backs. Regardless of whether they liked being rejected or not, the park was a private enterprise, and this allowed them set their own rules.

Laurent raised his hands up. "You, sir, are a disgrace! You cannot even recognize the literary treasure on this man's face. I presume you do not know Latin, do you? The children at this park should consider themselves lucky, were they to come into contact with such profound words. You would not find them in *Spongebob*, I assure you!"

Beast frowned, wondering where Laurent picked up the kid's cartoons from, but the overwhelming feeling of pride quickly replaced any other emotion as he gently pulled Laurent back. "It's fine. Let's just go somewhere else," he said.

Laurent was breathing hard, and his whole body spoke of tension. "It is *not* fine, but we will take our business elsewhere!"

The loss of fifty bucks fell on deaf ears. The manager rolled his eyes and walked off, leaving Laurent as shaken as if the water park were the gates to Heaven and he'd just been denied entry.

Beast pulled on his hand, leading them away from the entrance and the line of people ogling the commotion. Beast's life was no reality show. And yet, he'd closed so many doors when he chose to cover the burn scars with tattoos. He'd done it in anger and despair, but now that he had to live with everything that choice brought upon him, he was left to wonder what could have been. If it weren't for the tattoos, he'd still have people staring at him, but he could take Laurent anywhere he wanted, not be unwelcomed pretty much everywhere.

Laurent took a deep, shaky breath when they reached the parking lot, and he rubbed his eyes with his forearm. Was he… crying over this?

Beast stood still, watching Laurent as shame curled in his stomach and choked at his throat. "I'm sorry. I was young and stupid, okay? I can't just get rid of them. Sorry it spoiled your fun. Maybe someone else could take you another day?"

"No! I wanted to go today!" Laurent sniffed, and squeezed Beast's hands when they got to the motorbike. Beast wasn't sure if his actions were bratty, or erratic. "It doesn't matter. I would never change a thing about your ink unless you wanted to. It speaks about your soul."

The tenderness behind Laurent's words made Beast look away for a few seconds, but he squeezed Laurent's fingers even firmer. "Thanks. I like them. They stop people from pitying me because of the scars. But sometimes... this is just unbearable," Beast said and rubbed his face with his free hand.

Laurent just watched him in silence for a while. "Would it be possible to go somewhere today where I could get tattooed? I want to know how it feels. I want to understand it."

Beast stared at Laurent, not sure what to think. "It can hurt," he said softly, leaning in to kiss Laurent's forehead. He pushed back the long hair and rested his chin atop Laurent's head, bringing him closer.

"I'm ready to hurt," Laurent whispered, and Beast couldn't pinpoint why it felt like they were talking about different things.

He exhaled, watching Laurent with growing curiosity. He seemed completely sure of his idea. "What do you want to have tattooed?"

"This one." Laurent trailed his fingers over Beast's collar bones. "*The path to Paradise begins in Hell.*" Beast swallowed, trying to convince himself Laurent simply wanted a quote of Dante's *Inferno* because he had intimate knowledge of the text, yet it still felt as if Laurent was about to pick it off Beast's skin.

Beast couldn't bring himself to speak for several moments, then squeezed Laurent's hand firmly and nodded. Storm clouds were gathering on the horizon anyway, so maybe not going to the waterpark was a good thing after all.

*

After the fiasco at the waterpark, entering the tattoo shop was like coming home. Beast had spent endless hours here, having his skin covered in ink, inch after inch. Here, he was respected and greeted with smiles, not shunned like a leper.

Jabba, the owner, was still working on a client when they came over, but one word from Beast was enough for him to make the effort and move the next appointment to make a spot for Laurent. The steady buzz of the tattoo machine gave Beast a pleasant kick. Having had so much work done, he perceived the ache caused by the needle repeatedly stabbing at his skin somewhat pleasant, and he couldn't help but relax at the sound.

Nudity always made Laurent a bit flustered, so he looked away when Jabba's client slid off the tattooing bed and looked at her back in the mirror. As soon as Beast saw what it was that she had done, his good mood plummeted.

The tattoo was large yet simple, with no frills it read *Property of Claw*. And she wanted everyone to know so much she had it permanently etched in her skin.

When he glanced at a chair nearby, he noticed a leather vest with patches of a biker club from New Hampshire. He felt physically sick at the sight of it. As if Laurent's rejection hadn't been enough, and it now needed to be rubbed in even at a place he considered his safe haven.

The girl turned, watching her back in a mirror with a glow of happiness on her face. Put a veil on her, and she'd look like a bride without even donning a white dress.

Jabba shifted his corpulent body and smiled, looking at his client. “Happy?”

She grinned and rocked her hips to the sides, making the design move along with her muscles. “He’s gonna be so surprised.”

Laurent cleared his throat. “Do you not value your freedom?”

Beast scowled and looked out the window, not wanting to watch the property tattoo done as a tribute to some guy when he couldn’t even get patches on Laurent. It shouldn’t bother him so much but it did. It opened the barely closing gash in his heart and poked at it with spikes.

The girl laughed. “Oh, come on. You guys always say marriage is like prison, but it isn’t really. You’re just a bunch of complainers. This is a big deal for me. My man finally asked me to be his forever.”

Laurent groaned, making Beast want to stay out of this conversation altogether. “You cannot know what it will entail in a few years,” his voice was harsh, as if he had any right to scold a stranger. “When you are someone’s property, they can beat you to death, bury you, and no one would even know!”

Jabba frowned at him. “Whoa there! Chill out, man.”

But the girl got even more agitated. “What the fuck, asshole? What can you know about my relationship? I’m getting married, not entering into a pact with the devil.”

Laurent twisted his fingers together in frustration. “I’ve seen people punished for no fault of their own. Tossed into the gutter with no means of survival after years of living as *property*, and still, after a week or two they crawl back to their masters for even a glimmer of security!”

Jabba glanced at Beast. “Is he high?”

Beast listened to Laurent, completely stunned by the things coming out of his mouth. Was this what the rejection has been about? Laurent feared Beast would beat him to death and bury him in the garden? It was so fucked-up he might have preferred not to know the reasons behind Laurent’s rejection at all. That was exactly why they pretended the humiliation Beast had experienced at the party almost two weeks ago had never happened.

“Laurent, calm down. That is not what this means. A property... it’s like a wife for a biker,” he said in the end, fearing the girl could attack Laurent with her long nails otherwise.

Laurent gave him a weary glance. “Is it not like a servant?”

The girl hissed and put on a T-shirt despite the tattoo not being dressed yet. “What is wrong with you, you dumb fuck? It’s nothing like being a *servant*! It’s more than a wife even! It’s respect from the club, it’s protection, and a symbol of undying devotion.” She pulled on her vest, as if to make her point even clearer. “Everywhere I go, everyone knows who I belong to. Who would knock their teeth out if they touched me. I’m not just his. *He’s mine*. I’m done here.”

She shook her head, and left Laurent just sitting there without an answer.

Beast crossed his arms on his chest, unsure how to defuse this whole situation, but as the silence went on, he was forced to take a stand and looked at Jabba apologetically. "Sorry, man, he isn't from here."

They all had to suffer an uncomfortable silence while Jabba dressed the tattoo and accepted his fee. The girl then walked out, slamming the door so hard the glass in it jingled.

"I'm sorry," Laurent mumbled as soon as she was gone, but Beast wasn't sure who he was apologizing to.

Jabba waved his hand. "Don't worry about it. It's not like she's a repeat customer. I've seen worse scenes here than that. What are we doing for you, huh?"

Laurent chose to get the words tattooed over his collarbones, in the same place Beast wore them, and didn't back out even when his eyes watered at the beginning of the process. He held Beast's hand throughout, and sometimes glanced Beast's way with such an odd expression that Beast couldn't decipher what was going through Laurent's head. The three of them talked, laughed, and yet something seemed to have changed.

The weight of knowledge that Laurent didn't want to be with him because he was *afraid* of Beast kept him in low spirits, no matter how funny Jabba's stories were. Beast felt like he was faking a good mood for Laurent's sake, but he couldn't deny that watching the words appear on Laurent's skin in the same place Beast himself wore them was a thrill, maybe even a compromise on Laurent's part.

Would Laurent attach the same meaning to them that Beast did? What was his paradise, and what was his hell? For Beast, the words were an expression of hope that after the hell he'd gone through, he would find happiness again one day, that all the pain he'd gone through in recovery after the fire was worth something.

When the tattoo was done, Laurent still seemed to find it hard to smile, catching deep breaths and rubbing his eyes over and over until they were red. He got even more flustered when it turned out he didn't have enough money to cover the whole price.

Beast didn't mind stepping in.

By the time they needed to leave, rain was periodically drumming a frantic *staccato* against the windows of the parlor whenever the wind tossed the drops at the building. It was dark, wet, and unpleasant outside, but at least they had a meal to look forward to. Laurent insisted they have Chinese food from the same place where they'd gotten it the first time. Beast bought two slices of pie at the nearby diner for dessert, and they were off, both longing for the quiet warmth of their apartment.

Beast was surprised to see almost all the bikes gone from the garage, and even some of the cars, but he chose to not assume anything and led the way through the empty corridors. It was eerie to see the clubhouse so completely empty. There wasn't a soul left in the house, and if anyone had stayed behind, they were likely tucked into their own room, because without any music or chatter to be heard, without any lights on, the vast building felt abandoned.

Laurent held on to Beast's hand, but they were silent more often than not. Hound was already whining behind the door when they got to Beast's apartment, and Laurent greeted the dog tenderly, smiling at him and petting his muzzle. It was as if the presence of the dog alleviated the tension that hadn't left them since Laurent's heated discussion with the girl at the tattoo parlor.

They shared the food in silence, but Laurent kept close to Beast, constantly pressing against his side, and Beast didn't have the heart to ask him for a bit of space, so he could use his chopsticks comfortably. Hound lay at their feet, having fallen asleep soundly as soon as he realized he would not get any of the human food. It was all very homely and yet so odd. Beast couldn't remember Laurent being so subdued in recent weeks.

Thunder rumbled behind the windows, and the rain was a constant background noise. After they had dessert, they cuddled for a while, but then Laurent got up, checking his watch with lips pressed into a thin line.

"Can you please wait here for a moment?" he asked Beast, who watched him with a smile slowly surfacing on his face.

Laurent likely wanted to apologize for that horrendous fit at the tattoo parlor. And if that included some kind of sexy surprise for Beast's birthday, he would not say no. "Sure. Tell me when," he said with a widening grin.

Laurent smiled back, but then rushed out of the room in an oddly nervous fashion, which made Beast confident that he was up for a birthday treat. There were still two hours to go until midnight, so he was happy Laurent wasn't making him wait any longer. He thought back to the tattoo on Laurent's skin. How now no matter what happened, Laurent would have a piece of Beast with him. If that was a kind of compromise between just being boyfriends and becoming Beast's property, Beast could accept this. Clearly, Laurent cared for him if he wished to commemorate him in his own flesh, so maybe Beast should just chill out and stop overthinking everything so much.

Laurent's feet thudded against the floor as if he were wearing boots, but when he emerged from the corridor, he was in the same historical outfit as when they'd first met—indeed wearing boots—but without his glasses. Despite being happy to have it back after the dry clean, Laurent has never worn it since and just kept it in his room. From the tips of his boots, to the white collar of his shirt, he looked as if he'd stepped out of a costume drama. He was squeezing something in his hands.

Beast watched him, somewhat taken aback, and yet his brain was working at full speed, wondering what it was that Laurent expected. Did he wish to be fucked in those beautiful clothes that so complimented his natural beauty? "You look... lovely."

Laurent stepped closer, even though his smile remained tense. "I would like you to have this," he said and held out the pin that he'd gotten from his mother.

Beast looked at it, slowly growing cold. It was a priceless gift. One of such importance to Laurent that it should never be given away, and after a day of tense atmosphere the offer was getting Beast on edge. Something wasn't right, and he didn't know what.

All at once, his mind filled with horrible things, such as Laurent dumping him and wanting to leave behind something for Beast to remember him by. With his heart aching already, Beast asked, "What's going on?"

Laurent swallowed, and since Beast sat on the sofa, he was the one looking down at him for once. The outfit seemed to make him taller and more mature as well, even though it was just an impression, and a kid in suit was still just a kid in a suit.

"I want to apologize to you. Where I thought you wanted to trap me, all you were offering was protection and affection. You must understand that I had been property before. For years, I lived as a servant, and all that I dreamed of was freedom."

Beast's head felt light when he leaned forward and squeezed Laurent's hands above Hound's massive sleeping body. They were warm, and soft, and wonderful, and Beast wanted nothing more than to take Laurent in his arms and keep him like that forever.

"That's okay. That vest will be yours whenever you're ready for it. I still want to see you wear it."

Laurent's breaths were heavy as he spoke. "I can't take it. I don't deserve it. You've been so kind to me, you gave me the gift of healthy eyes, and I've kept so many secrets from you."

Beast exhaled and pulled Laurent closer where he eventually settled next to Beast on the sofa. Hound didn't even stir.

"Don't say that." Beast sighed, gently massaging Laurent's hands. They were so small, so full of grace when compared to Beast's paws that all Beast wanted was to cherish them. He brought them to his lips and kissed each knuckle, overwhelmed by tenderness. "I keep secrets too. Like... that I really do care that I look this way. That I have been searching for a way to connect to your demon, because I hoped if I were my old self again... you wouldn't want to leave," he said softly, not daring to look into Laurent's eyes and see disappointment. It sounded so pathetic, and yet there was such a visceral need in him to be truthful, to tell Laurent just how much he felt for him.

"Oh, Beast..." Laurent leaned closer and ran those perfect fingers over the grooves and scars on Beast's face. "I've misunderstood you so badly. You are perfect to me. I wish I could take away all your pain myself. If you could only see yourself the way I see you, you would know no change is needed."

Beast's heart beat so fast he could sense it all over his body. His neck felt tight, and the only relief came in the form of Laurent, whom Beast pulled close for a tight hug.

"I've been with so many guys, but I don't want to experiment anymore. I want you. I've never met anyone like that."

Laurent's deep sigh tickled Beast's neck. "And I've never realized love is more valuable than freedom. You are everything to me. Even though we were born centuries apart, I'm sure our souls are entwined."

Beast's mind might have stopped in that moment, stagnant as if bathed in the warmest, creamiest of happy thoughts. He reached out for Laurent and rubbed his shoulders, so overcome with joy he couldn't speak for several moments. "I-I love you too, Laurent."

Laurent leaned in for a gentle kiss where just their lips touched. "You will not like what I have to tell you, but it must be done, or I would forever live in misery. If whichever way I choose leaves me trapped, I choose this. Listen to me carefully. King... I know he's your father, but he is a cruel man. The deal he's made with the devil requires him to keep the Kings of Hell here, where the devil resides, so that he can feed on the primal urges people fulfil. That's why he is against moving despite danger and cost."

Beast stared at him, utterly stunned, and even though just weeks prior he would have dismissed such things as the ramblings of a mad person, now they made his skin crawl.

"But that's not all of it. He..." Laurent looked into Beast's eyes without blinking. "He lives on your vitality, my love. Anytime you hurt, he gets more of it, and whenever you are content, he is blocked from taking it. Tonight, after midnight, when you turn thirty three, he will be able to consume all of your life force and add it to his lifespan. He will kill you to stay young and healthy, Beast."

Beast shook his head in disbelief. The sudden onslaught of information left him confused and once again worried for Laurent's sanity. "That's... he's a jerk, but he's my father. He wouldn't do that. He is out there, preparing a party for me right now," Beast said, gesturing in the general direction of the town, but his mind stalled despite his best intentions. Because what if Laurent was right? What if he didn't simply have an overactive imagination?

Laurent stroked Beast's neck, and the sad little smile on his lips was already tugging at Beast's heart. "He's not. I know that what I say is true. I… the demon sent me here to aid him." Laurent frowned and Beast smelled smoke before he even saw it. Hound became alert as well, and he barked at Laurent, getting up and backing away slightly. White fumes started seeping through Laurent's clothes. "I don't have time. My task was to make sure you were here for your birthday. But I hadn't known what that meant. You have to believe me, Beast!" He choked on smoke coming out of his mouth.

Beast got to his feet, pulling Laurent into his arms in a desperate attempt to drag him to the nearest car before he fainted. He was hot as if fever were consuming his body, and Beast quickly picked him up, rushing to the door. The smell of sulphur bit into his nostrils as he leaned against the door in a vain attempt to press down the door handle. Hound tapped his feet on the floor, whining helplessly as he watched the scene unfold.

"Laurent, please, stay with me," whispered Beast.

"I wasn't allowed to tell you," Laurent rasped, his body becoming unnaturally light as if he was disappearing, turning into mist. "He's taking me back. It was either you or me, and I couldn't imagine a life without you anymore." He wrapped his arms around Beast's neck. "You must kill King, or leave now and never even come close to this house again. Promise me you will live."

Beast fell to his knees, cradling Laurent's body to his chest. It was light as a baby, as if with each passing second a part of Laurent was going up in flames. Frantic with fear, Beast cupped Laurent's cheeks and looked into his eyes. He didn't know where he was anymore. All that counted was to somehow keep Laurent by his side, to still hold him, even if his skin were to burn Beast's fingers. If he were to reach into flames once more to pull Laurent out of a burning car, he would, regardless of consequences.

"No, please."

"Don't let him have your precious life," the last words were only a whisper, and Laurent seemed to mouth something more, but his lips turned into gray fumes, his tongue went into a sudden burst of flame… and he was gone.

Beast uselessly tried to grasp at the cloud of smoke that was dispersing around him already, and Hound's barking came as if from behind a wall, as the dog frantically searched for Laurent.

But he was gone.

Chapter 27 - Beast

The room stank of burning flesh. A horrible, stomach-churning odor that had Beast curling up by the door and frantically clutching at the pale fumes, the last that remained of Laurent. And even that dispersed within seconds, rising to the ceiling in clouds of white smoke. With his mind dulled by shock, Beast tried to grasp at the air, but any traces of Laurent were soon gone, leaving him with an emptiness so profound he couldn't even find the voice to scream anymore. All of a sudden, his head spun, and he slid farther down the door, gasping for breath as his joints and muscles ached. He shuddered, nauseated by the bout of weakness that was gnawing through his bones.

Hound's soft whining was the only sane thing left in Beast's world.

It couldn't be happening. How was it possible that a man he'd just held in his arms could disperse into nothingness? Was he to wake up to an empty bed again, without Laurent curled up under his arm? But no matter how much Beast tried not to acknowledge what just happened, his hands were empty.

A glint of metal caught his attention, and he spotted Laurent's pin on the floor. He grabbed it and pulled it close to his face, overcome by a sense of doom the likes of which he'd never experienced before. Not when he lost his mother. Not when he realized he would never be the same man again. His life was about to end, and he couldn't even have Laurent by his side when that happened. With his throat swollen from a scream he couldn't voice, Beast took deep breaths, hoping they would somehow soothe his hurting body. It was all in vain, and hot wetness spilled down his cheek and into his hair.

Hound's expressive muzzle moved closer. The dog leaned down, first nuzzling Beast with its cold nose, and then licking his cheek. He didn't flinch away when Beast pulled him close for a hug he desperately needed. The dog kept making confused, whining noises in Beast's arms, as if Hound wished to voice what Beast was feeling.

A weakness spread through Beast's body, and all the way to his bones, turning into pain within his chest, intense as if his lungs were collapsing, his heart about to stop. The one person who could see Beast underneath the scars and tattoos, was gone, and with the devil ignoring Beast's pleading, there was no way for Beast to reach through time and grab Laurent before he fell.

Hound's brows gathered into a worried-looking frown when Beast forced himself to get up. He didn't remember ever feeling quite like he did now. The pain of burned skin had been horrid, so horrid in fact his brain blocked Beast from remembering it, but he did remember that at the time he could barely move, and even his fingers had remained motionless to avoid further skin breakage. The dull ache Beast was feeling right now wasn't nearly as bad, but it was a constant, throbbing discomfort spreading through his body like wildfire. Like having a bad case of the flu yet somehow much worse, as if his muscles were not only inflamed but had decided to stop cooperating altogether.

Walking to the bathroom was a feat in itself with his muscles trembling and strange aches appearing out of nowhere. He passed Laurent's room, and seeing the clothes folded on the bed made Beast hurt all the more. Even when Laurent had known he'd disappear, he'd still taken care to leave everything so neat.

Beast held on to the sink, panting to steady himself. Misery was taking over his body, leaving it unnaturally heavy and Beast's brain cooking inside his skull.

"Come out," he said, choking on words when he looked into the cracked mirror. Laurent had left it uncovered in the morning, and now Beast's own eyes were looking back at him, wet, dark, and tinted with red. Behind him, Hound paced nervously in the corridor, as if he wished to follow his master but was too afraid to.

There was no answer.

He raised his voice, repeating the same thing over and over, but the creature wouldn't respond. Beast could practically sense each tick of an invisible clock when Laurent's words slowly sank in at last. King had been feeding off him. It had been Beast's own life force that kept him youthful and healthy. As absurd as that sounded, there was no denying that the happier Beast was, the worse off King seemed to be. After seeing Laurent turn into smoke in his arms just minutes ago, there was nothing Beast would immediately dismiss as fiction. And so he believed his Laurent. He believed that King has been using him for years. That he'd purposefully let Beast waste his life away

Beast gritted his teeth, squeezing Laurent's pin so hard its sharp edges sank into the flesh of his palm. He leaned forward and grabbed both the doors of the mirror cupboard, tugging so hard the wood creaked. "Show yourself, or I'm gonna find you. I'm gonna destroy you. You can't play with my life!"

But nothing changed. There was no smoke, no odd noises, no darkness consuming the room. The devil had decided Beast was of no importance, and the fury that consumed Beast's chest had him punching the mirror over and over. Blood sprayed his face when a shard of glass tore through his skin, and Beast stumbled away, gathering his strength, resting with his back against the wall.

He gave his reflection one more glance in the broken, blood-stained mirror.

If he died tonight, he would be unable to destroy the infernal being. He would not give King the satisfaction, and he would not let Laurent's sacrifice go to waste. All that time, Laurent had been carrying this rock of a secret on his heart, unable to share the burden. That alone made Beast so furious that despite all the aches consuming his body, he walked out of the bathroom with a low growl that made Hound back away.

Beast looked at the pin and slowly attached it to the front of his cut. If this was the only thing he had left of Laurent, he would carry it into battle. The emptiness inside his chest was slowly being replaced by determination, and if hatred could be materialized, it would come in the form of Beast's heart.

He was too exhausted to cry or shout. He loaded two of his handguns, took his favorite knife, and left the house with Hound trailing behind him, visibly frightened and yet unwilling to abandon his master.

The clubhouse was quiet as a grave, and Beast now suspected King had somehow lured everyone away to complete his work.

Each of Beast's footsteps echoed in the silence despite the furious wind and rain outside, as if the empty corridors were a world of their own, in no way associated with the storm raging beyond the thick walls.

Beast didn't bother to switch on the light and marched through the empty hallways in complete silence that was broken only by the sounds of the weather, and six pairs of legs—his thumping loudly, and Hound's—quickly tapping against the resin floor. The tall windows were a blur of streaming water, and shadowy trees waved their arms with each powerful gust of wind.

A lightning bolt tore through the sky far away, and for a split second the corridor ahead of Beast was bright as if it were day. Hound gave a broken whine and pushed his heavy body close to his master's legs, but Beast himself grew roots in the floor. There was someone standing at the end of the corridor where the borders of the historic mansion began. Beast only registered the figure for a split second, but he saw that there was a spray of bright red across the front of a pale suit. When another flash of light brought the corridor back to life, the man was nowhere to be seen.

Beast ran, his gun ready for use, his head spinning so badly it was affecting the precision behind Beast's movements. But when he reached the doorway where the stranger had stood, and the thunder shook the walls around him, there was no trace of an intruder, no traces of blood on the pale floor, and no sound of footsteps rushing away to be heard.

His heart drummed as he tried to get to grips with the surreality of it all when Hound rushed past him, barking loudly, no longer afraid. Beast followed.

They both ran down the wide stairs as if a whole cavalcade of ghosts were after them. With the gun firmly in his hand, Beast crashed into the front door with his shoulder and shoved it open, hit by the smell of rain that had nothing pleasant about it. Instead of fresh, it seemed somehow stale, as if it wasn't water from the clouds but the juices from the ground beneath them raining upward. Centuries of evil—no, of something primal that didn't know good from evil—being soaked up into the clouds above them to now fall back down.

The thunder rolled over their heads, and as lightning spread its ghostly fingers over the dark sky, he saw King's motorbike parked in front of the stairs, as if it were a carriage waiting for William Fane himself. Beast stepped out of the house and into the rain that instantly drenched him to the bone, each heavy drop of water like a punch aimed to drain him of strength slowly and methodically.

The bike sure as hell hadn't been here when he'd arrived with Laurent, and without a reason for King to have left it where the machine was at the mercy of the horrid weather, it was a statement. A provocation.

Beast shot at it. Once. Twice. Three times. It fell into the mud with a sickening scream of wounded metal, and he watched, his breath shallow and fists tight.

"Where are you?" he asked quietly, slowly turning around to take in the dark shadows where King could remain hidden from Beast's wrath.

Hound circled the fallen bike, sniffing it even when thunder made him sink lower and bristle, as if danger was imminent.

The columns of trees provided shelter to shadows hidden just beyond the arch-like branches, and when Beast spun around, confused by the tricks of light and darkness, it almost felt like he was surrounded by architecture, not nature, and every spot that the weak glow wouldn't touch could hide a monster about to get him.

Beast panted, sensing his heart speeding up by the second, and when something bright flashed at the front of the building, he spun around, ready to fight. Lights were on in King's apartments in the second floor. The tall window was the frame to showcase the handsomest of monsters, whose dark silhouette moved languidly, as if King had all the time in the world.

Beast's phone rang.

He picked it up frantically, noticing that it was already half past eleven. Where had all that time gone? It seemed like just a minute ago he'd had two hours until midnight.

The line creaked, but the low voice that sneaked into Beast's ear was clear as day. Even King's voice was somehow deeper, throatier, tainted by greed. "I've waited for this so long."

Beast could feel his pulse even in his gums, and he raised his gun, shooting at the window.

The shadow flinched away from the glass that burst into shards, but then King laughed into the phone like a maniac. "I can feel you're weak. Can you even climb the stairs to get me? You have no idea how amazing I feel now. I think I actually got a boner."

Beast stepped forward, but his body swayed, as if pushed by invisible hands so suddenly he almost tripped over his own foot. Catching his breath, he made himself run back into the house, and yet the fact that holding on to a wall provided such comfort was already filling Beast's heart with worry. The first firearm was out of ammo, so Beast dropped it to the floor. He had no time to find spares.

"Fuck you. I know what you are. You're not getting away," he growled into the handset, pushing past the door. The presence of Hound, whose barrel-like body moved past him and rubbed against Beast's knees was more of a relief than he would have wanted it to be.

He could do this. The old staircase that would lead him straight to King was only a few steps across the hall, snaking around the gruesome gargoyle statue like a serpent. He took a deep breath and forced himself to move upstairs, knowing he could be watched. He wouldn't give King the satisfaction of seeing him struggle.

Each step was a challenge to Beast's legs, which seemed to have turned into lead. Never in his life had he felt so weak. The ground called out to him, and with his mind becoming cloudier the higher up the stairs he moved, a haze settled on his eyes. The last time he'd felt anything close to this was when he awoke from his surgery and the general anesthetic was still present in his veins. He wished to just curl up and rest, even if for a little while, but he knew that the moment he let himself lose focus, a moment of weakness would turn into eternal rest unrest.

The bannister seemed to move its black, snake-like body away from his grip, and when he finally got to the landing, he almost expected it to hiss at him. He would not let this devilish building suck all the will to live out of him. Laurent's sacrifice needed to have meaning. Beast had promised revenge, and he would unleash it on all the monsters hiding in the walls if it killed him.

King exhaled somewhere above Beast. "I have to say, keeping all these secrets to myself was *exhausting*. The constant arguments with your mother about why we couldn't just leave here, why I didn't want you to go away to college, yada yada. I always get my way, and I must say that the energy I drank from you this past hour seems even stronger than after your mother died, and that one was exquisite, if I do fucking say so myself."

It was like a punch to the gut, and Beast's damp boot slid off the edge of the step, making him stumble and fall hard on one knee. Hound moaned and pushed its soft muzzle against Beast's neck, unaware of the depth of the horror that was unfolding around them. Beast knew King hadn't been a good husband to his mother, but talking of her death in terms of something pleasurable was beyond anything he could have imagined.

"Shut the fuck up. Shut up!"

"You stupid boy, the Dark Riders never attacked her!" King laughed so loudly his voice drilled holes in Beast's ears as it echoed down the old walls. "I took her out, because she wanted to move you away. And I couldn't have my living, breathing steroid supply going anywhere, now could I? And when you burned to char on top of it? Now that was just priceless."

Beast's breath wheezed, and he leaned forward, resting his forehead on one of the steps as strength drained out of him like blood from a cut aorta. His eyes stung, closing despite Beast willing them not to, and the overwhelming need to just lie down—even if just for a while—weighed Beast's body down, making him sink to the polished wood that smelled of some kind of conservation product and dirt. He was sinking to the bottom of the world.

Hound wouldn't let him. The dog grabbed Beast's sleeve and tugged on it viciously, forcing Beast to keep his eyes open. In the corner of the landing stood a tall grandfather clock which Beast was sure hadn't been there before.

Tic tock.

"You're pathetic. To think that there was a time I was jealous of you, that I worried my sun was dying while yours was about to rise…" King's voice sounded sharper now, and it took Beast forever to understand that there was nothing blocking the sound anymore. He pried his eyes open and gazed along the stairs revolving around an empty space in the middle, all the way to where the staircase made another turn to climb above Beast's head. King leaned against the railing, but when Beast moved, so did King, partially hiding behind the old wood. The coward was likely still wary of Beast's other gun.

The surge of anger was like adrenaline kicking in and making Beast's heart beat firmly again. Cooled down by the dampness of Hound's tongue, he dragged himself to his feet and moved on all fours when the railing budged slightly under his weight with a vicious creak. His chest was one big burning core of pain by the time Beast managed to kneel on the stairs directly in front of King, laboriously catching his breath in hope that despite the horrid lightness in his head, his frantically beating heart would not give up.

He reached up, trying to grab at King, but as he moved, his other gun clattered down the stairs. Beast looked back, the image caught by his eyes not following his thoughts quick enough, and he howled with despair when he realized how far the weapon was. A whole flight of stairs below him.

The clock was still ticking. He couldn't waste any time retrieving it. Not now, when King was so close.

King put his hands on his hips and shook his head with a smile plastered to his lips. "You do know your little angel was in on this from the start, right?"

"And now he's gone," whispered Beast, reaching for the pin. It burned with a pleasant heat that streamed into his body like a surge of liquid energy to envelop Beast's aching heart in a plush cocoon. Beast dragged himself two more steps up, hand steady on the railing that he suddenly didn't need as desperately as just moments before. He let go before the unstable banister crumpled any further.

The frantic drumming of the rain against the roof above hid a marching rhythm for him to follow. When Beast stepped on the landing, into the light coming in through the tall window, he only had eyes for his target.

"A shame really, because I was planning to keep the boy around. Cocksucking lips like his could find a use in the club."

"He loved me," Beast said with confidence, through gritted teeth.

"You? You're lucky if your dog can love that hideous face," King laughed but took a few steps back, startled when the small windows in the upper part of the staircase slammed open one by one, letting in the howling wind and cold rain.

Rain rushed inside in a spray of water pushed in by the storm. The cold peeled sleepiness off Beast's mind, and he climbed the stairs fueled by rage growing inside him. He was by no means fast, and each movement felt like his skin was slowly about to break, but his eyes were fixed on a goal, and with Laurent gone, he had nothing to lose anymore.

"He loved me," he repeated, pushing forward as the lightning hit a tree just beyond the house. It exploded with fire, turning into a giant torch. In the bright glow of its flames, Beast saw something move above King, by the entrance to the attic space beyond the old roof. The smell of burning wood and sulphur spread in clouds of smoke as darkness expanded in the corner of the landing on top of the stairs, dull fire burning around a tar-black shadow with long horns.

Hound's bark tore through the air, as if he were about to jump the intruder and sink his teeth into the charred skin.

"I guess he must have had some love for you, but we also know he was as dumb as a rock if he chose going back to his world over a cozy spot on my dick. Especially if you consider that his loyalty to you won't save you anyway." King's grin widened when he looked up to the landing above him where a creature looking like a genderless giant dipped in tar took a step down. "This is why, Beast! The devil *needs* me. He will do right by me, so none of your bullets can touch me. I have infernal protection!"

"Really?" hissed Beast, forcing himself two more steps up. He was surprised that the malevolent being that watched them both from above instilled no fear in him. It just watched Beast and King with calm interest, as if it were a scientist and they—two rats in a cage. "Give me your gun then, and we will see."

King once more looked back at the creature that had eyes so hot they seemed white. "Why not?" He pulled his Magnum out of the holster and threw the gun down the stairs. It landed three steps above Beast, barrel aiming at Beast's head. "You've got..." he glanced at his watch. "I don't know. Thirty seconds?"

It was like having a noose finally put around Beast's neck. Had he not seen or heard the large standing clock ticking away loudly?

It synced in with his heart, and as he dashed forward to grab the gun, each beat inside his chest sounded like a number.

14.

13.

He grabbed the gun, pulled off the safety and shot.

King's body recoiled, and he gave a loud laugh, leaning against the railing, which shifted slightly beneath his weight. Red spread at the front of his white T-shirt, and in the faint light, with the wind tousling his hair and clothes, the blood soaking through the fabric made it look as if something was trying to crawl its way out of King's body.

King's laughter was gone as if it never resounded within the walls, and he rushed a few steps up the stairs in panic, passing the dark, horned creature. "You need me!" he yelled. "Protect me!"

10.

9.

Beast was losing all energy, and when he tried to shoot again, his grip on the Magnum faltered, and it dropped to the stairs. "Get him!" he urged Hound, and it was all the dog needed to act.

King's eyes went wide, and he reached to the back of his pants where he always kept a knife, but Hound's heavy bulk flew up the stairs, as if it weighed nothing, and crashed into King. The impact sent them both stumbling at the wonky railing. The sickening creak of breaking wood had Beast running, and in the bright light of the storm he saw the back of King's head meeting the hard step on the other side of the space in the middle of the spiraling staircase. Beast had his arms around the thick, furry form of his pet, holding on even as its weight pulled on his spine, but King fell, leaving behind a smear of blood and some hair on the edge of the step.

Beast yanked Hound back into safety, but his father's broken scream echoed in the staircase as if it were an empty cave at the entrance to hell. A sickening sound that was a crack and a splash at once was followed by the loud smash of breaking wood, although Beast's mind suggested split bones and mangled flesh. And then, nothing.

Hound whimpered, pulling free of the embrace and wiggling his tail so rapidly the movement made his whole body seem erratic, but Beast paid him no mind and moved back to the void left behind by the broken railing.

He looked down, and in the circular emptiness in the middle of the staircase he saw King draped over the gargoyle statue like a puppet whose strings had been cut. One of the statue's wings was down, and King's new expensive T-shirt was torn. Bright red slowly deemed the graphics at the front unreadable between the twin horns of the statue that now emerged from King's chest.

When the clock behind him struck midnight, its low bell resounding through the air time after time, Beast's body started burning. Still looking down, all the way to the bottom of the stairs, he sensed his joints stop creaking, his muscles feeling more confident by the minute. The broken shape three stories down was slowly secreting blood all over the white floor, and the moment the clock stopped chiming, Beast's mind became razor sharp.

He was elated.

He got to his feet as if it cost him no energy at all.

Nothing hurt and each sensation was pleasure.

Never in his life had he felt so good. He was on the verge of believing he could fly, and despite all the misery still in his heart, he choked out a laugh he couldn't contain.

The devilish monster watched him from the few steps above and it didn't seem like it was about to avenge King's death. Instead, it cocked its head slightly, pupil-less eyes pinning Beast.

It let out a low hum.

Beast looked up, slowly turning his body to face the creature. Even with the pleasure overcoming all his senses, he couldn't shake off the memory that this was the being that had taken Laurent away from him.

"You didn't protect him."

"I never promised that to him. I only promised that you would be here at the age of thirty three, and that I would allow for the exchange of energy," it spoke in a voice that had Beast's hairs bristling. As if it didn't care it was telling Beast it had been ready to kill him just seconds ago.

Beast took a deep breath, trying to clear his head out of hatred, grief, and pleasure all at once. Hound's body bumped into the side of his knee and stayed there, as if grounding Beast for a feat that might be beyond his capabilities. "He's not going to keep up his end of the bargain now."

"He is not." The black lips spread into an unnaturally wide smile so quickly bits of them fell off, revealing skin like lava and smoke coming out from behind charcoal teeth. "But I have you. And you have been pestering me long enough. Feel the energy inside your body now? I can ignite it further and restore you to your former glory, just as you wish. What I need from you is a promise that you will do for me what your father did. Keep the sinners satisfying their lust in this house. Keep conflict coming here, keep ego alive and intoxicating. Keep this place busy. Keep it alive and soaked in carnal pleasure for me."

Beast took a deep breath, his mind flooded with images from his past, with images of the future he'd dreamed of as a young man who had a face that made everyone tingle with lust. If he got the chance to once again become the man he once was, his life would be completely different. No one would send him away when he chose to patronise a business, girls would take secret pictures of him at the beach, he would make people uneasy with his attractive looks, and everyone capable of wanting a man would want a piece of him.

Laurent would never leave him.

His mind stalled, and with a hot flush spreading through his chest, he looked down at the pin attached to his leather cut.

His heart clenched in pain, and he took a few deep breaths to calm down. "No. That's not what I want. I want Laurent. Give him back to me," he said firmly, looking at the demon with new determination.

The monster's smile faltered, and it hissed, spitting red hot sparks at Beast. "He broke our agreement!"

"Take it or leave it. I don't give a flying fuck about your agreement with him. You either let me live with him, or this place will be abandoned for as long as it stays in the hands of my family. And I would have kids *just* to keep this place empty."

The demon huffed, and clouds of smoke erupted from more than one place under the skin of its face. "Are you trying to threaten me, mortal?"

The ground seemed to get hotter under Beast's feet, and Hound gave a warning bark.

Beast licked his lips. "Yes. And no tricks either. No other pacts aimed at harming me or Laurent." He must have been getting somewhere, because the thing seemed visibly agitated.

"But you will only get him and nothing more!" It roared, and Beast was wary of not taking a step back into the abyss like his father had.

"Only this," said Beast steadily, watching the creature without fear. He felt immortal. "Me and Laurent living out our lives together in good health, and in exchange I will make this place even more sinful than it was in my father's time."

The demon stepped back and hit the wall with it long claws. The plaster seemed to ripple, and the old, chipped surface turned into a mirror as wide and tall as the staircase.

"Go get him then."

Chapter 28 - Laurent

From behind the wooden bars of the cage mounted on the back of a horse-drawn wagon, life with Beast seemed like an elaborate dream. Curled up in the small space behind the sacks filled with dried corn, he watched the sun set above the dense forest. One of his captors drove the wagon while another rode next to them on a thin white horse.

The smell of fresh air couldn't soothe Laurent, nor did the last of the beautiful sunshine. In a few days, he would hang for the murder of William Fane, and there was nothing he could do to convince his jailers that he had been acting in self-defense once Fane's housekeeper took away Marcel's arm to hide her master's terrible secret.

The only notes he'd ever found on the matter of his hanging were vague, but they spoke volumes even if he'd never found the exact date of the execution. He'd been held in jail, was now being transported to another one, and would soon hang.

The wait was worse than death itself, which, as gruesome a perspective as it was, would be a brief affair.

The trees whispered softly above his head as the wagon rolled down the narrow road through the woods, letting Laurent breathe the scent of plant life freely for what likely was the last time. The cold air was a shock after spending the summer with Beast, but it was April here in 1805, and he carefully closed the coat around his aching body.

The servants in Fane's house had at first locked him in, then several of the young men of the household came by to pay their respects with fists. No matter how cruel, Fane had been their employer, and with no known heir to the estate, the future of everyone working there now hung on a loose thread.

Laurent pressed the cool back of his hand against the swollen skin on his jaw. He could only hope that by the time he faced the crowds gathered for his execution in Portland, he'd still have all his teeth. Even before he stood before the jury in Brecon, there was absolutely no doubt in his mind that he would die for having the audacity to fight for his life at all cost. With no capital to hire a decent lawyer, an indentured servant with no family to stand by him, he was utterly alone in his misery and could not count on anyone's protection.

"You seen his face?" One of the men said as if Laurent wasn't there to hear him. "He's got some bruises, but his lips are still plump. I will put them to good use tonight."

Laurent's hairs bristled, and his eyes widened as the two men laughed. Would there be no end to his indignity? Was this really the price he had to pay for defending himself? Or was it a price he was paying for having made a deal with the devil in the first place?

He curled his shoulders and lowered his head in a useless attempt to become invisible.

The man on the horse slammed his walking stick against the bars of the wooden cage, startling Laurent into looking back at him. "Cat got your tongue? Be nice, and maybe we'll feed you something besides stale bread."

Talk of food only reminded Laurent just how hungry he was. He glanced back at the man, finding it hard to gather his words. He'd gotten so used to living in a world where a giant man loved him and always had his back, but if he had to exchange his life for Beast's then so be it.

"May I please have some water?"

The two guards looked at one another. The one on the horse took a water bag attached to the saddle and sipped from it before putting it back where it belonged. "It's hot. You'll need to make do 'til we stop for the night."

Laurent sighed loudly and leaned his head against the thick wooden bars. All he had to console himself was the knowledge that his beloved had a chance at fighting for his life. And he surely defeated King or left. Beast was smarter and stronger than his cruel father.

A sob tore out of Laurent's throat all of a sudden when he remembered the Dante quote inked over Beast's forearm. *"There is no greater sorrow than to recall happiness in times of misery."* Laurent would never again feel the joy that overflowed in the heart when the man he loved smiled at him.

It took the men two seconds to burst out laughing, and the stick now poked at Laurent's shoulder, teasing him as if he were a wild animal, taken away from its home to serve as amusement to a cruel mob.

"Look at that. He really is a girl on the inside."

Every piece of Laurent wanted to lash out at them, yell that they didn't know where he'd been, and what he'd needed to do, but even though death awaited him at the end of the road, he didn't want to be beaten again. And if these men chose to, they could break each bone in his body.

He rubbed his eyes and pushed at the stick without much conviction.

The sun was already low, and the men stopped bothering him for a while after that, both clearly intent on getting to an inn before it got dark. Laurent watched the light turn a dark orange where it fell on his bound hands, and he simply waited, locked in his own miserable head more securely than he could ever be in the cage.

Something rustled in the bushes between the thick trees growing on both sides of the road, and the horse rider backed away to direct his mount to the other side of the wagon and look into the woods.

"That a deer?" asked the driver.

"Devil knows."

"Stop right there!" the driver yelled, pulling Laurent out of his thoughts.

Laurent turned to look, but the sacks of corn obscured his vision. The stranger cast the shadow of a giant, not only long but almost unnaturally broad in the chest and shoulders. Laurent squinted as the sun hurt his eyes, but even then he could see the man wore no coat, and the shirt clung to his body creating a distinctly unfashionable silhouette. *Unfashionable for 1805.*

Laurent's throat clenched when his mind told him he knew that figure, yet he refused to grasp at empty hopes.

"Step away, I said!" the driver repeated, and the sound of clinking metal had Laurent on pins and needles.

"We can do this the easy way, or the hard way. Give up your prisoner." Beast's voice had Laurent getting to his feet so fast he hit his head on the low ceiling of his cage.

"What in the devil's name are you?" the rider asked, pointing his pistol at Beast. Laurent gasped and was about to warn Beast of the danger when the more advanced 2017 pistol shot first. The man who tormented Laurent so cruelly not that long ago gave a choked cry and fell off his mount with a creak so horrid he was surely dead from a broken neck, even if Beast's bullet hadn't yet ended his life.

The driver hesitated, fumbling with his own gun, but something was off, and as Beast's titanic body approached, he frantically jumped off the wagon, intent on saving himself.

But Beast was stronger, bigger, faster, a more developed kind of human being brought up on meat and superfoods served on plastic, and he descended on the man like a harpy hungry for blood.

Laurent yelped when Beast turned the man's head sideways with a nasty crackle that made every joint in Laurent's body ache. When Beast released the limp body, it lifelessly slumped to the ground.

Laurent's eyes met Beast's, and the determined, furious expression of a man ready to do anything that needed to be done softened, as if there was a light switch to Beast that only Laurent knew how to operate.

"My Beast..." Laurent choked out, unable to find his full voice.

Beast slowly picked himself up, and at this angle the sun didn't spare Laurent any detail of his lover's handsome form. The Latin quotes on Beast's face were so clear over the scars, his powerful chest swelled with each deep breath, but the clear blue eyes became Laurent's sole focus when Beast left the body behind and stuck his hands into the cage, pulling Laurent close through the wooden bars.

If only Laurent's hands were free, he'd hug back so strongly he'd leave behind bruises. Instead, he had to settle on feeling Beast's touch and stroking his chest with the sides of his hands. Face buried in the front of Beast's shirt, he took a deep breath, and after days of pain, hunger, and degradation, the familiar scent of Beast's cologne brought tears to his eyes. But despite the painful longing to just let himself go end enjoy what he was given, he could not condemn Beast to his own fate.

"What are you doing here? You're not supposed to be here, Beast. This is not your time, you will not thrive here. And I will be a fugitive. This is all not how it's supposed to be." Still, Laurent rested his cheek against Beast's head.

Beast exhaled and twisted his neck, capturing Laurent's lips in a sweet, gentle kiss that made Laurent wish to forget his reason and just let himself be happy for those few more seconds.

"No. No, Laurent. I'm taking you back. You're coming home."

Laurent watched him, dumbstruck, but still gave him another kiss. "What do you mean? You surely cannot... I don't understand."

Beast licked his lips and drew back, letting go of Laurent before turning away from him. The brand on the back of Beast's neck made his skin look like finely worked leather, the imprint almost too perfect to be real.

The cogs of Laurent's brain felt rusty, but they did start moving. "You made... a deal? For me? What about King?"

Beast clenched his teeth, approaching the dead body of the driver. He stuck his hands into the man's coat and produced the large key used that morning to lock Laurent in the cage.

"Dead. The new king is me."

"Long live the king?" Laurent didn't spare any of the corpses another glance, thinking back to the terrible things those men promised to do to him at night. As soon as Beast unlocked the cage, Laurent stumbled out and pressed his body against Beast's firm chest. Nowhere did he feel as safe as in those arms.

Beast kissed his temple but was quick to cut the rope around Laurent's wrists. His fingers were so gentle when they skimmed over the dark bruises on the visible parts of Laurent's body. His blue eyes were bright and innocent as they looked back at Laurent. "Only if you come home with me. Will you stay with me forever?" he asked in the dying light.

Laurent nodded eagerly and wrapped his arms around Beast's waist. His heart soared, bating so fast he thought it might break from sheer happiness. "Nothing else will do."

Beast exhaled and slid his backpack down his arm, opening it quickly to produce a bundle of leather. Laurent's face flushed with heat even before Beast unfolded the pretty vest that had been made especially for him.

"Then I think you should have this."

Laurent turned around so that Beast could put it on for him, and he smiled when he looked over his shoulder. He didn't need to see the patches on the back of the garment to know what they read. "Yours."

"Forever," Beast said, taking hold of Laurent's hand. With the other, he pulled something small out of his jean pocket.

The mirror glinted in Beast's hand, reflecting the evening sun, but Laurent still managed to steal a kiss before the glass surface exploded with smoke and sucked them in.

Epilogue - Knight

Knight had taken the whole time-travel thing fairly well. The evidence was there, and as crazy as the truth was, he'd gotten on board with it as soon as he'd been presented with material proof in the unmarked grave by the rock. Seeing a horned devil appear in the mirror and fill the whole room with smoke was a whole new level of crazy.

Then again, it seemed that all the club members had been completely certain their new prez was not right in the head when he told them he'd made a pact with the devil, like his father before him, and that said pact involved lots of debauchery in the clubhouse.

The fact that they had all actually seen the demon was problematic but made the whole thing slightly easier to swallow. It still took several seconds of men glaring at each other with the same question in their eyes: *Did you see that too?*

Knight cleared his throat and tapped his fingers against the table. "You remember how when this place was still an asylum, they reported a mass hallucination about a demon walking the corridors?"

Joker groaned and massaged his temples. "So are you saying I should be fucking here more often or the devil will kill you?"

Davy snorted, adjusting his leg where it was lifted on a stool. "Right? Fucking nightmare."

Rev patted him on the back. "That's hardly an issue."

Fox shook his head with a frown. "Do we get shit too? Like superpowers, or something?"

Beast sighed. "I didn't get any powers. I have Laurent. And if you want to bargain with that thing, do it on your own, although I don't think it's such a great idea," he said.

Beast hadn't disclosed the truth about King to anyone but Knight, and while Knight agreed it was for the better if the patches believed the devil killed King over a broken pact, it still infuriated him to see all the tributes to their former prez.

"I'm good, thank you very much," Knight said and snickered Joker's way. "We will just have to fuck around so much there will be barely any time left for anything else."

Gray looked contemplative in his corner, but he did acknowledge what was being said with a nod. Maybe he'd reevaluate his own prolonged celibacy, because if he was fucking anyone, none of the members knew about it.

Beast took a deep breath. "As I've already said, it's not all about the fucking, so stop focusing on that like teenage boys. What it means is that the club needs to stay here. Our future is here. We keep parties going, and we keep this club like it's always been intended. A place for freedom in all aspects. As time passes, I'm sure we will find out more about this… thing, devil, demon, whatever, and we can then act as necessary."

Laurent sat to Beast's side despite not technically being allowed to participate in Church, but he had the most information about the secretive being that apparently owned their asses, and after saying all he could, he became quiet, just sitting next to Beast in the property vest that he never seemed to take off.

Beast tapped his fingers against the table and leaned back, watching all the members. "Now that you know everything, we can vote. Do you want me to take over after King?" he asked, steadily looking at the faces of his brothers. Their prospect, Jake wasn't present because of his status and because they hadn't agreed yet whether he should be told about the pact in the first place. For now, there were more important things to deal with.

Knight was the first to declare his support, and as each subsequent member voted for Beast becoming the club president, the atmosphere eased. Gray was the last one in line, and the only one of the men of whose decision Knight was not entirely sure, but he too supported Beast with a soft-spoken agreement.

Beast's shoulders relaxed as soon as his status has been confirmed, and he took the President's patch from the middle of the table. He then decided he wanted Rev, the oldest and most reliable of the men to keep his position as Sergeant-at-arms for the club. His gaze then wandered, stopping on Knight, who leaned back in the chair, unsure what to expect.

"Will you be my VP?" Beast asked.

Heat flared in Knight's chest. "Will we excavate the bodies?"

Joker snorted. "Are you guys gonna exchange vows now?"

Laurent rubbed his face. "Wouldn't it be better to leave those bodies to their eternal rest?"

Knight frowned. "There's history in that unmarked grave!"

Beast waved his hand. "Fine. We don't have any cargo coming this month, and I will need to make my own arrangement with Mr. Magpie now that King's gone. We can inform the authorities of those bodies in the meantime."

Not everyone was on board with police sniffing around the clubhouse, but at the end of the day, they all knew that just a few tests in the lab would establish the skeletons as much older than the biker club and clear them of any suspicion.

Knight folded his arms on his chest with a smile. He would now purposefully sign up to the forum for William Fane's fans to shove all the evidence into their stupid faces. Especially that crazyass Count, who had Fane's fucking face tattooed on his chest. He'd show all those 'Faneatics' what kind of man their idol really was, so there would be no doubt as to Laurent Mercier's role in the murders—or rather lack of it. Their family name would be finally cleared.

Gray glanced around the table. "With Davy out of the game for a longer time, King dead… isn't it time to think about patching in our prospect? Only six of us now are in working order. There's hangarounds, but that's not even close to being the same."

Knight laughed. "I don't know. He seems to *love* prospecting."

Joker threw a lighter at Knight. "You just like him sucking your dick."

"As if you don't!"

Beast slammed his hand on the table. "One step at a time. First, Mr. Magpie and business, then a steady stream of parties, then excavations, and *only then*, we can think about Jake."

Knight could live with that. "Can I suggest moving excavations before parties, prez?"

"No."

Knight shrugged. It was worth trying.

The end

Coming soon!

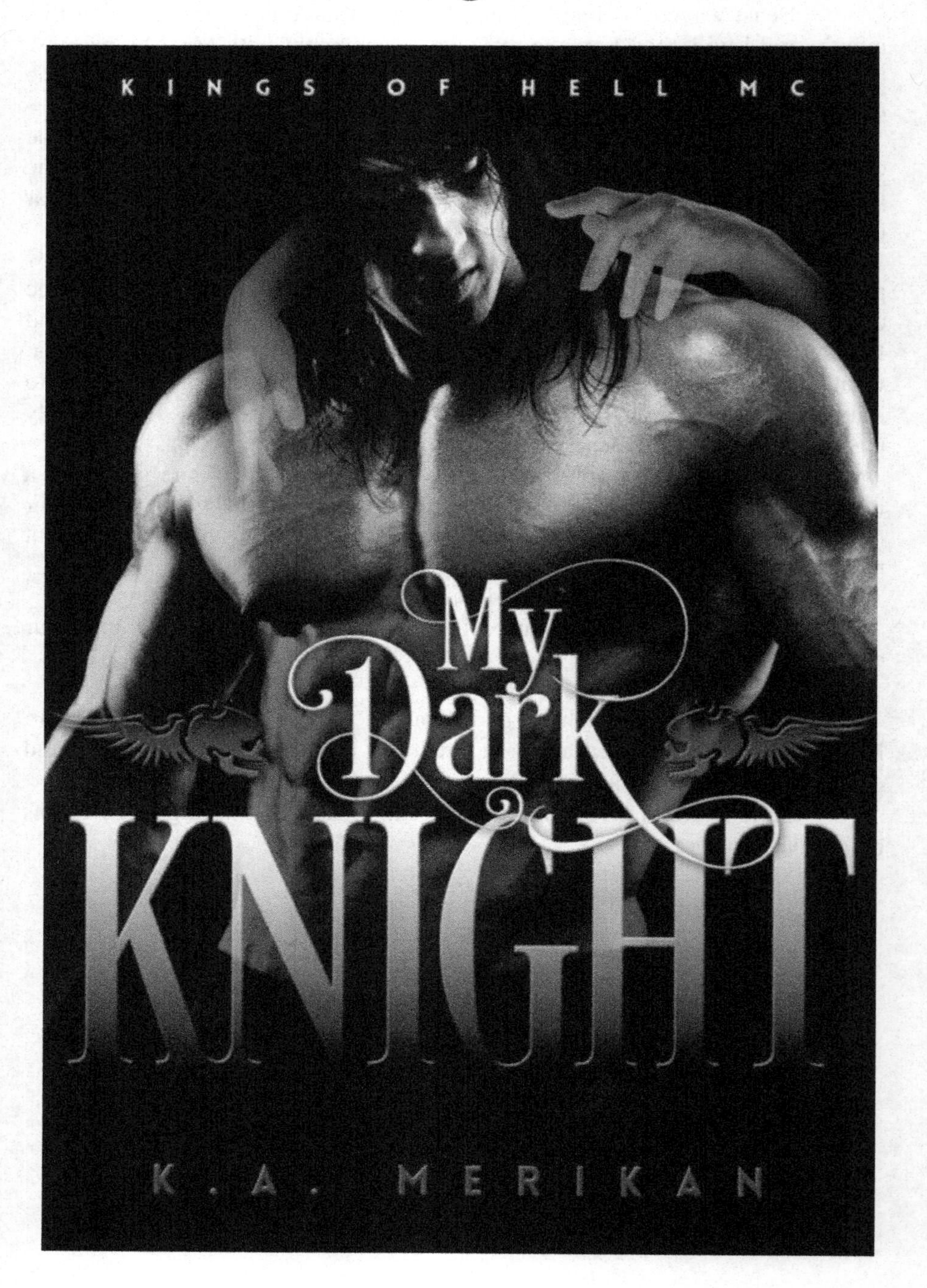

My Dark Knight

Kings of Hell MC #2

Newly single, Knight is done with relationships for now. All he's interested in is bringing down the Count, William Fane's biggest fan who is tarnishing the Mercier name by his insinuations against Laurent.

But things take a drastically new turn when the Count shows up at the clubhouse doorstep to investigate the bodies of Fane's victims, and under all the make-up and theatrics hides a handsome young guy with a passion for history to equal Knight's.

Thank you for reading *Laurent and the Beast.* If you enjoyed your time with our story, we would really appreciate it if you took a few minutes to leave a review on your favorite platform. It is especially important for us as self-publishing authors, who don't have the backing of an established press.
Not to mention we simply love hearing from readers! :)

Kat&Agnes AKA K.A. Merikan
kamerikan@gmail.com
http://kamerikan.com

NEWSLETTER

If you're interested in our upcoming releases, exclusive deals, extra content, freebies and the like, sign up for our newsletter.

http://kamerikan.com/newsletter

We promise not to spam you, and when you sign up, you can choose one of the following books for FREE. Win-Win!

Road of No Return by K.A. Merikan
Guns n' Boys Book 1 by K.A.Merikan
All Strings Attached by Miss Merikan
The Art of Mutual Pleasure by K.A. Merikan

Please, read the instructions in the welcoming e-mail to receive your free book :)

About the author

K.A. Merikan are a team of writers who try not to suck at adulting, with some success. Always eager to explore the murky waters of the weird and wonderful, K.A. Merikan don't follow fixed formulas and want each of their books to be a surprise for those who choose to hop on for the ride.

K.A. Merikan have a few sweeter M/M romances as well, but they specialize in the dark, dirty, and dangerous side of M/M, full of bikers, bad boys, mafiosi, and scorching hot romance.

http:/KAMerikan.com
https://twitter.com/#!/KA_Merikan
https://www.facebook.com/KAMerikan

Other books by K.A. Merikan

Guns n' Boys (single-couple series)
Road of No Return
The Devil's Ride
No Matter What
Red Hot
One Step Too Close
His Favorite Color is Blood
Heart Ripper
Diary of a Teenage Taxidermist
Bare-Knuckle Love
Mr. Jaguar
The Cattery
Werewolves of Chernobyl (written with L.A. Witt)
Break My Shell
Special Needs
The Copper Horse (single-couple trilogy)
Stung
Scavengers (single-couple series)
Crazy Kinky Dirty Love (single-couple series)
The Art of Mutual Pleasure
The Black Sheep and the Rotten Apple
Hipster Brothel

—- You don't fuck with the club president's son. —-

Tooth. Vice President of the Coffin Nails Motorcycle Club. On a neverending quest for vengeance. The last thing he needs is becoming a permanent babysitter for a male hooker.
Lucifer. Fallen. Lost. Alone.

After a childhood filled with neglect and abuse, followed by his mother's suicide, Lucifer set out into the world alone. There was nothing for him out there other than taking it one day at a time. As the bastard son of the Coffin Nails club president, Lucifer never got much fatherly love. So when the Nails show up at the strip joint Lucifer works in, the last thing he expects is to be put in the custody of Tooth, the Nails Vice President famous for his gruesome interrogation techniques. The man proves to be the sexiest beast Lucifer has ever met. He's also older, straight, and an itch Luci can't ever scratch.

Tooth's life came to a halt twelve years ago. His lover got brutally murdered, police never found the perpetrators, and all leads were dead ends. To find peace and his own justice, Tooth joined the Coffin Nails, but years on, he's gotten nowhere with the case, yet still lives on with the burning fire for revenge.

Babysitting a deeply scarred teenager with a talent for disappearing is the last thing on his bucket list. He promised himself to never get attached to someone like him again. To make sure the openly gay boy is safe in the clubhouse, Tooth is stuck keeping an eye on him. The big, blue, attention seeking gaze is drawing Tooth in, but fucking the president's son is a complete no-go, even when both their feelings go beyond lust.

What Tooth doesn't know is that Lucifer might hold the key to the closure Tooth so desperately needs.

WARNING Contains adult content: a gritty storyline, sex, explicit language, violence and abuse. Inappropriate use of dental tools and milk.

Themes: Prostitution, Outlaw Motorcycle Club, organized crime, homophobia, family issues, coming out, discipline/punishment, organ snatching, hurt-comfort, age gap

Genre: contemporary gay erotic dark romance

Length: ~ 125,000 words (Standalone novel, no cliffhanger.)

—- Love is sour like a Sicilian lemon. —-

The Family is always right.
The Family doesn't forget.
The Family pays for blood in blood.

Domenico Acerbi grew up in the shade of Sicilian lemon trees ready to give his life for the Family. Ready to follow orders and exceed expectations. A proud man of honor.
When Seth, the younger son of the Don is kidnapped, it's Domenico who is sent to get him back. The man he finds though, is not the boy he knew all those years ago. Lazy, annoying, spoiled, and as hot as a Sicilian summer.

Seth Villani wants nothing to do with the mafia. Unfortunately, he doesn't get a say when the Family pulls him right back into its fold after his mother's death. Thrown into a den of serpents otherwise known as the Villani Family, Seth has to find a way to navigate in the maze of lies. But when Domenico Acerbi, the most vicious snake of them all, sinks his fangs into Seth, the venom changes into an aphrodisiac that courses through Seth's veins.

Domenico knows his life is about to change when he gets the order to train Seth up to the role of future Don. Seth isn't made for it. He isn't even made. But a man Domenico knows he would never have to fear might just be someone he's always needed.

If Seth is doomed to follow in his father's footsteps, he might as well enjoy himself—with the most intoxicating man he's ever met. Maybe he can even fool himself into believing that Domenico isn't a handsome sociopath who kills for a living.

POSSIBLE SPOILERS:

Themes: Enemies to lovers, mafia, homophobia, assassin, organized crime

Genre: Dark, twisted erotic romance / crime thriller

Erotic content: Explicit gay sex, coercion

Length: ~110,000 words (book 1)

WARNING: Adult content. If you are easily offended, this book is not for you.
'Guns n' Boys' is a gritty story of extreme violence, offensive language, abuse, and morally ambiguous protagonists. Behind the morbid facade, there is a splash of inappropriate dark humor, and a love story that will crawl under your skin.

Made in the USA
Middletown, DE
12 May 2020

94489700R00179